MW01194779

THE SCOTSMAN FROM LUMBER RIVER

THE SCOTSMAN
FROM
LUMBER RIVER

Farmer, Industrialist, Banker
Public Servant

Mary Evelyn Underwood

PENTLAND PRESS, INC.
ENGLAND·USA·SCOTLAND

PUBLISHED BY PENTLAND PRESS, INC.
5124 Bur Oak Circle, Raleigh, North Carolina 27612
United States of America
919-782-0281

ISBN 1-57197-019-3
Library of Congress Catalog Card Number 96-67043

Copyright © 1996 Mary Evelyn Underwood
All rights reserved, which includes the right to reproduce this book
or portions thereof in any form whatsoever except as provided by
the U.S. Copyright Law.

Printed in the United States of America

To my professor, the late Hugh Talmadge Lefler,
who encouraged me to do this study.

CONTENTS

PREFACE

Highland Scots began coming to North Carolina as early as 1732 and continued to come in growing numbers throughout the century. They came to find new homes: The McQueens, McEachins, Gilchrists, McIntyres, Purcells, McNeils, McLaurins, Johnsons, Buies, McKinnons, McDonalds, McKays, McCorveys, McByrds, Matlocks, McPauls, McMillans, McLeans, McGehees, Grahams, McCalls, Campbells, McNeals, Torreys, Donalds, McLeods, and their friends and relatives.

They settled along the upper stretches of the Cape Fear River and its tributaries, also along Lumber River, a tributary of the Pee Dee River which flows through South Carolina. Within a few years there were settlements throughout the region now included in Anson, Bladen, Cumberland, Harnett, Hoke, Moore, Richmond, Robeson, Sampson, and Scotland counties.

At first the Highlanders came as families or in small groups, but by the 1760s large groups of several hundred began to arrive in Wilmington, reaching a peak number in 1773. In 1775, Governor Martin estimated that as many as twenty thousand were living in the area. Another large migration after the American Revolution and a continuing small stream over the next several decades added many more to that number.

Reasons for the great migration of Highlanders to America were both economic and political. Life in the highlands had always been hard and an ever increasing population, made possible by improvements in medicine and in the distribution of food, made conditions more difficult. The promise of land and a better life in America offered a solution to the problem as it did for most of the people who left Europe and undertook the hazardous journey to the New World.

Political conditions led others to leave the homeland. There had always been an alienation between Scotland and England, even when the Scottish House of Stuarts sat on the throne in London. In 1707, when the British Parliament passed the Act of Union, enforcing an alliance between the two, a smoldering reaction began to build immediately, especially among the highlanders. In 1745, when Prince Charles Edward Stuart ("Bonnie Prince Charlie"), the son of James II, who had been forced into exile in 1688, returned to Scotland and issued a "call" for highland clans to join him and restore the House of Stuart to the British throne, many of them raised their standards and joined his forces. His ill-trained and poorly equipped troops, however, were no match for the British army and they were decisively defeated at Culloden Moor on April 14, 1746.

While the British army hunted down the remnants of the rebel forces, Parliament in London took immediate action to prevent future uprisings. A series of laws were passed to break up the clan system: one ordered the confiscation of all weapons; another forbade highlanders to render military service for their chiefs; and, another made it illegal to wear the clan colors. Estates of rebel chiefs were confiscated and given to English officers and soldiers. A final action offered pardon to all rebels who would take an oath of allegiance to the House of Hanover and emigrate to America. Thousands accepted this offer and a mass exodus followed, sometimes as many as four thousand leaving Scotland in one month.

The greater number of these emigrants came to North Carolina, where Governor Gabriel Johnston (a native Scotsman), welcomed them and promised relief from taxes for ten years. Grants of land were also made available for permanent settlers.

As time passed, new economic developments added further incentive to leave the highlands. New landlords, who were no longer governed by the traditional loyalty of chieftains to members of their clans, began to evict tenants and fence their lands in order to raise sheep and provide wool for the textile mills. Others introduced new and better methods of agriculture and raised rents to pay for these. Tenants who could not pay the higher rent were forced to leave the farm and join the ranks of the unemployed. As economic distress increased throughout the highlands, many joined the trek to America.

The Highlanders who came to North Carolina were, for the most part, leaders among their own people, the most prosperous and energetic men and women of Scotland. They brought with them their church and southeastern North Carolina (along with the Piedmont areas settled by the Scotch Irish) became the stronghold of the Presbyterian church. The simple but beautiful architecture of churches preserved from the past century bear witness to both the deep faith and the culture of the Scottish settlers.

They also brought with them their interest in education. Wills preserved in the North Carolina State Archives often include money set aside to educate children or to help establish schools. Many of the Presbyterian ministers also served as school teachers. Such men as David Caldwell, Henry Patillo, Samuel E. McCorkle, and James Hall are well known leaders in the early history of education in North Carolina. Flora McDonald College (now St. Andrews College) remains as a monument to their interest in education.

Most of the Highlanders were farmers and many of them played an important role in the production of naval stores from the vast forests of longleaf pines. A smaller but significant number were mer-

chants, craftsmen, and skilled mechanics; while still others entered
the professions as doctors, lawyers, educators, and political leaders.
In fact, the title "The Scotsman from Lumber River" could well be
followed by any number of names, such as: John Charles McNeill,
poet laureate of North Carolina; or members of the Johnson family,
beginning with Livingston Johnson, editor of the *The Biblical
Recorder* and secretary of the State Baptist Convention, or Archibald
Johnson, journalist and editor of *Charity and Children*, or Jerald
Johnson, writer and journalist, or Wingate Johnson, chief of staff at
the North Carolina Baptist Hospital in Winston-Salem, or Lois
Johnson, dean of women at Wake Forest University. And, from only
a few miles farther up the Valley comes the name of Frank Porter
Graham, beloved president of the University of North Carolina at
Chapel Hill, an honored educator (recipient of honorary degrees
from twenty-one colleges and universities) and United States
Senator. Many other names could be added to this list; Angus Wilton
McLean was just one of the many able leaders whose Scottish fore-
bears settled the Cape Fear Valley.

Angus Wilton McLean
1879-1935

Chapter I

———•◦•●•◦•———

ANGUS WILTON MCLEAN,
A LEADER IN THE ECONOMIC RENAISSANCE
OF THE NEW SOUTH

———•◦•●•◦•———

Angus Wilton McLean was born April 20, 1870, on a farm in Robeson County near Floral College. He was the son of Archibald Alexander McLean and Caroline Amanda Purcell McLean and a descendant of a proud line of hardy Scots who came to live in the upper Cape Fear Valley. The first in the line to come to North Carolina was John McLean of Mull, who sailed from Greenock, port of Glasgow, in September of 1792 on the brig *Mally* and landed a month and a half later in Wilmington. From there he moved up the Cape Fear River past Fayetteville and on to upper Robeson to live near his friends, the Patrick McEachins. He bought land lying on the north side of Buck Pond and west of Gum Swamp in what is now Hoke County. Soon after he arrived, he married Effie McLean, the daughter of Hector and Jennet Murphy McLean, and they built a home. They reared a family of six children; a seventh died at birth. The descendants of these helped to people the upper Cape Fear Valley, and many of them as doctors, lawyers, merchants, farmers, bankers, businessmen, educators, and political leaders have contributed to the development of Eastern North Carolina. [1]

Angus Duart McLean, the fourth son of John and Effie, studied medicine at Jefferson Medical College in Philadelphia and returned to North Carolina to serve his people as a pioneer physician and surgeon. He was also interested in scientific farming and acquired considerable land and slaves. Being something of a scholar, he became a leader in building schools for the Valley. In 1841, he helped his neighbor John Gilchrist, Jr. and others to establish Floral College, a school for women. During the Civil War, like others living in the path of Sherman's march, he lost his horses, cattle, and other livestock, sharing in the hardships of a defeated South.

Archibald Alexander McLean, Angus Duart's second son, served as a gunner in Starr's Battery of Light Artillery and fought in a number of battles in Eastern North Carolina, including Bentonville. [2] When the war was over in 1865, Archibald returned to Robeson County and married Caroline Amanda Purcell, also of Scottish descent, [3] and took her to live on his farm near Floral College. It was into this home that Angus Wilton McLean was born in 1870, the first of seven children.

Life on the farm was hard in the 1870s and the years of Wilton's childhood were, for the most part, a matter of three months of school in a barren, one-room building and nine months of work on the farm, with Sundays always for religious services and instruction in the catechism. Nevertheless, he grew tall and strong of body and ambitious to accomplish and achieve. He had inherited qualities from his parents that stood him in good stead as he fought against poverty and limited educational opportunities. From his father, he inherited the Scotman's regard for thrift and frugality, courage, and sternness; from his mother, he inherited tenacity and perseverance. Living with his parents on the farm, he learned the value of hard work, and that a person does not always have to have everything he or she seems to need. With this legacy, he overcame the odds. His desire to succeed, however, did not destroy an inherent sense of fair play. [4] Among his friends and associates at school, he was long remembered as the big boy who took the side of smaller boys when they were being bullied, and this spirit of fair play and loyalty to friends was to be reflected in all his relationships as a man and public leader.

Born into a tradition of education and the stern culture of Scottish Presbyterianism, young Wilton was given the best education available at the time. After his early training in the local schools of Richmond, what is now Scotland County, he attended the Laurinburg Academy, which was directed by W. G. Quackenbush. At the age of seventeen, he left the academy and, for three years, he worked and saved his money to go to the University of North Carolina. He clerked in a store in Laurinburg, then taught school in Robeson County for $25 a month. [5] In the fall of 1890, he went to Chapel Hill, registered as a law student, and studied for two years under the direction of Dr. John Manning, Dr. Kemp P. Battle, Associate Justice James E. Shepherd, and Professor George T. Winston.

In 1892, McLean was admitted to the bar and began his practice in Lumberton, where for more than forty years he lived and worked, and contributed significantly to the growth and development of the town and the upper Cape Fear region. At the time, Lumberton was a small village with a population of 850 people, and the economy of the town and county was still tied to a one-crop (cotton) system of agriculture and a disappearing turpentine distillery business. Little change had come to the sleepy little community since the days of Reconstruction and brighter economic opportunities elsewhere had continued to drain the population. The streets were unpaved and open privies along the river were a menace to public health.

Electricity was unknown to the area, and all homes and public buildings depended on candles and kerosene lamps for lighting. [6]

The town's only public buildings were a red brick courthouse,
built in 1845, and a post office. A few stores carried the supplies
needed by the villagers and farm families of the larger community.
The general stores carried farm tools, turpentine dippers, scrapers,
and hacks, as well as cloth, needles, thread, hats, shoes, sugar, salt,
kerosene, and other items for the home. McMillan's drug store provided medical remedies prescribed by the two physicians, Dr. J. D.
McMillan and Dr. R. M. Norment. Mrs. Fannie Peterson's millinery
shop made hats for the wives of the more prosperous townsmen.
Fuller's mule and horse business (established in 1882), and A. E.
White's livery stable sold horses and mules as well as a line of wagons, buggies, and harness. [7]

There were a number of boarding houses and two hotels, The
Columbia and The Lumberton, and the town was very proud of its
newspaper, *The Robesonian.* The most interesting building in town
was the "opera house," which served as the center of entertainment
and provided a place for most of the public meetings. This so-called
opera house was built and owned by Dr. Rudolph Vampill, a
German doctor and musician who had come to the area and made
his home in the village. A well in front of the court house was also a
favorite gathering place for men who came to town on business, or
simply for those interested in getting the news.

There were three churches, Methodist, Baptist, and Presbyterian,
to provide spiritual guidance for the community, which over the
years had built a reputation as being devout in matters of religion.
One small public school provided a three-month term for those who
could not pay the fees at a private school. For those who could afford
it, the Robeson Institute, a Baptist school for boys, was opened in
1893 and served the community until it was replaced by a public
grade school in 1907. The Institute had an average enrollment of 160
students. Tuition at the school was $3.00 or $4.00 a month, with an
additional cost of fifty cents for those who wanted to study French,
bookkeeping, or commercial law. Instruction in art was also offered
for a monthly fee of $3.00. In addition to the Institute, there was the
Misses Rowland School for smaller children and girls and the
Thompson Institute for boys. The Whitin Normal School, under the
direction of Professor D. P. Allen, served the blacks of the community. [8]

As entertainment and diversion, the people of Lumberton looked
forward to commencement exercises at the Robeson Institute, an
occasion offering debates, oratorical contests, and musical programs;
for those who were interested in things academic, the events held
annually at nearby Flora Macdonald College were pleasurable and
profitable. There were also traveling minstrel shows and musicians

who appeared at the opera house. In October of 1913, Helen Leigh and Vernon Wallace played in George Cohan's musical farce, "The Little Millionaire" [9] and, in November, two comedies, "Nicodemus Glynn" and "Governor Bowen" were brought to town. [10] On other occasions, there were treats such as the exhibition of a "projecting kinetoscope" brought by a man from Charlotte, or the demonstration of a flying machine by John Kaminski of Milwaukee, the youngest licensed aviator in the world (an event watched by a crowd of 10,000). [11] For some, there were excursions to resort centers or a trip to Wilmington to hear and see actors such as Joe Jefferson, who toured southern towns in 1897. [12] Many of the men in town were members of the Masonic Lodge or the Knights of Pythias and found recreation in these group activities. McLean was a member and officer of the Knights of Pythias.

However, life was a very serious matter for the young lawyer, and aside from weekend trips to Maxton to visit his elderly parents, he allowed himself little time to play. When he came to Lumberton, McLean entered the office of a kinsman, Thomas A. McNeill, under whose tutelage he began his career as an attorney. In 1898, when McNeill was elected to the Superior Court bench, McLean joined another kinsman, Colonel Neil Archie McLean, in the firm of McLean and McLean, enlarged later by the addition of J. G. McCormick. W. B. Snow was also associated with them for a short period of time. On the death of his senior law partner in 1911, McLean invited L. R. Varser of Kinston to join him and his younger cousin, J. Dickson McLean, and the firm was reorganized as McLean, Varser, and McLean. [13]

McLean was never a great attorney, for he was not an eloquent speaker and his talents did not include debate and argument associated with courtroom cases. However, he was highly respected among his professional associates for his ability to plan the strategy for litigation and for his work as a corporate lawyer. His firm handled much of the legal business of the town of Lumberton and was counsel for the Atlantic Coast Line Railroad for a number of years. McLean practiced in all the courts of his section of the state and, on occasion, appeared in cases before the State Supreme Court. [14] In time, the partnership of McLean, Varser, and McLean came to be considered one of the best law firms in the state and its activities extended well beyond Robeson and the neighboring counties. In 1917, McLean was elected president of the North Carolina Bar Association. [15]

Soon after he came to Lumberton as a personable, though very shy, young lawyer, McLean met one of the town's attractive young women, Margaret Jones French, and they became friends. She had been reared by her maternal grandparents, Berry Godwin and Martha Faulk Godwin. Berry Godwin had come to Robeson County about 1855 and had gone into the turpentine business in St. Pauls township; but after the war, he had moved to Lumberton, where he became one of the town's most successful businessmen. Margaret, with whom the grandparents shared their good fortunes, enjoyed privileges of education beyond the usual custom of the day. She was a music student at the North Carolina State Normal and Industrial College when McLean met her and she later continued in advanced study at the Boston Conservatory of Music. [16]

The Godwins were opposed to Margaret's friendship with McLean, because they thought he was too old for her. He was already practicing law and starting a business, while their grand-daughter was still in school. Margaret loved and respected her grandparents, but she was unwilling to give up her friend. After seven years of courtship characterized by a very deep and sincere affection (as the box of letters Mrs. McLean kept until her death revealed), [17] they were married on April 14, 1904, in a simple cere-mony at the Godwin home with only a few intimate friends present. [18] The serious and prolonged illness of her grandmother led Margaret to choose an informal wedding. After a bridal trip to Canada and other points of interest, the McLeans returned to make their home in Lumberton. To them were born two sons and one daughter: Angus Wilton, Jr. in January 1913; Margaret French in September 1915; and Hector in September 1920.

Residence of the McLeans. "The Mansion" built in 1908.

The young couple quickly took their places in the life of the town. Margaret loved to entertain and, during the early years before their children were born, the McLeans became known for their unusual and beautiful parties. Holidays provided the incentive and motif for special events, as did the visits of out-of-town guests. Moreover, in a small town where there were few facilities for public entertainment, any evening was an appropriate time for a dinner party or a special gathering with friends. In spite of McLean's busy schedule as a lawyer and businessman, he and Margaret also enjoyed weekend trips to New York, Washington, and Richmond, and summer vacations at a resort on the East Coast or traveling through the West. During the summer of 1919, they spent several weeks in the British Isles and Europe.

In 1908, the McLeans built a new residence in the center of Lumberton. The house, known for years as "The Mansion," was a handsome structure, built in the columned style so popular around the turn of the century. Large stables on the back of the lot provided accommodations for the horses and carriage, and later for the touring car which McLean and his brother bought. In 1911, an Italian sculptor in New York, who had lived and worked as a stone mason in Lumberton in earlier years (and to whom McLean had given some financial assistance in a time of need), made two sleeping stone lions and sent them to rest on the front lawn. [19] The mansion and the lions were a source of pride in Lumberton, and even in the last days before it was torn down (by directions in Mrs. McLean's will), the house emitted a sort of grand elegance, reminiscent of the days when the McLeans entertained there and when their home served as the "Duart House," or center for the gathering of relatives from far and near.

A sense of loyalty and responsibility towards his kinsmen was one of the governing forces in McLean's life. He had inherited the Scotsman's affection for his relatives, and to him that meant an abiding interest in his extended family and help given to any member in need. He spent years collecting data on the McLean family history and, although he had not completed the research when he died, he left provisions in his will for finishing the work.

In 1919, when he and Mrs. McLean spent the summer in the British Isles and Europe, they visited the Isle of Mull, the original home of the McLean Clan, and paid their respects to Fitzroy Donald MacLean, the twenty-sixth Chief, in Duart Castle. At Glasgow, McLean was made a life member of the Clan MacLean Association of Scotland. [20] He was also a member of the Scottish Society of America, and, in 1924, he was invited to address the St. Andrews Society of New York on "The Highland Settlements in North Carolina." [21]

In the meantime, the young lawyer had become one of the leading businessmen in town. In 1892, there was no bank in Robeson County. Seeing the need for one, McLean persuaded a number of others to join him and, in 1897, they succeeded in establishing the Bank of Lumberton. [22] Thomas A. McNeill was elected as the first president, but the following year, when McNeill became a judge of the State Superior Court, McLean was selected to take his place. The bank prospered from the beginning. On opening day, June 14, 1897, a total of $5,000 was deposited and $10,000 was added the next day. By December 1900, the directors reported a capital stock of $20,000 and deposits of $98,325.70. [23]

Misfortune befell the bank in 1903, when the building burned and everything was destroyed, except the papers and money stored in the vault. However, three days after the fire, the bank was reopened for business in temporary quarters across the street, and within the next few months, a new building was completed. [24] In 1909, to provide greater financial resources for the growing town, the bank offered $50,000 worth of stock for sale. [25] By January 1911, its stock, which had a par value of $100 a share, was selling at $140, and the officials reported the sum of $665,803.43 in stock and reserves. [26] In 1914, the bank was rechartered as a national bank and became a part of the Federal Reserve System. [27] During the late 1920s, when other banks failed in North Carolina, the National Bank of Lumberton remained strong and secure, a witness to its efficient and sound management policies.

In 1922, McLean's interest in banking led him to participate in another venture. At that time he joined a group of financial leaders from various sections of the state in organizing the Atlantic Joint Stock Land Bank of Raleigh. Their purpose was to provide loans to farmers and landowners of North and South Carolina in much the same way as the banks organized under the Federal Farm Loan Act of 1916. Since the charter permitted the bank to float bonds to fifteen times its paid-in capital and surplus, they were able to grant as much as $7,500,000 in long-term loans. [28]

Even as he was seeking to establish a bank in Lumberton, McLean became interested in the textile industry as an additional source of wealth for Robeson County. With a number of local businessmen, he organized Lumberton's first textile factory, incorporated as Lumberton Cotton Mill in 1895, with a capital stock of $75,000 and a work capacity of 5,000 spindles. Robert D. Caldwell was elected president, McLean vice president, and H. B. Jennings secretary and treasurer.

In 1900, the mill opened for work and, within four years, it had more than doubled its equipment and its capital stock had increased to $175,000. [29] This mill produced coarse yarn which was used main-ly in the manufacture of heavy winter socks and underwear. In March 1906, McLean and a group of the stockholders of Lumberton Cotton Mill organized a second mill, Dresden Cotton Mill, with a capital stock of $160,000 and a potential load of 10,000 spindles. [30] In 1909, he joined H. B. Jennings, who had served as secretary and treasurer for the other two units, to organized still a third mill, Jennings Cotton Mill, with a capital stock of $250,000 and a work capacity of 10,000 spindles. [31] These two mills made fine yarns which could be used in a greater variety of woven goods. In 1922, the Lumberton and Dresden Mills were consolidated and reorganized as the Mansfield Mill, with a capital stock of $1,000,000. A weaving room was added and the Lumberton mills began producing unbleached sateens and shirtings; for a brief time they made striped and flowered goods. In 1924, the two mills, Jennings and Mansfield, reported an estimated yearly product valued at $2,300,000. [32]

Wages paid to the employees of the mills were low during the early years and remained so until the twenties. After the reorganization of the first two mills in 1922, there was a rapid climb, however, and the scale of wages which both Jennings Mill and Mansfield Mill reported to the commissioner of labor and printing in 1925 was well above the state average. [33] Moreover, from the beginning, the company officials had taken a personal interest in the workers and had tried to make East Lumberton something of a model industrial community. They built some sixty cottages to furnish housing for those who needed it. They erected a building and established a school in the village to provide educational opportunities for the workers and their families. In February 1909, the school opened with 190 children enrolled for daytime instruction. A night school was organized for the young men in the community and forty attended the opening sessions. With official invitation, ministers of Lumberton churches conducted worship services in the school's auditorium every Tuesday and Thursday evening. On Sundays, there was a Bible school for the children. [34] At Christmas, the mills were closed for a week of vacation and it was a regular custom for the management to send each family a basket of fruit and candies on Christmas morning. This paternalistic pattern of owner-labor relationships prevailed in many, if not most, of the textile communities in the state well into the second quarter of the twentieth century. McLean's mills demonstrated the better features of the system.

Industrial and agricultural expansion in Lumberton and Robeson County was handicapped by the lack of adequate transportation facilities. The area was served by the Seaboard Air Line Railroad, with no competition to force it to improve its facilities and with no connection at all to the North. In February 1906, several businessmen of Lumberton and St. Pauls met with the Lumberton Board of Trade to discuss the building of an independent railroad from

Lumberton to St. Pauls, where it would tap the Atlantic Coast Line and in this way give the Seaboard some competition. [35] Three men, McLean, J. F. L. Armfield (McLean's brother-in-law), and John Blue assumed leadership of the project. They put up $150,000 of their own money and borrowed $374,000, for a total capital investment of $524,000. McLean drew up a charter and worked with the state legislature to get it approved. In time, the Virginia and Carolina Southern Railroad was chartered and, before the Seaboard knew what was happening, the incorporators of the new line had ordered three carloads of rails to be delivered to Lumberton.

When the officials of the Seaboard discovered they were carrying the rails, they ordered the cars hauled eight miles into the country and put on the sidetrack to give them time to secure an injunction against the new road. The strategy did not work, however, because McLean and his associates rounded up twelve wagons and enough mules to pull them, drove down to the cars, unloaded the rails, and, in the darkness of night, started laying the line. By daylight, enough work had been done to make the Seaboard give up its attempt to stop the undertaking. [36]

The first part of the line was built to Hope Mills, by way of St. Pauls, a distance of about twenty-eight miles. This part was opened for passenger service in May 1909. [37] The second part of the road was planned to be a line from St. Pauls to Elizabethtown in Bladen County, but twice the citizens of Elizabethtown voted down a bond issue to provide their part of the money. [38] Discouraged by this apparent defeat and the depressed economic conditions following the panic of 1907, John Blue, who controlled 50 percent of the stock, decided to withdraw from the company. Rather than let the project go unfinished, McLean bought Blue's interest in the railroad, and he and his brother-in-law announced they would build the line to Elizabethtown, bonds or no bonds. [39]

They secured a force of convict labor to supplement a crew of more than 100 men and, in eleven months, the railroad was completed. On December 27, 1910, Elizabethtown greeted the first train; and on January 14, a great celebration was held, including an excursion trip on the train, a picnic for the crowd, and an auction in which McLean sold 110 lots near the new railway station. [40] Heretofore, Elizabethtown had had to depend solely on river boats for all traffic, both passenger and freight.

The builders of the new line had borrowed heavily and the returns from their investments were not adequate to hold off the creditors. Finally, in 1912, McLean worked out a plan whereby the Atlantic Coast Line Railroad agreed to take over the railroad's obligations, with the condition that the original company retain possession, operate the railroad, and pay the Coast Line five percent interest on its investments. In 1922, McLean reported that for the fifteen-year period the company had paid its five percent interest and made a total profit of $105,000, most of which the management had put back into maintenance and improvement of the property. [41] In spite of all his difficulties with the railroad, McLean took special pride in this project as one that made a contribution to the development of Robeson County and all of Eastern North Carolina.

In addition to these major undertakings, McLean promoted a number of other business ventures. In 1898, he and Albert Edward White organized the Lumberton Telephone Company, and this telephone system served the town until 1909, when the need for long distance connections led them to sell out to Bell Telephone Company. [42] In 1903, he organized the Lumberton Improvement Company to build the Waverly Hotel, [43] and, in 1910, he helped to organize a local Building and Loan Association. [44] He was also part owner and director of the Lumberton Drug Company. [45]

He went into the real estate business and initiated Lumberton's first city development project. With A. E. White, he bought a large area in Northeastern Lumberton, had it surveyed, streets laid out, and the land divided into 200 city lots. This area was called Lindell. They engaged the American Realty and Auction Company of Greensboro to take charge of the advertising and to conduct the most spectacular sale Lumberton had ever seen. There was a band; prizes were given out; and the auctioneers called the offers in unison. The nearby school dismissed classes and the ladies of the town added dignity to the occasion. The sale lasted from eleven in the morning until four in the afternoon, and during those five hours, bids were accepted for 143 lots. [46] This auction started a small land boom in Robeson County, and for months the county paper was filled with notices of sales and the records of private exchanges of real estate.

McLean's biggest real estate venture, however, was in farm and timber holdings of about four thousand acres in Bladen and Robeson counties. This was a joint project with his brother, Alexander T. McLean, who resigned his position as cashier of the Lumberton Bank to become vice president and general manager of the Robeson Development Company. The company opened offices in Lumberton and announced its business as a dealer in real estate, stocks, bonds, and other investments. [47]

In addition to his ventures in real estate development, McLean owned and cultivated more than a thousand acres of farmland. [48] Moreover, he took an active interest in the problems of southern agriculture. At a meeting of farmers from all the southern states in December of 1911, he delivered an address in which he denounced "time merchants" and the "crop lien system," asserting that, if he could control the merchants and abolish the lien laws, he could solve most of the farmers' problems. He called for an organization of merchants and businessmen to cooperate with farmers on these matters. [49] He went as a delegate to the second annual convention of the North Carolina Forestry Association meeting in Raleigh in February 1912, and, in 1915, he was elected vice president of the North Carolina Publicity Bureau for Development of Agriculture and Industry. [50]

McLean still found time for community and civic activities, in spite of all his business responsibilities. In April 1910, he and Mrs. McLean invited a number of their friends for an evening's visit and presented to them suggestions for a civic association, or organization to promote the general improvement of Lumberton. Their friends heartily endorsed the plan and that night they organized the Lumberton Civic Association and elected a tentative slate of officers. Two weeks later, at a public meeting, the temporary organization was made permanent, and upon McLean's suggestion, the group voted to join the American Civic Association. Within a few weeks, the membership had grown to 104 and a program of diversified activities was set in motion. The membership was divided into committees, each with a definite task. Among the tasks assigned were: public parks, cemeteries, trees and floral betterment, public libraries, recreation and entertainment, finance, public health, program, and finally, an advisory committee with McLean as the chairman. Mrs. McLean was chairman of the program committee. [51]

A date for a cleanup effort was set and the mayor and town commissioners were asked to cooperate. Pamphlets explaining the necessity of cleanliness and the use of disinfectants were distributed, and Dr. W. S. Rankin of the State Health Department and other public health officials were invited to speak at community gatherings on health and sanitation. The town commissioners undertook a program of improvement around the court house, and an ordinance was enacted requiring that property owners pave the sidewalks touching their land. The open privies along the railroad station were replaced with automatic flush toilets under the town hall, and the voluntary fire department was reorganized and enlarged. A movement was launched to give free medical and dental examinations to all school children and to report the findings to their parents. The committee on entertainment sponsored an art exhibit in the court house, a showing of engravings by English masters of the eighteenth century. The Industrial and Commercial Club, to which most of the businessmen of Lumberton belonged, cooperated with the Civic Association, and McLean, with the Lumberton Bank, undertook a plan of improvements at the Waverly Hotel. The Civic Association held regular monthly meetings, which were attended by a large number of local citizens, and their enthusiasm created an interest in community affairs that influenced the town for years.

The Civic Association and its work to improve Lumberton represented the spirit that had motivated McLean and other local leaders for two decades and more. As a result of their efforts and the cooperation of local people, Lumberton became a prosperous community and Robeson County became one of the richest counties in Eastern North Carolina. Adequate financial resources, textile mills, better transportation, and improved agriculture (introduction of a second staple crop, tobacco, and some truck farming) were both causes and results of the progress which had occurred.

The population of Lumberton grew from 849 in 1900 to 3,702 (including East Lumberton) in 1920. By 1920, the once sleepy little village along Lumber River had installed a sewer system and a complete system of water works (water came from twelve artesian wells rather than the river). Electric lights had replaced candles and oil lamps. A new court house had been erected. A grade school provided education to children grades one through seven, as well as three years of high school study. A fire department helped to make the town safe from destruction by fire and concrete sidewalks not only improved the appearance of the town, but made it easier for residents to move about the streets. The first two decades of the twentieth century had been a good period for Lumberton and Robeson County, and McLean had played a significant role in most of the efforts which made it possible.

What kind of a man was this Angus Wilton McLean, whose name was so indelibly inscribed on the story of Lumberton during the first quarter of the twentieth century? Ben Dixon MacNeill gave a discerning interpretation of the man and his works when he wrote: "The biography of Angus W. McLean . . . is not unlike that of dozens of other . . . men of his own age and his own times, who have wrought with their own communities, who have prospered for themselves and, in their own prosperity, have brought increase to their neighbors. He is typical of the generation that came after the war . . . men who have come up out of the meager circumstances that were the common lot of a formerly prosperous people in the two decades that followed the Civil War. They have been in the forefront of the economic renaissance . . . ." [52]

Physically, McLean was a big man, standing one inch over six feet and weighing around 225 pounds. He was also a man of great strength and energy. He required little sleep and could work several assistants to exhaustion before he began to tire. He was a proud man, always well dressed and immaculate in his grooming. For business, he customarily wore a conservative, double-breasted blue suit, with vest and spats, and he always carried a cane. A pair of little gold scissors on his watch chain was a reminder of his days as clerk in a store.

His life was guided by a philosophy which Judge H. Hoyle Sink, his close friend and associate for years, described as founded on the sanity and wisdom of work and a deep respect for truth and honesty. [53] He was a sincerely religious man and quietly practiced the principles handed down by a long line of devout Presbyterians. He and his family were faithful in attendance and support of the church; for years he was a ruling elder in the Lumberton Presbyterian Church. (Mrs. McLean was a faithful member of the Baptist church.) He served on the Board of Trustees for the University of North Carolina and for the Union Theological Seminary in Richmond, Virginia, and as chairman of the board of Flora MacDonald College.

By disposition serious and reserved, McLean never found it easy to meet people or to relax the barriers that separated him from all but his closest friends. He never learned to play or to respond lightly to any part of life. Even with his family, to which he was quite devoted, he remained the dignified head of the house until his son Hector was born; this birth helped McLean to unwind and enjoy having a vivacious baby boy in the house. [54] Time, however, mellowed the Scotsman and a letter written to Hector a short time before his death in 1935 reveals a deep love and affection for his children, and a gentle and caring nature usually hidden by his rather formal and stern bearing. [55]

Some called him a hard business man, but his generosity toward any who came to him for help revealed a very soft side to his nature, and those who knew him best saw beyond the stiffness to a man capable of great friendship and enduring loyalty. His neighbor, who saw him come and go through the years, said: "He was a leader of men . . . and a man of dignity." [56] Mark Sullivan wrote Martin Gillen, a mutual friend, in August 1923: "Remember me to Angus. That big Scotchman is the salt of the earth. He has the sure-footed common sense that could live up to high responsibilities if the people of this country knew how to pick men to serve them." [57] In 1924, the people of North Carolina picked him to serve them as their governor.

Chapter II

―‥•‥―

EARLY POLITICAL LIFE

―‥•‥―

McLean, who inherited a Scottish flair for politics, grew up in a family interested in public affairs. His father before him had served as treasurer for Robeson County for years before his death in 1906. McLean himself became actively involved in local politics soon after he opened a law office in Lumberton. In 1892, the year he returned to Robeson, he was made chairman of the County Democratic Executive Committee and, with this first post of duty, he began a lifelong participation in politics and government. Even as he was becoming one of Lumberton's foremost businessmen and community leaders, he was also emerging as a shrewd politician.

The 1890s was a turbulent period in North Carolina, and few people were able to remain indifferent, as highly emotional issues were debated on the hustings of one campaign after another. American farmers, who had suffered from a prolonged depression and from a lack of influence in government for three decades and more, found commonality with industrial workers and organized the People's, or Populist, party. In 1892, they nominated a president and vice president, and, in a number of states, they named a full slate of officers. They drew up a platform calling for an increase in the national currency and loans to farmers, tax reforms, election reforms, an eight-hour day for labor, and public ownership of railroads and utilities.

For conservatives of both regular parties, their platform was dangerously radical, but when Populist leaders encouraged Negro participation in the party, it raised for Southerners the memories of Reconstruction Days and "Republican-Negro rule." Consequently, Southern Democrats denounced the farmers as traitors and revived all the tactics once used against Republicans and Carpetbaggers. With a campaign of ruthless abuse (and sometimes violence) they defeated the Populists in the southern states, and contributed to their defeat in the national election. Having failed to win office or even Democratic acceptance of their program in 1892, the North Carolina Populists joined with the state Republican party in 1894 and won a sweeping victory, capturing both houses of the General Assembly. Only Governor Carr remained in office to carry the Democratic banner. Over the next six years, the story of North

Carolina politics continued to be a tale of partisan struggles and emotional bigotry.

The elections of 1896 and 1898 were held in the midst of confusion and bitter rivalries. In 1896, the Populists and Republicans failed to agree on a fusion ticket and three party tickets were presented to the voters. As a result of the split in the Democratic party and disarray within Populist ranks, the Republican candidate for governor, Daniel L. Russell, won by a narrow margin. This success was due, in part, to the large Negro vote in some of the eastern counties. To reward these supporters, he appointed a number of blacks to institutional boards and state agencies. In some of the eastern counties, several hundred Negroes were elected to minor offices. In 1898, the Democrats laid their plans well in advance, and, under the shrewd leadership of State Chairman Furnifold M. Simmons, launched a campaign to regain control of the state and local governments. With unprecedented organization, ruthless publicity, and a force of stump speakers, they carried the message of "White Supremacy" throughout the state. In November, they won control of the General Assembly and a majority of the North Carolina representatives in Congress, but scattered violence and a race riot in Wilmington marred the political image of the state.

Victory for the Democrats in 1898 served as a preview of the governor's race in 1900, when the "Negro question" was again a major issue. All of the tactics used to discredit the Republicans and Populists in 1898 were employed again, perhaps with more vigor. In the end, the Democrats carried the election and regained control of the Executive Office as well as the General Assembly. In that election, the voters also approved an amendment to the State Constitution, one which, in effect, disenfranchised blacks.

With its defeat in 1900, the Republican party was left without power in the state and the Populist party fell apart as white farmers and laborers returned to the Democratic party. Consequently, for the next two decades, North Carolina political campaigns were simply contests between "liberal" and "conservative" Democrats. The conservatives, who controlled the party for most of the time, promoted business as the best means of state development and gave reasonable support to educational, humanitarian, and social reform. The liberals, who were sympathetic to farmers, labor, and the common people in general, hoped to make business bear a greater part of the tax burden. The most spectacular battle between the two factions was in 1912, when Governor William W. Kitchen and Judge Walter Clark, both liberals, attempted to prevent the reelection of Senator Simmons, a staunch conservative.

During these strife-torn years, McLean served on the State Democratic Executive Committee and, working with Chairman Simmons, helped to make party policy. [1] It was during this period that he and Simmons became close friends and political allies. Meanwhile, he was active on the local level as well. He continued to serve on the Robeson County Democratic Executive Committee and, in 1902, was elected to the Board of Town Commissioners for Lumberton. [2] In 1904, he broadened his political interests when he was selected to go as delegate-at-large to the National Democratic Convention in St. Louis. His growing stature as a political leader in North Carolina was recognized in an appointment to the Committee on Rules for that Convention. [3]

In 1912, McLean emerged as a state and national leader in the Wilson campaign. In May of that year, the local precinct in Lumberton chose him as a delegate to the county convention and the county convention sent him as one of its forty delegates to the state convention in Raleigh. At that meeting, McLean was elected a delegate-at-large to the National Convention in Baltimore. He was again named to the State Democratic Executive Committee, and also to the State Credentials and Appeals Committee for the sixth district. [4] In Baltimore, McLean was appointed to the Committee on Permanent Organization and, from that position, he worked to have E. E. Britton of Raleigh made permanent secretary of the Convention. [5]

Woodrow Wilson was nominated at Baltimore to carry the Democratic party back to Washington. McLean, who had been a Wilson supporter from the beginning, worked very hard to ensure his victory in North Carolina. Early in August, he was appointed State Chairman of the Presidential Campaign Committee and given the task of raising funds for the Democrats. The committee met immediately to organize and make plans. Hugh McRae was elected secretary-treasurer and canvassers were appointed for each of the 100 counties. Plans were also made for a statewide publicity campaign. [6] In November, the Democrats carried the election, sending Wilson to Washington as President and Simmons to the United States Senate. The conservative candidate, Locke Craig, was elected Governor of North Carolina.

In 1916, McLean enthusiastically joined the campaign to keep Wilson in the White House. He was again elected to the State Democratic Executive Committee, and also to represent North Carolina on the National Committee, replacing Josephus Daniels, who had given up the post in 1913 to serve as Secretary of the Navy. [7] In June, McLean went as a delegate-at-large to the Democratic Convention in St. Louis and there supported Wilson's renomination. He was again appointed State Chairman of the Presidential Campaign Committee and helped raise $15,000 for the party. [8] Vance McCormick, National Democratic Chairman, said North Carolina was one of the four states to raise their quotas. During the campaign, McLean came to know the national leaders in

Washington and to be a close friend of Joseph P. Tumulty, Wilson's private secretary. He and Mrs. McLean were among the guests invited to a luncheon at the White House immediately following the inauguration in March. McLean was seated next to the President. [9]

By 1917, North Carolinians, along with other Americans, had turned their attention from politics to the war in Europe. As plans were initiated to provide food for the Allies, and for the American Expeditionary Forces in France, food conservation committees were formed throughout the nation. McLean headed the committee in Robeson County. In May, he called a meeting of all the farmers to make plans for the coming months. To implement their plans, they passed a resolution calling on the County Commissioners to appropriate up to $500 to enable the farm demonstration agent to wage a vigorous campaign to increase production of food crops and to teach the people how to save what they produced. [10] In response to this appeal, the commissioners hired a full-time Home Demonstration Agent. [11]

As chairman of the Liberty Loan Committee, McLean helped to organize the county into ten districts, each with a committee to solicit funds. A Liberty Bond Rally was held in Lumberton late in October and an all-out campaign was undertaken to raise the county's quota of $400,000. By the end of the month, the drive had been completed and the county had passed its allotment by $27,400. [12] In January 1918, McLean helped organize the Robeson County Chapter of the American Red Cross with a charter membership of 386. [13] He also served on the State War Relief Committee. [14]

After the United States declared war in April 1917, and men were being drafted to serve overseas, McLean was named to the Selective Service Advisory Commission and was appointed counsel in North Carolina for the Alien Property Custodian. [15] In April 1918, President Wilson called him to Washington to serve as one of four directors of the War Finance Corporation. His appointment was for four years with an annual salary of $12,000. W. P. G. Harding, governor of the Federal Reserve Board; Allen B. Farbes, a New York private banker and securities dealer; and Eugene Meyer, Jr., a New York banker and businessman, were the other three directors. [16] The Secretary of the Treasury, William Gibbs McAdoo, was an ex-officio member and chairman of the board. The appointment was confirmed by the Senate on May 4th. [17] McLean moved his family to Washington and took the oath of office on the 13th. The Corporation as a whole was sworn in and formally organized on May 17th. At that time, Harding was named Managing Director. Four lawyers and four financial experts were later employed to examine applications and to advise directors on technical matters. [18] The designated task of the agency was to deal with financial problems created by the war.

By the spring of 1918, the United States faced an impending crisis in capital markets. American business was expanding at a rapid rate in response to demands created by the war. More and more funds were needed for new facilities and to meet the rising costs of production. Moreover, large short-term loans to the Allies to finance their purchases in the United States during the early months of the war had placed a heavy burden on private banks. As the war continued and short-term loans failed to provide adequate funds, the Federal government had to assume responsibility for long-term assistance. To do this, Congress authorized the Treasury to sell bonds for several billion dollars—a total of twenty-three billion by 1920. Liberty Loan Campaigns were launched to sell the bonds to the public, rather than to banks whose resources had already been drained. With such demands on the capital markets, there was practically no available money for investment. Faced with this situation, the Administration decided that all financing of nonessential social and economics projects had to be curtailed so that more money would be available for wartime industries.

The Act by which the Corporation was created authorized the Board of Directors to formulate and implement plans to relieve the money shortage. It was empowered to make advances to banks willing to extend commercial credits to industries essential to the war efforts; to grant loans to individual applicants in exceptional cases; and to buy and sell government bonds. The Corporation was capitalized at $500,000,000 and given the authority to issue $3,000,000,000 in bonds if additional funds were needed. A new Capital Issues Committee, which was established concurrently with the Corporation, would investigate and determine whether any issue of bonds by a private company in excess of $100,000 would be compatible with the public interest. [19]

Applications flooded the Corporation from all quarters, but within the board's interpretation of its primary function, the directors rejected many of the requests. Careful scrutiny was made of all applications and proper collateral was demanded in all cases. The largest loans went to help the railroads, which were near the point of collapse. The revolving fund that Congress had created when the Federal government took them over in late December 1917 was exhausted. Increased cost of labor and supplies, and the extensive improvements which had been necessary to keep the roads in shape for the tremendous task of transporting troops and materials to the East Coast had eaten it up. Smaller loans were made to public utilities; to the United States Grain Corporation, which had been authorized to purchase and distribute wheat; the New York Canners' Warehouse, which could assist with the harvesting and preserving of fruits and vegetables; and to the cattle growers in the West, where three successive years without rain had created a shortage of food.

McLean went with some other members of the board to visit the cat-
tlemen and to evaluate their requests for assistance. [20]

The Corporation took steps to curtail its activities soon after the
Armistice was signed in November 1918, but in March 1919,
Congress amended the original Act and extended the life of the
agency for an additional year. The amendment authorized the
Corporation to make loans up to $1,000,000 to persons, corporations,
or associations engaged in exporting domestic products, and to
banks providing funds for this purpose. [21]

American exports had fallen dramatically as the war came to an
end. Because financial resources of war-torn countries in Europe
had been exhausted, they could not buy American farm or manufac-
tured goods without continued credit from the United States government. By December 1920, a growing depression in the American
farm community again called for government action. In January,
Congress extended the life of the War Finance Corporation for a second time, this time for three years, and authorized it to loan up to
$1,000,000,000 to stimulate the export of agricultural products.
During the fall and winter of 1921 to 1922 (the most critical period),
loans by the Corporation averaged more than $2,000,000 a day. [22]

McLean played an active role in the work of the Corporation. On
a number of occasions, he was asked to serve as Acting Managing
Director. In January 1919, he served in the absence of Managing
Director Meyer; in June 1920, he was again selected to serve for one
year in that post. [23] In June 1919, he represented the board before
the House Committee on Appropriations to give an account of the
activities of the Corporation. [24] During the summer of 1921, he
served on the Committee on Applications and, in August of that
summer, he was appointed to a special committee to investigate the
need for loans to banks, and to submit plans to the board for its consideration. [25] During the same time he was asked to look into a revision of the Bylaws of the Corporation. In March 1921, he offered his
resignation to the President, but Wilson asked him to reconsider his
decision as he was the only director from the South. Southern congressmen joined Wilson in urging that he stay. Although he had
already made plans to move his family back to Lumberton, he
accepted the President's request and remained on the board until
May 16, 1922. During this extended term, he worked diligently for
the cotton farmers of the South, who were experiencing great difficulties with a declining world market and with the ravages of the
boll weevil.

Upon receiving McLean's resignation in May 1922, the Board of
Directors passed the following resolution:

> Resolved, that the Board of Directors of the War Finance
> Corporation desire to enter [on] record an expression of the gen-
> uine regret and deep sense of loss occasioned by the retirement of

their colleague; their sincere admiration of the wisdom, courage and patriotism with which he has served his country during the stress of war and since in a fine spirit of self-sacrifice and devotion to the public interest and to duty; their grateful acknowledgment of the kindly and effective manner in which he has cooperated in every task and contributed to the solution of every problem; and their lasting appreciation of the treasured friendship of their colleague whose departure means a personal, as well as an official, loss to his associates . . . [26]

Expressions of appreciation for his work on the Corporation also came from United States Senators and Representatives: Senator John B. Kendrick of Wyoming, Senator Charles L. McNary of Oregon, Senator Harrold of Oklahoma, Senator Burson of New Mexico, Senator Arthur Capper of Kansas, Senator J. Thomas Heflin of Alabama, Senator Pat Harrison of Mississippi, Senator Furnifold M. Simmons of North Carolina, Representative W. F. Stevenson of South Carolina, and Representative Claude Kitchen of North Carolina. [27]

While McLean was in Washington as a director of the War Finance Corporation, he served in a number of other positions. In March 1920, he was appointed assistant secretary of the treasury, a post he held until March 1921. [28] In June 1920, the secretary of the treasury asked him to be his personal representative on the Railroad Advisory Committee, to review loans provided under the Transportation Act. [29]

When McLean resigned as assistant secretary of the treasury, President Wilson responded with a letter of appreciation for his work in that office and also as a member of the War Finance Corporation. He wrote:

> Allow me to take this occasion to express my sincere appreciation of your efficient services in this important executive position, and also of your loyal and effective work as a director, and later managing director, of the War Finance Corporation . . . .
>
> You have performed this duty with signal ability and devotion, and you are deserving of a large share of credit for the successful operation of the Corporation. I have known, particularly from the three secretaries of the treasury with whom you have been associated, of the great value of your contributions to the success of the war. I am grateful for your help and cooperation. [30]

On the same occasion, Secretary of the Treasury Houston wrote: "When Scotchmen break their reserve they are likely to go to extremes. I should have difficulty in going too far in my expression of appreciation of your work as assistant secretary of the treasury, as member and managing director of the War Finance Corporation, and as an adviser in respect to railway matters." [31]

Even while he was heavily involved in numerous activities in Washington, McLean still maintained close ties with North Carolina politics. Candidates seeking state appointment or assistance in running for office asked for his advice or endorsement even before they sought approval of Senator Simmons. McLean regularly attended the State Democratic Conventions as a delegate from Robeson County, and, in 1920, he went as a member of the North Carolina delegation to the National Democratic Convention in San Francisco. At that Convention, he supported William Gibbs McAdoo and helped launch a drive to secure his nomination.

By this time, McLean had become alarmed by the political scene as he saw national events working against the Democrats. He had been a staunch supporter of Wilson's programs and had spoken in favor of the League of Nations, but he understood the capriciousness of public opinion. In spite of conservative opposition to McAdoo—because of his relations with organized labor during the war—McLean felt that the democrats' best chance of winning the election in 1920 lay in McAdoo's candidacy. In a long letter to James O. Carr of Wilmington, North Carolina, he expressed his thinking on several issues vital to the Democratic party and its future. He wrote:

> As you know, my inclinations are conservative, and my position has always been that of an employer of labor in many capacities, yet I cannot overlook the fact that the interest of the laborers must be given more consideration now than ever. I know that during the war they have taken advantage of the situation and have profiteered, but as a matter of fact they have not profiteered half as much as the capitalists. I do not believe that any man, whether he be an employer of labor or not, can get along successfully in the future unless he assumes a more sympathetic attitude toward labor than has been assumed in the past . . . . I do not think it fair that railroad officials and those interested in railroad investments should hold Mr. McAdoo responsible for the trouble the railroad companies have had with the labor unions. As a matter of fact, if it had not been for the way in which he handled matters, we would have had a great deal more trouble during the war . . . . One reason I think McAdoo is a strong candidate is that he would be acceptable to labor as well as to a large element of the reasonable businessmen. The Democrats may as well realize that the Democratic party has no hope of success in the next election unless it receives a large percent of the labor vote. As a matter of fact, the Democratic party is the liberal party in this country, and to win it must secure the support of the liberal elements, including labor. [32]

This letter gives a remarkable insight into the ability of a self-proclaimed conservative to adapt to the changing times. If he had lived, McLean would, no doubt, have felt quite at home in the days of the New Deal.

McLean was also actively involved in the 1920 gubernatorial election in North Carolina. In February, he wrote to Carr in Wilmington, stating that he felt it was exceedingly important that "our friends" from the eastern counties control the delegates to the State Convention and asked Carr to look after the matter in Brunswick, New Hanover, and Columbus counties. [33] He feared that O. Max Gardner's organization was going to try to capture a majority of the state delegates.

At the Convention, McLean and Carr worked diligently to secure the nomination of Cameron Morrison. During the summer and fall, he campaigned for Morrison's election and continued to support him as Governor until his big spending programs and a growing state debt caused McLean grave concern. At that point, his instincts as a frugal Scotsman and a good businessman led him to become actively interested in running for the governorship in 1924.

Chapter III

―・◆・―

GUBERNATORIAL CAMPAIGN, 1924

―・◆・―

The 1920s in North Carolina could not be described as "roaring," but the state experienced most of the economic, social, and political developments which characterized this period throughout the nation. It was a time of both depression and prosperity. In general, North Carolina recovered rather quickly from the depression of 1920-21, but the farmers continued to suffer from the combination of low prices, the boll weevil, and the ever-increasing cost of living. Industry enjoyed a period of expansion, but the largest single manufacturing interest, textiles, was constantly plagued by the uncertainties of the world market.

The automobile brought the Good Roads Movement and the construction of an extensive system of state highways, and the mid-twenties saw one of the greatest building booms in North Carolina's history. Unfortunately, the state also experienced a series of labor strikes, a wave of crime, the rebirth of the Ku Klux Klan, and a bitter debate over evolution and Modernism in religion. Politically, the twenties saw the decline of the Simmons machine which had dominated state politics since 1898, with the single exception of its defeat by W. W. Kitchen in 1908, and the emergence of a new and younger group of politicians.

The year of 1924 opened with a note of uncertainty in the business world, with reports of deficits in government finances, and with the general conviction that it was time to follow a more conservative policy in public spending. In its report on 1923, the *Bradstreet Review* called for caution on the part of the nation's legislators during the coming year. On January 4, the management of textile mills in Gastonia announced they would have to curtail production unless there was rapid improvement within the next thirty days. Before the end of the month, Wake County found it necessary to issue bonds to cover a shortage of $155,000 for 1923, and reports already indicated that the state would end its fiscal year in June with a deficit of perhaps $5,000,000.

In the past three years, the state government had spent more lavishly than ever before in its history, having authorized an outlay of $65,000,000 for roads, $10,000,000 for loans to the counties for building school houses, and $17,500,000 for permanent improvements at the several state institutions. The counties and cities had indulged in programs even more costly. A *Raleigh News and Observer* survey of public opinion in January revealed hearty approval of the construction of highways and improvements in education, but also a distinct feeling that to keep up the pace of the past three years might not be the wisest course. [1] This frame of mind set the stage for the election of 1924 and helped to determine the platforms of the two candidates for governor.

As was so often true in North Carolina politics, plans for the gubernatorial campaign in 1924 had been in the making since the election of 1920 and before. In 1916, McLean had been discussed as a possible candidate for governor, but since he hoped to get a Federal appointment under the Wilson administration, he had withdrawn his name. However, while he was in Washington, from 1918 to 1922, he watched his record in view of the contest in 1924, and after his return home in the spring of 1922, he quietly but definitely made his plans to enter the race. [2] He secured the services of Charles H. England, who had been secretary for the late Claude Kitchen, to assist in laying the groundwork for a statewide organization. England visited several counties—among them Orange, Chatham, Alamance, Durham, Person, Guilford, Rockington, Caswell, Wilkes, Vance, Granville, and Stokes—to make contacts and obtain names of Democratic precinct committeemen, ladies interested in politics, and lists of prominent men and party leaders from each county. [3] In September 1923, McLean went to Washington for a conference with Senator Simmons and John G. Dawson, the State Democratic Chairman, to discuss plans for his candidacy. [4]

Early in 1924, McLean began to set his campaign in order. On February 4, he wrote letters to a few active Democrats in various sections of the state to ascertain their attitude toward him as a candidate and to get a picture of the general situation in each community. Later in February, he spent a week in the northeastern counties. On February 15, he visited Elizabeth City and made his first campaign speeches. At noon, he spoke to the Rotary Club on what he considered to be the three qualities of good government: honesty, wisdom, and efficiency. In the evening he delivered an address on education in its broader aspects at the formal opening of the city's million-dollar school building. [5] The subjects discussed in these two gatherings were major planks in the platform on which McLean would appeal for the support of the state's electorate.

Meanwhile, McLean's expected opponent, Josiah W. Bailey, had also been preparing for the campaign. Bailey was a brilliant man and endowed with an unusual ability to speak convincingly. In 1893, on his graduation from Wake Forest College, he succeeded his father as editor of the *Biblical Recorder* and ran the paper for almost fourteen years before he resigned to study law. As a young editor, he espoused the cause of public schools and worked with Dr. Charles D. McIver in the free school campaign of 1898. While editor, and later as a lawyer, he took an active part in state politics, and between 1913 and 1921, he served as United States Collector of Internal Revenue for North Carolina. Within a year after leaving the Collector's office, he made his plans to run for governor in 1924. In the summer of 1922, he visited Senator Simmons in Washington to secure his endorsement. Simmons, however, would promise nothing more than a friendly neutrality, and after Bailey broke with Governor Morrison in the winter of 1922-23, he withdrew even that agreement and gave public notice that he would support McLean. [6] Not discouraged by this rebuff, Bailey made his plans to run without the help of the party organization.

On December 30, 1923, he left the Raleigh law firm of Pou, Bailey, and Pou, and it was understood that he would make a formal announcement of his candidacy within a few days. For the sake of party solidarity, Chairman Dawson requested a short campaign, but Bailey decided to delay no longer than the middle of January. On the 12th, he gave a statement to the press, and five days later, he published his platform. [7]

McLean withheld his announcement until the middle of March. On March 17, he issued a statement, presenting the course of action he would follow if elected. He said: "In my judgment, a safe and sane, yet thoroughly progressive administration of the State's affairs is the paramount need at the present time. It is my ambition to give the State such an administration." He pledged his support for the following policies: continued improvement in public education; development of agriculture in such a way as to produce prosperity and contentment among the farmers; a survey of the tax situation with the view to removing defects and inequities, and a study of government expenses to the end that the state might be brought to live within its income; adoption of the budget system in every branch of the government; removal of all discrimination against North Carolina in the matter of freight rates; simplification of the judicial system; and continuation of the good roads program and other internal improvements. [8]

Meanwhile, On March 9, McLean had opened headquarters in the Yarborough Hotel at Raleigh and appointed W. J. Brogden, a Durham attorney who had never been closely associated with the Democratic machine, as state manager for his campaign. [9] He again consulted with Senator Simmons and other members of Congress from North Carolina and they gave their approval to his announced candidacy and to the platform on which he planned to run. [10] Early in April, he completed his statewide organization through which he would carry his appeal to the people. To work with State Manager Brogden, he appointed local managers in all 100 counties and enlisted influential leaders to support his cause in cities and towns across the state. [11]

In April, the attention of candidates and people alike turned toward the State Democratic Convention. From the time Chairman Dawson called the meeting to order at noon on April 17, it was evident that new forces were in control. The masters of the assemblage were not Senator Simmons, Governor Morrison, or even Col. Alston D. Watts. [12] Neither Senator Simmons nor Senator Overman had come down from Washington; Governor Morrison was in New York on a bridal tour; and Colonel Watts was in exile, due to a recent scandal. [13] In their places stood men such as Chairman Dawson, J. Elmer Long, D. G. Brummitt, Walter Murphy, W. A. Graham, O. Max Gardner, and N. A. Townshend, all representatives of the new and younger leadership in the Democratic party in North Carolina.

The election of delegates-at-large to the National Convention brought the only contest in the Convention and in that fight the women and the new men carried the day. Miss Mary C. Graham presented a resolution asking for an equally divided delegation of four men and four women. O. Max Gardner, who had been the champion of women's voting rights in 1920, threw his influence behind the proposal and the convention gave an overwhelming approval. Gardner also challenged the propriety of selecting both Senators for the panel; whereupon both Simmons and Overman had their names withdrawn. On the first vote, Chairman Dawson was elected by acclamation; on subsequent ballots Gardner, Morrison, and Josephus Daniels were chosen as the other men. The four women selected were: Miss Mary Henderson, Mrs. T. Palmer Jerman, Miss Hattie Morehead Berry, and Mrs. J. G. Fearing. Upon the request of William B. Umstead of Durham, Wiley C. Rodeman, State Commander of the American Legion, was added to the delegation. This was a gesture of honor to the Democratic servicemen. [14]

The convention was overwhelmingly in favor of McLean. "Not only did everybody look McLean with a button; everybody talked him," wrote the reporter for the *Greensboro Daily News*. [15] The Robeson delegation and other McLean forces exhibited an assertive confidence that irritated the Bailey people, even more so since the Raleigh man had not been elected as a delegate from his own county. However, Bailey himself was not greatly disturbed, for he could take courage from the convention of 1920; Gardner had been the popular candidate, but when the votes were cast, Cameron Morrison won the election. Speaking to the student body at Wake Forest College on the night of the eighteenth, Bailey declared he would fight to the end, win or lose. [16]

Undertones from the convention hall revealed a concern about the lavish spending of the Morrison administration and the feeling that it was time to take an inventory before the state continued the new progressivism. Furthermore, Secretary of State W. E. Everett, the keynote speaker, braved the wrath of his chief by "telling the truth" about the state's finances. He announced that by June 30, 1925, North Carolina would be faced with a deficit of $3,000,000 or more. [17] While that was not a cause for despair, he explained, it would mean that the government must find additional sources of revenue to pay for the new services demanded of it and must organize its finances with greater efficiency. He expressed his confidence in the willingness of North Carolina people to pay the bill and said they would not be stampeded by talk about taxes, but he declared a businesslike administration of public affairs by a governor with a great social vision was the necessity of the hour.

The platform approved by the convention included little or nothing of significance. The Greensboro paper called it "an abbreviated glorification of the party's past and not too lengthy promise to maintain the status quo." [18] The document of 2,000 words contained the usual praise of the Democratic party on both national and state levels; also the customary generalizations on promotion of the public welfare, all of which could be interpreted to please any faction or leader. The committee had discussed an eight-month school term and the restoration of the Cape Fear and Yadkin Valley Railroad, but decided not to mention these in the platform.

With the convention over, the two candidates renewed their campaigns with great energy and determination. For almost two months, North Carolinians saw and heard them as they presented their policies and views on what should be done for the state. Bailey had the advantage in this, for he was a fluent speaker and loved the challenge of a keen debate; but McLean tackled the job with the same tenacity and indefatigable will which had always been a part of the Scotsman's nature. He openly acknowledged his weakness as a speaker, but did not let that deter him from the task ahead. In a presentation at Wadesboro, he explained that he was no orator "as there were no schools of elocution or oratory on the farm where he was reared." He had spent his time, he said, "calling hogs and hollering gee-haw to a mule." This disadvantage on the speaker's platform notwithstanding, he moved ahead with his campaign plans. Early in April, he had begun his intensive campaign in the eastern and northeastern counties; in May, he moved on into the Piedmont and then into the mountain area. By the first of June, he had visited seventy counties and made a hundred speeches. For the final week, he returned from Western North Carolina to speak in Wilmington and to spend the last days in his home county of Robeson.

With a marked political shrewdness, Bailey succeeded in calling many of the plays and selecting the issues for the campaign. While McLean wanted to make his main appeal to the voters on economy in government and recasting the state's administrative machinery,

Bailey forced him to talk about taxes, freight rates, and machine politics, subjects of great popular appeal. In like manner, Bailey influenced the direction the campaign would follow by making an open appeal to the farmers who were suffering from a prolonged depression.

Even before the people of North Carolina were much concerned about another election, a Bailey-inspired writer launched a campaign to discredit McLean in the eyes of the farmers. An article, supported by editorial notation, appeared in the *Roxboro Courier* on December 12, 1923, charging that in 1920, after propaganda from Washington had led the farmers to plan the largest crop of cotton and tobacco in history, the War Finance Corporation, of which McLean was a member, had suspended its activities and left them with a crop they could not sell. The writer declared that due to this curtailment of credit, cotton, which had been bringing forty-two cents, fell to ten cents a pound, causing a net loss of $1,657,750,000 on the year's crop. He also charged that McLean and his associates made no effort to resume financing cotton exports until Congress, in January 1921, adopted a resolution directing the Corporation to resume activities; and that the Corporation had devoted its attention almost exclusively to big businesses, railroads, and public utilities, or to the cattle farmers of the West, and had ignored the cotton and tobacco farmers of the South. These were the facts, the editor of the *Courier* said, that the rank and file of the Democratic party should know since "it appears that the officeholding class, under the direction of Senator Simmons, Governor Morrison and A. D. Watts, seem to have determined to appoint Honorable Angus Wilton McLean Governor to succeed Morrison in 1925." [19] More than 11,000 copies of this article were mailed out to government agencies, civic organizations, church groups, and hundreds of individuals. [20] It was also reprinted in many local newspapers.

These charges represented a serious threat to McLean. If Bailey could win the farm vote, he would be able to carry the state, for North Carolina was largely rural. McLean denied the accusations, insisting that his work on the War Finance Corporation in 1918 had been almost entirely in the interest of the farmers. He said he had opposed the policy of the Federal Reserve Board in restricting credits in 1920 and had wanted to resign from his position, but Senator Simmons, Representative Claude Kitchen, Governor Morrison, and others had asked him to remain and continue his efforts to get relief for the cotton and tobacco growers through other channels. [21]

The Roxboro article caused indignation among McLean's followers, and Aubrey L. Brooks of Greensboro prepared an answer to the *Courier*. He sent a questionnaire to prominent men in government circles, asking them for information concerning the *Courier* charges and their opinions relative to McLean's record with the War Finance

Corporation. He asked them specifically if McLean had in any way been responsible for the deflation of 1920-1921 or had failed to serve the farmers of the South. Brooks received answers from senators and representatives, including Senators Simmons and Overman and Representatives R. L. Doughton and Charles Abernethy of North Carolina, and Senators Kenneth McKellar of Tennessee, John B. Kendrick of Wyoming, William J. Harris of Georgia, Pat Harrison of Mississippi, and J. Thomas Heflin of Alabama. McLean furnished Brooks with other letters from his files. All of these denied that McLean had in any way contributed to the deflation of 1920-1921, and testified that he had given himself completely and tirelessly to the cause of the farmers and their problems. Representative Doughton, the dirt farmer of the North Carolina delegation in Congress, expressed in substance the feelings of all when he wrote:

> I am familiar from personal contact and other ways with Mr. McLean's work as director of the War Finance Corporation, both during the war and after the war, and in my judgment he was one of the best friends that the agricultural and livestock industries had in official life at that time. He was understood to be one official who had the intimate knowledge of the agricultural and livestock situation . . . I heard many senators and representatives from the agricultural and livestock districts express themselves to the effect that Mr. McLean by his untiring efforts had demonstrated his real friendship for the farmers and livestock producers, and had been one of the most potential factors in bringing relief and help to them.
>
> In conclusion, I will say that in my opinion nothing could be more unjust than to charge Mr. McLean with the responsibility in any way for deflation and the disastrous conditions that resulted therefrom. It would be just as fair or reasonable to accuse George Washington with having been a Tory or Noah with having caused the flood as to charge A. W. McLean with the responsibility in any way for deflation. [22]

Bailey also posed the tax issue in a manner as to appeal to the farmers. He insisted that the burden of taxes, which had increased from approximately $10,000,000 in 1912 to more than $86,000,000 in 1922, had fallen in an unjust and injurious measure on the land, especially farmland and small homes. Under the existing system, he explained, the farmer paid out in taxes sixteen percent of his yearly income, while all other classes paid only eleven percent. He liked to describe North Carolina as a land of 560,000 families, 450,000 of them living on an income of less than $2,000 a year and 350,000 of them trying to live on less than $900 a year. In contrast to this, he added, the Atlantic Coast Line Railroad, which paid .1 percent in franchise tax, was making money at the rate of $2,000,000 a month on an investment of some $70,000,000; and R. J. Reynolds' Tobacco

Company was clearing a net profit of from $20,000,000 to $30,000,000 a year. [23]

To relieve the farmers of this unjust burden, Bailey presented a three-point program. He proposed the repeal of the legislative act exempting from taxation more than $116,000,000 worth of stock in foreign corporations held in the state, an increase in franchise rates on railroads, and a readjustment of the tax load by allocating to the counties other sources of revenue or by turning the schools over to the state for support. [24]

McLean and his friends realized the subject of taxes was dangerous if Bailey were allowed to exploit it unanswered. In February, James O. Carr wrote McLean: "We must realize that there is a large dissatisfied element on account of high local taxes, etc., and it might not be very hard for Bailey to stir up this element. I do not think his tax propaganda has taken root in the public mind generally, certainly not the thinking mind. However, if he can get it to the one 'gallus' fellow it might be harmful." [25]

In a counterattack with which they hoped to neutralize Bailey's appeal to the farmers, the McLean forces accused him of duplicity in his position on taxes. G. K. Grantham, who had served in the General Assembly of 1919 from Harnett County, published charges of bad faith in an article entitled, "When Did Mr. Bailey Become the Friend of the Farmer?" He asserted that in 1919, when the legislature was considering the income tax as a means of relieving the tax burden on land, Bailey as a representative for the capitalists and corporations appeared before the Finance Committee and fought the proposal. When he was asked how sufficient money could be raised otherwise, Grantham said Bailey replied: "If you want some revenue right badly, assess the lands of North Carolina, 33,000,000 acres of them . . . and you will get some revenue, all you need. Why don't you do it? Is it easier to make North Carolina corporations shell out once more? Why, in North Carolina, hogs are valued at less than I pay for a ham . . . !" And to another question Bailey had made the remarkable declaration that "dogs in Durham are taxed higher than mules," Grantham reported. [26]

In answering Grantham's imputations, Bailey declared he was being quoted out of context and his position thus completely misrepresented. He admitted he had opposed the income tax in 1919, but insisted he did so because the Federal government at that time levied heavy income taxes and he did think it an opportune time for the state to impose more. Now that the Federal taxes had been reduced, he had changed his mind. The statement about "the mules and dogs" and "hogs and ham," he said, was also being misinterpreted. He had not been advocating increased taxes on farmers, but was trying to show the disparities existing between tax evaluation of personal and real property in the several counties, that hogs were taxed at sixty cents a piece in one county and $3.00 in another. His main purpose, he explained, had been to point out that the Tax Commission was not properly exerting its powers to equalize taxes. [27] Yet for all Bailey and his friends could do to discount Grantham's charges, the "mules and dogs" and "hogs and ham" circulars caused him more trouble perhaps than anything the McLean forces did.

McLean himself did not enter the war of circulars and campaign pamphlets, but dealt with the tax issue in a more constructive manner—in his speeches. He approved the income tax amendment of 1920 and the policy of reserving all levies on personal and real property to the counties for local purposes and allocating the income, inheritance, and other special taxes to the state. He recognized, however, that there were gross inequities in tax rates of the several counties. Some lands were valued too high, a considerable amount of land was never listed for taxes, and the rates were excessive in some counties. These defects must be worked out with the assistance of the General Assembly, he declared. [28]

Moreover, the crux of the problem of finance, McLean insisted, was not in the tax laws or even in the collection of taxes, but in the application of sound business methods to spending the money collected. A reduction of taxes could best be achieved through "economy from extravagance" and careful supervision of both state and local revenues. To an audience at Wadesboro he said, "We are watching the tax collectors, and shutting our eyes to the tax spenders . . . we will have to recognize and apply business methods to government and private affairs." [29]

To achieve efficiency and economy in government, he recommended the establishment of an Executive Budget Commission. He believed that such a body headed by the governor could effect economies, which would reduce expenses without interfering with necessary and wholesome progress. The readjustment in administrative machinery could be effected by converting the existing Legislative Budget Commission into an Executive Commission and giving it sufficient power to supervise all fiscal affairs of the state government. The reorganized body would serve as a department of finance, functioning not only when the legislature was in session, but in the interim between sessions. As such, the Commission would draft the revenue and machinery acts for the General Assembly, coordinate the work of all state departments, and, by closely supervising the state's finances, maintain a balanced budget and prevent accumulated deficits. This was McLean's real answer to the tax problem. [30]

Another issue that Bailey introduced into the campaign, freight rates, was also a timely subject. The problem of rate discrimination against North Carolina had been a matter of concern for years, but during the early twenties it had become a serious threat to the new industrial development as well as a source of hardship to farmers and consumers in general. Governor Morrison had appealed to the Interstate Commerce Commission to secure readjustment of rates and, in 1924, sponsored a plan for the development of water transportation, including the construction of public terminals and improved ports and the establishment of a state-owned boat line.

Bailey took up the cause and inveighed against the railroads with great fervor. They were wealthy and powerful and must be regulated, he said. To clinch their control over North Carolina shipping, they had bought and dismembered the Cape Fear and Yadkin Valley Railroad, the one line that could have made connections with the roads of the west and brought throughline rates from the middle west to a deep water port at Wilmington. If anything were ever to be done about this, he concluded, the state could not afford to take the chances involved in electing a railroad man as governor; and "one of the candidates for Governor had been president of an Atlantic Coast Line subsidiary" for years and had resigned in January 1924 in full view of his candidacy. [31]

McLean was in favor of doing everything possible to secure rates fair to the state. He had long advocated the development of water transportation in competition with the railroads and he saw the need for a trunk line to the west. [32] But, to him these were matters to be fought out in the courts and in the halls of the legislature and not subjects that could be decided on the stump in a political campaign. Nevertheless, he dealt with the issue in his major addresses and pledged himself to see that the cases before the Interstate Commerce Commission and the courts were prosecuted with vigor and every effort made to remove discrimination and put North Carolina on a parity with neighboring states. [33]

In an address at Greensboro in late June, McLean defended his connection to the Atlantic Coast Line. He said he saw the needs of Robeson County and sought to do something about them. The area, he stated, was "bottled up by a branch of the Seaboard" and its services to a growing community were inadequate. "We needed railroad competition and we couldn't get it," he declared. To solve the problem, he told how he had persuaded two friends to join him and help build a line to connect with the Atlantic Coast Line about twenty-seven miles from Lumberton. In spite of Seaboard opposition, they built the road, he said, and opened up that section of Robeson and a good part of Bladen county. As a result, population in towns along the line increased tenfold and the whole southeastern section of the state shared in the benefits. "My neighbors down there have said it was the most constructive thing I have ever done and I believe it is so," he said. [34]

As for his serving as divisional counsel for the Atlantic Coast Line, that relationship had ended in 1918, he stated. He had appeared in court for the Coast Line but it was in the open, he declared. At the same time, he had prosecuted suits against the Southern and Seaboard, he explained, and had made more money in those cases than he had ever earned in retainer fees from the Coast Line.

Bailey's third issue, machine politics, was not only a threat to Democratic solidarity, but also gave aid and comfort to the Republicans. Because he was waging the contest of a political Ishmaelite, Bailey attempted to capitalize on the growing disapproval of the Simmons machine and thereby gain the votes of all the disgruntled, as well as the liberals of the state. Recent misdeeds within the party's inner circle had brought reproach upon the figurative head of the machine. Lieutenant Governor William B. Cooper and his brother, Thomas E. Cooper, had been charged with misuse of funds in the Commercial National Bank of Wilmington; the state democratic chairman, J. D. Norwood, had "found a conflict between the Federal court and other duties" and had resigned; and the revenue commissioner and long-time party king-pin, Alston D. Watts, had gone out under a very dark moral shadow. These unfortunate episodes furnished materials for the Republican rebuttal to the Democratic censure of the Harding scandals, and added a note of political righteousness to Bailey's revolt against the so-called machine.

Bailey described the machine as "an organization of politicians . . . who seek to maintain themselves in power by organization and patronage, rather than by the freely-expressed will of the people," [35] and he denounced with great vigor the attempt of any group to so do. He denied the right of one governor to name his successor or of senators and representatives in Washington to control the election of the state's officials. The machine, he said, was trying to perpetuate itself and, in doing so, had stolen the birthright of the people, the right of self government. He repeated that it was not a campaign between McLean and himself, but one between the people and the machine. In order to restore the party and government to the voters, he proposed the adoption of the secret or Australian ballot. Almost all of the other states in the Union had already initiated some form of the protected ballot. [36]

McLean was well aware of the harm that the Watts-Cooper wrongdoings could do him if his opponents succeeded in connecting him too closely with the Simmons organization, but he was not unfaithful to Simmons, his friend. In McLean's philosophy of life there was nothing that could justify being disloyal to a friend. Nor had a more faithful supporter of the Democratic party ever asked the approval of its members in North Carolina. [37] Personally, he deplored the conduct of such men as Watts and the Coopers, who brought discredit not only to themselves but also to the organization with which they were associated; but they were not the Democratic party. [38] He understood the confusion and apparent disintegration that was threatening the national party and was greatly disturbed by it. He devoted major portions of his speeches to an appeal for solidarity in Democratic ranks, and his call to harmony was perhaps as much for the party's sake as an attempt to nullify Bailey's arraignments against machine-controlled politics in North Carolina.

Although McLean refrained from using personal abuse in answering Bailey's charges, he responded to the attack in a number of campaign speeches. At Henderson in Vance County, on May 11, he asked: "What is the machine?" As an answer he declared: "If it is the fighting militant Democrats who swept Russelism and Butlerism into discard, then I am proud that I have its support, for that means that every Democrat in North Carolina who loves his party is for me . . ." [39] At Salisbury and again at Greensboro he defended the state election laws, saying he doubted all the talk about dishonesty in the way elections were administered but assured the people of the state that, if elected, he would use every means at his command to prosecute offenders. [40] He tried to avoid a clear-cut stand on the secret ballot, but statements made during the campaign indicated that he opposed the system. At Greensboro on June 3, he said, "I am a Democrat and not ashamed for any man to see me vote, but I have no objection to the Australian ballot." [41] The next day, at Wilmington, he came near to taking a definite stand, saying, "I always feel when a man wants to hide his ballot that he wants to slip over and vote the Republican ticket." [42]

Meanwhile, McLean's friends had few scruples in their counterattacks. Former state senator, R. S. McCoin, and O. M. Mull, McLean's manager in Cleveland County, rushed into the fray with gloves off. McCoin called Bailey another Marion Butler who was going around the state "raving about the so-called 'machine,' the Democratic organization from which he drew $45,000 in salary in a nice, fat job over a period of twenty-five years of almost continuous office-holding." [43] In a letter to the *Cleveland Star* on March 14, Mull declared Bailey had used the machine to defeat Gardner in 1920, and had himself been the one to recommend A. D. Watts for office as Commissioner of Revenue. Furthermore, Mull added, if Bailey had now deserted the machine, he should prove his conversion in the ranks of the privates before he assumed command. [44] And even before McCoin and Mull responded, Brock Barkley, Raleigh reporter for the *Charlotte Observer*, had attacked with sword unsheathed. In a public letter in February, he wrote:

> In 1919, Mr. Bailey, you were mired down to your neck in fellowship with Colonel Alston D. Watts and the 'machine.' Now you seek to make the public believe you have put on a clean shirt. Only a short time before 1919 you were sitting on the throne of the rev-

enue collector's kingdom in eastern North Carolina while Colonel Watts was ruling in the western realm. As a matter of fact, you and Colonel Watts were 'machine buddies' until sometime in 1921 when you got the gubernatorial bee and Colonel Watts refused to go out and get honey for you. [45]

McLean was in favor of continued improvement of the public schools, with the ultimate goal of equal opportunities for every child to enjoy the best educational advantages (both academic and vocational), that the state could afford. While most of the counties were able, for the time being, to provide school for only six months, he believed that, with the expected increase in wealth and development of material resources, all of North Carolina could move into an eight-month program in the near future. The most pressing need, he maintained, was for better educational facilities in the rural communities. Every plan for improving agriculture, for bringing a better life to the people on the farm, he insisted, must include provisions for schools and training in both scientific and practical agriculture. [46]

Bailey spoke very little about education, for all his professed liberalism. However, some of Bailey's friends attempted to turn the discussion to his benefit by forcing McLean to take a definite stand on an eight-month term for the whole state. By so doing, they could either negate the influence that McLean's advocacy of more and better educational opportunities was having on the liberals or discredit him in the eyes of the numerous voters who were opposed to additional spending for schools. To this end, they spread rumors that McLean had announced he would support an immediate extension of the six-month term. Those who were set against increasing local taxes were so upset that McLean had to take a public stand against the proposal. At Sanford on May 19, he said: "I know, as every other intelligent man knows, that we are not in shape at the present time to assume the tax burden of an eight-month school term." [47] He went on to explain that he was looking to that as an ultimate goal, but that it might be many years before it could be realized. It would be up to the people to decide when the state could afford it. He reaffirmed this position in other speeches.

Although organized labor was of minor significance in North Carolina, recent strikes and labor unrest caused politicians to give more attention to the laboring class in the new industrial centers. Bailey made a direct bid for its support; but the labor leaders, who could not agree on a common policy, were never able to mobilize even their small organizations for either candidate. [48] McLean warned against the demagogues who tried to stir up class against class and promised a fair and just treatment for both capital and labor. [49]

In his campaign McLean had the support of all the leading daily papers in the state except the *Greensboro Daily News*, which sympathized with Bailey's candidacy. The *Asheville Citizen, Charlotte Observer, Winston-Salem Journal,* and *Wilmington Star* ardently favored McLean. The *Raleigh News and Observer* gave equal coverage to both candidates. Many weeklies and smaller daily papers wrote on behalf of Bailey or used his materials in their columns. Among the more outspoken and zealous Bailey organs were the *Roxboro Courier, The Independent* of Elizabeth City, the *Dunn Dispatch,* the *Kinston Free Press,* and the *People's Advocate* of Fayetteville.

Although in late May there appeared to be a surge toward the Bailey camp and McLean became quite concerned about the over confidence which he sensed among his followers, in the minds of those who knew North Carolina politics, there was never any doubt about a McLean victory. [50] Even the *Greensboro Daily News,* commenting on McLean's distress, admitted Bailey had things going his way at the moment but declared "a Bailey triumph would be a phenomenon so weird that we are unable to visualize it imaginatively." [51] And, save for an eleventh-hour attempt on the part of Bailey forces to influence voters by injecting the Ku Klux Klan into the contest, the campaign moved successfully to a close. When the returns were in, the vote stood 151,197 for McLean and 83,574 for Bailey. [52] McLean had carried eighty-three of the one hundred counties; he had found approval in the rural counties of the mountain area and the coastal plain as well as in the urban and industrial sections of the Piedmont.

On the surface it is difficult to account for so decisive a victory. From the beginning, McLean had two disadvantages which few candidates in North Carolina have been able to overcome: he was a poor speaker and he had associated with the railroads and "capitalists" much of his life. On the other hand, Bailey was one of the most able speakers the state had ever produced—and he had been associated with a church publication much of his life. Furthermore, Bailey had the outside man's advantage, in that he could capitalize on the mistakes of the incumbents and profit by the growing revolt against so-called extravagance in government spending; while McLean was supported by the administration and could not afford to criticize Morrison's program.

The *Greensboro Daily News* found an explanation for McLean's victory in the general prosperity that North Carolina had been enjoying since 1921. This paper contended that people, by and large, were not going to worry much about political machines, as long as business was good. [53] For the *Asheville Citizen,* the McLean victory meant that North Carolinians were committed to the stride of progress that had been made in recent years. [54] It was true that, in spite of all the complaints about tax burdens and a "spending administration," few things in the history of the state had found such universal approval as the Good Roads Movement—and McLean had promised to continue that program. The warmth of pride in new school buildings, city streets, modern courthouses, and other community improvements, and the satisfaction received from reports of a growing industry, made a rather good insulation against the chilling words about high taxes and machine politics.

Another explanation for the election returns lies in the individual character of the candidates themselves. Although McLean was not a good speaker, he presented his program in such an honest and frank manner that people believed he meant what he said. On the other hand, there was a streak of demagoguery in Bailey's approach that made many afraid to trust him. In May, the *Asheville Citizen* wrote that as "a statesman he [Bailey] is without the stability which thinks out a policy in statecraft and sticks to it. He is blown about by too many winds of doctrine ever to reach a safe harbor." [55]

A final factor in McLean's victory was his efficient statewide organization. Since campaigns are won or lost in the local precincts, the success of a candidate frequently depends on the zeal and ability of the party workers. Without a doubt, McLean's corps of helpers contributed immeasurably to his victory. His organization had been completed early and was supported by the experienced men and women in the Democratic party. Although Bailey was the better speaker, he lacked the auxiliary force of field workers to carry his campaign to the individual voters. He poured out a veritable flood of literature, but as one of his supporters wrote, "An ardent worker on the highways and hedges is much more effective than printed matter."

In the weeks following the primary, the political leaders and the candidates turned their attention to preparations for the general election in November. The Democrats knew that the fall campaign for state officers would perhaps be overshadowed by the presidential election and this caused them great concern. Although the Republican party had been tarnished by the revelation of scandal in the Harding administration, improvements in the economy by 1923 seemed to make that party synonymous with prosperity. Furthermore, the Republicans had met in convention and, without dissent, nominated Calvin Coolidge for another term; while the Democratic Convention had become involved in a long and bitter contest between William Gibbs McAdoo and Alfred S. Smith, the idol of New York City. When neither of the two could win a two-thirds vote, the convention had nominated John W. Davis, a brilliant but conservative lawyer, whose connections with J. Pierpont Morgan Company completely disqualified him in the eyes of labor and western liberals. Moreover, as a dark-horse candidate and a man unknown to most Americans, Davis aroused little enthusiasm, even among eastern conservatives.

The introduction of a third ticket headed by Robert M. LaFollotte, a progressive Republican of Wisconsin, and Burton K. Wheeler, a liberal Democrat of Montana, threatened to draw farm-labor support from the Democratic party. The bitterness engendered at the national convention, the Progressive appeal to labor and farmers, and the lackluster nature of the party's leader made 1924 a bleak year for Democrats.

To counter general apathy among Democrats and to offset current advantages of the Republicans, State Chairman John G. Dawson and the Democratic Executive Committee launched a major campaign on behalf of the party and all of its candidates. The shortage of funds and of volunteer workers, however, made their task more difficult. Campaign contributions were slow in coming in, leaving an unusually heavy financial burden on the candidates themselves. [56] Not dismayed by these problems, Dawson set up a statewide organization and sent out a veritable army of speakers to carry the Democratic message into every section of the state. [57] He enlisted candidates seeking office as well as loyal Democrats from the one hundred counties, and he also invited out-of-state leaders to make keynote speeches. Senator Pat Harrison of Mississippi came to open the campaign in September; [58] Senator Cole L. Blease of South Carolina came in October. [59] Senators Simmons and Overman, Congressman Edward W. Pou, and Josephus Daniels also came down from Washington to take an active part in the campaign. The list of other speakers included J. C. B. Ehringhaus, A. L. Brooks, Josiah W. Bailey, O. Max Gardner, Dennis G. Brummitt, Major Walter Murphy, Clyde R. Hoey, D. F. Giles, Baxter Durham, and Francis D. Winston—all leaders or future leaders in North Carolina. [60]

On March 20, the Republican State Convention had announced the candidacy of Isaac Meekins for governor and adopted a platform approving the program of the National Republican Party and endorsing the major policies on which both McLean and Bailey were seeking nomination: continuation of the Good Roads Program, better schools, reduction of taxes through economy and efficiency in government, restoration of the Cape Fear and Yadkin Railroad, progressive labor legislation, and fair election laws. [61] In his campaign, Meekins challenged McLean to a public debate on taxes and other issues; and he made a bid for the defeated Bailey forces, inviting them to join the Republicans and help defeat McLean and the Democratic party machine. [62]

Late in August, McLean opened his fall campaign and for ten weeks he again visited most of the one hundred counties. He had learned much from his experience in the spring; so he was more at ease with the crowds he met in September and October than he had been in April and May. He pledged his administration to continue the road-building program and to increase state appropriations for public schools. He made no promises to reduce taxes or to sponsor the favorite project of any particular community, but he renewed his promise to administer the state efficiently and to secure the best possible returns from all tax dollars spent.

In addition to the platform on which he sought election, McLean discussed matters of common interest to all Americans. Frequently, he spoke on what he considered the important issues of the day: prevention of war, increased world trade, the preservation of democratic government free of corruption, the insidious usurpation of power by an "invisible empire," and a more equitable distribution of the tax burden. In response to the Progressive party's effort to attract the farm vote, he addressed the problems of rural families. He agreed that net returns on their work were too small. To change that situation, he advised farmers to raise their own food and feed instead of buying these items, to grow less cotton and a greater variety of other crops, and to seek education and training in scientific and practical agriculture. These changes, he insisted, would bring prosperity to the farm. [63] Wherever he went, he defended his party, declaring that although Democrats had been out of power, they had done more for the country during the last four years than the Republicans had done while in control. [64]

As he toured the state, McLean seldom had a capacity crowd and was never able to stir any great enthusiasm for his cause, but his straightforward manner left the feeling that he would be a safe leader. [65] Of additional assistance to his candidacy was the excellent coverage he received from a friendly press. In the spring, L. J. Hampton had been employed and paid by the *Wilmington Star*, the *Charlotte Observer*, the *Asheville Citizen*, and a number of other dailies to report on his meetings. Ben Dixson MacNeill and Jonathan Daniels followed him during the fall campaign. MacNeill, in particular, tried to create a new, more positive image for McLean. Instead of the formal, reserved person, who had difficulty making friends, MacNeill pictured him as a devoted and affectionate husband and father. He reported that McLean called home almost daily after dinner to have contact with his family. On the day after the election in November he even published a story describing how McLean had gone to the polls and cast his ballot, but instead of staying to hear the outcome that evening, he went home and gathered his children to take them on an opossum hunt. [66] These press reviews did not make McLean a charismatic leader, but they encouraged many voters to trust him as their governor.

McLean finished his tour of the western counties on November 1 and returned home to await the results of the election. On November 4, he carried the state by a vote of 294,441 against a total of 185,627 for Meekins. [67] On November 6, in a message expressing his gratitude to the electorate, he repeated the pledge he had made when he announced his candidacy: to subordinate every personal interest and to strive earnestly and wholeheartedly for the welfare of the state. And, there was the widespread conviction that he meant it.

Chapter IV

―――――•••●•••―――――

AN ADMINISTRATION OF EFFICIENCY AND ECONOMY: THE EXECUTIVE BUDGET SYSTEM

―――――•••●•••―――――

At noon on January 14, 1925, Angus Wilton McLean took the oath of office and entered upon his duties as the 55th governor of North Carolina. At 11:00 A.M. legislative committees met him as he arrived by special train from Lumberton and escorted him along streets lined with troops to the Executive Mansion, where Governor Morrison and other officials joined his party for the drive to the city auditorium and the inauguration ceremonies.

Shortly after noon Governor Morrison gave his Farewell Address and presented Governor-elect McLean to the state. Having been duly sworn by Chief Justice W. A. Hoke, the new chief executive delivered his Inaugural Address, a simple, straightforward message to the people of North Carolina. He said it was time for the state to take stock of its resources and liabilities, to consolidate the gains already won, and to put on a sound operating basis the permanent investments that had been made. This, he insisted, could best be done by improving the efficiency of each branch of the government so as to produce maximum service at minimum cost.

He promised to work toward equalizing the educational opportunities of all children, those on farms as well as those in towns and cities. He expressed his desire to complete the system of public highways, but he said he would approve no more bonds than could be safely issued without destroying the credit of the state.

During the past three years approximately $90,000,000 worth of North Carolina securities had been placed on the market, bringing the total debt to $110,000,000. It was evident to even the most optimistic, he declared, that such an unprecedented scale of expenditures could not be continued. Further spending on roads and permanent improvements at the several institutions would be necessary, but these programs should be kept within the bounds of business prudence and safety to the state's credit. He promised to use all his energy and accumulated experience to give North Carolina "an administration characterized by efficiency, economy, and rational progress," and that two elementary rules of sound finance would never be violated during his term of office: one, that current expen-

ditures must never exceed current revenues applicable to such out-
lays and second, that bonds should never be issued except for necessary permanent improvements and then with definite provision for
payment of interest and amortization of the principal. [1]

From the city auditorium, Morrison and McLean moved to a
stand on Fayetteville Street, where they viewed the inaugural
parade. Leading the procession was the governor's honor guard,
Battery B of the 262nd Coast Artillery from Lumberton and the
Service Company and band of the 120th Infantry of Raleigh. These
were followed by other units of the National Guard and a detach-
ment of the regular army artillery from Fort Bragg. The State College
R.O.T.C. battalion brought up the rear. Two three-inch guns boomed
the gubernatorial salute as the troops marched past the reviewing
stand with bands playing and colors flying.

Following the parade, McLean and his party were guests at a luncheon arranged by legislative committees and the Woman's Club of
Raleigh. In the evening, the festivities were concluded with a reception at the Mansion and a ball held in the city auditorium. Since
Mrs. McLean had not been able to come to Raleigh for the inauguration because of illness, McLean did not attend the ball but asked
Lieutenant Governor and Mrs. J. Elmer Long to go in his place.

It had been a great day for all the "Macs" and their friends and
neighbors from Lumber River. A large delegation, which had accom-
panied McLean to Raleigh on the special train, occupied a reserved
section in the auditorium, just to the left of the platform, during the
formal ceremonies at noon and had participated in all the festivities
of the day. It was quite apparent that these people from Robeson
were proud of the county's First Son; and none were prouder than
William McNeill and Abe Purdie, two black farmers on the McLean
lands, who came to see McLean inaugurated and stayed close by all
day to see it performed.

For the most part, both the new governor and his message were
approved by the entire state. Men who had believed in pay-as-you-go
were sure his plan of rational progress was the way to security and
safety, and those who had been for liberal appropriations in the
sweep of the "program of progress" were now convinced the time
had come to take stock. An administration characterized by efficiency, economy, and rational progress was what the people wanted and
they were ready to sustain the governor who promised these things. [2]
Indeed, few executives have taken office in North Carolina with as
nearly an unanimous approval as did Governor McLean.

Perhaps the main reason for such hearty endorsement of
McLean's program of economy and sound finance was the alarm
over a deficit in the general fund, a deficit which was growing larger
every year; also, a state debt of $113,868,000, as one of the heaviest
per capita in the United States. [3] In 1923, Commissioner of Revenue

A. J. Maxwell had shocked the state in the midst of its great spending spree by announcing there was a shortage, [4] but Governor Morrison denied it and the public was too pleased with new roads, more school buildings, street lights, and sewage systems to pay much attention. However, when Secretary of State William N. Everett reported the same thing to the State Democratic Convention in April 1924, more people stopped to think. By January 1925, when the General Assembly convened and the Budget Report of the biennium gave an estimated shortage of $9,515,787.63 by the end of the fiscal year in June, thus confirming all earlier predictions, the state was upset by the possibility of higher taxes and was ready to listen to counsel on economies of government spending. [5]

There were two main causes for the deficit and the growing state debt: namely, a fiscal system that had developed haphazardly and the legislative practice of making appropriations without providing the necessary revenue. The Budget Act of 1921 applied to only a limited part of the state government; some sixteen departments and numbers of commissions and other agencies operated under general authorizations. Approximately twenty-two units or divisions operated on their own revenues and made no statements of receipts or expenditures. Moreover, the legislature frequently approved laws carrying special grants in addition to the general appropriations, and there were numbers of continuing or hidden appropriations which were not included in the biennial estimates. Also, due to a policy of repeatedly "refunding" bonds, the state was still paying debts contracted before the Civil War. A change in dates for the fiscal year created other problems. In January of 1921, the General Assembly had moved the fiscal year forward, setting the beginning date for July 1 (instead of December 1), but had provided no special funds to take care of the seven months between the old and new fiscal periods. [6] The same session surrendered to the counties all taxes on property and substituted for state use a levy on personal and corporate income. This tax, however, was not collectible until 1922 and the government was left one entire year without revenue from either property or income tax. [7]

The Budget Commission's report and Governor McLean's recommendation that the deficit be funded and that the state go on a cash basis brought an angry protest from former Governor Morrison, who felt that an attempt was being made to discredit his administration. He insisted that North Carolina's financial affairs were in good condition and that the statements relative to a shortage in funds were unfounded in fact and based only on theories of accounting. In spite of the efforts of his friends to prevent his doing so, Morrison went to Raleigh for a hearing before a joint session of the House and Senate finance committees on February 4. He told them that his administration was due all taxes levied by the two revenue bills of his term, regardless of when they were collected, and demanded an audit on that basis. [8] The committees listened respectfully but acted on the recommendations of the Budget Commission. Unfortunately, Morrison and a few of his friends continued the fight, and for almost a year, the state heard their protests from platforms and through the press. McLean refused to be drawn into the controversy, knowing that any statement from him would only prolong the dispute; but when the attacks against the new administration continued through the summer and on into the fall, Charles A. Webb, editor of the *Asheville Citizen*, decided someone should answer the charges and try to bring the matter to a close. On September 28, he addressed a public letter to Morrison in which he assured him no one had accused his administration of wastefulness or extravagance and that he had many loyal friends throughout the state, but that people were getting tired of the controversy and his outbursts against McLean. [9] Santford Martin of the *Winston-Salem Journal* wrote him a few days later, saying almost the same thing. [10]

Meanwhile, McLean had turned his attention to the task of reorganizing the administrative machinery so as to help prevent future deficits. During the weeks following the election in November, he began conferring with state officials and visiting state institutions. In December, he met with the Legislative Budget Committee as it was drawing up the budget for 1925-1926. On January 21, a week after his inauguration, he went before the General Assembly to deliver a preliminary message on the economy and to set forth the general policies he would seek to follow as governor. He declared the cardinal principle of fiscal policy to be that the budget must be balanced for each operating period. He stated that he believed the state was entering upon a less spectacular period, because there must be less money spent on expansion and permanent improvements. Equally beneficial results could be achieved, however, by "constructive administrative work and continuous striving to apply to government those principles and methods of thrift and broad economy which the businessman applies to his own affairs." [11] To achieve this end, he urged the General Assembly to provide for an executive budget system, which would give the governor and a budget bureau the authority to supervise fiscal affairs of the state. This system had been the principal plank in the platform on which he had appealed to the voters and it was the foundation on which he as governor would build his hopes for a successful administration.

On January 30, when he delivered his official "State of Affairs" message, he renewed his request for a law converting the Legislative Budget Commission into an Executive Budget Commission with enlarged and more effective powers over fiscal affairs. The Legislative Budget Commission had been of great service, he said, but it was impossible for the members to give continuous attention and direction to the numerous state departments, agencies, and institutions. The Executive Budget Commission as a permanent body and headed by the governor would be able to meet this need. It would be able to prepare the annual budget based on estimated receipts and expenditures of the state as a whole, always guided by the principle that expenses must not exceed income. It would also have authority to investigate and supervise the management of funds by the state agencies and institutions. It would, in fact, provide the central organization that had been lacking in state government, and would achieve a level of efficiency and economy that could keep the state and its institutions and agencies on a sound financial basis.

To make the system operative, McLean recommended that the assembly repeal all statutes carrying special appropriations and to include every item to be funded in the general appropriation bill passed each biennium. He also stated that, to make the system work, the fiscal year must begin on July 1 and end on June 30 in each succeeding year. All revenues actually collected during this period would be applicable to that fiscal year, and all expenditures made during the period would be applicable to that period only. [12]

To prepare a bill providing for an Executive Budget Commission, one that he would present to the General Assembly, Governor McLean secured assistance wherever it was available. He gathered information from other states already trying such a system and from the Legislative Bureau of the United States Senate, and, to help write the law, he employed legislative draftsmen from the Bureau of Municipal Research in New York and the Federal Budget Bureau in Washington. Martin Gillen, a personal friend and a financial expert from Wisconsin, came and lived in the Executive Mansion during the entire session to help with the proposed measure. [13] R. L. Varser, the acting chairman of the Legislative Budget Commission, and other members of the General Assembly also gave many hours to working out the details.

On February 14, Representative Henry Groves Connor, Jr. introduced the bill and on February 28, "The Act to Establish an Executive Budget System for all State Departments, Bureaus, Divisions, Officers, Boards, Commissions, Institutions, and other State Agencies or Undertakings . . . " became law. The act made the governor *ex officio* director of the budget and head of a budget bureau established in connection with his office and converted the Legislative Budget Commission into an Advisory Budget Commission. This Advisory Budget Commission would meet in January and July of each year, or upon call of the director, for the biennial consideration of the state's finances. As director of the budget, the governor was given the power and authority to examine under oath any office or head of any department or institution; to compel the production of papers, books, and documents in the possession or under control of such officials; to have the books and accounts of all agencies audited, and to require that all institutions and divisions of the state government maintain a system of accounting and auditing which could be expected to provide correct information concerning their financial conditions; and to examine any state institution or agency, inspect its property, and inquire into its methods of operation and management. As director, it would also be his duty to recommend to the General Assembly such changes in the management of the several departments and institutions as, in his judgment, would promote a more efficient and economical operation of those agencies.

The act provided that all money should be appropriated and all funds disbursed from the State Treasury according to a biennial budget approved and adopted by the General Assembly at its regular sessions, and it made the preparation of such a budget one of the chief duties of the new bureau and advisory commission. It directed the heads of all departments and state agencies to cooperate in this preparation by furnishing, on or before September 1 of each nonlegislative year, reports of disbursements made during the past and current years and estimates of needs for the coming biennium. It also required the state auditor to supply quarterly and yearly statements of both the expenditures and revenues of all departments, institutions, and other agencies and a complete financial balance sheet for the state at the close of each fiscal period. From these estimates and reports, the director and the Advisory Budget Commission were instructed to draw up the biennial budget report and prepare an appropriation bill and a revenue bill to bring the report formally before the General Assembly. [14]

A number of other measures supplemented the Executive Budget Act and helped to establish the new arrangements for administering finances in the state. The General Fund Note Act of 1925 authorized the state treasurer, by and with the consent of the governor and Council of State, to sell up to $5,000,000 worth of notes to cover the expected deficit and balance the books at the close of the current fiscal year on June 30, 1925. This would facilitate the placing of all financial operations on a budgetary basis, whereby the cash revenue collected in each fiscal year could be applicable to and sufficient for the cash expense disbursements of the same period. [15] The appropriations act of 1925 repealed all laws carrying general and unlimited grants and placed all institutions, departments, and agencies upon a biennial appropriations basis. It also declared the allotments to be maximum and only available to the extent that they were necessary for the maintenance of the institutions and departments, and provided that if any part of the money allowed should be used for causes other than those specified in the act, the responsible persons would be subject to suit for recovery of the misused funds with interest and costs. And finally, it placed the supervision of all funds in the hands of the governor as director of the budget and authorized him to reduce all allotments pro rata when necessary in order to bring the appropriations within the revenue actually collected during the fiscal period. [16]

A third act, the Daily Deposit Act, required that all agencies receiving or collecting public funds deposit their collections daily with some bank or trust company officially designated and to the credit of the state treasurer. [17] By doing so, the government would not only be able to eliminate the cost of borrowing money in anticipation of revenue from taxes, but would also realize an added income from interest on the deposits.

A fourth act provided for the investment of all sinking funds. Under a constitutional provision, approved by the voters in the election in November of 1924, the sinking funds set up for the amortization of all state bonds were declared inviolate. To fulfill the purpose of that amendment, the General Assembly created a Sinking Fund Commission, composed of the governor, state treasurer, and state auditor, and directed it, under severe penalties for malfeasance, to invest the reserves. [18]

Soon after the legislature adjourned on March 10, Governor McLean set to work preparing for the inauguration of the new fiscal program. As he did not secure an assistant director until after the law went into effect in July, it was necessary for him to assume the chief responsibility for the bureau. He converted part of the Executive Mansion into a workshop and installed a staff of secretaries there to supplement the regular force at his office. A number of accountants were put to work in rooms on the third floor of the Capitol and others were sent out to audit the books and financial records of the state institutions. Meanwhile, McLean himself began holding conferences with the heads of departments and representatives of all state agencies to help them make a transition to the new system. Only his tremendous physical strength and tireless energy made it possible for him to accomplish the task. However, by laboring twelve to fourteen hours a day and with the enthusiastic cooperation of the men around him, he had the government and all its subdivisions ready to make the change by the last of June. [19]

The most important step in initiating the new plan was to put each administrative unit on a budgetary system of its own. To this end, McLean prepared forms and sets of instructions and asked all departments, institutions, and other agencies to begin work on their reports of expenditures for 1924-1925, their budgets for the next biennium, and their estimated requests for the first quarter of the incoming year. [20] Prior to 1925, appropriations made to the various units had usually become available in toto, and the board of directors and administrative head of each institution and agency had been left free to decide how the funds could be spent to the best advantage of the organization for which they were responsible. [21] Under the new system, however, all moneys granted were to be distributed in quarterly allotments and expenditures restricted to the amounts necessary to carry on the specific activities authorized by the General Assembly. Grants beyond the original allotments could be secured by petitioning the director, but all departments and agencies were required to stay within the legislative appropriations and to return any unexpended funds to the state treasurer at the close of the fiscal year.

Another important step in reorganizing the state's business was achieved by standardizing the methods used in buying supplies for the several departments and institutions. As director, McLean instructed these units to each appoint a purchasing agent and to make him directly responsible for all materials ordered and for the prices paid. All requests for supplies and services were to be presented to him as formal requisitions, in triplicate form, and he would grant authorization to purchase or hire, subject to the final approval of the head of the department or institution. [22] The separate units were also encouraged to take advantage of the benefits to be derived from buying in large lots and from using the facilities of the several departments in securing equipment and services. For instance, arrangements were made with the State Highway Department to take care of repairs and furnish supplies for all state-owned motor vehicles at actual cost. [23]

The introduction of new machinery and new methods for administering the state's fiscal affairs was not accomplished without difficulty, and of all the problems which Governor McLean encountered, the most serious one was trying to close the gap which the General Assembly left between the estimated income of 1925-1926 and the appropriations provided for the same period. He had worked for days with the House and Senate committees trying to pare requests for appropriations and to find additional sources of revenue, but in spite of their efforts, they failed to achieve a balanced budget. They had explored numerous suggestions for new taxes, but none were approved. The railroads protested against increasing their franchise fees; the merchants and manufacturers opposed a levy on tobacco products; and both the House and Senate had flatly rejected a general sales tax. The revenue bill as passed provided for an increase of 33 1/3 percent in the tax on corporate income, increases from 25 to 66 1/3 percent on personal income, and some minor increases in the inheritance tax. However, even with these higher rates and further cuts in appropriations, there still remained an estimated deficit of $558,290 for 1925-1926 and $1,151,719 for 1926-1927. [24]

Neither did developments during the spring months offer any hope that revenues would exceed the estimates and thus effect a balance in state finances. Each month the returns from taxes fell far short of expectations, and in April the total income ran behind by a million dollars. Under these circumstances, there seemed to be no way to meet the expenditures for the incoming year but to exercise the authority granted to the director of the budget to cut appropriations in proportion to the deficiency in revenues. To prepare for such a possible course of action, on April 27, McLean sent a memorandum to the heads of all departments and institutions explaining the situation in detail and warning them that in all probability there would have to be a pro rata reduction in their allotments. [25] By the middle of May, he was able to make a final statement and on May 20, he instructed all agencies to plan their expenditures on the basis of a five percent cut. [26]

There were complaints about the cut and every department of government found itself struggling to keep expenses within the reduced allotments. On November 6, Assistant Director Henry Burke sent a memorandum to McLean explaining that the Board of Public Buildings and Grounds was having problems. They had already discontinued the service of five janitors and would have to drop four more by the end of the month. The twenty remaining workers would be redistributed to serve all the departments. They had also attempted to cut expenses by discontinuing the supply of towels (except paper ones), matches, and drinking cups in public buildings. They hoped to save $1,800 a year by using a central telephone exchange for all departments. They were also considering the possibility of moving state offices from rental space into quarters in the Old Blind School building, once these were repaired. [27] McLean himself cut the staff at the mansion and took other measures to reduce the cost of maintenance at that facility.

There were other vigorous protests against the cut in appropriations and a few ugly incidents got considerable publicity. Dr. C. Banks McNairy, Superintendent of Caswell Training School, told reporters that his institution would have to reduce its staff and turn out some thirty or possibly seventy of its inmates to stay within the funds it had received. [28] In August, an article was released to the press saying that sixteen patients, all suffering from the worst stages of tuberculosis, had been requested to leave the North Carolina Sanatorium for the Treatment of Tuberculosis because there was no room for them. The lack of room, the article stated, was due to the reduction of appropriations for the institution. Superintendent P. P. McCain declared he had been misquoted and that there was no such emergency, but the article caused some to wonder if "rational progress" was what the state needed after all. [29]

A continuing problem that McLean and his staff encountered was that of keeping the several institutions and state agencies within the bounds of their annual appropriations. As the first financial reports came to the governor's desk in June of 1925, they revealed the fact that some departments and institutions had already overspent all of their allotments for 1924-1925 and were piling up debts in both current and capital outlay. The General Assembly of 1923 had tried to stop such imprudent practices by adding a clause to the Act to Provide Bonds for Permanent Improvements at the State Institutions, a clause which made any official who voted for or aided in spending more than was appropriated for his institution liable to removal by the governor. [30]

McLean declined to take action under this provision, but gave notice that he expected to follow the more exact law of 1925 strictly and to keep a close check on all expenditures. However, in spite of careful supervision, keeping all the agencies within the limits of their allotments was a continuous problem, and on occasion Henry Burke had to deal rather vigorously with some of them. In October 1926, he reported that five of the institutions had gone beyond their appropriations, and, in the spring of 1927, at least one exceeded its allotments. [31] The worst offender, according to Burke's standards, was the State Hospital at Raleigh. In February 1927, he declared that as to housekeeping the institution was run perfectly, but that neither the officials nor the employees knew the first thing about good business methods. There were no records kept of their supplies, he said, and no proper requisitions were required for withdrawals from the stores. [32] And in March he wrote Governor McLean stating that the Hospital had simply "repudiated the Budget system" and had overdrawn its appropriations again. [33]

As could be expected, there were mutterings and complaints about the numerous reports and the new system of supervision, and some directors and administrators expressed bitter resentment toward the Bureau and its control over appropriations. C. F. Harvey, president of the Board of Directors for State Hospital in Raleigh, wrote McLean and said that his board intended to see that the hospital received all the money which had been appropriated for its use and that the directors would take full responsibility for all the institution spent. [34] Nathan O'Berry, a director of the State Hospital in Goldsboro, tendered his resignation, declaring he could not waste his time merely signing vouchers. [35] The University of North Carolina keenly resented the budgetary controls. Dr. E. C. Branson of the Department of Rural Social Economics wrote Governor McLean protesting that the authority of the director to make pro rata reductions in appropriations created an uncertainty as to the actual amount the school could expect for current expenses and thus made it difficult to operate on contracts. He also claimed that the loss of independence in making decisions about the distribution of funds provided for buildings, equipment, and repairs rendered it impossible to make the adjustments frequently needed in a growing institution. [36]

In spite of the criticism from all these sources, the governor's perseverance and hard work were rewarded. By the summer of 1926, the worst financial difficulties were over and the annual reports told the good news—that the state was ending the first half of the biennium with a surplus in the treasury. In his annual statement in July 1926, McLean cited a cash balance of $1,269,824 for the year, a balance substantial enough to take care of the $900,000 gap between the appropriations and the estimated revenues for 1926-27. [37]

Benefiting from his experiences during his first year and a half as governor, McLean asked the General Assembly in 1927 to provide new powers for the director of the budget, powers which would enable him, with the consent of the majority of the Advisory Budget Commission, to cut allotments when they were too large or when they exceeded the actual revenue applicable to such grants, and to distribute any necessary reductions among the departments and institutions at his own discretion. [38] Stirred by jealousy of the governor's increased powers, the legislators refused to approve these requests. They left the power to cut appropriations, but only in the case of insufficient revenue and with the provisions that such reductions must be made pro rata, as the 1925 law had provided.

"Deliberate progress" was still the slogan of most of the members of the General Assembly in 1927, but the deficit-provoked gloom of 1926 had been dispelled by the gratifying news of a surplus. In a more generous frame of mind, they loosened the purse strings and voted an appropriation of $72,247,790 for the biennial period, while they approved a revenue bill which differed very little from the bill of 1925. They included an estate tax to take advantage of the act of Congress which permitted the Federal government to abandon eighty percent of its estate tax to states making an equal levy; they also added a graduated license tax on contractors and raised the rate on corporate incomes by one half of one percent. Otherwise, the state taxes remained approximately as they had been, [39] and the estimated revenues for the biennium again fell short of the appropriations by $1,419,279. The treasury was in a better condition in 1927, however, and a credit balance estimated at $1,400,000 would take care of the expected deficit.

The administration had adopted the policy of issuing no bonds except for useful and permanent improvements and always with a plan for payment of interest and amortizing the principal within the life of the improvement. This policy, with the installation of the new budget machinery, improved the state's credit in the money markets, and McLean's experience as a banker and member of the War

Finance Corporation also proved to be a valuable asset when he and State Treasurer Ben R. Lacy opened negotiations for the sale of North Carolina securities. [40] The men on Wall Street knew and trusted McLean and appreciated the fact that he understood what he was talking about when he discussed money. In turn, McLean understood the temperament of the bond markets, how important it was to watch for the right moment, and the importance of preparation before attempting a sale. With this in mind, he informed the financial world about the new laws that tightened up the sinking funds, provided for a balanced budget, and promoted an efficient, businesslike administration of state affairs. He mailed copies of his financial statements to banks, insurance companies, and other potential investors throughout the country. His reports were well received and the beneficial effects of his labor were soon reflected in better rates for the state's bonds.

In June 1925, Governor McLean and State Treasurer Lacy went to New York with $5,000,000 of long-term notes, authorized to fund the deficit in the general fund, and $10,000,000 in short-term notes issued in anticipation of the collection of taxes. Although the market had been quiet and the prospects did not look favorable, McLean made a personal appeal to a group of bankers and brokers and asked them to grant North Carolina more favorable terms than those offered. When bids were taken, he sold the long-term notes at par for 4-1/4 percent, which was 1/4th of a percent under the current price, and the short-term notes at equally good rates. [41] In December of the same year, he had again negotiated a sale of over $20,000,000 worth of bonds at 4-1/2 percent, [42] and, in December 1926, he sold another $20,000,000 for 4-1/4 percent. [43] By the spring of 1927, McLean secured a rate of 4 percent, the most satisfactory rate the state had received in years. [44] The 1928 sale went for the same price. [45] According to McLean's estimates, the state would have been able to save from $40,000,000 to $50,000,000 between 1920 and 1928 if such a rate had been secured for all the highway and permanent improvement bonds that had been sold during that time.

When McLean made his third financial report to the people in July of 1928, he was able to show a cash surplus of $1,749,495 for the year, a surplus that, with the credit balance of the two preceding years, meant a savings of over $3,000,000 during the three-year period. [46] In the main, these savings had been effected through the coordination of some seventy departments and state agencies into one administrative unit. By making regular budgets and plans the several agencies had been able to carry out their programs with less money than before, when there had been no systematic planning and control over spending. Systematized buying through central purchasing agents had not only secured better prices, but had promoted more judicious spending of funds. Use of convict labor in making improvements at certain institutions and in the execution of some state projects had both reduced the cost of construction and given employment to the surplus labor at the central prison. This cheap labor had saved money in erecting a building at the Farm Colony for Women at Kinston, in rebuilding a wing of the State Hospital in Raleigh, and in making improvements at the Executive Mansion and on Capitol Square.

The Budget Bureau had also been able to reduce expenditures by transferring unused equipment from one institution to another. Furthermore, with state funds made readily available by the daily deposit of all collections, the government had not been forced to borrow in anticipation of taxes, and the interest paid on deposits had brought a net earning of $1,174,412 during the two years from June 30, 1926 to June 30, 1928. [47]

His financial statement also included an inventory of all the state's assets and debts. This accounting showed a total of $223,347,629 invested in public highways, institutions, department buildings, and other fixed assets; holdings in railroad stock valued at $5,233,584; and current or working assets of $23,681,682.65. On the other side of the ledger was a funded debt of more than $170,000,000. Of this debt approximately $111,000,000 had been appropriated for the highway system and would be funded with revenues realized from gasoline taxes and license fees. Over $15,500,000 had been loans to counties for the construction of school buildings and would be repaid in annual installments. Sinking funds for amortizing the funded indebtedness held cash and securities of over $21,000,000. [48] Although the debt was well secured, as the inventory indicates, McLean knew that a large debt on the state's credit was potentially dangerous, and he refused to approve any requests for more issues in 1929.

By the beginning of 1928, signs of a serious depression were already evident in North Carolina. Farm prices were still low and the textile industry was being forced to curtail production and run on a part-time schedule. That left large numbers of unemployed in many communities and the loss of their wages affected other businesses. Realizing the significance of these conditions and anticipating a decrease in state revenues in 1928-1929, Governor McLean undertook to cushion the state from the worst effects of a financial shortage by leaving a surplus of $2,500,000 in the treasury for the incoming administration. In January 1928, with the consent and approval of the Advisory Budget Commission, he called a conference of the heads of all state departments and institutions to discuss the matter; other meetings were held in July and December. In session with these leaders, McLean explained the conditions and made a plea for their help in building a credit balance. If there should have to be a horizontal cut in 1929-1930, it would be more easily absorbed if there were a surplus to supplement the regular income, he told them. He also spoke of the need for a greatly increased Equalization Fund to relieve the tax burden in some of the poorer counties and to equalize the educational opportunities for all children, both rural and urban. If there were no surplus left to help with this and other expenses, taxes would have to be increased. It was his opinion, McLean told the conference, that conditions in agriculture and industries did not warrant additional levies in the near future. [49]

On December 15, 1928, as director of the budget, McLean mailed the biennial report and copies of the budget bills to his successor, O. Max Gardner. Because he and the Advisory Budget Commission had been reluctant to increase taxes, the recommended appropriations of $34,982,419 for current expenses, including $10,000,000 for the Equalization Fund, exceeded the income expected by about $2,500,000. However, to cover the deficiency, McLean explained, there would be on June 30, 1929, an estimated cash surplus in the general fund of $2,587,011, a sum sufficient to balance the budget and leave $85,782 in the treasury on June 30, 1931. [50]

The governor who had told a newspaper reporter the day after his inauguration in January 1925 that he had never had many thrills in his life must have experienced a special kind of Scottish elation when he made this accounting to the governor-elect.

Chapter V

—◦◦•◦◦—

AT HOME IN RALEIGH: WILTON AND MARGARET MCLEAN

—◦◦•◦◦—

While the Governor was working hard to get state finances on a sound and efficient basis, he was also trying to get his family settled in their new home, the Governor's Mansion. Mrs. McLean, who had been ill and unable to attend the inauguration, was delayed in bringing the children to join him. In fact, it was April before she was able to take over her duties as First Lady. Following a bout of pneumonia, she had developed a nasal problem for which she received treatment at Johns Hopkins Hospital.

Upon assuming office in January, McLean asked the Board of Public Buildings and Grounds to renovate a suite of rooms on the second floor of the mansion so his family could move in. Atwood and Nash, architects for the board, received bids and gave a contract to James A. Davidson to do the work for $7,094. [1] McLean asked H. Pier Giovanni of Wilmington to confer with Mrs. McLean and to draw up plans for the renovation. [2]

The mansion was the second residence provided for governors of North Carolina. The first "Governor's Palace," as it was sometimes called, was built in 1816 during the brief wave of national pride that followed the War of 1812. It was located at the southern end of Fayetteville Street, an elite section of Raleigh at that time. Well before the Civil War, however, the city had moved away from that end of the street and the governor's residence had been left in a section becoming more and more undesirable. William W. Holden, appointed to the office in 1865, refused to live in it and his successors followed his example and rented other facilities. For more than a decade after the war, nothing was done to improve or replace the residence because there were no funds available.

By 1883, the state's economy was improving and Thomas J. Jarvis, a very popular governor, had plans drawn for a new executive residence at Burke Square on Blount Street and asked the General Assembly to appropriate the necessary funds. In February, the legislators approved the plans but provided no money for the building. In lieu of the requested funds, they stipulated that certain city lots, owned by the state, could be sold and the proceeds applied to the project. Meanwhile, Mrs. Jarvis had won an ally in Captain W. J. Hicks, superintendent of State Prison, who agreed to use convicts to make the bricks and do the construction work. That would allow the money raised from selling the lots to go toward furnishings. Hicks, who was also an architect and construction engineer, worked tirelessly to carry out the plans, but funds were inadequate and Governor Jarvis left office before the mansion was completed.

Newly-elected Governor Alfred M. Scales twice requested appropriations to complete the building and the legislature again responded by authorizing the sale of lots, including the old mansion. Only $10,000 was realized from these sales and Hicks had to carry on with convict labor and cheap materials. Brownstone for trimming was brought from quarries in Anson County and pink marble for the front steps from Cherokee County. As Scale's term moved toward a close, Hicks rushed to finish the job. He was forced to use the cheapest kind of plumbing fixtures and the electrical wiring was put in over the ceiling. Plain dirt was piled between the floors to deaden the sounds of walking. The basement and the third floor were left unfinished. Altogether, the state had spent $21,860 on the project.

The new Executive Mansion was an imposing Victorian-style structure. It was the largest building in the city, measuring 110 feet by 125 feet. The main reception hall was ninety feet by twenty feet and many of the forty rooms were twenty feet by twenty-five feet. All ceilings were sixteen feet high. The entire first floor, except the kitchen and butler's pantry, could be opened up to provide 8,000 square feet of floor space for official functions or major social gatherings. Unfortunately, the interior construction was of poor quality and left unfinished. It was also drafty and cold, as it depended solely on open fireplaces for heating. [3]

By the 1920s the structure had become so obsolete and was in such a state of deterioration that many were in favor of scrapping it and building another residence for the governor. Almost every Chief Executive since David G. Fowler, the first to live in the mansion, had added another covering of wall paper or paint. Many conveniences had been provided, but the plumbing remained a constant problem and the electrical wiring a danger to the residents. As the dirt between the floors dried and the planks shrank, clouds of dust followed anyone walking across the rooms. The *Raleigh News and Observer*, in November 1925, described the building as "a great bulk of an exterior, done on barbarian lines" and declared the bedrooms and living quarters on the second floor were "Medieval in their appointments and fixtures." [4]

To counter the proposal to scrap the building, Secretary of State W. N. Everett initiated a plan to repair and refurnish it. McLean gave his support to the plan. Early in February, Everett had the mansion inspected and on February 13, H. E. Miller, director of the Bureau of Sanitary Engineering and Inspection, reported to the State Department of Health that he had graded the residence by a score card used for hotels, and that it had rated seventy-one, a grade which would make any hotel subject to indictment. His main concern was the lack of cleanliness due to conditions of the building and an inadequate staff of housekeepers. The report described in detail the conditions of the building. The basement, which had never been finished, had a dirt floor except for two rooms, where the wooden floors were decayed from the dampness, and a small brick-floored room for the hot water heater. Inches of dust from the dirt floor, he noted, could find its way up through openings in the wall left for registers in a proposed hot air heating system. On the first level, the walls and floor of the kitchen, butler's pantry, and storerooms were worn and rough, making it almost impossible to clean them. The kitchen was too small and poorly equipped, and lack of ventilation allowed food odors to penetrate the whole house. In the reception room, the walls and ceiling were in severe need of refinishing and painting; in some areas the paint had blistered and was falling away.

The second story was in even worse condition than the first. The floors, made of five to six inch boards and now with one-half-inch cracks between them, were extremely difficult to keep clean. The rug in the master bedroom was almost worn through in spots because of the uneven surface. There were still openings in the floor cut by plumbers and steam fitters, loose boards not jointed or nailed down, all as the workmen had left them in 1889. The woodwork was in bad condition and the wallpaper faded and cracked. The third floor and attic had remained unfinished through the years and loads of old mortar and accumulated dust continued to sift through into the rooms below. [5] Following the inspection, the Health Department condemned the plumbing and the State Insurance Department ordered the electrical system replaced. [6]

The inspectors recommended extensive repairs and renovations. As absolute necessities, they listed concrete floors and proper drainage in the basement, the refinishing and waxing of floors on the first level, new floors for most of the second story, the removal of old hot air registers and the closing of holes, installation of electrical connections so as to allow the use of a vacuum cleaner, and proper sealing of openings for light fixtures. Other repairs and improvements were also recommended. [7]

In response to this report, the General Assembly appropriated $50,000 for renovations and new furnishings. [8] In June, when the funds became available, the Board of Public Buildings and Grounds advertised for bids and gave contracts for the work. Atwood and Nash, architects for the board, were employed to do the structural repair and H. Pier Giovanni of Wilmington was asked to do the interior decorations. Contracts were given to Thompson Electrical Company for the rewiring and Biemann and Rewells for the plumbing. J. H. Davidson received a contract for renovation of the kitchen area, and Holloway's Cabinet Shop was employed to repair, refinish, and upholster old furniture. Nine worn rugs were sent to Olson Rug Company for reweaving (at a cost of $37.80). [9]

Mrs. McLean worked closely with Giovanni to redecorate the interior. She selected simple, substantial furnishings and equipment. She chose white as the basic color and sought to make the building elegant and formal. Hangings at the windows were of high-quality materials, but not elaborate. She salvaged all she could from pieces of furniture remaining in the mansion. Of particular interest to her and the governor was an old sideboard in the dining room which had been buried for many years under successive coats of varnish. The piece had been built originally for the British steamer *Lord Clyde*, which North Carolina had purchased during the Civil War and rechristened the *Advance*. It was made of native Scottish wood and intricately carved with Highland symbols: roses, thistles, fruits, vegetables, fish, and game. The McLeans had it refinished and moved, along with a large accompanying mirror, into the reception room. Mrs. McLean had a fine silver service set which had been used on the battleship *North Carolina* returned to the mansion for display on the sideboard.

Mrs. McLean also had a number of portraits of North Carolina leaders restored and hung in appropriate places. They had hung directly over radiators and were badly damaged. She reclaimed worn rugs that had been stored in the attic and had them rewoven by the Olson Rug Company. A few new oriental rugs were purchased for the main rooms on the first floor. As there were insufficient funds for additional furniture, she brought several pieces from their home in Lumberton, including some tapestried Jacobean chairs, some French Court gilded pieces, some Spanish-style leather chairs, and a long library table. [10]

The Governor bought new china for the mansion: a dozen each of dinner plates ($175) and entree plates ($125), dessert cups ($115), bouillon cups and saucers ($150), soup cups ($120), Sheffield double-egg cups ($288), and an alternate set of plates ($100)—a total expenditure of $1073. The original order had been for two dozen each, but to save money, McLean reduced the order. The china was purchased from Delaney-Varney Company, engravers, of Baltimore. [11]

McLean's policy toward spending was evident in his expenditures for the mansion. Holloway's Cabinet Shop had been employed to repair, refinish, and upholster a number of pieces of old furniture on the assurance that costs would be reasonable, but when McLean received a bill for $1,427.30, he rejected the charge as being unacceptable. He sent a check for $500 as an interim payment until the matter could be settled. He suggested that disinterested persons be asked to decide on a proper billing, or that the company use whatever course it deemed proper to collect the debt. He assured them that he intended to give the state the same consideration in paying this public bill that he would a personal transaction. [12]

This policy was followed in all expenditures for the mansion. In preparing for his family to move to Raleigh in January 1925, McLean asked the Board of Buildings and Grounds to allow him to employ two additional persons for the housekeeping staff. He suggested that they hire Richard Anderson and Marie Hayden for this work, each at $15 a week. That would make a total payment of $107.50 a week for servants, including a gardener and chauffeur (McLean never learned to drive a car). [13] In August, he asked the board's approval for his dismissal of one servant, as she was no longer needed. He also replaced one cook who was receiving $21 a week with one at $15 a week. He told the board he "was not willing to pay any houseservant for the present over $15 a week," as that was as much as he had ever paid one at his home. He asked the keeper of the Capitol to dispense with the gardener and to transfer the night watchman to another place, as these servants were no longer necessary—that would save $48.50 on mansion expenses. He also asked that he be allowed to dismiss Ernest Dixon, who was employed to clean the windows for $18 to $21 a week, observing that this work could be done by the regular houseservants. He attempted another saving for the state when he requested that the Building and Grounds Board discontinue the practice of providing spring water for drinking at the mansion and in the public offices. He said he had investigated the matter and found that the city water was free from contamination and was available at a much more reasonable cost, thirty cents per thousand gallons in contrast to ten cents a gallon for spring water. [14]

For the McLeans, the mansion was not only the official residence of the governor; it was a real home for their family. Mrs. McLean managed the household for her husband and children and for frequent visitors—especially McLean relatives who came to Raleigh. She did little or none of the cooking herself, but she knew foods and carefully supervised the buying and preparation of all meals. Every week she had six dozen fresh eggs shipped to Raleigh from the Singletary Farm in Robeson County, and she was equally selective in buying meats and vegetables. All of the meals were "company meals" and unexpected guests were always welcome. The children's birthdays and all holidays were occasions for celebration, with appropriate decorations and parties or special dinners. Thanksgiving and Christmas were highlights of the year for the family. [15]

Mrs. McLean loved to entertain and had a dramatic flair for planning and executing festive occasions. She was always a gracious hostess, presiding with a simple, quiet dignity. Some thought her aloof because she was not given to much chatter, but it was a matter of reticence and not a lack of interest. As official hostess for the governor, she gave two major receptions for the General Assembly each year and others for various organizations or groups meeting in Raleigh, including the United Confederate Veterans, the United Daughters of the Confederacy, the Daughters of the American Revolution, the Order of the Eastern Star, the North Carolina Garden Clubs, and the North Carolina Art Society. She also entertained smaller groups at dinners or luncheons. Such groups included members of the Gettysburg Memorial Committee, Justices of the State Supreme Court, legislative committees, state officers and heads of departments, and members of the State Democratic Executive Committee. Dignitaries who came to Raleigh on official visits were always received as guests at the mansion and entertained with appropriate receptions or dinners.

The biggest social event of the year in Raleigh was the annual New Year's Eve Reception and Open House to which all residents of the city were invited, as well as hundreds of special guests from across the state. On these occasions, the mansion was beautifully decorated with holiday greens and flowers. For each event, Mrs. McLean planned a central motif completed with elaborate decorations and attractive refreshments. On one such occasion, she created a massive snow scene in the main dinning room. Green trees formed a background for snow-covered hills, while on the banquet table miniature children were sleigh riding and playing in the snow and Santa's sleigh was being drawn by eight miniature reindeer. Ice cream molded in the shape of snowballs was served with little cakes. [16] On another occasion, she used cupids and bells interspersed with baskets of pink roses and pink tapers in silver candlesticks. [17] Orchestras provided music for these receptions, while cheerful fires in the large fireplaces invited guests to linger and visit. As many as 3,000 people attended these annual events.

Mrs. McLean never served wine at any of her meals or receptions, but ice would be furnished for any guests of the mansion who wanted to drink in their rooms. Sometimes she arranged for dancing at the small parties but more often she planned interesting games. At one formal buffet supper in March 1928, she placed "tuberettes" (cigarettes sealed in straw holders) beside the plates of all the female guests. Although women in Raleigh and elsewhere smoked cigarettes at bridge parties and private teas, none were willing to be seen smoking at an official party in the Executive Mansion. Instead, all of the tuberettes, which were attached to small match boxes with red, white, and blue rubber bands, disappeared into coat pockets or purses as souvenirs or for use at home. [18]

Mrs. McLean managed her household and all of the entertainment with the assistance of one secretary (borrowed from the governor's office) and the servants allotted to the mansion, but the cost of maintaining the home and for all the official entertainment was very great. The governor's salary of $6500 was insufficient to cover all the expenses. In spite of McLean's careful planning and strict economies, it was often necessary for him to supplement his salary with monies from his own private funds. [19]

Entertainment at the mansion was largely the responsibility of the First Lady. The Governor, who grew up on the farm in a day when there was little time for fun or frolic, had never learned to "play." He did not know how to take part in a casual conversation of "small talk," so he was never at ease in social gatherings. Judge H. Hoyle Sink, with whom he worked, recalled watching him at formal dinners nervously twirling the little gold scissors on his watch chain as he sat bored and unable to enter into the conversations around him. Judge Sink also stated that he was often summoned to the Governor's office to "talk" with visiting dignitaries, and always if the visitor was a woman. [20] McLean was not a good golfer and he did little hunting and fishing. He did like to ride and kept a horse, "Governor," for this purpose at the prison farm in Raleigh. He joined the Vanguard Bible Class at the First Presbyterian Church in Raleigh, but that was one of the few activities in which he became involved beyond his duties as the chief executive. [21]

To his official duties, however, McLean gave his full attention. He had two stenographers at his office in the Capitol and two in his office at the mansion, and he often worked these in relays from eight o'clock in the morning until one o'clock at night. [22] This kind of schedule was particularly true of his first year in office, when he was working on the Executive Budget Bill, and then trying to bring all State institutions, departments, and agencies into the new system. When out-of-state experts in finance and management came to advise him, the tempo became even more strenuous.

McLean's one concession to himself was an annual vacation at some time during the summer months. As he had done for a number of years, he would spend a few weeks as a guest of Martin J. Gillen at a camp near Land of Lakes in Wisconsin. [23] He usually took the two older children with him and an attendant to take care of them. Mrs. McLean used this time for her own vacation plans with Hector, the youngest child. Even these summer trips were never a time of rest and recreation, as most people would interpret them, for he spent from six to eight hours each day in hard manual labor, cutting down trees, building roads, and similar tasks. His self indulgence was restricted to four hours of rest, eight hours of sleep, and perhaps some time for fishing. This time spent out of doors in strenuous activity, however, did prepare him for his demanding schedule as governor.

Besides these limited vacation experiences, the only time McLean was away from the office was when official business took him out of town. He usually took his family with him on these trips. In fact,

Mrs. McLean kept a "going dress" of knit material ready and an overnight bag packed with lingerie and toiletries for unexpected trips. Since the family traveled by car, Mrs. McLean had large flat suitcases (black to match the color of the car) made to fit on the running board of the sedan. This arrangement left plenty of room inside the car for the children, and, if necessary, picnic baskets of food. [24]

Chapter VI

————••◆◆••————

REORGANIZATION OF STATE DEPARTMENTS

————••◆◆••————

For more than a half century, the executive branch of the state government in North Carolina had grown more and more complex as new administrative services had been added one after another. By 1925, there were more than seventy-five departments, bureaus, boards, commissions, and agencies, each with considerable authority to go its own way, performing the several tasks assumed by the government. With such division of authority and responsibility resulting in an overlap and duplication of functions and organization, it had become increasingly difficult to formulate any broad policy and program for the whole of state activities or to achieve a desired efficiency and economy in the administration of public affairs.

In 1915, Governor Locke Craig and in 1917, his successor, Thomas Walter Bickett, called attention to the problem and recommended the short ballot as a means of centralizing responsibility and promoting the intelligent selection of officials who would be directly accountable to the people. In a special message to the General Assembly on January 28, 1921, Governor Cameron Morrison made a plea for drastic changes in the administrative machinery, and because of Morrison's promptings, State Auditor Baxter Durham made a survey of North Carolina's government and formulated a plan for the reorganization of departments, institutions, and other agencies. [1] Based on this study, a bill was drafted and introduced at the 1923 session of the General Assembly, but the measure received little consideration, as no group made a serious effort to secure its enactment.

In his campaign in 1924, McLean attempted to focus public attention on the outdated system still in use and the need to overhaul and simplify the executive structure; in his first message to the General Assembly on January 21, 1925, he restated his desire to modernize the organs of government and to improve the methods used in managing the state's affairs. He told the legislators that the antiquated system was one of the major factors responsible for the ever-increasing costs of government and asked them to give careful consideration to a reorganization of administrative machinery in both state

and county governments. He urged them to centralize responsibility
and to reduce the number of elective officials. [2]

Repeated efforts had been made during the past decade to have
the General Assembly call a constitutional convention—but all had
failed. Encouraged by Governor McLean's strong appeal for reorganization, Representative Edward F. Butler, on January 29, introduced a resolution calling for a convention in May 1927, and a few
days later, seven senators, among them some of the most influential
members of that body, presented a bill providing for a convention in
October 1925. A substitute measure combining both bills received a
favorable report in the Joint Committee on Constitutional
Amendments, but was killed in the House and postponed indefinite-
ly in the Senate on a motion of the men who introduced it. [3]

Thus, the attempt to effect a general review and reorganization of
the state government had failed again. As soon as it became known
that Governor McLean would back the measures calling for a convention, petitions from conservative forces inside and outside the
state poured into his office, asking him to withdraw his support.
These appeals all expressed a fear that, if a convention was called
and delegates elected while there was so much dissatisfaction over
taxes and the agricultural depression, he as governor would not be
able to control the body and direct the changes it would make. The
New York bond attorneys became disturbed and Senator Simmons,
responding to the anxious letters coming into his office, wrote to
advise against calling a convention at the time. [4] Under this pressure, McLean withdrew his support and the movement came to an
end.

Meanwhile, Senator William L. Foushee of Durham had introduced a bill providing for a constitutional amendment which would
leave only three elective officers in the executive branch: the governor, lieutenant governor, and secretary of state. His measure, however, was no more successful than the efforts to provide for a constitutional convention to examine the whole document. [5]

Apart from this initial failure, Governor McLean's program for
administrative reform received wholehearted approval and, during
his four-year term, several significant steps were taken toward the
unification and reorganization of the state government. The most
significant was the installation of the Executive Budget System, but
other measures also effected important changes in several departments and in the administration of the state's business. Among
these were: (1) the classification of all state employees and the establishment of a uniform salary and wage schedule for comparable
work in all public offices; (2) the consolidation of functions and reassignment of duties performed by the state departments; and (3) the
creation of a new department of conservation and development.

In a special message to the General Assembly on February 27, Governor McLean discussed the matter of public service and cost of government as related to the salary and wages of officials and employees. He explained that with the growing complexity of state services, new assistants had been added and salaries set without regard to the compensation paid for comparable work done elsewhere. As a result of this practice, there was wide disparity in the salaries and wages paid and in the number of persons employed to do similar work in the several departments, and the cost of conducting public business in North Carolina was exceeding such expenditures by private industry. This situation must not be allowed to continue, McLean told them, for it was unfair to the people of the state to expend more of their money than a proper execution of the public services required. To help remedy the problem, he asked the legislators to enact a law authorizing him to appoint a commission of competent and fair-minded citizens to study the salaries paid by the state, to abolish offices which they considered unnecessary, and to recommend a revised salary and wage scale; moreover, he asked them to empower him as governor to put these changes into effect. [6]

Later in the day, Senator Oscar Lee Clark presented a bill to provide for a Salary and Wage Commission and it was passed without opposition; on March 4, the lower house gave its approval. [7] On April 1, Governor McLean appointed the commission, naming Julian E. Price of Greensboro as chairman, and Samuel L. Rogers of Franklin as executive secretary. George A. Holderness of Tarboro, P. H. Hanes, Jr. of Winston-Salem, R. N. Page of Aberdeen, and Frank Tate of Morganton were named to serve with them. Rogers, who lived only a month after his appointment, was succeeded in the position of executive secretary by H. Hoyle Sink of Lexington. It was the task of these men to make a study of working conditions among the state's employees and to develop, install, and administer a scientific and equitable plan of compensation for these workers. To assist them in this undertaking, McLean secured the services of Lewis Meriam from the Institute of Government Research in Washington, Yale O. Millington, assistant librarian at State College, and two graduate students from the University of North Carolina. [8] These people gathered information concerning the work of every employee in the non-institutional executive agencies and the functions and organization of every such unit. On the basis of this data, and under the direction of Meriam and Millington, the commission classified all workers according to position and qualifications and fixed a schedule of salaries and wages for each group.

By October, the original work was completed and Executive Secretary Sink submitted the commission's report to Governor McLean, who proceeded to put its recommendations into effect. Of the 1,601 employees involved in the study, twenty-nine were given raises in salary and 108 received cuts. The commission abolished only seven positions, all of these in the Insurance Department. The Revenue Office, in anticipation of the commission's statement, had already reduced its staff and made heavy cuts in salaries. [9] Other positions had also been voluntarily eliminated by department heads who did not fill vacancies which occurred from time to time. From all these changes, Sink recorded that there had been a net saving of $25,181.40 in salaries since July 1, 1924. [10]

In its report on October 1, the commission also prescribed uniform working hours, sick leaves, and vacation time for all state employees. It set a minimum work day of seven hours for Monday through Friday and four hours on Saturday, but ruled that overtime without compensation could be required to keep the necessary work current. The calendar of vacation time for all workers with one year's service included two weeks or twelve working days of free time, two days petty leave, ten days for sick leave, and six and one half holidays: January 1, May 10, July 4, Labor Day, December 25 and one-half day on December 24, and Thanksgiving Day. State employees had been receiving twelve days of vacation, unlimited sick leave, half-time on Saturdays, and twelve legal holidays. The commission also ruled that no employee was to engage in outside work which would be inconsistent with his obligation to the state or interfere with his time and energy. [11]

Upon the publication of this report, Secretary Sink was immediately besieged by the dissatisfied—nearly 1,000 persons making requests for changes in salary within the next two days. Late in October, the commission sat to hear appeals and tried to explain all the changes that had been made, but it granted few modifications of the published schedule. [12] When, in November, the American Legion made a determined protest, the commission agreed to recognize Armistice Day as a legal holiday for all employees; [13] but it stood firm when some of the offices demanded Lee-Jackson Day also. In response to their request, the commission ruled that the departments could close on any of the other state and national holidays, but if they did so, the employees should have their annual vacations curtailed by that same number of days. The attorney general upheld this ruling, and in a conference with the governor and the members of the commission, the departments heads agreed to the seven approved days. [14]

Despite its commendable work in putting state workers on a uniform salary schedule and in eliminating a number of abuses in the public service, it soon became apparent that the commission's usefulness was very greatly limited by its lack of authority to deal with personnel problems, and especially with the matter of recruitment and selection of trained and efficient persons for the various offices. In making its study of the administrative agencies, the commission had found individuals employed and assigned to work for which they had little or no training and they found one group of positions filled by boys and girls sixteen and seventeen, and in one case fifteen, years of age. In its report to the governor in December 1926, the commission recommended that the act of 1925 be amended to empower it to pass upon the qualifications, including the age and training, of all applicants and to require the department heads to employ only those persons whom it had approved. [15] The General Assembly of 1927 failed to act favorably on these suggestions, however, or to take any steps toward changing the agency into a real department of personnel.

From its beginning, the commission had been the center of controversy. The *Raleigh News and Observer*, as spokesman for the office-holding groups in Raleigh, had kept up a running criticism of its work, and the opposition gathered such strength that a bill which would have abolished the organization altogether and transferred its duties to the Council of State and the elective heads of the departments was presented to the General Assembly in 1927. [16] Governor McLean intervened and saved the agency, but because of the pressure from those who had been affected by the commission's rulings, he decided not to endanger his major program by making a last ditch fight for its control over the selection of employees. [17] The legislators rejected the commission's request for the additional authority and the House even tabled a Senate bill to prevent nepotism in state offices.

The explanation for such antagonism toward the commission and the determined stand against giving it power over appointments can be found, perhaps, in the fear that an impersonal system of recruitment would hinder the use of political patronage and impose a disadvantage upon the professional office-seekers, and in a natural reluctance to change the old way of doing things. Yet, in spite of its failure to develop into anything more than an advisory board, the commission laid a good foundation and the task was easier when the state moved forward again in the field of civil service.

Although it was not a part of the program to improve the public service, a law restricting the use of state-owned automobiles was passed in 1925, and was frequently associated with the regulations made by the Salary and Wage Commission. On January 28, Senator Hugh M. Humphrey of Wayne County introduced a resolution calling for a detailed statement from each department and institution, showing the persons on the payroll, the salaries or wages paid them and the duties assigned each, as well as the number and price of motor vehicles bought since January 1, 1923 and the expenses incurred in their upkeep. [18] The resolution was promptly approved with little opposition. A few days later, Josiah W. Bailey aroused more interest in the matter by making charges of extravagances in some of the departments and of misuse of publicly-owned cars. On February 25, the *Raleigh News and Observer* published the Humphrey report on expenditures in the state government, and on March 7, the General Assembly passed a bill prohibiting the private use of automobiles bought with state or county funds and limiting the purchase price of all such motor vehicles to $1,500, except with the approval of the governor and Council of State. [19]

The first major action in the reorganization of the state departments and the reassignment of administrative duties involved the consolidation of all revenue collecting forces in the Revenue Department. In his message on February 27, Governor McLean asked the legislators to provide for this revision and, on March 6, they gave their final approval to "An Act to Unify and Consolidate the Tax Collecting Forces of the State . . . " By this act, the Automobile Division and the Automobile Theft Division of the State Department were transferred to the Department of Revenue and, along with them, the responsibility for collecting automobile license fees and gasoline taxes imposed by the Highway Act of 1921, the Motor Vehicles Registration Act of 1923, and the act to regulate motor vehicles used as common carriers passed by the current session. In like manner, the collection of insurance taxes and fees was moved from the Insurance Department to the Revenue Office. [20] The centralization of these duties eliminated a duplication of activity in three departments and effected both efficiency and economy in administering the tax laws.

The second revision placed upon the Corporation Commission all responsibility for the supervision and regulation of business, financial, and industrial organizations operating in the state and strengthened its authority for the performance of the added functions. Among the new duties imposed upon the department was the regulation of corporate stock issued in North Carolina. The increased sale of fraudulent and worthless securities during the early twenties had aroused great concern and many persons were demanding that the government take steps to protect investors. [21] To provide a remedy for this situation, Governor McLean, on January 21, asked the General Assembly to revise the Capital Issues Law and, to bring the matter directly before the legislators, he had a bill prepared and presented for their consideration. In his biennial report for 1924, Insurance Commissioner Stacy W. Wade had also recommended a new and more stringent law and, in January, he prepared a bill incorporating the changes he had suggested. His measure, however, was rejected for the governor's bill, which transferred the administration of the law from the Insurance Department to the Corporation Commission.

The new Capital Issues or Blue Sky Law required that all corporations, except a group listed as being exempt from the statute, make application to the Corporation Commission and have their stock listed on the register of qualified securities; moreover, it authorized the corporation commissioner, designated by the governor to enforce the law, to examine the finances and business of corporations making application and to refuse registration or to remove securities from the register if he at any time should find evidence of an attempt to defraud the public or to evade the regulations imposed by the statute. The act required that all advertising be submitted to the commissioner before it was made public, and that all contracts be in writing and include the statement that no more than five percent of the amount annually paid on separate subscriptions would be used for promotional purposes. A permanent listing of securities and all information in the hands of the Corporation Commission concerning them was to be kept open for public inspection at all times. Dealers and salesmen were also required to register with the commission and sales made in violation of the law would be voidable at the election of the purchaser. Furthermore, the agent or salesman who made such sales would be held responsible for the full amount paid by the purchaser and be liable to punishment by fine or imprisonment or both. [22]

In April, Governor McLean designated Commissioner Allen J. Maxwell to administer the law and he in turn appointed I. M. Bailey as his assistant and counsel to the commission. [23] Within days, Maxwell and his staff began receiving applications, making examinations, and granting registration certificates to those corporations, dealers, and agents who could qualify to do business in the state. On June 16, the commission reported that only thirty-four dealers and salesmen had succeeded in meeting the requirements under the new law. [24]

The Corporation Commission was also given greater responsibilities in the supervision of North Carolina banks; although, for some time there had been considerable criticism of its work in administering the banking laws and a large faction wanted to transfer this function to another state agency. Between 1921 and 1925, there had been fifty-seven state and six national bank failures in North Carolina, with losses to depositors amounting to $12,555,048. Many people were ready to place the blame for these losses on the Corporation Commission. [25] In February 1925, Representative James E. L. Wade of New Hanover County introduced a bill which would have removed the supervision of state banks from the Corporation Commission to a new banking commission and would have created a depositor's guaranty fund, but the measure was killed in a House committee. [26] The demand for an independent banking commission was renewed in 1926 and 1927, but when Governor McLean made an inquiry and found there was no unanimity of opinion or active interest in the proposal among the bankers themselves, he refused to give his support to the plan. [27]

After the movement to create a state banking commission failed, the General Assembly, in 1925, passed a number of measures which increased the powers of the Corporation Commission to enforce the state laws and, in 1927, the Assembly expanded its jurisdiction to include the liquidation of insolvent banks. Many of the banks that had gone to pieces had done so because officers and directors borrowed money for business ventures or loaned money to their friends to make similar investments. Senator Thomas L. Johnson of Robeson County presented a bill devised to prevent these practices and the legislators accepted his proposal with hearty approval. His measure limited the loans that could be made, providing that no sum of more than 20 percent of the capital and surplus of any bank could be granted to any one person, unless by a two-thirds vote of the Board of Directors, and of no more than 25 percent under any circumstances. No loans of any amount could be made to officers or employees of a bank except upon good collateral or other ample security, as well as the written approval of the Board of Directors. [28] Another bill sponsored by Senator Patrick H. Williams and approved by the General Assembly discouraged other irresponsible practices by making stockholders in industrial banks liable for twice the par value of stock held in such institutions. [29] Both of these statutes strengthened the hands of the Corporation Commission in its supervision of the state's banks.

During the 1925 session, Senator Williams also tried to create a law authorizing the Corporation Commission to appoint a receiver to take over any bank that refused to make reports to the Commission, had violated the provisions of the laws, or was in an insolvent, unsafe or unsound condition to transact business; but he failed to win sufficient support for the measure. In 1927, a similar bill was passed, however, and the Corporation Commission was directed to assume the responsibility for the liquidation of all insolvent banks as well as those that had refused to comply with the state banking laws. [30] Under this new system, the process of liquidation could be achieved in a much shorter time than had been required for action by court-appointed receivers.

The banking laws were not a part of the administration's legislative program. Although he did not oppose the bills, Governor McLean did not request or sponsor any measures to change the existing statutes. During the debates on the Johnson and Williams bills in 1925, he wrote to the Federal Reserve Board and secured an expert's opinion on the state laws and suggestions for amendments, but otherwise he took no active part in securing these reforms. [31]

Faithfulness to the public in banking practices, however, was a subject on which McLean held very firm convictions. During the first two years of his term of office, he did not extend executive clemency to a single official who had been convicted of breaking the banking laws. In response to the Commissioner of Pardons regarding such a matter he wrote: "I do not feel that I would be justified in acting favorable in this case at the present time. In my opinion, men who are responsible for bank failures, rendering innocent people penniless, are much worse than highway robbers or burglars. The case would have to be unusually strong to influence me to extend clemency." [32] He, in like manner, refused to take any action to save Thomas E. Cooper, brother of the former lieutenant governor and prominent state politician, from a term in the federal penitentiary in Atlanta or to prevent Cooper's further humiliation of serving a second term on the chain gang in New Hanover County.

A third measure imposed upon the Corporation Commission the duty of regulating bus lines and trucks used as common carriers in the state. The 1925 Act Providing the Supervision and Control of . . . Motor Vehicles used in the Business of Transporting Persons or Property for Compensation . . . vested in the commission the power and authority to supervise and regulate every motor vehicle carrier in the state, to fix or approve rates, fares, charges, classifications, rules, and regulations for each such carrier; to fix and prescribe speed limits; to regulate accounts, service, and safety of operation; to require all carriers to file annual and other reports and data; and to supervise and regulate carriers in all matters affecting the relationship between such carriers and the traveling and shipping public. [33] Since the business of motor transportation would exceed that of the railroads within the next few years, this new task was a significant addition to the commission's work.

A third consolidation of executive functions centralized the legal activities of all state agencies under one head, the attorney-general, and eliminated the employment of additional lawyers in several departments. The new statute, which was approved and sponsored by Governor McLean, provided that the attorney-general be given three more assistants and such clerical help as might be needed for the increased duties. One of the assistants was to be assigned to serve as counsel for the State Highway Commission, another for the Department of Revenue, and a third would perform such duties as the attorney-general might appoint. Henceforth, the law stated, the attorney-general and these assistants would serve as legal advisors for all departments and institutions and no agency would employ other attorneys except by and with the consent of the governor. [34]

Among the administrative reforms achieved by the McLean administration, few were more important than the consolidation of all agencies dealing with the natural resources of the state into a new Department of Conservation and Development. Speaking to the General Assembly on January 21, 1925, McLean explained the grow-

ing need for such a department (1) to serve as a press agent and
properly advertise the state, (2) to educate the people as to the value
of the forest lands and how to take care of them, (3) to encourage the
proper use of the potential assets in undeveloped water power, and
(4) to promote the establishment of new manufacturing industries
by serving as a clearinghouse for reliable information on all natural
and artificial resources in North Carolina. [35] A bill incorporating his
suggestions was prepared and presented to the House by
Representative Thomas E. Whitaker of Guilford County and was
passed without opposition.

The act created the Department of Conservation and
Development and transferred to it all the powers and authority formerly exercised by the Geological and Economic Survey, the State
Geological Board, and the state geologist. The management of the
department was to be vested in a board of six directors and the governor as *ex officio* chairman. [36] In 1927, the State Fisheries
Commission and the State Game Commission were added to the
department and the Board of Directors, which was increased to
twelve members with a term of six years, was authorized to appoint
a state game warden and to assume the administration of the fish
and game laws. [37]

Governor McLean was very anxious to find the best man available to organize and direct the new agency, and his appointment of
Wade H. Phillips as administrative director proved satisfactory in
every way. In 1927, J. K. Dixon, who had served as chairman of the
Fisheries Commission, was elected as assistant director in charge of
inland fisheries. [38] To take care of the many and varied services committed to its charge, the department was organized into six divisions
with one member of the board immediately responsible for each,
and all serving under Phillips as chief administrative head. The six
divisions were administration, geological survey, forestry, parks and
public land, game and inland fisheries, coastal fisheries and water
resources.

When the department assumed the responsibility for enforcing
the statewide game law, McLean asked Phillips to act as state game
warden until it could be ascertained if sufficient revenue would be
realized from the operation of the statute to pay the salary of a full-
time warden and his assistants. By July 1928, however, the work of
administering the law had expanded so as to consume almost three-
fourths of the director's time and the receipts from hunting and fishing licenses had proved to be twice the original estimates. In
response to Phillips' request, the board, at its meeting in July 1928,
elected Charles H. England as full-time game warden and reorganized the machinery for enforcing the state law. It reduced the number of assistants from seven to four and converted this smaller group
into a mobile force under the immediate direction of the state game

warden. In order that the five wardens might be able to devote their time fully to the enforcement of the laws, they were relieved of the job of issuing hunting and fishing licenses and this task was assigned to the clerk of Superior Court and a special agent in each county. [39]

To coordinate the work of all the state departments and to serve as a link between the government in Raleigh and the rural communities of the one hundred counties, Governor McLean came up with a plan for a publicly owned and operated radio broadcasting station at State College. At a conference of representatives from the Department of Agriculture, Public Health and Public Welfare, the Agricultural Extension Service, and State College on February 5, 1925, he reviewed his proposals. With receiving sets installed in rural school houses, where the community could gather to listen, he told the conference there was an unlimited possibility for presenting the problems of the state and giving information relative to markets, agricultural extension work, public health, highway construction, and other services of the various agencies. Furthermore, the system could be used to bring extension courses in college work to those unable to continue their education beyond the public schools. [40]

Following the February conference, Governor McLean asked the engineers of the Highway Department and of State College to work out plans and determine the costs of such a project. To assist them, he secured the services of a special engineer from the Radio Corporation of America in New York City. Meanwhile, he sent Frank Page to Washington to confer with officials in the Commerce Department and he himself made a personal appeal to Commerce Secretary Herbert Hoover concerning the allocation of a wavelength for the station. [41] The Commerce Department was sympathetic, but it could promise nothing until pending legislation was approved by Congress. The White Radio Bill, which was planned with the idea of giving a special wavelength to each state, did not pass, however, and the matter of supervision and regulation of the radio business was left undecided. Yet, in spite of the discouraging outlook, Governor McLean continued to gather information and to make plans, hoping that the Commerce Department would be able to provide a wavelength as it reorganized its work and expanded radio services throughout the nation.

When the engineer from the Radio Corporation of America completed his survey, he recommended the installation of a fifty kilowatt station to insure regular and reliable statewide coverage, and estimates from different sources quoted costs of equipment and installation at over $100,000. [42] In preparing the budget recommendations for 1927, Governor McLean included an appropriation of $120,000 for the original costs of setting up the station. He estimated that the expense for maintenance would be comparatively small, since the station would be operated largely by State College students. [43]

The governor's plan was received with mixed feelings. Most of the administrative heads in Raleigh, and other individuals scattered throughout the state, gave their enthusiastic approval. Superintendent of Public Instruction A. T. Allen predicted 500 schoolhouses would install receiving sets as soon as the broadcasting system was established; but others were skeptical. They believed listeners wanted to hear music, prize fights, or athletic events and were not interested in educational programs. Some contended that the project was too great an expense for the state to undertake while so much emphasis was being placed on economy in government. One newspaper expressed its disapproval in the following words:

> It has been apparent for some time that the present administration would have a radio broadcasting station or know the reason why. Every administration must have at least one tangent upon which it can fly off to wherever it can fly to. Undoubtedly we have arrived at the particular tangent upon which the McLean administration is destined to ride to kingdom come. It is to be, not the economy administration, or even the budget administration, but the radio administration—static and the votes of the legislature permitting.
>
> A good deal has been said about the wonders of the radio and a good deal more will be said. But if the people of North Carolina and the General Assembly discover wisdom in the radio proposal of Governor McLean it will be a wonder, beside which the transatlantic telephone is a child's toy. [44]

When the appropriations bill came up for their consideration, a majority of the members of the General Assembly did not find wisdom in the project and refused to approve the allotment. [45]

The establishment of a state-owned radio broadcasting system was, without a doubt, the most progressive part of Governor McLean's program, and perhaps it was too revolutionary to have a chance of adoption by a state traditionally opposed to rapid change. The real surprise is not that the proposal was rejected, but that a governor who was considered to be so well founded in Scottish conservatism conceived of the plan in 1925 and fought so hard to have it enacted. His vision of what such a station could mean to a rural state as a publicity agent, in the coordination of government activities, and as a program for improving the life of its farm people, gave him one claim to a place among those honored as progressive governors in the post-war twenties.

Chapter VII

———•◆•◆•———

Social Issues: Public Health and Prison Reform

———•◆•◆•———

For several decades, North Carolina had been a leader in the promotion of public health and, in 1927, it was still ranked sixth among the states in the amount of money appropriated for that work. [1] Through the efforts of the State Board of Health and of local health officers, significant progress had been made in the prevention of epidemics, in the control of malaria in some eastern counties, in the fight against hookworm, and in providing medical care for school children. Yet, there were weak spots in the record of achievement, for North Carolina ranked fortieth in hospital facilities and reported a death rate among mothers and infants which far exceeded the national average, a situation due in large part to the scarcity of both hospitals and doctors in many sections of the state. Happily, during the last half of the twenties, an increased attention to public health work in local communities, some improvements in hospital services, and the provision of more adequate facilities for medical training promised relief for the most serious problems.

Governor McLean did not sponsor a specific plan of action on behalf of public health, but he gave official encouragement to the efforts of the State Board and stood ready to help when and in whatever ways he could. Expressing his interest in the matter, he told the General Assembly in January 1925:

> Good health is more than the concern of the individual; it is an important requisite of good citizenship, and therefore, it is the duty of the state to do its part in preserving and protecting the health of the individual citizen and the communities also. An intelligent and industrial competency, as well as civic efficiency, is of little avail if there is any serious impairment of the health of the citizenry. Good health is not only essential to the progressive development of the State, but is now generally admitted to be one of the most important aspects of modern conservation . . . Greater efforts must be made to render the children in our public schools physically fit to benefit from the more abundant advantages offered them.
>
> In my opinion you can make no more profitable expenditure than to continue and gradually increase this branch of our public service. [2]

The General Assembly, with McLean's approval, more than doubled funds for public health, but, without the governor's leadership and prompting, the legislators did very little toward health care reform. Only three minor bills affecting public health were passed during the four years. On February 16, 1925, Representative James R. Boyd of Haywood County introduced a bill requiring that all persons and firms engaged in the slaughter and sale of meat-producing animals secure a permit from the Commissioner of Agriculture, whose duty it would be to make a thorough investigation of the sanitary conditions existing in each establishment, judge the efficiency of the inspection provided, and examine the manner in which the animals were slaughtered and the meat prepared for market. Moreover, the act stipulated that all inspections must be conducted under the supervision of a graduate veterinarian, approved by State Veterinarian of North Carolina or the North Carolina Veterinary Medical Examining Board, and that all meat inspected must bear the inscription, "N. C. Inspected and Passed" branded on it with a rubber stamp. The act also authorized cities, towns, and counties to establish and maintain inspection at establishments located within the limits of their designated boundaries and to fix and collect fees necessary to the maintenance of such inspection. The Commissioner of Agriculture was, furthermore, empowered to make all necessary rules and regulations to govern the inspection, preparation, and handling of meat products at all establishments operating in North Carolina. [3]

On February 24, Thomas Creekmore of Wake County presented an amendment to the 1921 law which established a system of inspection for bakeries. Creekmore's measure provided precautions against the spreading of certain diseases and infections commonly associated with bakery products and forbade any baker to pick up or receive bread which had been placed in open stocks where it might have been subject to contamination. [4]

A third measure sponsored by Representative Thomas J. Graham of Graham County made it unlawful for any carrier to transport foods intended for human consumption in cars or vehicles which had not been cleaned in such a manner as to meet common rules of sanitation. [5] (He had watched farmers bring cattle to the slaughter house in trucks and then carry the meat to market in the same vehicle without even washing out the bed.)

Although it would be two decades before North Carolina would undertake a well-organized plan to provide adequate hospital and medical service, the state continued to move forward with a commendable program of work in public health and sanitation. The Bureau of Engineering and Inspection supervised the construction and maintenance of public water supplies and sewage systems and enforced the sanitation laws; the Bureau of Public Health Nursing

and Infant Hygiene offered mothers instruction in the care of themselves and their babies. Each year the Bureau of Medical Inspection
of Schools examined some 90,000 children in those counties which
did not have local health departments, provided dental treatment
for some 36,000 children, and provided surgery for the removal of
tonsils and adenoids for another 2,000 in summer clinics. The State
Laboratory of Hygiene supplied sera and vaccines for smallpox,
typhoid fever, diphtheria, etc., a public service that, at commercial
rates, would have cost in excess of $1,250,000 a year. In January
1928, the State Board of Health organized the Life Extension
Division and began a campaign to educate the public as to the
importance of periodic examinations in the fight against cancer and
degenerative diseases. Through the efforts of the division of County
Health Work, a number of new county health departments were
organized, bringing the total to thirty-nine or approximately one-
eighth of all such units with full-time staff in the United States. [6]
These accomplishments were largely the work of Dr. W. S. Rankin
and then of Dr. Charles O'H. Laughinghouse who succeeded him in
1925.

Perhaps the greatest boon to the cause of good health in the state
during McLean's administration was the establishment of an extensive hospitalization program under the Duke Foundation in 1925.
According to the provisions governing the Endowment created by
James B. Duke in December 1924, and by the terms of his will pro-
bated after his death in October 1925, thirty-two percent of a trust
estate of more than $40,000,000 and ninety percent of the residuary
estate bequeathed to the Endowment in 1925 was to be used to furnish hospitalization for persons who could not pay for such care and
to build and equip additional hospitals. The will also included a gift
of $4,000,000 to be used to provide a medical school, hospital, and
nurses' home at Duke University. [7] In June 1925, Dr. W. S. Rankin,
who had been with the State Board of Health since 1909, resigned
his position in Raleigh and became director of the Duke program.

While Governor McLean contributed little more than official
encouragement toward the work in public health, he took active
steps to improve the state's services in caring for the disadvantaged.
Either at his suggestion or with his approval, the General Assembly
in 1925 enacted a number of measures which increased the governor's power to supervise the work of the state institutions and made
some significant steps toward creating a uniform policy for the management and operation of the several units. The Executive Budget
Act gave the governor the authority to oversee financial affairs, and
another act empowered him to appoint the trustees, directors, and
managers for all institutions and to remove them with or without
cause. [8]

McLean supplemented this last act with an executive order directing all boards to meet at least quarterly and to keep in close touch with the needs of the organizations for which they were responsible. [9] In the past, there had been no rule regarding meetings and some boards had convened only once a year and took very little interest in the welfare of the institutions. McLean also initiated the practice of having semiannual conferences for the administrative heads and directors, thus giving them an opportunity to study and plan the work of each unit in terms of a statewide program.

Representative Henry Groves Connor, Jr. sponsored a measure which provided a uniform policy relative to charges for patients in charitable institutions; formerly the matter had been left more or less to the decision of each organization. As passed on March 4, this statute required the trustees or directors of each institution to fix rates of actual costs and to levy charges based on these for all patients, except indigents. All money received in payment of these fees was to be deposited with the State Treasury, where it would be credited to the school or hospital making the collection. [10] This law put all units on an equal basis and relieved the state of the growing expenses for the care of persons who were able to pay for treatment. Critics of the measure, nevertheless, called attention to the fact that the state furnished a free education for the able-bodied while they were charging the less fortunate for the same opportunities.

One of the weakest spots in the administration of the several institutions, and especially in the hospitals and other establishments caring for the mentally and physically disabled, lay in the poor management of business affairs. This deficiency was due in part to the practice of selecting a doctor or other professional trained in the medical sciences as superintendent and holding him or her responsible for directing the business of the institution, as well as the treatment of the patients and inmates.

An unfortunate example of this injudicious practice came to light early in 1925 at Caswell Training School, the state institution for the mentally retarded. Dr. C. Banks McNairy, a beloved and able physician, who had given himself completely and efficiently to the care of the persons committed to his keeping, lacked the qualities of a business administrator, and the general management and operation of the school suffered accordingly. To help solve this problem, Governor McLean sought a new ruling on the existing law and Attorney General Dennis G. Brummitt returned an opinion authorizing the directors of the several institutions to elect a business manager in addition to the regular administrative head. [11] This innovation assured more efficiency in business affairs and left the superintendents free to direct the professional and technical duties of their establishments.

By the mid-twenties, providing care for the mentally retarded had become a big responsibility in North Carolina, and the facilities at Caswell Training School were inadequate to accommodate even the very difficult cases. With a capacity for 575 residents, there was never room for all of the patients seeking admission. There were some 700 mentally retarded individuals still living in county homes, where they received no training. In July 1925, Governor McLean appointed an Advisory Committee to investigate and survey the scope of the work to be done at this institution, with reference to the patients to be accepted and the type of training and treatments to be undertaken. The committee, with Dr. W. S. Rankin as chairman, conducted the study and made its report to the governor in September 1926. As a result of its findings, the committee recommended that the management continue to give preference to cases most burdensome to the patient's families, but that a sufficient number of the different types of cases be included to effect a sound economy in the operation of the establishment. It was the committee's opinion that the least disabled patients could be trained to help care for the less able ones, to work in the kitchens, in the dairy, and on the farm— thus cutting expenses. It suggested that patients with higher levels of intelligence be placed in colonies apart from the other inmates and that they be paroled to their families after a period of three years training in these groups.

The committee further recommended that legislation be passed to provide physical and mental examinations for all school children retarded by one year and that the superintendent of public instruction and the secretary of the State Board of Health be directed to plan measures for their relief. And finally, the committee requested a more satisfactory law authorizing sterilization for the inmates of State Prison, all hospitals for the insane, and Caswell Training School, and larger appropriations to provide additional facilities for the mentally ill. [12]

Frequent disputes arose over the responsibility for specific cases among those seeking admission on their own initiative as well as those committed to an institution by order of the courts. At a conference of the administrative heads in January 1928, it was agreed that a special committee be appointed to serve as a clearinghouse of information and to make recommendations relative to the assignment of patients to hospitals or other places for custodial or therapeutic care. It would also define the duties and responsibilities for the disabled (as these obligations were shared by the state and county), codify the statutes governing each institution and the rules and regulations adopted for its operation, and put this material in pamphlet form for the use of welfare officers and others concerned. [13]

Governor McLean's work with the penal institutions and the state's services for criminals was perhaps more significant than his efforts on behalf of the mentally and physically disadvantaged. Almost his first action as chief executive was to secure additional personnel to help review all the requests for pardons and to direct rehabilitation work with discharged prisoners. The duty of the governor to grant pardons and reprieves had caused him much concern, even before he took office. He was willing to accept the responsibility for making the decisions, but he felt that, with all the duties of the office, it would be physically impossible for him to give proper attention to the details involved in all the appeals for clemency. There was a real need, he believed, for some official who could investigate the cases, get the papers in order, and summarize the evidence for the governor's final review. When the General Assembly met in 1925, the first measure that he had prepared for its consideration was a bill authorizing him to appoint a Commissioner of Pardons. Sponsored by Representative Bunyan S. Womble of Forsyth and supported by a number of leaders in both houses, the measure was approved and became law on February 8, 1925. [14] On April 1, he appointed H. Hoyle Sink of Lexington, who served as Commissioner until he resigned to accept a position as special judge of the superior court on May 1, 1927. Edwin B. Bridges of Charlotte was then selected to fill the vacancy. [15]

The establishment of a Commissioner of Pardons was unique in that all other states had used parole boards or similar organizations. The experiment worked successfully, however, and, although the name was changed in 1929, the office remained a permanent part of the executive structure. As a full-time worker, the Commissioner was able to make personal first-hand investigations at the scene of the crime in all special cases begging clemency, and in his capacity as a public official, he was able to serve the poor as well as the rich. Moreover, he provided an even more important social service in his follow-up and rehabilitation work with paroled prisoners.

Governor McLean came to believe that a system of paroles was the most effective way to handle the majority of cases seeking relief from prison sentences and of assisting the discharged prisoners in their return to a regular community life. A full pardon freed a man from further responsibility to the law and experience had shown that, either from choice or an unfortunate combination of circumstances, many of those released in this manner drifted back into their old ways of life. Under a parole system, on the other hand, the individuals would have supervision and aid during the difficult transition from prison life to freedom. For this reason, McLean granted few pardons, but chose rather to release worthy prisoners under an arrangement of conditional freedom. Each prisoner paroled was placed under the supervision of the welfare officer of the county in which he or she lived, or some other suitable person who was expected to keep in contact and make regular reports to the

Commissioner of Pardons. At the same time, the Commissioner endeavored to help each released person find a permanent place in the community. Working through committees from civic clubs in fifty counties that volunteered their services and through local welfare officers, he found jobs for many of these men and women. The fact that only thirty-nine such paroles were revoked out of the 811 granted during the four years of McLean's administration suggests that the system worked. [16]

McLean also took definite steps to overhaul the administration of Central Prison in Raleigh and to improve conditions in the convict camps and local jails. For a number of years, there had been considerable pressure for prison reform in North Carolina, and many individuals had come to believe that the state's penal system was failing to either protect society or to reclaim the criminals. Through the efforts of the Conference for Social Service, repeated demands had been made for changes in the state prison and for improvements in the camps and local jails. Moved both by his own interest and by many outside requests for action, Governor Morrison, in 1922, appointed the Citizens Committee of One Hundred to study the state's plan and facilities for taking care of its criminal charges, and three of its recommendations had been enacted into law by the General Assembly in 1923. [17] At the extra session in August 1924, the Assembly appointed a second committee to investigate Central Prison and the convict camps and to report to the regular session in 1925. During the fall, this group made its study (including a tour of prisons in five southern states to compare their facilities with those in North Carolina), and, in January, presented its findings and recommendations to Governor McLean.

Based on its study, the committee recommended that control and management of Central Prison be clearly defined and that the prison system be placed under a state prison board. It also recommended that inspection of all county prisons be made by the State Department of Public Welfare. To provide work for the inmates of Central Prison, it recommended that a prison factory be established to produce clothes for inmates, as well as a printing press and a plant for making city, county, and state automobile license tags. The committee also recommended that permanent housing facilities be erected at Caledonia Prison Farm. Finally, it recommended that a dentist, an additional doctor, and a chaplain be added to the staff at Central Prison. [18]

To implement the recommendation, McLean had a number of bills drafted and presented to the General Assembly for action. Representative George R. Ward of Duplin County introduced a prison reorganization bill, [19] and Senator Simon J. Everett of Pitt County presented a measure authorizing the establishment of a State Bureau of Identification at State Prison, where it was to be maintained as a part of the machinery for locating and effecting the arrest and conviction of criminals. [20] The bills were approved without significant opposition.

The Prison Reorganization Act revised Chapter 130 of the Consolidated Statutes of 1919 to incorporate the recommendations made by Governor McLean, Superintendent Pou, and others. It provided that the corporation known as State Prison be made a regular department, governed by a Board of Directors consisting of a chairman and six other members—all to be appointed by the governor and subject to his removal with or without cause.

The new department would operate on legislative appropriations under the Executive Budget System and all monies collected by prison authorities were to be paid into the State Treasury. The prison board was directed to make provision for receiving and keeping all persons sentenced to Central Prison and to provide employment for all those able to work, either in the penitentiary and on farms owned or leased by the state, or by contracting for the hire of able-bodied convicts with outside concerns. All prisoners were to remain under the control and care of the Board of Directors at all times. The board would have charge of and manage all property of the Prison Department and would adopt and enforce rules and regulations for the governance of the department, its agents and employees, and the convicts under its care.

The act also provided for the classification of all male prisoners into three groups, according to their attitude toward the rules and regulations, their willingness to work, and whether they could be expected to maintain themselves by honest industry after their discharge. The uniforms, the type of work in which they would be employed, and the degree of restrictions on their freedom would vary according to these three classifications. [21]

Governor McLean selected a board of able men to direct the department and, on April 7, the members convened for an organizational meeting. The new board reselected George Ross Pou as superintendent, in spite of the attempt of the *Raleigh News and Observer* to discredit his administration and to prevent his reselection, and Dr. J. H. Norman as a combined warden and physician, an arrangement which was expected to save $4,000 a year. In previous years, food and household furnishings had been included as a part of the compensation to prison officials, but the new board decided to let the members of the staff secure their own supplies and to pay them fixed salaries accordingly. [22]

Meanwhile, Prison Superintendent George Ross Pou, in his biennial report of 1923-24, had given a detailed picture of an accumulated deficit in operating expenses at Central Prison and recommended a number of changes in both the organization and the policies of that institution. [23] In his special message to the General Assembly in

February, McLean urged the legislators to consider the immediate need and to find some constructive remedy for the growing deficit. He told then that in a little more than three years (since November 20, 1921), the deficiency in current expenses had grown to a sum of $298,847.42 and by June 30, 1925, it would probably reach a total of $430,842.42. Furthermore, it appeared that there would continue to be a shortage of $275,200 per year if the prison continued to run under the existing plan. [24]

One reason for the financial difficulties, as Governor McLean explained to the General Assembly, was the losses sustained from the sale and repossession of Caledonia Prison Farm. In 1918, the farm had been sold; but in 1923, it had been repossessed because the purchasers were unable to meet their payments. When the farm was returned, however, it was in such a dilapidated condition that the prison administration was forced to spend more than $70,000 to put even a part of it into a state of cultivation; more than 1,200 acres were still to be reclaimed. These unexpected expenses had eaten up most of the profits made from the prison lands.

An even more significant reason for the operating deficit could be found in the number and nature of persons being sentenced to terms in Central Prison and to other factors which made it more and more difficult to find employment for all the convicts. Not only was there a rather sharp increase in prison population, but a greater number of the persons committed during the past few years had been mentally and physically impaired and the expenses for these prisoners absorbed the profits made by revenue-producing prisoners. In the total population of approximately 1,200 inmates at Central Prison, only about 900 could be gainfully employed, even when steady work was available. Moreover, there was no longer the demand for convict labor that there had been in earlier years when the railroads and first public highways were being built. Construction companies using the new machinery and improved materials preferred to employ free labor. Not only did they need more skilled workers, but they insisted that since the humanitarian laws of recent years had deprived them of any effective discipline for the convicts, they could not obtain a normal day's work from persons currently filling the prisons.

To remedy the situation and prevent the penitentiary from becoming a permanent burden on the taxpayers of the state, Governor McLean recommended (1) that the prison be maintained on an appropriation basis, and financed just like other state institutions; (2) that the Board of Directors, by and with the consent of the governor and council of state, be authorized to purchase machinery and equipment needed to enable the management to provide employment for the persons confined in Central Prison; and (3) that the accumulated deficit of $298,847.42, the $40,000 due for fertilizer, and any shortages occurring in the operating expenses before July 1, 1925, be transferred to the general fund of the State Treasury. [25] In response to the governor's requests, Senators Mark Squires and W. C. Heath sponsored a measure which provided for funding the prison deficit and directed the management to purchase fertilizer and industrial equipment to furnish work for the convicts in Central Prison. [26] The bill was approved.

In the spring of 1925, Governor McLean made an investigation which revealed that in only six states in the Union were the penal institutions maintained on a self-supporting basis and that these were able to do so because they enjoyed near monopolies on certain industries. However, in spite of these findings, he was determined to make North Carolina's state prison self-sustaining, and during the next several months, he and the Board of Directors made a concentrated effort to achieve that objective. Wide publicity was given through the press and several hundred letters were written in an attempt to secure employment for the prison's surplus labor. [27] From these contacts a considerable number of convicts were put to work on roads and quarries in the western part of the state; [28] others were used in the construction of buildings at some of the institutions and in work on the Mansion and Capitol Square in Raleigh. They also made investigations and explored the possibilities of creating additional employment through the establishment of new industries, such as brick-making, the manufacturing of automobile license plates, a prison printing press, and the maintenance of a floral hothouse. State Geologist Jasper L. Stuckey and A. F. Greaves-Walker, professor of Ceramic Engineering at State College in Raleigh, were asked to investigate the quality of clay deposits on prison lands and in other areas where the state might buy sites for brick plants. [29] They conducted the study, though the project was not realized during the McLean administration.

In 1926, the Board of Directors gave its approval to the construction of a floral hothouse and the establishment of a printing plant. In February 1928, Superintendent Pou considered submitting a bid for the state's 1929 automobile license plates, with a view to installing the necessary machinery if the prison were awarded the bid; but after reviewing all the factors involved, he decided the department was not yet ready to undertake such a project. [30]

Later in the spring of 1928, Pou found work for a hundred or more convicts in North Carolina's two active coal mines, the Carolina Mine at Coal Glen near Sanford and the Erskine-Ramsey at Cumnock. However, when four of these men were killed and seven injured in a mine accident at the Carolina Mine in December 1928, a wave of public censure condemned this use of the state's prisoners in places of danger. In 1925, fifty-three miners had been killed by an explosion at the Carolina Mine and a similar explosion had killed a number of men in the Erskine-Ramsey Mine several years earlier. Critics contended that the state had no right to force prisoners to work in places which involved such risks. [31] They asserted that a desire to make the prison self-sustaining had overshadowed all concern for the welfare of the prisoners.

The campaign to make State Prison self-supporting was successful beyond hopes. By the end of 1925, its income was more than sufficient to meet all operating expenses and, in January 1929, the Board of Directors reported an estimated balance of more than $250,000 for the four preceding years. [32] Employment had been found for all the able-bodied convicts; and Caledonia Prison Farm, which had been made into one of the most profitable farming units in North Carolina, was raising food for Central Prison and the fourteen prison camps scattered over the state, in addition to several thousand bales of cotton and large quantities of peanuts. Despite a 275 percent increase in prison population during the last eight years, Central Prison had become the seventh state penitentiary in the nation to operate on a self-supporting basis and could report a profit exceeded by only one other institution. [33]

Governor McLean's interest in the prison department included more than its financial problems. He was also concerned for the well-being of the inmates. The reorganization act of 1925 placed the department under the supervision of the State Board of Charities and Public Welfare, and through the services of this agency and the work of department officials, efforts were made to help prisoners with personal problems and provide a more satisfactory rehabilitation of all those committed to the state's care. With the cooperation of the Commissioner of Pardons, contacts were maintained between prisoners and their families, assistance was given to wives and children left in need by the absence of husbands and fathers, and work was found for prisoners after their release. When Governor McLean discovered that there were young boys among the inmates at the penitentiary and on the prison farms, he took immediate steps to have them removed. He directed Commissioner Bridges to gather the records of prisoners under sixteen and to parole them as soon as possible to one of the institutions for juvenile delinquents. [34] In December 1927, when a fourteen-year-old boy was convicted of murdering a neighbor and sentenced to six years in the state penitentiary, he declared the prison was no place for boys and paroled him to Stonewall Jackson Training School. [35] As soon as employment was found for all the able-bodied black convicts at Camp Polk Farm near Raleigh, that establishment was set aside for white offenders under twenty years of age. [36]

In 1925, the Legislative Council of North Carolina Women, representing the several business and professional women's clubs and organizations in the state, asked the General Assembly to establish a place of detention for white women over sixteen, or those too old to be cared for at Samarcand in Moore County, and to assume the responsibility for Efland Industrial School for Negro Girls in Orange County. The legislative committees refused to approve the bills and nothing was done about either project. [37] In 1927, Governor McLean gave his support to the measures and, on March 9, the legislators approved a bill which provided for the Industrial Farm Colony for Women and directed the governor to appoint a Board of Directors. The board was authorized to choose a site for the colony on land owned by the state and to have plans and specifications drawn up for the necessary buildings and equipment. It was also to have full responsibility for determining the policies, making the rules and regulations, and directing the administration of the institution. The State Treasury was instructed to sell bonds up to $60,000 to pay for the buildings and equipment. [38]

On June 4, Governor McLean appointed the Board of Directors and within the next several weeks, they selected 500 acres of land belonging to Caswell Training School near Kinston as a site for the farm colony. [39] A brick dormitory, equipped for thirty inmates, a residence for the chief administrator, an infirmary, and other service plants were constructed and ready for occupancy by the middle of January 1929. Meanwhile, a Board of Trustees and a superintendent were selected to take charge of the institution when it opened. In the budget message presented to his successor and the General Assembly in 1929, Governor McLean recommended an appropriation for maintenance and an additional grant for a second dormitory.

The proposal, offered by Negro Club Women of North Carolina, that the state accept the Industrial School for Negro Girls at Efland and make it into a state reformatory for black girls was again rejected in 1927. The General Assembly, however, did provide an annual appropriation of $2,000 to help with the expenses of the institution. [40]

Along with his efforts toward the reorganization of Central Prison and the establishment of a detention home for female prisoners, Governor McLean took steps to provide more effective inspection of the fourteen convict camps scattered over the state. In a conference with Mrs. Kate Burr Johnson, Commissioner of Charities and Public Welfare, and Dr. G. M. Cooper of the State Board of Health in July 1925, McLean suggested a plan for combining the efforts of both offices in performing the regular inspections of state and county prison camps as required by law. With the consent of Mrs. Johnson and Dr. Cooper, an arrangement was worked out whereby L. G. Whitley, chief sanitary inspector of the Health Department, would serve both agencies and his salary and expenses would be supplied equally by the two departments. [41] The plan proved to be economical and satisfactory, as it not only prevented duplication of effort but provided more regular service than had been possible before. Until this cooperative arrangement was made, neither department had been able to keep a full-time inspector in the field and the work had suffered as a consequence. To provide an improved standard on which Whitley could base his examinations, the State Board of Health, in June 1926, adopted rules and regulations governing the sanitary and hygienic management of convict camps and county jails and copies of these were mailed to prison officials and sheriffs in each county. On the basis of these regulations, Whitley graded the various penal establishments and reported deficiencies to local authorities, the State Department of Welfare, and the State Board of Health. When they were informed of unsatisfactory conditions, some officials took immediate steps to bring about improvements, while others refused to cooperate until they were threatened with state action.

Although the new regulations helped to improve conditions in state and county facilities, there were many lingering problems. One of these was the lack of proper facilities and care for the criminally insane. In January 1925, fifty-five such persons were transferred from State Prison to a new building erected at State Hospital for the Insane, but, in constructing this facility, no provisions had been made for the security of these residents. [42] Furthermore, there were repeated escapes from the prison farms, where men could easily cut themselves out of old buildings and temporary structures. In February 1925, nineteen prisoners escaped from Caledonia Prison Farm (four of them convicted murderers and the others desperate criminals). [43] During a two-week period in February, thirty prisoners escaped from State Prison in Raleigh. [44] In March 1925, there was a mutiny among the forty-four black prisoners from Caledonia working in a quarry; two were killed and ten wounded as they tried to escape. [45] In August, six convicts escaped (after shooting a guard) from Caledonia. [46]

There were repeated charges that prison guards were brutal and inhumane. There were claims of favoritism for those who had "pull," while others who were kept in solitary were so weak and starved they were near death. In July 1927, E. E. Dudding, president of Prisoners' Relief Society, wrote McLean that "An outpost of Hell" would be a good name for Halifax Prison Farm. He described mistreatment of convicts and charged that six men were killed while trying to escape and two were shot while wearing irons. [47] Kate Burr Johnson, state commissioner of public welfare, was highly critical of living conditions and treatment of prisoners and led a crusade to change these conditions. Some accused her of being a fanatic (and some of her ideas perhaps were unwise), but her efforts were generally positive and constructive.

McLean backed Mrs. Johnson and the Department of Welfare in its efforts to prevent mistreatment of prisoners and in its actions against persons charged with such conduct. A few notorious cases aroused statewide concern, among them an affair in Stanly County, where N. C. Cranford, supervisor of the local prison camp, was charged with brutal treatment of convicts and the murder of two men; and an instance in Nash County where the camp foreman and a guard at the Rocky Mount Prison Camp beat a black prisoner to death.

Governor McLean appointed special counsel to assist with the prosecution in each case and at least five members of the Department of Welfare made fifteen trips to Albemarle to investigate the charges against Cranford and to help with the trial. In Stanly County, local opinion, mostly in defense of the county's name, was in favor of Cranford, and the jury let him go free, while in Nash County, the foreman and guard were convicted and sentenced to terms of up to twenty years of hard labor. [48] According to Mrs. Johnson, this conviction was the second ever secured against a North Carolina prison official and marked a definite change in public attitude toward the treatment of prisoners. Following the trials, the Stanly Camp was closed; the Rocky Mount Camp was retained but it was completely reorganized and brought into line with regulations from the Health Department.

Governor McLean took just as strong a stand on all matters of law enforcement. When, in March 1925, a mob of white men mutilated a Jewish salesman in Martin County, he denounced the mutilation as a "horrible crime against the laws of our state" and issued a proclamation offering a $400 reward for each person arrested and convicted. [49] Twenty-eight men were arrested and tried; ten were given sentences from six to thirty years, and the others were fined. [50]

Again in September 1925, when an Asheville mob stormed the Buncombe County jail in an attempt to take a black boy who was charged with assaulting a white woman, the governor ordered the arrest of all those participating and sent a unit of the State Guard to maintain order. Fifteen members of the mob were found guilty and given sentences ranging from twelve months on the county roads to eight years in the state penitentiary. [51] In the weeks following the trial in November, some 6,800 requests that he pardon or commute the sentences of those convicted poured into his office, but McLean refused to be swayed. On February 10, he issued a statement in which he made it clear that as long as he was governor, he intended to see that any prisoner in the custody of the law received the same protection as the judge on the bench or the solicitor who represented the state in the prosecution, and he warned those who might consider taking the law into their own hands that they would be punished severely, just as had been done in the Asheville and Martin County cases. [52]

Chapter VIII

—••◆••—

THE PUBLIC SCHOOL SYSTEM: EQUAL OPPORTUNITIES
FOR RURAL CHILDREN

—••◆••—

In his Inaugural Address, delivered on January 14, 1925, Governor McLean said:

> I favor progress in public education, because it is the foundation stone of our civilization. The classic utterance of a great North Carolinian, 'A democracy cannot be built on the backs of ignorant men,' sounded an everlasting truth.
>
> We have long taken to heart this great lesson, so that today our system of public education is the delight of our citizenship and the glorious hope of our future progress. We should carry on this program, because it means advancement, development, democracy.
>
> In the rate of progress made in public education in the past 25 years, North Carolina has outstripped every state in the country; yet we are forced to admit that education is still the most pressing need of our Commonwealth.
>
> The fundamental factor in our system of education is the public school system, because every process of educational development must begin at the bottom. Therefore, we need to stress more and more the work of our elementary and high schools.
>
> The principal requisite in our present educational system is to equalize the school facilities of the rural children, particularly those who live in the less wealthy counties, so that we may provide equality of opportunity in educational advantages for all children in the rural districts as fast as it is possible to do so. I hope that day will soon come when every boy and girl in the most remote rural sections of the state will have the opportunity for at least a high school education. We must constantly strive to reach this goal. [1]

McLean could never have been called a crusader, but in his businesslike manner and with his philosophy that a state, no more than an individual, should spend beyond the reasonable limits of its ability to pay, he worked hard for the cause of education during his four years as chief executive. He not only recognized that schools must furnish leaders for the new industrial development which was rapidly placing North Carolina in the forefront among her southern neighbors, but he also saw, in the rural school, the state's best chances for building a better agricultural community. It was his firm belief that there could be no permanent or well-balanced progress along any line, material or social, until the farmers and their families were brought up to a higher level in education, general culture, and material prosperity. So that there might be adequate schools for the needs of the state and all its people, he worked to bring about an equal distribution of the tax burden among the counties, and the steps he achieved toward this end paved the way for a state-supported uniform system of public schools.

It was true that great progress had been made since 1900, when Governor Charles B. Aycock encouraged an interest in education and launched his campaign to provide schools and equal opportunities for all children in North Carolina. Between 1900 and 1924, public school enrollment had doubled and the number of teachers employed had increased threefold. Expenditures for education had grown from approximately $1,250,000 in 1900 to almost $34,000,000 in 1924-1925. In 1900, North Carolina could count about thirty public high schools with an enrollment of approximately 2,000, but in 1924, there were 712 such schools with an enrollment of 73,593. In 1918, a constitutional amendment had extended the minimum school term from four to six months; by 1924, all urban areas enjoyed at least eight months of school. [2]

In spite of this commendable record of achievement, the goals set in 1900 had not been realized. Thirteen percent of the population over ten years of age still could not read or write, and, according to Dr. Samuel Huntington Hobbs, Jr., in *North Carolina Economic and Social*, the illiteracy rate of the Carolina Highlands in the western part of the state was surpassed by no area within the bounds of the United States unless it was the nearby mountain regions of Kentucky and Tennessee. [3] Per capita expenditures for children enrolled in the public schools were still less than half the national average and the term of slightly over seven months was exceeded in forty-one states. There was a grave shortage of teachers and, of those employed, more than 24 percent had less than a high school education and fewer than 14 percent had completed a four-year college course. [4]

The reasons for this low level of education, however, were not hard to find. In the first place, North Carolina was a rural state. In 1920, seventy-one of every one hundred inhabitants lived outside an incorporated town with a population of 2,500 or more, [5] and, until the Good Roads Program of the 1920s provided a system of state highways to connect the cities and towns and better county roads for the rural areas, the one-room school located in walking distance was about all that was possible for many children in the state.

In the second place, North Carolina was a poor state. In total wealth produced in factories, farms, forests, and mines, North

Carolina ranked 15th in the Union, but forty states exceeded her in the distribution of true wealth. [6] National statistics also indicated that, between 1902 and 1922, the state had made the largest percentage increase in wealth per capita of all the states, but only 1.24 percent of the entire population filed income tax returns as compared to 3.52 percent for the nation. [7] The majority of North Carolinians were small farmers and almost half of these farmers were tenants who did not own the land on which they lived. Nearly one-third of the population was black and represented a small proportion of the wealth; while the laboring classes of the cities and towns seldom had more than their weekly wages. [8] Moreover, the uneven distribution of wealth from county to county was almost as great a handicap to the development of a uniform system of schools as was the general low level of income. With a variation in taxable wealth of $8,358 per child in Forsyth County to $1,598 in Wilkes County, [9] the obligation to provide equal educational opportunities for all children presented problems of major import.

And finally, North Carolina had proportionately more children to educate than any other state in the Union. With a growing school population and limited sources of wealth from which to draw support, the odds seemed to be stacked against North Carolina's educational system. Only through the judicious development of all natural resources and the accumulation of greater true wealth could the state hope to provide educational programs which would meet national standards.

The imperative needs of North Carolina schools in 1925 were: a stringent compulsory attendance law, faithfully enforced; an extended term of eight months; more competent and trained teachers; and more state aid to make these possible. Finding a way to provide these essentials consumed the attention of North Carolina leaders for more than two decades, but between 1925 and 1929, the McLean administration made significant steps to that end.

Early in 1924, as they looked ahead to the 1925 session of the General Assembly, those who hoped for educational changes in North Carolina launched a campaign to win support for a program of legislation on behalf of the public schools. At its regular meeting in March the North Carolina Educational Association endorsed resolutions calling for an eight-month term, a uniform system for enforcing the compulsory attendance law, and eight additional normal schools for the training of teachers. [10] In May, a group of interested citizens met in Raleigh and selected a Central Committee of One Hundred, with A. D. Broadhurst of Greensboro as chairman, to direct the organization of local committees and to carry the fight for an eight-month term directly to the people. [11] From these beginnings and on through the summer and fall, groups of teachers and citizens in communities all over the state urged the voting public to demand some positive action by the General Assembly in 1925.

In his biennial report to the governor, Superintendent of Public Instruction A. T. Allen also recommended an eight-month term, further consolidation of rural schools, a uniform curriculum for the entire state, more school buildings, and additional facilities for training teachers. He pointed out that, while all children living in towns and cities attended school for eight months, 71.3 percent of the white children and 92.4 percent of the African-American children living in rural areas did not enjoy a similar opportunity. Moreover, since it was almost impossible to secure competent teachers to work only six months in the year, the children who attended these short-term schools were not only deprived of the additional time for learning, but of competent teachers as well. As a result of these conditions, he reported, 66.7 percent of all white rural children were educationally retarded from one to eight years by the time they reached the seventh grade and less than ten percent ever went on to high school. Discouraged by repeated failures, thousands dropped out of school to work on the farm or simply because they lost interest. For the black children, the story was even worse. [12]

Yet, for all the efforts to inform the public and to secure the election of men who would serve the cause of education, the school leaders found their program eclipsed by a concern for state finances. When the General Assembly convened in January, a widespread conviction that North Carolina must spend less money made its members reluctant to undertake any program which would mean additional expenses. As to the need for better schools and an extended term, there was almost unanimous agreement, but no one seemed to know where to secure the extra funds. The legislators rejected all suggestions for new excise taxes or a general sales tax, and the bill to provide a state tax on property for the support of all schools was tabled in the House. [13]

On January 22, a committee from the State Association of County Commissioners appeared before the Budget Commission to give its approval to an increased Equalization Fund, but expressed reservations about an eight-month term at county expense. [14] Governor McLean also felt that it would not be right to compel the less wealthy agricultural counties to assume the responsibility for eight months of education until the tax burden for the shorter term had been fairly and adequately distributed. With no support from the governor and no influential leader to sponsor it in either house, it was not surprising, then, that the proposal for a longer school term died, as did the other suggestions for a state-supported system and a compulsory attendance law.

Although the General Assembly failed to take positive action on the eight-month term, it did provide some appropriations for educational services and approved a number of other measures on behalf of the state's schools. It increased the Equalization Fund by $500,000 to make it $1,500,000 for each year of the biennium, the distribution conditioned on a levy of at least forty-four cents on the hundred valuation of taxable property in the county receiving such aid, [15] and it approved an issue of $5,000,000 worth of bonds to help counties in the construction and equipment of school buildings. [16] It also enacted two laws to protect the children being transported by bus to the consolidated schools. One bill limited the speed of such buses to twenty-five miles per hour, [17] and another measure required all automobiles to stop at least fifty feet behind a school bus picking up or dropping off children on the highways. [18] Moreover, in what perhaps was its most important action, it authorized the appointment of an Educational Commission to make a study of the school system and to report back to the governor and General Assembly in 1927.

In a message to both houses on February 28, Governor McLean asked the legislators to provide for such a commission. He said: "The expansion of our educational facilities, the ever-increasing costs, and a firm and steady appreciation of the necessity of further advancement involve problems of costs, economic administration, the elimination of overlapping in effort and expense, the standardization of equipment, and the correlation of all educational efforts. To solve these problems by applying constructive policies and methods, intensive study is imperatively necessary." [19] Senator A. A. F. Seawell of Lee County introduced a bill embodying his suggestions and it was passed without opposition; on March 7, the lower house gave its approval. [20]

On March 3, 1926, Governor McLean appointed the Educational Commission, naming as members Charles A. Webb of Asheville, Mrs. E. L. McKee of Sylva, James O. Carr of Wilmington, James K. Norfleet of Winston-Salem, Mrs. Joseph A. Brown of Chadbourn, Thomas D. Warren of New Bern, Dr. J. Y. Joyner of Raleigh, C. E. Teague of Sanford, Mrs. J. G. Fearing of Elizabeth City, T. Wingate Andrews of High Point, L. S. Robinson of Wadesboro, and S. E. Lattimore of Shelby. [21] On March 22, the commission convened in the governor's office for its organizational meeting. J. O. Carr was chosen to serve as chairman and Dr. J. Y. Joyner as executive secretary. Dr. Fred W. Morrison was selected as an assistant to Dr. Joyner and director of the investigations. [22] It was expected that it would take the group six months to complete its assignment.

Meanwhile, the school leaders who believed that the Educational Commission would find facts to support their demand for an eight-month term, made plans for another fight in the General Assembly. To arouse the public interest they sent speakers through the state and, in local communities, civic groups joined with teachers' organizations to win support for the extended term. Dr. Edgar W. Knight, as president of the North Carolina Educational Association, campaigned with vigor and determination. Speaking to the Raleigh Civitan Club on August 25, he said:

> Educationally North Carolina is marked by mediocrity. Mediocrity means weakness, and in public education mediocrity is equivalent to downright public immorality.
>
> Mediocre ability and inferior effort in education are reproaches enough, but indifference to our shortcomings and satisfaction with our low place are more disgraceful. In education and cultural interests in North Carolina today there is evident a deadly complacency. It often dwells on the tongue and lingers on the pen of those who brag or write of North Carolina. Complacency beams in the countenances of some of our school officials. The rather generous publicity which we have received and encouraged at home and abroad during the recent years has helped make us satisfied with feeble efforts which we think of as real achievements, but which would pass unnoticed in any other parts of the United States except our own provincial South.

> We have the shortest school legal term in the entire United States, and probably no one of the entire 48 so boasted and so boastful does so little to train teachers for the public schools. None apparently has been so remiss in this important work and we still piddle aimlessly about the task.
>
> Many of our county superintendents of schools are inferior in ability and training and sadly deficient in qualities of leadership. Too many of them are pitiable political appendages, uninspired and uninspiring to teachers or the public. Some of our city superintendents are little if any better. [23]

In October, Knight told the joint meeting of the Rotary and Kiwanis clubs in Raleigh that real equality of educational opportunity could never be achieved by subsidizing the counties through a fund which was founded on poverty and served only to create and perpetuate distinction in class and rank. The Equalization Fund, he insisted, should be entitled "an act for branding and marking the poor, so that they may be known from the prosperous and the proud." [24]

Other speakers included A. T. Allen, superintendent of public instruction, Julius B. Warren, secretary of the North Carolina Educational Association, and William N. Everett, secretary of state. Most of the daily papers gave considerable space to the cause and Clarence Poe, editor of the *Progressive Farmer*, urged that some way be found to relieve the farmers from their burden of taxes and to make it possible for the rural areas to have schools comparable to those of the urban centers. [25]

Without a doubt, a majority of public opinion was in agreement that the state should extend its school term, though an occasional voice expressed some objections. In January, The Farmers' Union, at its annual convention, passed a resolution against lengthening the term to eight months. Farmers could not bear the burden of additional taxes, it said; moreover, they needed the children to work at home. [26] A similar pronouncement before a mass meeting of Mecklenburg County citizens indicated that this opinion was not just the thinking of a small group. [27] In its annual session at Morehead City in August, the Association of County Commissioners listened to Superintendent Allen present the case for an eight-month term, but the members refused to commit themselves until the state would provide the necessary funds. [28] Even as the General Assembly began to debate the issue in January, the *Charlotte Observer*, which often spoke for the industrial interests of North Carolina, declared there was no need for an extended term. Whatever gap existed between the education provided for the rural child and the city child, the paper insisted, was being filled adequately by the activities of the farm agents. [29]

During the months of discussion, Governor McLean remained silent for the most part. He watched the campaigners with some uneasiness, however, for he felt they were unconcerned about the costs or where the state could find the money, and, in August, he counseled Chairman Carr of the Educational Commission to take care, lest the "professional school people" take charge of the study. [30] McLean favored equal opportunities for all children, but he did not see how the state could, at the moment, finance the additional months for all schools. He was strongly opposed to a state tax on real property, because he believed the assessments on land were already as heavy as the farmers could bear; and he feared that additional levies on corporate wealth would drive industry away.

The final realization of a uniform and adequate school system could be achieved, he insisted, only as the growth of industrial wealth and improved conditions in the agricultural community brought a natural increase in state revenues through the existing channels of income, inheritance, and privilege taxes. Meanwhile, he advocated that the burden of a six-month term be equalized and that state aid be gradually increased to enable the counties to move into an eight-month term as fast as their financial means would allow. This was a policy of caution and too conservative to satisfy the educational forces who wanted to achieve an immediate extension by constitutional amendment and to leave the responsibility for finding funds to the state's legislators.

Soon after the General Assembly convened in January, the
Educational Commission completed a report on the first part of its
work and, on the 26th, Governor McLean submitted its findings to
the two houses, with a message requesting their careful consideration of the recommendations included. [31] The report summarized
the progress made since 1900 and discussed at length the problems
still to be solved: the wide variations in educational opportunities
for children in rural and urban areas, the scarcity of trained teachers, and the unjust burden of taxes borne by the poorer counties.

To provide some assistance with these problems, the commission
recommended: (1) that the existing plan for joint county and state
support of the minimum six-month term be continued, but that
state aid be extended to equalize the total expense for schools and no
longer be confined to the outlay for salaries alone; (2) that the
General Assembly provide for a complete, thorough, and fair revalu-
ation of all property in North Carolina, and that the reassessment be
kept up to date; (3) that the Equalization Fund be increased to
$4,000,000 and that this fund be given precedence in the budget
over all other appropriations for education; (4) that to participate in
the Equalization Fund, counties be required to keep a uniform system of books and reports, to observe the salary schedules prescribed
by the state, to levy an ad valorem tax of 35 or 40 cents per $100
value on all taxable property for the support of schools, and to provide an additional levy for maintaining sinking funds and debt service; (5) that $300,000 of the Fund be reserved to equalize the burden
of expenses for two extra months and, thus, encourage the adoption
of an eight-month term; (6) that the state expand the facilities for
training teachers and add other normal schools, especially for the
training of black teachers; (7) and that the school term be extended
to eight months by legislative enactment, not by constitutional
amendment, upon the approval of the several communities and at
such time as a definite and constant source of revenue could be provided. [32]

On this last point, the commission was divided seven to five, the
dissenting group filing a minority report recommending the immediate adoption of an eight-month term by constitutional amendment. These five members, three women and two city school superintendents, believed the findings from their study called for immediate action on behalf of the rural children and they refused to
accept the argument that levying additional taxes to provide better
educational facilities might cripple the state and check progress in
other fields. [33] On March 4, when their report was brought to the
Senate, J. M. Broughton offered a bill proposing a constitutional
amendment to be voted on in the general election of 1928. His measure was tabled without discussion—the attempt to secure an extended term had failed again. [34]

In the meantime, both houses had become deadlocked in a controversy over providing aid for the six-month term. The question in dispute was whether the legislature should provide a statewide tax to help the counties support their schools or adopt a greatly-increased Equalization Fund, as recommended by both the governor and the Educational Commission. In the House, the poorer counties, led by Representative A. D. MacLean of Beaufort, A. M. Graham of Sampson, Judge Francis D. Winston of Bertie, N. A. Townsend of Harnett, and John H. Folger of Surry, consolidated their strength behind a bill presented by Representative Graham. His measure would provide a statewide ad valorem tax on property to supplement the Equalization Fund and other appropriations for operating expenses. The counties, then, would only be responsible for capital outlay, equipment, and debt service. [35] As a companion measure, this group supported Judge Winston's bill creating a $4,000,000 equalization fund. [36] The Senate, in which the more prosperous counties had a stronger position, voted down all attempts to levy a statewide tax and, with an overwhelming majority, passed the administration's request for a $2,500,000 equalization fund. [37]

Needless to say, the controversy over an additional property tax was one in which the whole state was interested. Delegations came to make personal appeals and to lobby for one side or the other. J. L. Skinner, secretary of the State Association of County Commissioners, came to Raleigh to make known the views of his organization. He reported that, with a few exceptions from the larger counties, all county commissioners were enthusiastically in favor of a statewide tax for the support of public schools and, while they did not object to an eight-month term, they were opposed to an extension supported by the counties from local levies on land. [38]

Letters expressing strong convictions on both sides sought Governor McLean's help in turning the vote of the General Assembly. One came from A. H. Bahnson of the Washington Mills Company of Winston-Salem, who said it was difficult for him to understand why sentiment was so strong in favor of such a tax, in view of the fact that the last state levy on land was a complete failure. The business people were against it, he declared, and were doing all they could to block the measure. [39] A similar opinion came from J. O. Carr of Wilmington. He insisted it would be disastrous to revive the statewide property tax, because the school people would never stop demanding higher rates once the tax was allowed. [40] Another letter pleading the opposite view came from William W. Dawson of Pitt County, who wrote expressing his hearty approval of the tax proposal and asking McLean to assist in securing such a measure. [41]

In an evening session of the House on February 28, attended by a crowd that packed the galleries and jammed the lobbies, the tax debate came to a climax. As the members were finding their places, Judge Winston sent to the desk an amendment which would increase his proposed equalization fund from $4,000,000 to $5,000,000. Others also presented measures, new bills or amendments, bringing the total to nine educational bills on the desk by the time the session opened. When the preliminaries were over and the debate was called, Representative Graham took charge and led off in defense of his bill. He was not there to match the poor counties against the richer ones, he said, but to help provide a uniform system of schools for North Carolina. This, however, could never be done as long as eight of the 100 counties possessed more than one-half of the wealth of the state, but had fewer than two-fifths of the children. Representative MacLean followed, speaking at length in support of the state tax and urging the legislators to provide larger appropriations for the Equalization Fund; others joined the defense as the debate continued through the evening.

Reuben O. Everett of Durham spoke against the tax. It would not relieve the burdened farmers, he said, but rather the big corporations and the railroads. The farmers, he said, should not be required to pay any more ad valorem taxes for the support of schools; the load should be transferred to the earnings of big business and persons who could afford to pay. Representative Thomas J. Gold of Guilford said he saw no reason for changing the system that had worked so well since it was initiated by Aycock and McIver, and declared the plan for state-supported schools would mean such centralization that it would destroy "state's rights," and could well lead to a national educational system. He said the people of his county were willing to support their own schools and to help other counties through large income taxes, and special privilege taxes, but that they would not accept an ad valorem tax on land.

When the debate finally ended and the vote was called, the Graham bill passed by a count of sixty-eight to forty-two, while Judge Winston's $5,000,000 equalization fund was defeated by ten votes. [42]

The Senate, meanwhile, had passed a bill which, in the end, replaced Graham's. This bill, sponsored by Senator A. E. Woltz of Gaston County and backed by Governor McLean, incorporated the administration's earlier bill appropriating $2,500,000 for the Equalization Fund and authorized the appointment of a State Board of Equalization to administer the Fund. The duties of this board would be twofold: (1) to determine the true value of all property subject to taxation; this value was to serve as the basis on which taxes would be levied and collected and the basis on which state grants would be apportioned among the counties; and (2) to allocate the appropriations. Any county desiring to participate in the program must provide an ad valorem tax of forty-two cents, levied on the basis of the board's assessment, as its part of the expenses for a six-month school term. Moreover, in making the apportionments to the several counties, the board was to determine the difference between the actual expenditures for salaries and operating expenses and the amount to be raised by this forty-two cent tax and to allocate a sum sufficient to cover the deficit. In case the Equalization Fund did not prove to be adequate for this purpose in all counties, the commissioners would be required to levy an additional tax to take care of the shortage. To give special aid and to encourage counties to improve their schools, the bill provided that $100,000 of the $2,500,000 fund be set aside and distributed among participating units, for the employment of additional instructors where an increased attendance required them, for relief to counties suffering some misfortune, and for extra grants to those having made marked improvements in their teaching personnel. [43]

With the two houses each adamant in defense of its own measure, it looked as if the session might close without any action on the Educational Commission's report. However, on the evening of March 2, the stalemate was broken and a compromise was reached. When the House Committee on Education returned the Woltz Bill with a favorable report, the insurgents from the poorer counties gave up what appeared to be a hopeless struggle and agreed to accept the Senate's measure with two amendments, one increasing the Equalization Fund to $3,250,000 and the other reducing the county tax to forty cents. On the following day the Senate voted an increase of one half of one percent in income tax on corporations to raise the additional $750,000 and, on March 8, gave its final approval to the House amendments. [44] Thus ended what the correspondent of the *Greensboro Daily News* described as the most furious debate the General Assembly had seen in a quarter of a century.

One final measure renewed the building loan fund and completed the session's work on behalf of the public schools. Although, in providing the $3,250,000 Equalization Fund, the legislators had voted the largest appropriation that had ever been made for public education in North Carolina, they retreated from this high moment of generosity to assume quite a miserly attitude toward the loan fund. Beginning in 1921, each regular session of the General Assembly had approved a fund of $5,000,000 to be loaned to counties for the construction and equipment of school buildings, but when a bill providing a similar appropriation was presented to the House on March 3, it ran into determined opposition. Some of the members had heard complaints of extravagance, and Representative Marvin W. Nash of Richmond County objected to the fund because Hamlet had borrowed $25,000 for a black school. After an appeal by Superintendent Allen, in which he told the legislators that unless some communities got additional buildings, they would not be able to take care of the increased school population, the House passed the bill; but not before it had cut the appropriation in half. The Senate approved the cut a few days later. [45]

The dispute over the funding of public education did not end with the passage of the appropriation bills in March. In 1925, an appointed board allotted the equalization funds in the same amounts and on the same basis as the 1923-1924 distribution, [46] but there was considerable dissatisfaction with this method. To avoid this trouble in 1927, steps were taken to achieve a more equitable apportionment of monies. In March, the new and enlarged Equalization Board met and its members were sent out to visit every county, confer with local authorities, examine records, and make investigations. Based on their findings, the board decided to use the last valuation on property (1926) as a basis for distribution of funds for the first year of the biennium, but that a more accurate valuation would be made for the second year. Forms and maps for such a survey were prepared and sent to all the counties. Some of these counties had already started an evaluation on their own; three-fourths made an effort to cooperate with the state.

When the new report came in, however, it was apparent that there remained great disparities in assessed needs and valuation figures from county to county. Moreover, tentative requests from ninety-one counties seeking help by far exceeded the appropriation of $3,250,000. The board did its best to allocate the monies on what it considered an equitable basis and instructed a number of counties to raise their tax rates to cover expected shortages. Ninety counties were given increased allotments; twenty-five of these received double their previous grants; five received eight times their last grant. Quotas for Currituck and Jackson Counties were only slightly better than earlier allotments, and funds for Camden and Dare Counties were actually reduced. [47]

As could be expected, there were many protests. There were charges that some of the counties receiving the most money were the richest counties in the state. An editorial in the *Raleigh News and Observer* stated that, although the Equalization Fund was supposed to even out the tax burden, a greater portion of the money had been distributed among counties whose tax rates were already below average, while many counties with a rate far above average received small amounts. Several counties threatened to carry their protests into court.

On July 8, the Equalization Board held a public hearing and many counties came to present their cause. Camden County made the most strenuous protest, but twenty others brought accusations of unfair treatment. Members of the board listened and tried to explain their position. Only two counties, Chatham and Rockingham, were promised relief. [48]

On July 22, the board met in Morehead City to begin a study of tax data and to canvass all complaints. To appease Camden and several other counties, they agreed to allot each of them $5,000 from the stimulating fund; in all they distributed $35,000 from the $100,000 fund. They canvassed the entire state, but made few changes in the 1927 allotments—except for Camden, Dare, Pitt, and Rockingham Counties. [49]

In June 1929, the board met to distribute funds for the 1928-1929 biennium and made a few changes in the previous allotments. Whatever increases were made were very small and counties continued their protests against what they considered to be unfair treatment. [50] This dissatisfaction over the distribution of the Equalization Fund helped to fuel the demand for a state-supported school term of eight months.

Although it was not always considered a part of the public school system, a program to reduce or eliminate adult illiteracy was initiated during the 1920s. In fact, the General Assembly of 1919 made schools for adults, often referred to as "moonlight schools," a part of the public school system. In 1919-1920, fifty-two counties organized schools for adults and had regularly employed teachers. There were a total of 272 schools with 5,580 persons enrolled. The costs were shared equally by the state and the counties. The State Department of Education prepared a reader and other texts. [51] Unfortunately, when the state property tax was abolished in 1921, these early efforts died due to a lack of funds.

The program was renewed during the late twenties. At a conference of school superintendents held in Asheville in 1927, the problem of adult illiteracy was included on the agenda. Governor McLean attended the conference and, in his address, he declared that no greater goal could be reached during his administration than the abolition of adult illiteracy and he gave his promise to support all efforts made to that end.

Meanwhile, Buncombe County and the City of Asheville, under the leadership of Mrs. Elizabeth C. Morris, developed a model program. In 1919, a survey of the county and the City of Asheville found 7000 illiterate adults, but by 1925, Mrs. Morris's efforts had enjoyed remarkable success in reducing that number. One thousand persons had gone through the first three grades; another 1,000 had mastered the first two grades; and 2,000 had completed the first grade. The average age of these students was thirty years. [52]

With renewed interest in the program during the late twenties Asheville and Buncombe County expanded its efforts. Five full-time teachers and sixteen part-time workers were added to the existing staff. It was their goal to reach the remaining 1,361 adults, white and black, who could not read or write. In 1926, the county was honored for its program by the National Education Association and Mrs.

Morris was asked to present her textbook for adult beginners to the Department of Adult Education. [53]

In 1927, the National Bureau of Education and the General Federation of Women's Clubs joined the national crusade to move the United States up from tenth place in education among the nations of the world. Each state was asked to conduct a survey of adult illiteracy and to work out a plan for dealing with the problem. [54] In April 1927, McLean appointed a committee on adult illiteracy to survey North Carolina, locate the centers of illiteracy, and prepare a plan for community or night schools. He also agreed to asked the General Assembly for an appropriation of $50,000 or $60,000 for the work.

The increased appropriations for public schools and the crusade against adult illiteracy indicated a growing conviction that the state must accept more responsibility for the education of all its people, a conviction which was also reflected, though to a lesser degree, in the grants for higher education. In 1921, under the leadership of Governor Morrison, North Carolina had entered upon a six-year, $20,000,000 program of improvements and expansion for the state's institutions, and the schools had been promised a proportionately large share of the money. For the first biennial period, the General Assembly approved almost $4,000,000 in bonds for the several institutions of higher learning and the 1923 session added a little more than $7,000,000. By the time the 1925 session convened, however, there was a widespread feeling that such outlays could not be continued, and that the third installment would have to be delayed; moreover, there was the general belief that appropriations for the colleges must give way for the moment to larger grants for the public schools.

A number of factors were responsible for this change of attitude. The campaign on behalf of secondary schools, of course, was one factor, but economic conditions in North Carolina had perhaps an even greater influence on public thinking. The state as a whole had been stirred by the reports of deficits and bonded debts and businesses had begun to feel the burden of increased state services through the income, inheritance, franchise, and other taxes on corporate wealth. Speaking on behalf of the business community in February 1925, the *Charlotte Observer* said: "The people of the state are too well-informed to be willing to sacrifice our further industrial and business expansion in order to enable any department of the state government or any state institutions to put on at this time a more ambitious program of work . . . ." [55]

A third factor was the public reaction against the size of the estimates which the several institutions presented to the Budget Commission in the fall of 1924. When information supplied to the press revealed that the requests in aggregate amounted to almost

$40,000,000, there was a wave of angry protests from all directions. Governor Morrison, who had helped initiate the six-year program, declared the institutions were endangering the whole plan by trying to go too fast; and Governor-elect McLean characterized the requests as "reckless" and representing a "mania for spending as much money as possible." [56] The legislators, whose task it was to appropriate the funds, were subject to the same reaction as their neighbors at home.

Upon the suggestion of the Budget Commission, the institutions revised their original requests, but in the revised estimates, the educational institutions asked for an appropriation of more than $5,900,000 for maintenance—an amount almost double that received for the preceding biennium; and for permanent improvements, they asked for almost $8,500,000. [57] Governor Morrison and the Budget Commission slashed these requests and recommended to the General Assembly an appropriation of slightly over $4,500,000 for maintenance and $2,770,000 for permanent improvements. The legislators in 1925 cut the recommendations for maintenance by another $200,000, but accepted the suggestions for permanent improvements. Moreover, to make certain that the institutions lived within their allotments, they were placed under the Executive Budget System and administrative officials were made lawfully liable for any money spent for purposes other than those specified in the appropriations act. [58]

In 1927, the Budget Commission again cut the requests of the educational institutions but recommended a 13 percent increase in the grants for the preceding biennium. [59] After an unsuccessful attempt by some of the house leaders to cut the appropriations and give half the sum to the Equalization Fund, the General Assembly approved an appropriation of $5,542,900 for maintenance during the biennium of 1927-1929 and something over $3,500,000 for permanent improvements. [60]

None of the schools had been satisfied with their apportionments, but the University of North Carolina, insisting that its future as a first-class institution was at stake, fought back with great resolution. The administration and faculty made a statewide appeal to the alumni to speak out in support of the university. Speaking to a meeting of former students in Greensboro on October 11, 1926, University President Harry W. Chase declared that to wait any longer in moving forward with the program begun in 1921 would be to invite disaster. The university, he said, could not hope to keep good professors at the current salaries, and to lose them would reduce its standing to that of a second-rate school. [61] Again in November, President Chase presented the cause of the university to a conference of alumni meeting in Chapel Hill, and the persons present pledged themselves to stand solidly behind every request for appropriations at the next session of the General Assembly. [62]

It goes without saying that Governor McLean resented the university's campaign to place pressure on the legislature, as well as its criticism of him as director of the budget, and he was very frank in saying so. [63] The controversy between the governor and the university continued to the end, and although the university laid down its cudgels long enough to honor McLean with a Doctor of Laws degree at commencement in June 1926, the citation read at the time of the conferment disclosed the school's continued irritation with the governor's program of economy and efficiency. It read: "Under his regime as governor, a far-sighted policy of rigid retrenchment and strict economy has been inaugurated which, while jarring the state vehicle through the sudden arrest of its careering progress, will doubtless eventuate in the permanent stabilization of the intricate and delicate finances of the commonwealth. In recognition of his service to the state and nation, the university will now confer upon him the degree of Doctor of Laws."

While the McLean administration had not initiated another multimillion dollar program for the colleges, the appropriations for maintenance had been increased and a total of $6,325,000 had been provided for permanent improvements. [64] Moreover, a significant contribution had been made toward improving the institutions for training teachers. In 1926, the Educational Commission made a special study of these schools and found that both facilities and the type of training being offered were quite inadequate for the state's needs. A rather large number of institutions offered courses in education: the University of North Carolina and North Carolina College for Women both maintained schools of education; three normal schools offered training for white teachers and four for black teachers; more than twenty-five private institutions included courses in education; and thirteen high schools had departments for training teachers. However, many of these schools were providing only one or two years of college work and, in some cases, the work was still at a secondary level. In fact, the commission reported, only 67.22 percent of the white teachers and 49.07 percent of the black teachers in the public high schools in North Carolina could measure up to the national standard of four-year college work, and only 38.57 percent of the white elementary teachers and 15.1 percent of the black elementary teachers could meet the national standard of two-year college work. Moreover, the commission found that the number being trained, not considering the inadequate programs, fell short of the number needed. In 1926, the schools had been forced to employ 2,331 white teachers and 1,000 black teachers who had not had as much as one year of education beyond high school. [65]

In a two-day conference, November 22-23, the heads of the several colleges and normal schools met with the Educational Commission and together they formulated a series of recommendations to be presented to the General Assembly in 1927. Some of the more important of these were: (1) that the teacher training departments of the high schools be discontinued as fast as more adequate provisions could be made; (2) that the facilities at Appalachian State Normal School and Cullowhee Normal School be expanded to take care of a total of 500 or 600 students at each institution; (3) that North Carolina College for Women and Eastern Carolina Teachers College be enlarged and equipped to the extent of a maximum production for their locations; (4) that the University of North Carolina undertake the training of elementary teachers as well as high school teachers; (5) that within the next four or five years, an additional institution be provided; (6) that the facilities at the black state normal schools be enlarged; (7) that the State Department and institutions of higher learning continue to raise educational requirements for teachers so that North Carolina's educational standards might equal the best in the nation. [66]

In response to these findings and upon the recommendations of Governor McLean and the Budget Commission, the General Assembly, in 1927, voted sufficient funds to provide facilities for 300 additional students at North Carolina College for Women and Eastern Carolina Teachers College, for 140 additional students at Appalachian State Normal School, and facilities to enable Cullowhee Normal School to increase its student body to 400. [67] The University of North Carolina was encouraged to expand its training program for teachers to include elementary teachers. [68]

Increased allotments were also provided for black colleges and normal schools. The legislators voted $85,000 for the three normal schools, the Winston-Salem Teachers College, the State Normal School at Fayetteville, and the North Carolina State Normal School at Elizabeth City, and $240,000 for the Agricultural and Technical College at Greensboro and the North Carolina College for Afro-Americans at Durham. They likewise increased the appropriations for maintenance at the five institutions, voting a total of $514,990, or an increment of $40,000 over the 1925 allotment. With the extra funds for more buildings and operating expenses, the Winston-Salem Teachers College extended its term to a four-year program and the State Normal School at Fayetteville and the North Carolina State Normal at Elizabeth City were able to meet the standards required for two-year training schools before the year was over. [69]

As the new facilities became available, the State Board of Education took steps to shift the emphasis in training for teachers from summer schools and extension work to more adequate and thorough study in the four-year colleges, or at least in the accredited two-year normal schools. As a result, the number of teachers holding an "A" certificate, or a diploma from a four-year college, increased almost seventeen percent between 1924 and 1929. [70] In June 1928, the State Board ruled that it would grant no more sub-standard certificates to elementary teachers and that high school teachers would

be certified by subjects and be authorized to teach only those subjects. [71]

In the overall picture, publicly-supported education made significant progress on all levels during the four years of McLean's administration. The university and larger colleges did not receive all the
funding they requested, but appropriations for them increased year
after year and there was marked expansion of institutions for training teachers, both black and white. Secondary and elementary
schools received financial support that enabled them to make great
strides toward an equitable system for all children in the state. By
1928, fourteen counties had a uniform eight-month term and many
communities within other counties had also added the two extra
months, thus making it possible for forty-five percent more children
to attend schools with at least an eight-month term than had been
able to do so in 1924. [72] Moreover, in leaving a $2,500,000 surplus in
the treasury at the end of his term, Governor McLean hoped to make
it possible for the state government to complete the distribution of
the financial burden in all counties and to enable the poorer ones to
extend their terms to eight months within the next four years.

Expenditures per child enrolled in the public schools increased from
$25.97 to $32.67 during the four-year period. State aid to public education had more than doubled and for the three years, between 1926-1928,
the expenditures for public education in North Carolina exceeded all
previous records, totaling more than $41,000,000 a year. [73]

Rapid progress had been made in the public high school movement. Between 1924 and 1929, the enrollment in high schools had
increased from 67,086 to 96,739 and the number of graduates from
8,246 to 12,145. [74] The movement to consolidate the small schools
had also moved with considerable speed. More than 290 new consol-
idations were effected and the number of children transported to
these larger schools grew from 69,295 to 165,328. [75]

There was still much to be done to bring the educational program
in North Carolina up to national standards, but the record of steady
progress made during the last half of the twenties was one for which
the state did not have to be ashamed. As statistics indicated, North
Carolina was spending approximately 52.18 percent of her income
from taxes on education, an amount surpassed by only four states in
the Union. [76] With the development of industry and the accumulation of greater wealth, the state could look forward to a brighter
future for its schools. McLean's work to establish a sound financial
system, to promote industry, and to improve the conditions in the
farming community also contributed to this end.

Chapter IX

―・・●・・―

REFORMS IN COUNTRY GOVERNMENT

―・・●・・―

By the twenties, county government had become big business in North Carolina, as it had in other states of the United States. Within the fifteen-year period between 1910 and 1925, expenditures in the 100 counties had grown from $5,000,000 to $38,000,000 and the bonded debt from $5,000,000 to $102,000,000. [1] This increase in expenditures meant, of course, that North Carolinians were enjoying more services than ever before; but because of an excessive overhead in the cost of administration, the taxpayers were not receiving a maximum return on their money.

Waste and inefficiency appeared all too often because governments, organized when administrative functions were few and simple and expenditures amounted to a few thousand dollars, could not meet the responsibilities required of them when such functions became more technical and disbursements added up to several hundred thousand dollars per year. During the early years of the twentieth century, cities and states had begun to reorganize, to simplify, and to centralize control in order to achieve efficiency in government; but counties all over the nation remained the bailiwicks of petty politicians, or at best, the field for untrained officials who knew little about the administration of public affairs.

The constitution of North Carolina provided for some eight or ten county officials and boards, each authorized to perform certain functions, but no one official or executive body had authority to direct or coordinate all the work. The Board of Commissioners, which was nominally the head of the county, had little control over policies of the separate agencies except through its power to levy taxes and appropriate money, and even this power could be limited by action of the state legislature. Moreover, the commissioners, who were in most cases farmers or small town businessmen, seldom had the social vision and professional training needed to direct the complex functions demanded of governments in the twentieth century.

The weaknesses of county government were revealed most clearly in the lax administration of tax laws and the uncontrolled disbursements of funds. Since more than ninety percent of all county revenues were derived from property taxes, one of the most important duties of a county administration was the discovery, appraisal, and listing of taxable property. However, officials had been deficient in performing this work. Very little land was assessed at its real value, much land had escaped listing at all, and rarely were there any penalties imposed for failures to give proper information to the tax assessors.

The laxness of collecting taxes was, perhaps, an even greater weakness in the taxing procedures. Because of the lack of regularity and firmness on the part of officials, Dr. Paul N. Wager in his study on county government declared that many taxpayers had lost all respect for the laws, and delinquency had become so common that it had lost its reproach. [2] Each year, hundreds of people in every county defaulted in their payments and actions to foreclose seldom meant anything more than an extension of time.

Finally, wasteful spending and careless handling of public funds added greatly to the costs of county government. Officials frequently spent money on their own initiative and made no statement of the transaction until the debt had been incurred. From the sheriff and the clerk of court to the jailer and superintendent of the county home, all officials bought their own supplies. Even if all were shrewd traders, a loss would have been sustained from buying retail. In few counties were there adequate records kept of "claims allowed" and funds disbursed, of bonds sold, or taxes uncollected. At times, the commissioners themselves were completely in the dark as to the financial conditions of the county for which they were responsible.

For a number of years, leaders in the state had been aware of the loose, disjointed system and the outdated methods used in county administration, and had been seeking reform. As early as 1914, Dr. Eugene G. Branson, founder of the Department of Rural Social Economics at the University of North Carolina, began collecting materials on the antiquated and wasteful practices and working through his seminars and the North Carolina Club to train young leaders to make changes. His work was augmented in 1924, when the Institute for Research in Social Science was founded and adopted county affairs as one of its chief problems. By their joint efforts, intensive studies of some forty-three counties were made within the next three years and an excellent library of source materials was built up at the university. [3]

Dr. Eugene Clyde Brooks had also been for years a strong advocate of reform in county government. In his work as editor of *North Carolina Education*, 1906-1923, and then as superintendent of public instruction, 1919-1923, he saw the crippling effects that careless handling of funds and haphazard methods of conducting public business had on the school system, and he began urging the counties to adopt a standard system of bookkeeping and fixed salaries for all officials. In 1921, while Branson was gathering materials at the university, Brooks launched a speaking campaign and, for one entire year, he toured the state on behalf of good government. [4] Then, believing that the power of example would be a great force in winning support for the movement, he selected Pitt County as a field for experiment and, for two years, worked closely with its officials to demonstrate what could be done if the people had the desire to do it. In this project, he found willing and able cooperation from the board of commissioners headed by Dr. William W. Dawson, and the result of their efforts was a splendid record of efficiency and a well-ordered government. [5]

McLean's first contact with the reform movement came in 1922, when he served on a commission appointed by Governor Morrison to conduct a study and recommend changes in the county government laws. In 1923, the legislature ignored the commission's report, but the study made McLean aware of the need for reform, and in 1925, when he became governor, he made the reorganization of county government one of the chief objectives of his administration.

In his message to the General Assembly on January 21, 1925, McLean spoke of the need to improve the administration of county affairs and asked the legislators to give careful attention to the matter. In response to this request, Senator A. F. Sams of Winston-Salem introduced a bill authorizing the appointment of a commission to consult with county officials and to make recommendations to the General Assembly in 1927. Dr. Brooks supported the measure and worked for its enactment, but the Committee on Counties, Cities, and Towns refused to approve it. [6] Senator W. L. Foushee of Durham also drafted a bill providing for a commission to study and report on county government in 1927, and Dr. Branson urged McLean to back it. However, for some reason Senator Foushee decided to withhold his bill and it did not come up for discussion. [7]

Governor McLean did not push either measure nor did he recommend one of his own. As the 1925 session opened, the problem of state finances and the reorganization of state government consumed so much of his time and energy that he had no opportunity to prepare legislation on county affairs. Moreover, he found that the reform leaders were divided and could not agree on a plan of procedure. Branson wanted to call a constitutional convention and overhaul both state and county governments, while Brooks wanted to work for gradual reform through legislative action. With such division among the leaders and no carefully-planned legislation ready to present to the General Assembly, there was little chance of securing a constructive program in 1925. Perhaps for this reason, Governor McLean decided to wait until 1927 to make his fight for county reform.

He did not wait long to begin preparation for 1927, however. In a message to the State Association of County Commissioners meeting at Blowing Rock in August 1925, McLean explained the need for changes in the management of county affairs and suggested that he would appoint a commission to study the problem if the association approved. He said: "Many counties have already made great progress in improving their methods and it seems to me that a commission, by studying the best practices and observing the best functions of a number of counties, might be able to set up general standards by which the officials of each county may measure the efficiency of their own county government." [8] The association approved his suggestion and asked that he appoint such a commission.

On September 14, McLean appointed the commission, naming twelve men who were well acquainted with county government, among them Dr. E. C. Brooks, who had become president of State College, Professor A. C. McIntosh of the University Law School, and F. P. Spruill, president of the State Association of County Commissioners. At a meeting held in the governor's office a short time later, the commission elected Brooks as chairman and McIntosh as secretary, and organized itself into five subcommittees, each to examine a particular program involved in its proposed work. These special studies were: (1) how each of a certain group of counties was organized and governed; (2) the business methods in these counties; (3) the managerial forms of government; (4) the nature of the reports required to be made to state departments; and (5) the laws relating to county governments. [9]

For approximately ten months, the subcommittees gathered data on their assigned problems, assembling on occasion to report their findings and to review the entire project. Dr. Branson and the Institute for Research in Social Science at the University of North Carolina made all their materials available for the survey and members of the subcommittees used these to supplement their own investigations. By late summer of 1926, the commission had completed its work and had its report ready to present to the State Association of County Commissioners. On August 11, at its meeting in Morehead City, the association endorsed the report with a few minor changes and recommended that it be submitted to the General Assembly in 1927. [10]

Meanwhile, Governor McLean had begun working with the commission and with other advisers preparing bills to present to the legislature in January. To assist with the drafting, he called upon members of the Institute of Research at the University of North Carolina, the state's bond attorney in New York, Chester B. Masslich, government experts from the Bureau of Municipal Research in New York and the Institute of Government Research in Washington. [11] By the time the legislators convened in Raleigh, these workers had three bills drafted and other bills were in the advanced stages of preparation.

In a special message to the General Assembly on February 15, Governor McLean submitted the commission's report with recommendations for appropriate legislation. The commission had found that the most urgent need for reform was in the administration of fiscal affairs and had concluded that the following functions would ensure good business management of a county: (1) maintaining unity in the official family through a system of fiscal control; (2) preserving all taxables through proper assessment and listing of property at an equitable value; (3) collecting the revenue fairly and justly; (4) safeguarding the revenue through proper accounting; (5) safeguarding expenditures through budget control and a central purchasing agent; (6) protecting the physical property of the county; and (7) providing properly for the administration of justice.

To secure the efficient administration of these functions, the commission recommended that the machinery of government be so organized as to give the Board of Commissioners greater authority to supervise all county business; that the board be authorized to employ or select a business manager to coordinate the activities of the entire official family and to appoint administrative officials such as tax supervisor, collector of revenue, auditor, purchasing agent, treasurer, and custodian of county property; that all boards be required to furnish the commissioners a detailed statement of their expenditures at the end of each year. It also recommended that the Bar Association be asked to review the machinery for preserving law and order and to make recommendations for improvements, and that the General Assembly adopt rules to safeguard county government from the interference of individual legislators. Finally, it recommended that the General Assembly create a Department of Finance and Accounting to aid the counties in adjusting to an improved plan of fiscal control, and that it provide for the preparation of a code of county government law and a manual of county government for the use of local officials. [12]

In his special message accompanying the report, Governor McLean asked the General Assembly to enact five measures, including the three bills which had already been drafted and two others which he promised to submit in a few days. The measures for which he requested approval were: an act to provide improved methods of county government, an act to provide for the administration of fiscal affairs, an act to provide for the issuance of bonds and notes and for proper taxation for the payment of these, an act to amend the constitutional limits on county debt, and an act to amend the Consolidated Statutes in respect to the collection of taxes. [13] These measures, he told the legislators, would be the "first definite step toward reducing the constantly increasing burden of local taxes."

The three prepared bills were promptly introduced in both houses and referred to appropriate committees for study. A week later, on February 21, Senator Kenneth C. Royall presented a constitutional amendment limiting the debt of counties and their subdivisions, and on February 24, a group of representatives presented two measures to the lower house, one to regulate the collection of taxes and another to amend the Consolidated Statutes relative to tax deeds and foreclosure certificates. All of these bills were approved before the end of the session and with little or no opposition, except the measure to limit county debt by constitutional amendment. [14] Some statutory limitations were included in the Act to Provide for Issuance of Bonds and Notes, but it was not until the depression of the early 1930s brought a near crisis in local finances that the General Assembly was willing to make this limitation a part of the constitution.

The Act to Provide Improved Methods of County Government had been planned with three objectives: (1) to establish a way by which counties might change the structure of their governments without a special act of legislation, (2) to confer certain duties and powers upon the Board of Commissioners irrespective of the form of government, and (3) to provide for state supervision and assistance in the conduct of county affairs. Two forms of county government, the traditional commissioners form and the newer manager plan, were recognized, and counties were permitted to choose either plan or to modify or combine both plans in order to meet their needs.

Counties retaining the traditional form would elect a Board of Commissioners as before, but the number of commissioners could be increased or decreased and their terms fixed as each county might decide. Under the manager plan, the Board of Commissioners was authorized to appoint a person trained for the work to serve as administrative head of the county and to be responsible for the management of all departments over which the board had control. It would be his specific duty: (1) to execute all orders, resolutions, or regulations issued by the commissioners; (2) to recommend for the board's consideration any measures he or she might deem necessary for the satisfactory administration of county business; (3) to make reports and keep the commissioners well informed as to the financial conditions of the county and its future needs; (4) to appoint such subordinate officials, agents, and employees as the board might consider necessary; and (5) to perform such other duties as the office might require. The manager was to be selected on the basis of merit only and did not have to be a resident of the county at the time of his appointment. In lieu of the employment of a manager, the board might impose the duties and powers of the office upon the chairman of the board or some other officer of the county who was qualified to perform such duties.

Whichever form the counties chose, the Board of Commissioners was to be held responsible for certain administrative functions. It would be the duty of the commissioners to provide as soon as possible "for unifying fiscal management of county affairs, for preserving the sources of revenue, for safeguarding the collection of all revenue, for guarding adequately all expenditures, for securing proper accounting of all funds, and for preserving the physical property of the county." They were also to initiate a plan of centralized purchasing for all departments of the government so that waste could be eliminated and that the county might obtain the advantages of buying in larger quantities. Furthermore, the commissioners were to provide for regular inspection and care of all property of the county.

To provide state supervision and assistance in the administration of county government, the act established a special commission, the County Government Advisory Commission, to be composed of five members and appointed by the governor for a term of not more than four years. At least three of the members must be county commissioners at the time of appointment and all must be qualified by knowledge and experience to advise and assist county officials in the proper administration of public affairs. The duties of the commission as prescribed by the act were: to advise with the county boards as to the best methods of administering local government; to prepare and recommend to the governing authorities simple and efficient methods of accounting; to suggest and help put into operation such changes in the organization of departments as would best promote the public interest; and to make recommendations to the governor and General Assembly concerning any modifications in county laws which it might deem advisable. The commission was also authorized to appoint an executive secretary and such assistants as he might need to carry out this program. Finally, the act authorized the governor to request the attorney general or his staff to codify all laws relating to county government, to arrange and classify them with reference to the different boards and departments, and to make the code manual available to all county officials. [15]

Governor McLean's second proposal, An Act to Provide for the Administration of the Fiscal Affairs of Counties, was designed to accomplish two main objectives: to centralize the administration of financial affairs in one office, and to place every county on a budget. To achieve the first purpose, the act directed the Board of Commissioners in each county to appoint, biennially, a person who was trained and experienced in modern methods of accounting as county accountant or to impose the duties of the office on the county auditor or any other official except the tax collector or treasurer. The accountant would be responsible for supervising and controlling all the expenditures so that they would not exceed the resources available. Specifically, his or her duties would be: to act as accountant for the county and its subdivisions in settling with all officials; to keep a record of all disbursements, receipts, and contracts; to require every officer receiving or disbursing money to keep accurate

records; to file with the Board of Commissioners an annual statement of the financial conditions of the county; to advise with the
officers and departments as to the best methods of keeping accounts,
so as to bring about a simple, accurate, and uniform system throughout the state; and to perform such other duties as the act imposed.

To give the accountant power to control and supervise all com-
mitments and disbursements of money, the act forbade that any
contract requiring the payment of money or requisition for supplies
or materials be made, or warrant or order drawn on the treasury,
without a certificate of the availability of funds from the county
accountant. Moreover, the accountant was directed to withhold his
signature from such a certificate if, after investigation, he found that
there was not a sufficient balance of the specific appropriation to
cover the payment, or if bonds or notes had not been properly
authorized for the purpose. The act also required that every officer
or employee collecting or receiving funds belonging to the county
must make daily deposits of these funds in a bank or banks designated by the Board of Commissioners, and must report deposits daily to
the county accountant by means of a duplicate deposit ticket signed
by the depository.

The second important feature of the act placed all counties on a
budget and provided the machinery for making the periodic appropriations of revenue and the annual tax levies. The act specified that
by the first day of June, every official and head of every department
must submit to the county accountant an estimate of the needs of
his office or department for the ensuing year, as well as a statement
of the amounts to be expended during the current year. Upon the
basis of these computations and reports, the accountant would prepare and present to the Board of Commissioners by the first Monday
in July a budget estimate of amounts to be needed for the next year,
an estimate of the revenue to be available during the same year, and
a statement on the unencumbered surplus revenue of the current
year. Upon receipt of the budget estimates, the board was to file one
copy in the office of the clerk, where it would be open for public
inspection, to furnish a copy to each newspaper in the county, and
to have a summary of the estimates published in at least one newspaper. No later than the fourth Monday in July of each year, the
board must adopt and record on its minutes a resolution, which
would make appropriations for all county purposes upon the basis
of the estimates and statements presented by the county accountant.
The commissioners would be free to make any changes in the budget estimates, except that they must make provisions for the six-
month school term and they must appropriate the full amount of
any deficits and the full amount necessary for the payment of principal and interest on bonds and for sinking funds. Moreover, they
were forbidden to make any appropriations in excess of the estimated revenues to be derived from county taxes. Finally, the board was
to levy, by the Wednesday after the third Monday in August of each

year, taxes sufficient to produce the revenue needed to cover the appropriations and to take care of probable delinquencies in tax collection. [16]

The third measure, An Act to Provide for the Issuance of Bonds and Notes and for Proper Taxation for the Payment of These, or the County Finance Act, was designed to prevent an unwarranted county debt and to otherwise safeguard county credit. By this act, counties would be permitted to borrow money for both temporary and permanent financing, but under limitations restricting the amount of debt and the time for repayment. For current needs, counties were authorized to sell short-term notes for sums of not more than eighty percent of the uncollected taxes and other revenues expected during the year, but the loan was to be repaid in no more than thirty days after the expiration of the same fiscal year. Counties could borrow by means of short-term notes for paying the interest or principal on bonds or notes due, but the loans must be repaid no later than the end of following fiscal year. They would also borrow in anticipation of the sale of bonds but the sums must not exceed the amount authorized for the bonds and must be repaid within three years after the bonds had been approved.

For permanent financing, the act approved the sale of bonds and long-term notes for the following purposes:

(1) Erection and purchase of schoolhouses
(2) Highway construction and reconstruction, including ridges and culverts
(3) Bridge construction
(4) Erection and purchase of courthouse and jails, including a public auditorium within and as a part of the courthouse
(5) Erection and purchase of county homes for the indigent and infirm
(6) Erection and purchase of hospitals
(7) Erection and purchase of public auditoriums
(8) Elimination of grade crossings in cooperation with railroad companies
(9) Acquisition and improvement of lands for public parks and playgrounds
(10) Funding or refunding of valid debt incurred before July 1, 1927
(11) A portion of the cost of bridges to be constructed at county boundaries
(12) A portion of the cost of public buildings to be constructed or acquired jointly by the county and a municipality within the county

The act carried a number of stipulations that provided security for investors and protected the credit of the whole state. It required, in the first place, that counties pledge full faith and credit for all bonds and that they levy and collect annually a tax sufficient to pay both principal and interest on bonds when due. Furthermore, a definite time limit was placed on all issues. The act specified that bonds must mature in annual series, and the first installment of funding bonds must be payable no more than two years after the date of issue and other bonds in no more than three years after date of issue. Moreover, all bonds must mature within the period estimated as the life of the improvement for which they were ordered. Finally, the act forbade any county to issue bonds which would create an aggregate debt in excess of five percent of its property valuation, except that it permitted bonds for the refunding of earlier bonds, and it allowed an additional two percent debt for counties with debts already in excess of four percent of their property valuation and an eight percent limitation for any county assuming the school debt of all its subdivisions.

Another important feature of the law required full publicity concerning every proposed bond issue, including a sworn statement on the financial conditions of the county and what percentage of the assessed valuation of county wealth the new debt would represent. Such a statement was to be filed in the office of the clerk and remain there for public inspection for at least ten days before the final passage of an order to issue bonds. Moreover, at a public hearing, held after the first publication of the order, the county board or other governing body was required to hear any and all citizens who might want to make a protest against the sale, and any bond sale opposed by fifteen percent of the voters would have to be referred to a vote of the people. [17]

The Act to Provide for the Collection of Taxes within the Counties of the State and for Settlement of Same, which was largely a rewriting of former laws, was planned to the end that taxes would be collected and settlement completed within the same fiscal year in which the levy was imposed, thus making it possible for counties to go on the budget system as required in the Fiscal Control Act. It required that on or before the first Monday in October of each year, the county Board of Commissioners prepare duplicate lists of the taxes for each township, as well as the proper receipt books, and that on that date, these be delivered to the sheriff or other tax-collecting official. Moreover, it required that by the same date, the sheriff or tax collector should have made a full and complete settlement and accounting for taxes collected during the preceding year and should have prepared bond as security for the collection and settlement in the ensuing year. No tax lists or receipt books were to be submitted to any tax collecting official who had not made such a settlement. The act also required that the collector make monthly reports to the county Board of Commissioners and that, on the first Monday of the following May, he or she submit a full and itemized statement concerning uncollected taxes. At that time, the commissioners were to order sale of all property for which taxes had not been paid, the sale to be held on the first Monday in June. On the first Monday in July, the sheriff or collector was to make a complete settlement with the county for all taxes due. Commissioners who failed to provide for the collecting of taxes according to the schedule provided would be liable to a fine of $10 a day for each day of delay in carrying out the law, and other officials failing to perform their duties in enforcing the statute would be punishable by fine or imprisonment or both. [18]

The fifth act amended the Consolidated Statutes relating to tax deeds and foreclosure of certificates of sale. Under the existing law, the purchaser of lands sold for delinquent taxes received a certificate of sale and was entitled to a deed and full ownership if the property was not redeemed in one year. [19] Since most people considered it unethical to bid for the land of a fellow citizen in this manner, the county usually became the purchaser. However, by practice, counties rarely foreclosed but continued to carry the back taxes on the books, hoping to collect eventually. Under the 1927 law, no tax deeds were to be granted, but any person or firm purchasing lands at a tax sale would be given a lien on the real estate with a right to foreclosure by civil action after one year. In such action, the purchaser would be entitled to a sum equal to the amount paid for the land, any taxes or money expended on the property after purchase, the sheriff's cost, and twenty percent interest on these for a period of twelve months and thereafter ten percent until the final settlement was made. In the case of purchase by the county, it would be the duty of the county accountant to collect, and if at the end of fourteen months collection had not been made, he was directed to take foreclosure action. The Board of Commissioners could not reduce the rate of interest or interfere in the procedure. [20]

In addition to these five major pieces of legislation, Governor McLean sponsored another bill designed to restore the credit standing of local governments and to prevent defaulting on county and municipal bonds. The Public Securities Recording Act of 1927 declared that "the default in payment for a single day of the interest or principal of bonds or notes issued by any county, township, school district, municipal corporation, or taxing district results, not only is discredit to the obligor, but is often interpreted by bondholders and investors as a reflection upon the credit of the state itself and all of its municipalities and political subdivisions . . . "

To remedy this, the act made it the duty of the recording officer of every board which had issued bonds, or would do so in the future, to file with the state auditor a statement giving the name and amount of such bonds, the purpose of the issue, the rate of interest, the dates of issues, and the time fixed for payment of both principal and interest. It then became the duty of the state auditor to furnish each board authorized to levy taxes at least thirty days before the time for the annual levy a statement of the amount to be provided for the payment of interest due and for the bonds then maturing. He was likewise required to give a notice to the treasurer or disbursing officer of every county, town, or district at least thirty days before the payments would become due. Heavy penalties were provided for any officer failing in his duty under this law. [21]

There was widespread approval of the county government laws, but the *Raleigh News and Observer* expressed the feelings of some who were not fully convinced that the new laws would solve the counties' problems. On June 15, an editorial expressed the opinion that:

> Unfortunately good county government is more than bookkeeping. It is more than an intelligent and efficient system of keeping records. These efficiency experts can doubtless show the county administrations over the state a great deal that will simplify their work and that will give them an opportunity of at least knowing whether or not they are making the county ends meet.
>
> While this is not to be scorned, probably the worst enemy of county government in North Carolina will never be touched by the abstract discussion of administrative methods. It is simply the brand of politics that controls many county elections and will continue to control them until people who pay taxes year in and year out and vote occasionally take the government into their hands.
>
> It's going to take sterner measures than efficiency lectures to make the courthouse rings behave. [22]

On March 12, Governor McLean appointed the County Government Advisory Commission, naming E. C. Brooks (as chairman), J. E. Woodland, D. W. Newsom, E. M. Lyda, and A. C. McIntosh. On March 17, the Commission met in the governor's office to organize and formulate general policies and plans. In mid-April, it appointed Charles M. Johnson as executive secretary and W. E. Easterling as his assistant. [23]

As an area in which its assistance might be most effective, the Commission decided to work with the county accountants in making budgets and setting their records in order. Immediately it sent letters to the county boards, one advising them as to their duty under the County Government Act, that of appointing a county accountant, and another instructing them concerning the budget which must be made out before July 1. [24] On April 20, the Commission met with the commissioners from some eight counties who came to Raleigh to discuss budgeting [25] and, in July, it conducted a four and a half day county government institute at State College. A model county, Number 101, was set up to demonstrate the administration of the 1927 laws, and instruction was offered in budgeting and accounting procedures and in the practical application of these in the several counties. Representatives from about eighty counties attended the sessions. [26]

The Advisory Commission also compiled and published a number of important aids for county officials. It drew up a uniform classification of accounts to use in making budgets and keeping county records, and designed and printed budget and bookkeeping forms. It prepared a county calendar, showing the forty-two duties required of fiscal officials, the date when each must be performed, and the officer or officers charged with the responsibility. On the request of Governor McLean, the attorney general had a Fiscal Code for County Officials compiled and the Commission had it printed. An adequate supply of all these materials was furnished each county without cost, and forms for use in the publication of information pertaining to budgets and statements of the financial condition of the counties were provided later. [27]

As soon as it became practical for them to do so, the executive secretary and his assistants began visiting the several counties to help the commissioners and accountants inaugurate the new fiscal program. To hasten the work, five additional men were employed during November and December 1927, when many of the counties were drawing up their first budgets and learning to keep classified records for the first time in their history. By the end of 1928, these representatives had visited every county in the state at least once and many had been visited several times in response to requests from county officials. [28]

Handicapped by political lethargy and a traditional reluctance to make changes in either state or county government, as well as the resistance of courthouse rings, the Advisory Commission was forced to move slowly and to be satisfied with partial success in the early months of its activities. A few counties, especially those with acts prohibiting the issuance of bonds for any cause without a vote of the people, had trouble in securing approval for bonds to pay their floating debts and make it possible for them to go on a budget system. [29] Some still defaulted in payment of principal and interest on bonds, largely because no records of bond issues had been kept in the past and no official had been responsible for making the proper preparations for meeting payments as they came due. With some assistance from the state auditor, these cases were brought into line, however, and the debts were settled. [30]

There was particularly strong opposition to the new laws in some of the eastern counties where the postwar depression among farmers had been felt most keenly. Their chief objections related to tax deeds and foreclosure of certificates for sale. In June 1928, taxpayers of Duplin, Craven, Pamlico, and Carteret Counties petitioned Judge Henry A. Grady to grant injunctions against the sheriff's sales. They justified their requests on the grounds that the strawberry and other truck crops had failed during the spring and summer and that the cotton and tobacco farmers could not pay until their crops were sold in late fall. Judge Grady complied with their petitions and, in a public letter to Governor McLean, he stated the reasons for his action:

> I have granted injunctions to Craven, Pamlico, Carteret and Duplin . . . . There is no law that I know of that will support such injunctive relief; but when the execution of the tax law means destruction to the people, I feel that I should come to their relief, and I am doing so as far as possible.
>
> This law that requires the sheriffs in the several counties to advertise on the first Monday in May, and sell on the first Monday in June, all lands where taxes have not been paid, and the additional penalty of 20 percent which the statute requires, is simply an outrage on the people of Eastern North Carolina.
>
> I understand that this law was carefully prepared and engineered through the General Assembly by a certain well-known educator, who pays practically no taxes at all, and who evidently has little regard for the welfare of the great masses of the people.

> I am but a novice in the matter of taxation; but I am well educated in the matter of paying taxes. I cannot have any say in what is being done, but I am now calling upon you as Governor of the State to recommend to the next General Assembly the repeal of this iniquitous law . . . . It is unjust, inequitable, contrary to the spirit of a free and honorable people. [31]

Charles M. Johnson, speaking for the Advisory Commission, appealed to Governor McLean to answer Grady's statement before other counties sought relief from paying taxes through such injunctions. On June 11, McLean gave his reply to the press. He denied Grady's charge that the county government laws had been engineered through the General Assembly by any one person, stating that the measures had been framed after intensive consideration by many individuals and that the provisions had been widely discussed prior to final passage. He stressed the fact that the June date for sale of property was one month later than the old law required and that the 20 percent charge for redeeming land sold in a tax sale was not new but had been in North Carolina laws for forty years. The 1927 statute limited it to the first twelve months following the sale. He declared that he could not see the justice in granting an injunction to protect one-third of the people from the necessity of paying taxes when the county had collected the full amount from the other two-thirds. Furthermore, since the Board of Commissioners would be required to levy a rate sufficient to cover all deficits as well as the current expenses, the failure of the counties to collect from the delinquent minority would mean a higher rate for all in the coming year. [32]

A wave of popular reaction followed McLean's public statement. Letters of approval poured into his office, and a number of influential daily newspapers gave him a vote of confidence. His stand and the fact that the State Supreme Court had upheld the County Finance Act in two or more separate cases tended to weaken the opposition and to strengthen the support for the new laws. [33]

The County Advisory Commission made its first report in December 1928. Though there were discouraging parts, the Commission stated that every county in the state had made some effort to improve its government and to follow the laws. Only six counties had complied completely with tax laws, but only one had refused to order a sale for the collection of delinquent taxes. Only thirty-four had given their tax lists to the sheriffs on time, but a large percentage of them had done so within six weeks of the date. Only forty-four had made full and complete settlements with the sheriffs within six weeks of the required date, but some of the delays were for justifiable reasons. Two more counties, Cleveland and Davidson, had employed managers and others were considering such an addition to their governments. Improvements were reflected in the manner in which budgets were prepared and records set up. Some sixty-six counties had adopted a system of classified reports and accounts, and seventy-five had adopted the recommended bookkeeping forms or had adjusted their own to meet the Commission's requirements. [34]

Honest mistakes continued to be made and gross irregularities continued to occur all too often, especially in the improper and incomplete settlements with officers handling county money. Counties still failed to live within their budgets and debts continued to pile up. Many places of authority were still filled with men unqualified to perform the duties expected of them. However, a significant beginning had been made toward reforming local government in North Carolina. Marked improvements had been made in at least sixty-five counties, and the Advisory Commission reported that wherever the new laws had been diligently applied, there had been gratifying results. [35] Perhaps the most encouraging sign of progress was the fact that many officials had begun to realize the need for reform and were taking their problems to the County Advisory Commission. Before the end of 1928, the Commission was in great need of an enlarged staff and more money to supply the services requested of it.

The enactment of the five county government laws, which represented the first significant attempt to reform county government in North Carolina since Reconstruction, was one of the most important achievements of the McLean administration. This action ranks in importance with the establishment of the Executive Budget System and the reorganization of the state departments. All of the statutes were planned to meet specific needs, but perhaps the County Fiscal Control Act and the Act to Provide Improved Methods of County Government were the most constructive contributions toward effecting a better administration of county affairs. In his book on county government, Dr. Wager describes the County Fiscal Control Act as "one of the most far-reaching acts in the interest of sound financial practice in county government" that had been enacted in any state. [36] The County Government Act, even though it was optional, opened the way for progressive units to move ahead as fast as they wished, and as long as North Carolina counties continued to insist on filling all administrative offices by popular election, the establishment of an Advisory Commission of trained men to assist local officials offered the best chance for achieving any appreciable degree of efficiency in county government.

Chapter X

-----•◆•-----

AGRICULTURE AND INDUSTRY:
ADJUSTING TO POSTWAR ECONOMY

-----•◆•-----

Although Governor McLean is best known for his fiscal reforms and the reorganization of the administrative machinery of state and county governments, he made significant contributions in the promotion of improved methods of marketing and diversification in agriculture and industry. As a lifelong farmer, he knew the problems of the farmers and understood their need to adjust to the revolutionary changes which had been taking place in American agriculture for several decades. As an industrialist, he was also aware of the difficulties being encountered by the textile industry and of its need to adjust to postwar markets and to the competition of a new age of synthetics.

The problems of agriculture in North Carolina could be largely solved, he believed, by a program of diversification, more judicious marketing practices, and the application of better business methods. He called on the farmers of the state to abandon the one-crop system and to diversify their plantings. Instead of putting all their acres in tobacco and cotton, he urged them to plant food crops, to take advantage of the fine grazing lands and raise dairy cattle, and to raise poultry and hogs. By producing food for their families and feed for the livestock, they could save their earnings from money crops; whereas, on the one-crop system, those profits were drained off to pay other states more than $250,000,000 each year for the food which North Carolina had to import.

Since changes in both the domestic and foreign markets were major factors in the current depression, farmers must study the markets and adjust to their demands, he insisted. In an address delivered on opening day of the state fair in October 1925, he spoke on the need for substituting higher-grade agricultural products for lower-grade commodities, and for using more efficient methods of preparing goods for market. He reminded the cotton farmers that while they were producing large quantities of low-grade staple, which often did not bring enough to cover the cost of production, the textile mills of North Carolina were importing almost all of their supplies of better cotton. Instead of hanging on to outdated methods of bailing and ginning, and using shiftless tenant labor, the modern cotton grower, he declared, must "seek his profit in better quality, cleaner handling, and more economic methods of intensive production."

And, what was true of cotton was perhaps even more so of tobacco, he added. Even though North Carolina had the soil and climate to produce the highest grades of bright tobacco, most of the farmers were still planting the poorer grades and receiving the lowest prices. That was unnecessary, he told his state fair audience, for with attention to better plantings, more careful curing and grading, the yearly returns could be doubled and more. In like manner, crops of corn fed to hogs and cattle could double the rewards through the sale of meat and dairy products. [1]

Governor McLean was also convinced that if farmers would learn to count the cost of production and use simple methods of accounting, they could run their farms like a business and eliminate blind adherence to practices which were bringing economic ruin to so many. In a radio address to high school agricultural students all over the state in March 1928, he said:

> Many of our farmers are making what I consider a very serious mistake. I refer to the too frequent lack of business methods in the operation of the farm. If the farmers as a whole [would] adopt and follow closely a simple form of cost accounting, many of the troubles they now experience would disappear. When a manufacturer produces an article he knows to the fraction of a cent just what it cost him and he makes his price accordingly. If the market is glutted, he abandons that article and manufactures something else. The farmer should keep records that would show him what every pound of cotton or tobacco, every bushel of corn or wheat, every pound of pork or beef, and every sale of milk and butter cost him. He should record his sale price and check it against this cost, so he will know whether he has made or lost money on each item. By the introduction of simple cost accounting methods, this can be done. I know of no more important and more neglected phase of farming. [2]

In a final analysis, then, it was Governor McLean's contention that the solution of the farmers' problems depended largely on the farmers themselves. He was opposed to pegged prices or government regulation of the markets. He believed that, with thrift and industry on the part of the individual, the laws of the marketplace could still be counted on to regulate the flow of goods and the rewards for honest labor. To the General Assembly in 1927 he said: "No General Assembly, no government agency, no practice of good will for the farmer will greatly aid him until he decides to work out his own salvation. He can do that only when he learns to appreciate his situation, take stock of his advantages, and realize the necessity of improving his methods by thinking and acting in his own interest, as do his competitors in other vocations." [3]

The duty of the government toward the farmer and his problems, he contended, was to maintain the proper facilities for research in agriculture, to furnish easy credit, and to provide schools for training in better methods of farming and farm management. In 1925, he asked the General Assembly to provide additional facilities for research and experimental work in agriculture and he pledged himself to cooperate with the State Department of Agriculture and State College in devising special means of improving the agricultural industry in the state. In response to McLean's request, the legislature approved a plan, presented by Commissioner William A. Graham and President E. C. Brooks, for reorganizing the joint activities of the Department of Agriculture and State College. The plan placed all extension and research work under the direction of State College and left farm marketing and police and regulatory activities required in agricultural work with the Department of Agriculture. A joint committee was to be appointed and given authority to settle all questions of jurisdiction and to make recommendations for improving the cooperative efforts of the two agencies. Revenues from the Department of Agriculture would help finance the research conducted by State College. [4] In 1927, the General Assembly appropriated $60,000 for two test farms, one in the Sandhill area and one in the northeastern counties. [5]

To furnish easier credit for the farmers, the General Assembly of 1925 authorized and directed the State Department of Agriculture to establish land mortgage associations which would be able to grant loans on agricultural lands, forest lands, and dwellings. [6] In 1927, the Assembly forbade credit organizations to charge an interest rate of more than two percent in excess of the rate charged by the Federal Intermediate Banks, and never more than a total of eight percent. [7]

In his plan for helping the farmers of North Carolina, Governor McLean pinned his highest hopes on public schools. For this reason, his work for public education focused on providing equal opportunities for all rural children. He knew the conservative nature of the rural population and the farmers' reluctance to accept information and make changes. The hope for the future, he believed, was to educate the children and, through them, win cooperation from their parents. It was his desire to make high schools in rural sections into community centers through which agricultural extension work and agricultural education could be brought, not only to the children enrolled in the schools, but also to the farmers and their wives. In the first of a series of radio messages to the vocational high schools of the state in February 1927, he said:

The rural school succeeds to the degree in which it becomes a center of country life in its social relations. Every rural school needs to be at the service of the entire community. It needs to be a common forum for the community thought . . . . It has its distinct role in entertainment as well as instruction. It should be made into an all-the—year asset—a school by day, a gathering place in the evening. It should be near to the soil and its problems, its joys and its difficulties. It should be for agriculture the means of its better understanding through becoming a common ground for experience and experiment to meet and confer in a common interest. [8]

Governor McLean's plan for a state radio was designed to reach "the rural districts in a continuous educational campaign of publicity for advancement of agriculture and rural betterment." Because the farmers were generally poor readers, they subscribed to few journals and read very little of the free materials sent them from the agricultural departments in Washington and Raleigh. Furthermore, it was exceedingly difficult to get them to attend meetings and demonstrations which were provided for their benefit. Under such circumstances, Governor McLean believed the only chance of capturing the farmers' interest would be through the public schools and through the medium of radio.

In 1926, cotton prices dropped to twelve cents and below, and the farmers of the South faced a year of starvation and ruin. [9] Governor H. L. Whitfield of Mississippi asked Southern governors to join him in calling a conference to formulate plans for both temporary and long-term relief. He suggested as subjects for consideration the formation of financial pools in the several states to take surplus cotton off the market, regulations of acreage for the 1927 crop, and the establishment of permanent machinery for advising with southern states on problems pertaining to the section. [10] The governors agreed and the conference was called to meet in Memphis on October 13.

There was widespread enthusiasm about this conference and a general confidence that some plan of relief could be found through the cooperative action of all the cotton-growing states. The conference had barely begun, however, when the delegates became aligned in two hostile camps contending over the means to be used in relieving the depressed market. One rather determined faction introduced and secured approval for a resolution asking all state legislatures to reduce cotton acreage by statute. Another group vigorously opposed any plan of government interference or subsidy. The North Carolina delegation split over the question also, with Dr. B. W. Kilgore leading those advocating legislative limitation of acreage and William A. Graham directing those who opposed such action. Graham proposed that the 1926 crop be held on the farms, if possible, as long as the prices remained low and the cotton exports be restricted until such a time as the world demand would be acute enough to ensure a fair price. If the crops were held, he maintained, prices would naturally rise and adjust themselves. This also represented the opinion of Governor McLean. [11]

The delegates did agree on general plans for crop reduction in 1927. They agreed to ask the farmers to sign a contract to reduce plantings by 25 percent, and to ask bankers to make no loans to those who would not cooperate. They approved the formation of financial pools to hold 4,000,000 bales of the 1926 crop off the market, and they recommended long-term financing for more permanent stabilization of cotton prices. Permanent headquarters were established in Memphis and provisions were made to employ an executive secretary to direct the cooperative efforts to regulate production. The conference also appointed committees to organize crop reduction campaigns in the several states. [12]

Meanwhile, McLean had already been working on plans for a financial pool in North Carolina. At the suggestion of Julius W. Cone of the Cone Textile Mills of Greensboro, he had invited a number of bankers and businessmen to meet with him in Greensboro on October 11 to consider plans for a joint fund to stabilize prices at a reasonable level. The group approved his plan and instructed the North Carolina delegates in Memphis to vote for such a program for the entire South. After a trip to Washington to confer with Eugene Meyer, Jr., chairman of the Cotton Commission appointed by President Coolidge, and Carl Williams, chairman of the Federal Farm Loan Board, Governor McLean called a second conference for October 23. At that meeting, definite plans were made for a super-bank, the North Carolina Finance Corporation, with a capital stock of $1,000,000. Within days, the full $1,000,000 was subscribed and, early in November, the bank was opened for business. [13]

The project proved to be a disappointment, however, for the bank did very little business. Several reasons were suggested as possible explanations for the failure. Governor McLean thought the terms offered were too harsh, but John W. Simpson, president of the corporation, believed the explanation was in the farmers' resentment of what they felt was a plan to coerce them into borrowing money and holding their crops off the market. [14] Perhaps another reason was simply that those who could afford to hold their crops over the winter did not need to borrow money.

The Memphis plan to canvass the state and ask the farmers to sign an agreement to reduce their acreage for 1927 was delayed in North Carolina by factional disputes among the agricultural leaders. Commissioner Graham refused to serve as chairman of the state committee, and by the time the committee was reorganized, Dr. E. C. Brooks of State College had presented an alternate plan, one providing reduction indirectly through a program of diversified farming. [15] On October 28, Brooks wrote McLean, suggesting that he call a special conference to formulate plans for permanent diversification of crops, and for improving the marketing facilities of the state. This, he said, should accompany the organization of the Cotton Finance Corporation and the efforts to hold the 1926 surplus off the market. [16] McLean heartily approved the suggestion and immediately called a meeting for November 8. He urged the attendance of farmers and representatives of all organizations interested in the state's farming.

On the appointed date, representatives from thirty-five counties met in Raleigh. Although a rather strong faction of those in attendance thought North Carolina should cooperate with the other southern states as planned at Memphis, in its final decision, the conference dropped the individual sign-up campaign and adopted Brooks' plan to achieve reduction through a statewide campaign to encourage diversification of crops. It agreed on a goal of 25 percent reduction for the state as a whole and a specific quota for each county. A Central Committee was appointed, with Brooks as chairman, to inaugurate and direct the campaign, and this committee in turn was instructed to appoint a committee in each county to work directly with the cotton growers. The conference also agreed to ask bankers and merchants to sign pledges to give credit only to those farmers who were willing to cooperate. [17]

On November 19, the Central Committee met in the offices at the State Department of Agriculture and completed its plans to begin the campaign as soon as the proper blanks could be printed. A subcommittee, composed of H. M. Cox of the Central Committee and Dr. G. W. Forster of State College, was appointed to prepare the forms. The forms were to contain suggestions for a diversified program for farms of different sizes and operated under varying conditions, as the straight cotton farms, the cotton and tobacco farms, or the cotton and peanut farms. Along with the suggested standard, there were to be spaces for each individual farmer to list his crop acreage for 1926 and his proposed acreage for 1927. There was also to be space to indicate the number of livestock maintained and a suggested minimum for economical operation. Plans for the campaign included a preliminary survey for pledges during the first week in December and an intensive canvass in January and February to cover all the cotton-growing counties. [18]

The campaign was carried out under the direction of Dr. Brooks and with the active cooperation of the county farm agents. Central committees were organized in the several counties, each composed of representatives from the county Board of Commissioners, the county Board of Agriculture, the local Chamber of Commerce, each bank in the county, the supply merchants, the county farm agent, the cotton association field agent, and one or more representative farmers. Beginning in January, meetings were held in each of the counties and great efforts were made to get all the farmers to attend.

At these meetings, extension specialists from State College and the county agents explained the program and how it would work to the benefit of all. Dr. Brooks told the cotton growers in several of the early meetings that Texas was already raising enough cotton to supply almost half the world's needs, and that it would be very unwise for farmers of the East to try to compete with the Southwest, where the cost of production could be greatly reduced by the use of machinery. [19]

A reduction of thirteen percent in cotton acreage was achieved by the campaign, and the cotton farmers were rewarded with a price average of 19.6 cents, as compared with 12.7 cents for the 1926 crop. [20] Of much greater significance than this reduction in acreage, however, was the progress made in diversification of crops and in the application of business methods to farm management. The Better Farming Questionnaire sent out in April 1927 revealed that, for the first time, 1,434 farmers were keeping cost and production records. It also indicated that many farmers were producing four or more money crops and that their holdings in poultry, swine, and dairy cows were growing larger. During 1927, fifty-three counties made car lot shipment of fruits or vegetables. Altogether, more than 18,000 carloads where shipped by train, in addition to large quantities carried by trucks. Duplin County led with 1,126 car loads of strawberries and 1,176 of vegetables. [21] A strawberry festival at Chadbourn and a peanut festival at Ahoskie emphasized the increased importance of those two crops.

Governor McLean's interests in the economic progress of North Carolina included the development of a sound industrial economy as well as a prosperous farm community. In 1925, he called on the General Assembly to protect industry from any unjust or inequitable burden by way of excessive taxes or ill-advised legislation which might hamper its growth, and he backed his request with a policy of caution and economy in state spending. [22] Moreover, during his four years as governor, he made an intensive effort to encourage the development of diversified industries, to advertise the natural resources and other economic assets of North Carolina, and to invite outside capital to finance new and larger enterprises.

The ruling principle of McLean's industrial program was diversification and the wise and profitable utilization of all natural resources. He urged the development of home industries, or the manufacture of products that were needed for home consumption, instead of concentration on three or four export industries as textiles, tobacco, and furniture. Among the more important home industries he named those producing structural products, such as face brick, hollow tile, building stone, structural steel, and sewer pipe. These products were needed badly in North Carolina for the building programs being carried out in every town and county.

Moreover, abundant supplies of all the materials except for steel could be found in the state. For Eastern North Carolina, he urged a program of reforestation and production of timber for industrial purposes, as well as the expansion of fisheries and oyster beds. He stressed the importance of developing the potential water power of the Piedmont and mountain streams to furnish power for a great industrial state. And for the whole state, he urged the promotion of the tourist trade. "Our wonderful climate, our unsurpassed natural scenery, and our splendid highway system should make North Carolina the premier recreational and resort section of Eastern America," he told the General Assembly in 1925. [23]

For the depressed textile industry, McLean advised readjustment of production to meet the needs of the market. Instead of confining their efforts to making yarns and cheap grades of cloth, he advised the mill owners to manufacture finished goods and finer fabrics. At the second annual diversification banquet at the Made-in Carolinas Exposition in Charlotte on September 29, 1925, he said:

> It is a recognized fact that, in the depression which textile mills have been suffering, those suffered most whose products represent-ed the least mutation from the raw to the finished products. Yarns and other unfinished goods of all sorts . . . have felt the depression acutely.
>
> Mills, on the other hand, which have specialized in the higher grades that sell for a higher price have managed to keep their heads above water and to keep away from the red ink side of the ledger . . . . North Carolina has taken the first step and is now ready for the second, which is the establishment of a textile economy to produce in the finished state anything that can be made of cotton. Whether it be to meet the new demands of fine fabrics, of bleached cloths, of mercerized goods, we have not done the most with our cotton crop . . . until we have spun and woven and processed it in the forms the ultimate consumer is most eager to obtain and to pay for. [24]

The establishment of the State Department of Conservation and Development was Governor McLean's most important contribution toward the promotion of diversified industry and toward a wise con-servation and utilization of the state's natural resources. The func-tions of this department, when established in 1925, were to aid: (1) in promoting the conservation and development of the natural resources of the state; (2) in promoting a more profitable use of lands, forests, and water; (3) in promoting the development of com-merce and industry; (4) in coordinating all scientific investigations and the related activities of state agencies in formulating and pro-moting sound policies of conservation and development. It was also to collect and classify facts derived from such investigations as a source of information easily accessible to the public, setting forth the natural, economic, industrial, and commercial advantages of the state. [25]

In 1927, the department was expanded to include the State Fisheries Commission and the State Game Commission and its powers were increased to correspond with the new duties. Other statutes enacted in 1925 and 1927 provided legal protection for fish and wild game and gave the department authority to regulate the exploitation of these resources. [26] A law in 1925 increased the penalties for setting forest fires and provided for a program of education on fire prevention, a program to be carried on through the public schools. [27]

To encourage the development of the state's potential water power, the General Assembly, in 1925, approved a law granting power companies the right of eminent domain for undeveloped water sites. John H. Small, former congressman from the first district, asked Governor McLean to seek measures which would protect the state's rights in its water power resources, but McLean was too strong a defender of free enterprise to follow the example of Wisconsin's Bob LaFollette in a fight against the power companies. [28]

Soon after its organization in 1925, the Department of Conservation and Development conducted a survey of existing industries and of the natural resources of the state; later surveys were conducted of the state's water power facilities. The purpose of these studies was to uncover minerals and other resources which could be utilized profitably in industry, and in this objective they were quite successful. The department geologists and the engineers of the Department of Ceramic Engineering at State College discovered that the gray stone in Orange County, three miles from Hillsboro, was the same kind of stone that was being imported for building purposes for $17 a ton. The Orange County stone could be quarried and sold within the state for $2.70 a ton. Presented with these findings, the officials of Duke University purchased 350 acres containing the deposits to provide materials for buildings on their new campus. This project in Durham pointed the way to further development of the building stone industry in North Carolina. [29]

A number of other new industries grew out of the department's surveys, especially from its work on clay products. In two years time, brickkilns at Pine Hall, Thomasville, Hendersonville, New London, Sanford, Norwood, and Monroe had begun to turn out polychrome texture brick of the highest quality and finish in reds, blacks, browns, and greens. Two plants, representing an investment of $667,000, were built at Sanford to produce shale hollow tile. [30]

In cooperation with the Department of Conservation, Governor McLean worked to promote the fishing industry of Eastern North Carolina. In April 1925, he appointed a delegate to a conference of state officials from the Atlantic and Gulf States, a conference called to initiate a program of cooperation between the states and the fed-

eral government in the conservation and development of all fisheries. [31] He cooperated with the State Fisheries Commission in maintaining a laboratory and in providing inspection of the oyster beds
in the waters of Pamlico and adjacent sounds. In 1924, the market
for oysters had almost closed when a case of typhoid fever was
traced to oysters taken from contaminated waters. Although immediate examination proved North Carolina oysters pure and the
waters free of contamination, it was necessary to maintain regular
inspection and certification of oysters and other shellfish to ensure a
market for the state's products. To make the inspection more effective, McLean and the State Board of Health worked out an agreement with the other states to cooperate in enforcing the sanitary regulations approved by the United States Health Service. [32]

Looking to the promotion of more woodworking industries in
North Carolina and to a more economical use of timber and wood
resources, McLean asked Axel H. Oxholm, director of a National
Commission on Wood Utilization, to conduct a survey of the wood
industries in the state. He appointed a committee, with Reuben
Robertson of the Champion Fibre Company in Canton as chairman,
to work with Director Oxholm and his commission. The Department
of Conservation also cooperated in conducting the survey. [33]

Governor McLean was particularly distressed by the tremendous
losses every year from forest fires. In September 1925, he wrote the
chairman of the board of county commissioners in every county,
urging them to cooperate with the Department of Conservation in
matching funds for protection of the forests. [34] In 1927, he supported
legislation directing the counties to pay the department for sup-
pressing fires within their own boundaries, but the measure was
defeated. When this attempt to secure county support failed, McLean
asked Director Wade Phillips to work out a plan by which all state
agencies in the field could cooperate in fire prevention. [35]
Furthermore, to make the state more aware of the problem, he pro-
claimed the last week in April as American Forest Week, to be
observed with special attention to the prevention of forest fires.

McLean recognized the need for outside capital if North Carolina
was to develop major industry in the near future. There had never
been any great accumulations of surplus money in the state, and the
building of new industries, as well as the expansion of existing ones,
called for large investments. To attract outside investors, he joined
with the Department of Conservation and Development in a campaign to inform the nation of the accomplishments, the resources,
and economic assets of North Carolina. The department published a
number of booklets: *The Path of Progress, North Carolina: The Fifth
State,* and *North Carolina: A Good Place to Live.* These were sent to governors of the several states, to representative businessmen, and to
schools and libraries. The department also published a great deal of

material giving the results of their surveys and their findings from research and experiments. All of these publications were made available to the public and many of them were placed in schools and public libraries.

In addition to these materials from the Department of Conservation, Governor McLean published his annual financial statements and sent these out to banking houses, insurance companies, bond syndicates, and big business houses. He wrote articles for both state and national periodicals and newspapers. He wrote "North Carolina Today" for the North Carolina supplement of the *Christian Science Monitor*; "North Carolina Continues Its Forward March of Progress" for the *Electrical World*. He also wrote articles for the *United States Investor* of Boston, *The Index* of New York, *The Atlantic Constitution*, the *New York Evening Post*, and the *New York Herald Tribune*, as well as articles for most of the state papers.

In the spring of 1926, North Carolinians, Incorporated, was organized as a special agency to advertise the state. [36] This was a private undertaking, but it was endorsed by Governor McLean and other officials. The public also responded to the new organization's appeal for support with considerable enthusiasm, and at a mass meeting held in Raleigh in late November, plans were made for raising $150,000 annually for the next three years to advertise North Carolina on a national scale. [37] "Good Will" tours from Asheville to Canada and Florida advertised the state to both the north and the south. Eastern North Carolina expositions, sponsored by the Eastern Carolina Chamber of Commerce, and road shows organized by Commissioner Frank Page furnished other valuable advertising. For several years, the idea of a state homecoming week had been discussed; in June 1928, Governor McLean issued a proclamation, calling for general cooperation in the observance of such a week in late October. All boards of county commissioners, members of the press, women's clubs, the Chamber of Commerce, and other civic groups were asked to unite in inviting the estimated 160,000 North Carolinians living in other parts of the country to come home and see the progress their native state had made. [38]

Through correspondence and personal contacts, Governor McLean invited specific enterprises to North Carolina and helped other groups that were working to bring industry to the state. In this way, several important new industries were secured for the various sections, such as the American Enka Corporation for the Asheville area and other rayon mills for the Burlington and Charlotte areas. He gave special invitations to Pet Milk Company, Carnation Milk Company, and other companies involved in processing dairy products. He also approached the Goodyear Tire and Rubber Company, the International Paper Company, and similar organizations which used products native to North Carolina. [39]

No doubt, the action that provided the most effective advertising and brought more people to North Carolina than any other single undertaking was the creation of the Smoky Mountain National Park in Western North Carolina and Eastern Tennessee. This was not only the most spectacular conservation project in the state's history, but was the greatest impetus to the tourist trade ever provided by government action. Governor McLean, however, cannot be given much credit for this undertaking. As early as 1899, the Asheville Board of Trade had launched a movement to secure a park for the mountain area, but the efforts of the lumbering interests and the opposition of David Henderson and Joseph Cannon, speakers of the House of Representatives in Washington, blocked any such project. The idea was kept alive by Horace Kephart's *Our Southern Highlanders* and Margaret Morley's *The Carolina Mountains*, both first-hand pictures of the Appalachians. The creation of the National Park Service in the Department of Interior in 1917 and the organization of the National Parks Association in 1919 provided further impetus for the park movement. In February 1924, Secretary of the Interior Hubert Work appointed a committee of five prominent conservationists to survey lands east of the Mississippi River to locate areas that could be used for parks. Encouraged by this awakening of national interest in parks, North Carolina officials and congressmen renewed their fight for a park in the Great Smoky Mountains. [40]

In the summer of 1924, the extra session of the General Assembly authorized the appointment of a special commission to present North Carolina's claims for a national park. Among those appointed to serve on the commission were House Speaker John G. Dawson, Dr. E. C. Brooks, Mark Squires, Plato Ebbs, and Harry Nettles. [41] This group worked closely with Senator Simmons and other North Carolina congressmen to forestall a movement (encouraged by Virginia) to locate the one national park in Eastern United States in the Shenandoah Valley, and to have Western North Carolina and Eastern Tennessee approved as a second site. They also intensified their efforts to arouse interest in the park among North Carolinians themselves. In October 1925, the Great Smoky Mountains, Incorporated, was organized to direct the park campaign; P. Roger Miller of the Asheville Chamber of Commerce and Horace Kephart were put in charge of the publicity. At about the same time, the park commissions of North Carolina and Tennessee employed a New York firm to raise money for securing the lands. [42]

In May 1926, the Temple Bill, which provided for two parks, one in the Shenandoah Valley and one in the Great Smoky Mountains of North Carolina and Tennessee, was approved and signed by President Coolidge. [43] The task of the state commission, then, was to secure the needed funds. Because efforts to raise money by private subscription had produced pledges but not much cash, the commission became convinced that a state appropriation would be necessary. To that end, it began planning its strategy for a fight in the General Assembly in 1927, and, at the same time, friends and foes of the park began to bring pressures on Governor McLean to use his influence for one side or the other.

In February, Senators Squires and Ebbs introduced a bill providing an appropriation of $2,000,000 to be used for the purchase of ark lands. [44] A large delegation of Asheville people came to Raleigh to attend the hearings of the appropriation committees and to lobby for the measure. Attorneys for the Champion Fibre Company and other lumber companies owning land within the area of the proposed park also attended the hearing, and stayed to oppose the bill. Although Governor McLean was very much interested in conserving North Carolina forests, his respect for the rights of private property made him hesitate to back the park movement. Furthermore, his inherent tendency to be cautious and to follow a safe road made him reluctant to undertake so large a project without some guarantee that it could be carried through to a satisfactory conclusion. In February 1927, he wrote Charles A. Webb, who had undertaken a personal campaign to win McLean's support for the pending legislation, that he was in favor of parks, but that he could not ask the legislature to appropriate $2,000,000 unless it was so hedged that the money could not be spent until success of the project was assured. If they did and it failed, it "would forever damn all of those who had a part in it," he said. With no guarantee that the people would subscribe enough additional funds, that Tennessee would do its part, or that the federal government would develop a park on the lands donated, the risks involved were too great to be taken without appropriate measures to insure the state against loss. [45]

However, the park leaders won the battle. On January 27, the Senate voted unanimously to invite Congressman H. W. Temple of Texas and Arno B. Cammerer, assistant director of the National Park Service, to come to Raleigh and present the matter to the legislators. Aware of the pressures being made on the General Assembly, McLean went to Washington on February 12 to confer with Secretary Work and North Carolina congressmen about the issue. [46] Encouraged by his findings, he returned to Raleigh to work with the legislative committees on amendments for the original bill which would provide adequate protection for the state's money. The bill as amended created the North Carolina Park Commission and empowered it to acquire land for the park, and it authorized the issuance of $2,000,000 of bonds for use in purchasing lands. The bonds could not be sold, however, until (1) the Secretary of the Interior had designated areas to be acquired; (2) Tennessee had made adequate financial provisions to purchase her part of the land; (3) and adequate financial provisions, including the $2,000,000 in bonds, had been made for North Carolina to purchase her part of the land. With these amendments, Governor McLean gave his approval to the bill and it was passed on February 22. [47]

On February 28, 1928, John D. Rockefeller, Jr. offered $5,000,000 from the Laura Spelman Rockefeller Memorial to match funds raised by North Carolina and Tennessee for the establishment of a national park in the Great Smokies. [48] This gift made it possible to begin actual work on the park. After what seemed to be months of unnecessary delays, on September 12, 1928, Governor McLean and the Council of State found that all legal conditions had been fulfilled and a motion was passed to authorize the state treasurer to negotiate a loan for $2,000,000 as provided in the law of 1927. [49]

Other actions taken by the McLean administration to encourage farming and industry and to promote the general welfare of the state included a continuation of Governor Morrison's Good Roads Program, cooperative action with the federal government in the completion of the Inland Waterway from Beaufort to Wilmington, and renewed efforts to achieve better freight rates for the shippers of the state. The Good Roads Program had been, without a doubt, one of the most popular movements in North Carolina's history. Although there was a general demand for curtailing government spending in 1925, the demand did not include a retrenchment in road building. When the General Assembly convened in 1925, Representative T. C. Bowie and Senator W. C. Heath introduced a bill calling for $35,000,000 for highway construction, and immediately a flood of telegrams and resolutions from civic organizations, newspaper editors, public officials, and other community leaders requesting support for the program poured into McLean's office. On the other hand, the bond attorneys and bankers of New York and Boston warned that such an appropriation would damage the state's credit. [50]

As a compromise, Governor McLean asked for $20,000,000 in bonds. This sum, supplemented by funds from other state sources and from the federal government, would mean a total of about $31,000,000, he told the legislators. [51] Backed by Frank Page, state highway commissioner, who said $20,000,000 would be all the state could judiciously spend during the next two years, McLean carried the day. [52] The bonds were to mature in installments at two and three years intervals, the last to be due January 1, 1947. [53] A supplementary bill amended the 1921 and 1923 statutes dealing with collection and use of highway revenues. The new amendment changed the tax on gasoline from three cents to four cents, reduced the funds allowed for overhead expenses of the Highway Commission and the collection of revenue, and increased the annual payments to the highway sinking fund from $250,000 to $500,000. [54] A special appropriation of $600,000 was provided for building a bridge across the lower Chowan River. [55]

In 1927, Governor McLean supported a bond issue of $30,000,000 for highway construction, $12,000,000 of it to be used to repay the counties for money they had loaned the state to spend on roads. The act forbade the Highway Commission to accept future loans, but authorized the state to take over at least ten percent of the 6,000 miles of county roads for maintenance and improvement during the next two years. [56] Another act provided $1,250,000 of bonds to build a bridge, or bridges, across the Cape Fear River and North East River at Wilmington. [57]

In November 1927, Frank Page reported to Governor McLean that the highway system had reached a state of being able to perpetuate and increase itself with the funds from gasoline tax and other highway revenues. [58] On the basis of this report, McLean gave a statement to the press in April 1928, reviewing the state's program of highway improvement. By June 1, 1929, North Carolina would have spent an approximate total of $140,000,000 on the highway system, he explained, and $116,850,000 of it had been spent within the preceding eight years. The system, with the additional mileage authorized by the General Assembly in 1927, would have 7,700 miles of dependable highways connecting county seats and principal towns and cities in the state, and about half of the total would be hard surfaced. By January 1, 1929, the bonded debt of North Carolina would be approximately $185,000,000, he stated, and all of it but $11,000,000 had been incurred during the current decade for highway construction, and permanent improvements at the state institutions, and as loans to counties for school buildings. In light of these facts, McLean said he believed the time had come when there should be no further bonds issues for highways and that the necessary extensions and improvements should be provided from the highway revenues derived from the motor license fees and the gasoline taxes. [59] The budget report to the 1929 General Assembly carried no recommendation for additional highway bonds.

For some years, Senator Simmons had been agitating in congressional committees to get the Intercoastal Waterway extended from Beaufort to the Cape Fear River, and then on to St. John's River in Florida. Such an inland canal would provide a protected and weather-free water lane for coastal shipping and enable barge traffic to flow freely to all the North Atlantic ports. Moreover, low water rates would be an important factor in securing better freight rates for North Carolina shippers. Finally, in January 1927, he secured approval of an extension from Beaufort to the Cape Fear River, with the condition that North Carolina provide the right of way. [60] The Rivers and Harbors Bill, which was passed in March 1927, appropriated about $750,000 to finance the project. [61] Governor McLean had promised Simmons that he would do everything he could to see that the state furnished the required land. In February 1927, at McLean's request, the General Assembly approved the necessary measure and appropriated $75,000 for the undertaking. [62]

As another approach to the problem of oppressive freight rates charged by the railroads, Governor McLean asked the General Assembly in 1925 to authorize the appointment of an Advisory Transportation Commission to investigate and report on discriminations against North Carolina and to make recommendations relative to more adequate water transportation for the state. Many of the legislators and leaders opposed the measure because they felt it was an attempt to dodge the issue. They held that the commission appointed by Governor Morrison in 1923 had made all the investigations necessary and that another such group would only repeat work already done. In the end, however, a new commission was approved, and the 1927 General Assembly renewed the appropriation to enable it to study the matter of trunk line transportation into the West. This issue centered on the fact that North Carolina needed a direct railroad connection with the West and the charge that the railroad companies had intentionally prevented such a connection. [63] A final report was made in January 1929.

For some time, there had been the general conviction that North Carolina farmers were bearing more than their share of the tax burden, and, by 1925, the manufacturing interests in the state were also becoming concerned about the higher rates on corporate wealth. In late 1926, the industrialists joined the farmers in an intensive campaign to get the General Assembly of 1927 to take some positive action on the matter. In November, Bernard M. Cone, chairman of the Committee on Taxation for the North Carolina Cotton Manufacturers Association, told the textile men at their fall meeting in Pinehurst that taxes were eating up the profits of the industry. [64] H. Smith Richardson, president of the Vick Chemical Company of Greensboro, stumped the state and waged an extended campaign (through the press) against North Carolina's corporation taxes. Many others appealed directly to Governor McLean, imploring him to do something about the situation. In fact, the agitation to save North Carolina industry by reducing taxes was sufficient to influence McLean's attitude toward increased appropriations for public services. [65]

As the legislators convened in 1927, they were under pressure from the several groups to overhaul the state tax system and to give relief to the farmers and industry. At the same time, demand for an extended school term and increased equalization funds, more money for roads, and appropriations for other public services made general reduction of taxes impossible. As a compromise, the General Assembly approved Governor McLean's request for a commission to study taxation in North Carolina and to report to the legislature in 1929. [66] The legislature did take two other important steps toward reorganizing the taxing procedures. It created a Board of Assessment and gave it the power and authority to supervise assessment and collection of taxes in the state, [67] and as a gesture toward corporate interests, it approved a constitutional amendment to allow a special classification of intangible taxes. The amendment was to be submitted to the people in the general election of 1928. [68] In January 1929, the Tax Commission submitted its findings to the legislature with a number of very general recommendations. It reported that while taxes on farm lands were high, they were not excessive. It reviewed the local and state debts and expressed approval for the large expenditures for roads, schools, and other public improvements as sound investments. However, it recommended that, for the time being, the state's credit should not be extended by further bond issues, except in cases of grave public necessity. [69]

Chapter XI

---•◆•---

REMEMBERING THE PAST

---•◆•---

For many years, North Carolinians seemed to have forgotten their history. Too much of their time and effort had been consumed in the struggle to deal with major political, economic, and social problems. Following World War I, however, the state emerged as a leader in the Southern Progressive Movement and a new pride in the state and the role it was playing in the nation awakened an interest in its past. Guided by this new spirit and under the leadership of a governor who had an appreciation for history, some significant steps were initiated to recognize and commemorate events of the past and to help preserve the state's historical legacy.

Throughout his life, Governor McLean had been intensely interested in history and had spent years doing research and writing the story of the Highland Scots in North Carolina. [1] Now, as governor, he had an opportunity to promote this interest on a much broader scale. One of his first actions as the chief executive demonstrated his commitment to this cause. Instead of demolishing the Governor's Mansion, which was in a bad state of deterioration, he chose to renovate the 1880s structure and to reclaim valuable pieces of furniture long hidden under layers of dust in the attic, as well as damaged portraits of earlier leaders. (This story has been told in an earlier chapter.)

With the mansion restored, McLean turned his attention to the State Capitol and other historic buildings in Raleigh. The Capitol, which was completed in 1840, was one of the finest and best preserved examples of Greek Revival-style architecture in the nation. Except for minor damages made during Sherman's occupation of the building in April 1865, the structure remained sturdy and in basically good condition. The grounds, on the other had, had never been landscaped and were poorly tended. By 1925, only twenty-one of the original 200 beautiful oak trees on the six-acre plot remained, and some of these were in varying degrees of decay due to the lack of care. [2] Ladies in the Raleigh Garden Club had planted beds of petunias and cannas around the Capitol, but as Charles F. Gillette, a landscape architect visiting Raleigh in August 1925 said, the effect this picture gave was that of a "dignified old gentleman with a frill around his pants." [3] The nobility of the structure called for formal

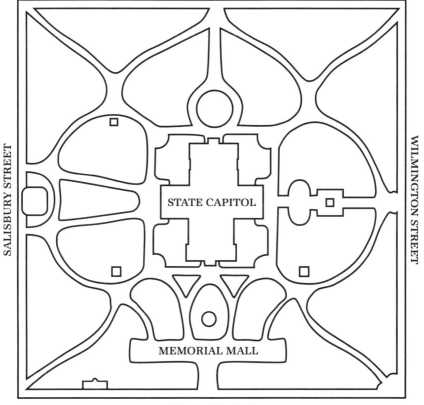

EDENTON STREET

SALISBURY STREET

WILMINGTON STREET

STATE CAPITOL

MEMORIAL MALL

MORGAN STREET

FAYETTEVILLE STREET ENTRANCE

Union Square

(ca. 1928)

landscaping, not a "frill." Aroused by Gillette's remarks, McLean, on September 23, appointed a committee to take charge of beautifying and preserving the Capitol grounds and public buildings downtown. He asked W. C. Coker, professor of Botany at the University of North Carolina, H. M. Curran, forester for the State Department of Agriculture, and C. D. Matthews, horticulturist at State College, to accept this responsibility. [4]

In the meantime, McLean contacted the Olmstead Brothers, landscape architects of Brookline, Massachusetts and asked them to draft a plan for landscaping Capitol Square. [5] The plans they drew up included serpentine walks gracefully running through the grounds, leaving well-defined areas for grass, trees, and shrubs, as well as appropriate sites for placing historic monuments and markers. A memorial mall was drawn on the south lawn. In October 1928, McLean presented the plans to the Board of Public Buildings and Grounds and asked them to undertake the development of one unit at the Fayetteville Street entrance. This unit included the memorial mall, walks on the south lawn, and the setting of the McIver and Aycock monuments. [6] With this directive and $7,000 the General Assembly had appropriated for the project, the board began work. One of the first tasks was to try to save the beautiful old oaks. Men filled cavities, pruned, braced, fertilized, and sprayed. They poured walkways, installed a system of irrigation, and began planting a variety of new trees and shrubs. By November, the memorial mall, a rectangle 216 feet long and thirty feet wide, had been completed, new serpentine fashion walkways had been poured on the south lawn, and part of the permanent planting had been done. By the middle of December, the first unit was ready to be opened to the public. On December 16, McLean presided over a formal opening ceremony. [7] Other governors would complete the project.

McLean wanted to secure a reproduction of the Canova statue of George Washington which the state had acquired in 1821 to stand in the rotunda of the first State House. When that building burned in 1831, the statue was damaged beyond repair and no real effort had been made to replace it when the new Capitol was erected a few years later. Now, McLean wanted to redeem that failure. In February 1925, Representative R. O. Everett of Durham introduced a bill to provide $4,000 to secure a reproduction, but the measure failed to pass. A second bill was introduced in March, this one reducing the sum requested to $2,000. Governor McLean, John Sprunt Hill, and R. O. Everett offered to personally underwrite any expense beyond that amount. This bill passed the House but the Senate refused to approve the appropriation. [8] In spite of this legislative rebuff, McLean did not give up. In December 1928, he asked Secretary of State Frank B. Kellogg to secure names of reputable Italian sculptors who could reproduce the statue. Unfortunately, time ran out for him as governor and the realization of this dream had to be deferred more than six decades.

Appreciating a study of the past as he did, McLean was concerned that generations of children were growing up without any knowledge of North Carolina history. In September 1928, he called a conference of college presidents, professors involved in the teaching of history, and representatives of state departments and agencies. [9] He voiced his concerns and asked them to undertake the writing of appropriate textbooks and to introduce North Carolina History as a course of study in the curriculum for all schools. In response to the governor's appeal, a number of new history books were published. Dr. Alex M. Arnette, professor of history at Women's College in Greensboro, published a simple text, *The Story of North Carolina*, in 1933. Dr. Albert Ray Newsome and Dr. Hugh Talmadge Lefler, professors at the University of North Carolina, brought out a more comprehensive textbook for high school classes later in the thirties and a college text in 1954. With textbooks available, the State Department of Public Education incorporated the study into the curriculum for public schools and a number of colleges made the course available.

The awakening interest in North Carolina history led to the identification and preservation of a number of historic sites. In February 1925, the General Assembly passed a resolution authorizing the cession of Moore's Creek Battleground to the United States Government to be established as a national park. Representative Charles L. Abernethy introduced a bill in Congress recommending that the government accept the property, and on August 4, 1926, the thirty acres were transferred to the federal government as a part of the Sesquicentennial Celebration of the Battle of Moore's Creek Bridge. [10] At the same time, the Roanoke Colony Memorial Association asked Congress to accept as a gift the Fort Raleigh property on Roanoke Island and to erect a monument at the site of the first English settlement in America. The North Carolina Department of Conservation and Development opposed this move and sought to retain the property as a state park, but the association prevailed and the property became a national park. [11]

In March 1925, the General Assembly appropriated $102,000 for the purchase of Fort Caswell Military Reservation. [12] The fort had been lost to the United States Government during the Civil War. Representative Abernethy presented the request for purchase of the fort to Congress and the War Department. The request was granted, and due to the efforts of Representative Abernethy, the state was able to purchase the property for one dollar.

In July 1925, McLean accepted for North Carolina Fort Macon and 400 acres of land surrounding it in Carteret County. [13] The fort, named for Nathaniel Macon, an outstanding leader in the colony, was built during the colonial period to defend Beaufort Inlet against the Spanish and was rebuilt after being heavily battered during the War of 1812. In April 1862, it was captured by federal forces and had remained the property of the United States Government since that time. In 1924, the U. S. Department of War placed it on a list of abandoned fortifications and ordered that it be sold. Representative Abernethy presented a request from North Carolina and through his efforts, the state was again able to secure the property for one dollar. The General Assembly approved the purchase and Governor McLean appointed a committee to draw up a plan of restoration.

As governor, McLean initiated steps to have Bentonville Battlefield established as a national military park. He asked Senator Simmons to introduce legislation authorizing the establishment of such a park and to press Congress for its approval. He assured Simmons that North Carolina would buy the land and donate it to the federal government. Congress failed to approve the idea, however, and Bentonville was left to be developed as a state park. [14] On September 15, 1927, McLean delivered an address accepting a marker for the field presented by the United Daughters of the Confederacy. [15]

In January 1927, the legislature voted to restore the cottage where Andrew Johnson was born. For many years, bitterness in the aftermath of the Civil War had left the citizens of Raleigh indifferent to the preservation of the home. Meanwhile, the house had been bought by Julius Lewis to use as rental property, and black tenants were living in it when George Foster Peabody visited Raleigh and expressed fear that it might be burned. His visit stimulated interest in the building and the city had it moved to Pullen Park. On March 9, 1927, the legislature created a committee to make plans for restoring the structure and to petition Congress for assistance with the expenses. On September 3, 1928, at 10:00 A.M., a formal program commemorating Johnson was held in the House of Representatives and, later in the day, the Andrew Johnson Memorial Association unveiled a bronze tablet marking the site of Johnson's birth. [16]

A number of celebrations were held to commemorate important events in the history of the state. The Sesquicentennial Celebration of the Battle of Moore's Creek Bridge in August 1926 has already been mentioned. Two other celebrations were of special importance: the Sesquicentennial Celebration of the signing of the Mecklenburg Declaration of Independence, and the Celebration of the Birthday of American Aviation at Kill Devil Hill. In May 1925, Charlotte celebrated the most significant event in its history. [17] Local preparations were begun early in the year. The Charlotte Pageant Association asked members of Congress to participate and to take official action recognizing the event as one of national importance. Representative Bulwinkle introduced legislation authorizing the appointment of a national committee to cooperate with Charlotte officials and granting on appropriation of $10,000 to cover its expenses. The bill was passed and President Coolidge named the committee with Senator Overman as chairman. [18]

The Pageant Association organized a five-day celebration in May, featuring "A Pageant of Mecklenburg's Gift to the Nation." Preceding the premier presentation of the pageant on May 18, Governor McLean welcomed the National Committee and special guests, and former Senator Hoke Smith brought greetings from the President. Other events of the day included a luncheon for the governor and his guests and a military parade in the afternoon. A formal dinner in the evening was followed by a second performance of the pageant. [19] Similar schedules filled the other four days.

Certainly one of the most important celebrations of the 1920s was held on Kill Devil Hill at Kitty Hawk on December 17, 1928. In December 1926, Senator Hiram Bingham of Connecticut and Representative Lindsay Warren of North Carolina introduced bills authorizing the erection of a monument on Kill Devil Hill to commemorate the first flight in air by the Wright brothers on December 17, 1903. President Coolidge signed the combined bill into law on March 2, 1927. [20] Meanwhile, there was quite a controversy going on between Orville Wright and the Smithsonian Institute over the recognition of the Wright plane as the first to make a successful flight. At the time, the Institute had already accepted the Langley plane and tagged it as the first. Refusing to accept a second place, Orville sent the Wright plane to the British Museum in London. [21] In spite of this controversy, plans proceeded for the erection of an appropriate monument, and on December 17, some 5,000 persons gathered for the unveiling of a tablet of commemoration and to participate in the laying of a cornerstone for an obelisk on Kill Devil Hill. [22]

Fifty nations sent representatives for the occasion. Orville Wright was there, as was Secretary of War Dwight F. Davis, Senator Bingham, Assistant Secretary of Commerce for Aviation W. P. McCracken, and Assistant Secretary of War for Aviation F. Truber Davison. Other special guests included Count Igot Sikorsky, the celebrated Russian designer of planes, the telegraph operator who had sent out the story of the first flight, congressmen and other public officials, as well as everyone known in aviation except Charles A. Lindberg, who had declined because he wanted the Wrights to have the day for themselves. [23] Among the aviators present were Amelia M. Earhart and Reid Landis, who, next to Edward R. (Eddie) Rickenbacker, was America's foremost ace in World War I. [24]

Governor McLean met the official party at the Virginia state line. The group then moved down Currituck Peninsula to Point Harbor, where they entered boats to carry them across Albemarle Sound to

Kitty Hawk. A welcoming committee met others at Elizabeth City and arranged for boats to take them across the sound to the island. The official guests rode by wagon to Kill Devil Hill; others walked as there were no roads or transportation available on the island. At the opening ceremony, Governor McLean welcomed the guests and thanked the War Department and the members of Congress for their action in providing for a permanent memorial. [25] Senator Bingham, who was president of the National Aeronautical Association, delivered the principal address and unveiled the tablet marking the actual site where the flight took place. Secretary of War Davis laid the cornerstone for a massive obelisk to be erected on the hill. [26]

Langley Field and Hampton Roads naval air station had squadrons of planes groomed for flight over Kitty Hawk in the greatest demonstration of modern aeronautics staged thus far in America, but they had to cancel their plans. It was duck-hunting season and the hunters protested, declaring the planes would scare all the ducks away. They protested with such vigor that the Birthday of American Aviation was celebrated without the appearance of a single plane in the air. [27]

There were other celebrations, all of them significant but none receiving the acclaim of the Kitty Hawk event. On August 18, 1926, a Virginia Dare Celebration commemorated the 339th birthday of the first white child born in North Carolina. Stanley Baldwin, Prime Minister of England, sent a message of support to President Coolidge, and the British Ambassador, Sir Esme Howard, gave the principal address. [28] Congress had projected plans for a monument to be erected in memory of the little girl. There was also a celebration in Halifax County commemorating the 150th birthday of the adoption of the Halifax Resolves on April 12, 1776. The Halifax Resolves were passed by the fourth provincial Congress and authorized delegates to the Continental Congress to vote for independence from England. [29] These resolutions placed North Carolina as the first colony to openly advocate breaking ties with Britain.

In September 1927, more than 300 North Carolina veterans of World War I, along with other American veterans, returned to France to visit military cemeteries and to take part in a memorial exercise at the Tomb of the Unknown Soldier in Paris. Each man was asked to carry a small amount of soil from his hometown to sprinkle on graves of former buddies. Captain Paul Younts of Charlotte, Commander of the American Legion in the Department of North Carolina, and General Albert L. Cox of Raleigh led the state contingent. [30]

Early in 1925, the North Carolina Chapter of the United Daughters of the Confederacy began a campaign to raise funds to provide a memorial to North Carolina soldiers who died in the Battle of Gettysburg. In February 1927, the General Assembly passed legislation creating a Gettysburg Memorial Commission and authorizing it to secure an appropriate monument to be placed on the field. The Commission employed Gutzon Borglum, the well-known sculptor from Connecticut, to make the monument. [31]

In a ceremony held on the Capitol steps in Washington, D. C. on December 16, 1927, a group of North Carolina veterans met a color guard of veterans from Maine and New Jersey to receive state flags which had been captured during the Civil War. [32] At that time, only one other North Carolina flag remained in the possession of another state.

In February 1927, the General Assembly endorsed "The Old North State," written by Judge William Gaston in 1840, as the state song. [33] The Daughters of the American Revolution proposed the action, but a number of persons, including Dr. Hubert Poteat and other prominent musicians, opposed the selection, saying both music and words were commonplace.

North Carolina also participated in a number of national projects to honor past leaders and historic events. In 1926, a committee was appointed to help raise the state's quota of a fund to buy and restore Jefferson's home at Monticello. Walter Murphy served as chairman. [34] A. T. Allen headed another committee to raise funds to establish a Woodrow Wilson Birthplace Memorial. [35] In 1927, the General Assembly authorized the naming of a committee to work with other states and the federal government in arranging for the celebration of the 200th anniversary of George Washington's birthday. [36]

In 1926, North Carolina was asked to participate in the Sesquicentennial Exposition in Philadelphia. Following up on this invitation, McLean directed the several departments of state government to plan and arrange a North Carolina Bay at the Cloister of Colonies at Valley Forge, a memorial to Washington and his troops erected under the auspices of the Episcopal Church. He asked that they allocate $6,870 to the project with the understanding that more money would be available if needed. McLean was invited to take part in the opening of the Exposition on June 14 and to assist in the unveiling of a monument honoring the signers of the Declaration of Independence. [37] The Fayetteville Light Infantry, the Wilmington Light Infantry, and the Hornet's Nest Riflemen of Charlotte accompanied him and marched in the Flag Day parade. On June 17, McLean delivered a dedicatory address opening the North Carolina Bay in the Cloister of Colonies. In October, he returned to Philadelphia to deliver an address on North Carolina Day at the Exposition. [38]

Chapter XII

———•◦•———●———•◦•———

OTHER SUCCESSES AND FAILURES OF
THE MCLEAN ADMINISTRATION

———•◦•———●———•◦•———

The twenties were a transition period in American society, a time when government and social institutions were challenged to deal with old problems grown worse, and with new problems created by social and economic change. The automobile brought better transportation but with it problems involving highway safety; the war had left a wake of increased crime and racial bigotry; expanding industrialization created a need for social legislation to protect the growing labor force; and continuing abuse of the voting process called for reform in election laws. The McLean administration dealt successfully with some of these problems; in other cases, it experienced its worst failures.

The building of good roads brought in the day of motor transportation and with it a multitude of traffic problems. By 1925, there were 340,287 cars registered in North Carolina, representing a threefold increase in two years. [1] With this great increase in the number of private cars, and with the establishment of motor bus and truck lines for public transportation, the problems with traffic accidents multiplied at a distressing rate. In 1925 and again in 1927, the General Assembly gave time and serious effort to formulating laws which would eliminate traffic hazards and protect the lives and property of people traveling on the public roads.

In 1925, the assembly passed laws limiting speed to thirty-five miles per hour on the open highways and increasing the penalties for driving while intoxicated. In 1927, the legislators rewrote much of the state's traffic legislation and added a number of new bills. One of the most important of these measures, An Act Regulating the Operation of Vehicles on Highways . . ., included a code of general rules, speed limits for towns and open road, restrictions as to the type and size of vehicles that could be used on the highways, requirements for traffic signs, and penalties for violations of these. [2] This measure was sponsored by Governor McLean, the State Revenue Department, the Carolina Motor Club, and the Automotive Trade Dealers' Association. Senator J. S. Hargett from Jones County steered the bill through the Senate; in the House, R. O. Everett of Durham and others gave active support.

A second measure, also presented by Senator Hargett, provided for the registration of all motor vehicles and the proper display of license plates. It also provided penalties for stealing or damaging automotive vehicles, and prescribed official action for the recovery of such property. A uniform fee of fifty cents was fixed for certificates of ownership, but registration fees varied according to the size and type of vehicle. Funds from the title fees were to be set aside for an Auto Theft Fund and were to be used to cover the necessary expenses incurred in the recovery of stolen cars. All other fees were to be used for maintenance of the state roads. [3]

Other bills dealt with specific problems of safety on the highways. One required that all vehicles driven on the highways at night must shine lights; [4] another made the failure to stop at a stop sign contributory negligence in any action for injury to a person or property. [5] Representative Everett sponsored a bill making the use of smoke screens illegal and a violation punishable by imprisonment for one to ten years in State Prison. [6] Devices for emitting screens of smoke and gas had been used by rum runners and were a serious traffic hazard.

Representative O. F. Mason of Gaston County secured a measure to increase penalties for driving while under the influence of drugs, opiates, or intoxicating liquors. [7] Senators Hargett and Clayton Moore introduced a bill requiring a license of all drivers, but unfortunately their bill was tabled just before the third reading. [8] Governor McLean had also requested this bill, but for some reason the legislators were unwilling to approve it.

In August 1924, the General Assembly (in extra session) appointed a committee of five state officials to study the conditions concerning the operation of buses, trucks, and other vehicles for hire and to report to the next regular session. It was also to draft and present a bill to regulate the operation and management of such motor vehicles on public roads and streets. Early in January 1925, Representative T. C. Bowie of Ashe County presented the committee's report and its proposed legislation.

The Committee on Public Roads and Turnpikes rejected the committee's bill but reported a substitute measure that was approved and ratified by both houses on February 20. This act required all motor vehicles used as common carriers in the transportation of persons or property to register with the State Corporation Commission and to secure a license to operate. It vested the Corporation Commission with power and authority to supervise and regulate all such carriers; to prescribe speed limits; to regulate the accounts, services, and safety of all motor carriers; to require regular reports; and to supervise and regulate these carriers in all other matters affecting their relationship with the public. The commission could revoke, alter, or amend a certificate of permission at any time for violation of traffic laws. No person was to operate such carriers until he or she had passed an examination and obtained a driver's permit. For the privilege of operation, a tax of six percent of the gross amount received from all fares and charges was required in quarterly payments, and the books and records of all licensees were to be open for inspection at all times. [9] A supplemental act directed that all funds collected through the franchise tax be paid to the state treasurer and credited to the general fund. [10]

In 1927, the bus owners in the state asked for an extension of their franchise rights from three to ten years and for the permission to increase the width of buses from eighty-six to ninety inches. The legislature rejected these requests but passed a new law to replace the act of 1925. Additional clauses in this law granted the Corporation Commission authority to designate towns and cities in which carriers must provide stations and to prescribe rules and regulations governing the maintenance and operation of these. Other new regulations limited the load capacity for passengers and baggage, and forbade carriers to charge rates higher than the tariffs filed with and approved by the Corporation Commission. [11]

A mounting toll of lives and property lost in accidents on public roads, and the increased use of automobiles in criminal activities conducted on a statewide scale, convinced many that North Carolina needed a state police force to assist the counties and towns in the enforcement of law and order on the highways. The Extra Session in August 1924 rejected a bill providing such a system, but to appease those urging action, it appointed a special committee to investigate the feasibility and advisability of establishing a state patrol and to report to the legislature in 1925. The committee conducted a study and drafted a bill providing a police force. On February 9, 1925, Representative J. E. L. Wade, Jr., and Senator C. P. Harris presented the measure, but, as in 1924, the bill was killed in committee. [12]

During 1926, Frank Page of the Highway Commission, Attorney General Brummitt, and others conducted a campaign throughout the state, trying to inform the people of the need of a state patrol system. Commissioner Page advocated a measure requiring all drivers to stand a test for competency and to secure a license, and the establishment of a constabulary of 100 patrolmen to enforce the traffic laws. In his plan, the license fees would cover the expenses of the police force. [13] In a referendum vote, an overwhelming majority of the Carolina Motor Club members endorsed his proposals. Governor McLean also favored a state patrol and a statement proposing such a system is found in his papers. However, in his message to the assembly on January 6, 1927, he asked for legislation requiring all drivers to stand an examination and secure a license, but did not mention a highway patrol.

In January 1927, Senator Lloyd J. Lawrence and Representative A. D. MacLean again introduced bills requiring all drivers to secure licenses and providing a force of police under the control of the State Highway Commission. A license fee of $1.50 would be used to pay for the state police. Both bills were rejected, however, on the grounds that North Carolina was not ready for a state patrol system. [14] Governor McLean's refusal to support the measures certainly strengthened the opposition and contributed to their defeat.

An increase in crime during the postwar years had created pressing problems of law enforcement throughout the United States. In North Carolina, the problem was no less serious; in fact, the state's homicide rate was one of the highest in the nation. At the same time, the record of convictions was exceedingly low and sentences for the convicted were usually light. Court dockets were crowded and, in many counties, cases were left unsettled for months and even years. Everywhere people were demanding a simpler, less technical, and more effective system of procedures that would enable the courts to administer justice with greater speed and efficiency. In his message to the General Assembly in January 1925, Governor McLean discussed the problem of increased crime and of the need for changes in court procedures. He spoke of crowded dockets and long trial delays. To remedy the situation, he asked the legislature to provide for a standing judicial conference, to be composed of the judges of the Supreme Court and the several superior courts, the attorney general, and at least one member of the bar from each judicial district, and to assign that conference the task of repairing the judicial machinery from within. When 75 percent of the cases carried to the appellate courts involved only matters of practice and procedure, he said, the indications were that the judicial machinery had bogged down from defects inherent in itself. A standing conference of judges and lawyers would put the work of reforming the machinery ,in the hands of those most responsible for achieving an effective and equitable administration of justice. [15]

Weeks before the legislators convened in 1925, preparations were under way to fight for additional judicial districts and more judges. In November, Senator J. M. Sharpe of Rockingham County sent out a letter to all state senators asking them to gather information on the condition of court dockets in the several districts and a letter to all the superior court judges asking them to suggest the best methods for remedying the situation. [16] Governor McLean also made a survey of the courts. In late November, he asked A. B. Andrews of Raleigh, who had been working on the problem for years, and Henry M. London, the legislative reference librarian, to collect information on the courts and compile it for the use of legislative committees. [17]

Furthermore, when the General Assembly convened in January, both the House and Senate appointed committees to gather information concerning the need for additional judicial districts in the state. On the basis of the findings from these several investigations, three plans for relieving congestion in the courts were introduced: (1) the appointment of four circuit judges to supplement the work of the superior court judges, a measure presented by Representative I. M. Bailey of Onslow County; (2) provision for seven additional judicial districts with seven judges and solicitors, a bill sponsored by Representative R. O. Everett of Durham; and (3) the appointment of emergency judges as needed, a plan presented by Senator Frank Dunlap.

Representative Bailey's bill passed the House but was abandoned when the Supreme Court gave an informal ruling that it would be unconstitutional. [18] The legislators then turned to Everett's bill, which called for seven additional judicial districts and the same number of judges and solicitors. Although the measure was backed by the North Carolina Bar Association and a strong faction in both houses, it met bitter opposition when it came up for debate. The opposition referred to the deficit in the state treasury and declared the salaries of seven additional solicitors would impose an undue burden on the taxpayers. Their real reason for opposing the bill, however, was the fear that changes in the district lines would permit the election of some Republican solicitors in the western part of the state. Governor McLean took no part in the discussions, but as a straight-line Democrat, he was also reluctant to upset Democratic control of the judicial districts. [19] On February 10, the House rejected the bill on its second reading by a vote of forty-eight to fifty-eight, [20] but on a motion to reconsider the bill was placed back on the calendar. As a compromise, Representative A. H. Graham of Orange County offered an amendment providing for four new districts with four judges and solicitors in place of seven. The House approved the bill as amended, but the Senate voted it down on the third reading. [21]

When the legislators failed to reach an agreement on a permanent reorganization of the judicial districts, they turned to Senator Dunlap's bill. His measure would authorize the governor to appoint lawyers to hold court as emergency judges in any county in the state. The appointments would be for specific terms only and the judges would receive $150 and expenses for each week or part of a week that they were engaged. Many opposed the bill because they did not like an emergency program by lawyers, but the measure had two strong arguments in its favor. It would avoid the political difficulties expected in redistricting the state, and it would eliminate the salaries of four solicitors. Feeling that something must be done to relieve the congested court dockets, the opposition reluctantly surrendered and, on March 2, the Senate gave its approval. On March 9, the House rushed the bill through with little discussion. [22]

Those who opposed the emergency plan pinned their hopes on Governor McLean's measure providing for a judicial conference. With recommendations from the conference of judges, they would be able to make a stronger fight in 1927. On February 14, Representative Graham introduced the administration's bill providing for such a conference, and the House passed it without discussion. On the final day of the session, the Senate gave its approval. [23]

In April 1925, Governor McLean selected a lawyer from each of the twenty judicial districts to sit with the judges, and, on June 25, the Judicial Conference had its first meeting. For the next two years, the members studied and worked on recommendations for improvements in court organization and procedures. By January 1927, they had their report ready and had drafted seven bills to put their recommendations into effect. On January 20, Representative H. G. Connor, Jr. presented the bills. The most important of the measures had been planned with the view of improving the jury system. The Jury Reform Bill would repeal the law requiring the County Board of Commissioners to select the names of persons for jury service and would make every person over twenty-one years of age who had lived in the state two years and in the county one year liable for jury service. Jury lists would be compiled by a commission of five members to be appointed in each county every two years by the resident judge of the judicial district. Among the other bills presented, one would give judges the authority to limit the argument of lawyers before juries, except in cases of capital felonies. Another would authorize the State Supreme Court to establish general rules for the process, court practice, and procedure to be used in all courts. A third would amend the constitution so as to allow separate judicial districts for trial and civil cases and thus to make it possible to have additional superior courts without additional solicitors. A fourth would provide one meeting each year for the Judicial Conference. Other bills contained changes in court procedures. [24]

Of the seven bills, only the measure providing one yearly meeting for the Judicial Conference passed. The jury reform bill, which represented the outstanding work of the Judicial Conference, met the most hostile criticism. Representative I. C. Moser of Randolph County declared the proposal assumed that the juror under the existing system was not only ignorant but without moral character. Representative M. W. Nash of Richmond County saw in the bill a grave danger that women might be selected to sit on juries. On February 14, after two hours of debate, the House tabled the measure. [25] The defeat of this bill practically nullified the work of the Judicial Conference; the defeat of the other five bills made the nullification complete.

Rejection of the conference bills was a major defeat for the administration and other bills were to follow. In his message to the legislature on January 6, Governor McLean recommended a constitutional amendment, providing that the Supreme Court be the only constitutional court and giving the General Assembly full power to provide such inferior courts as the state might need. For temporary relief, he recommended either the appointment of a larger number of regular judges or the renewal of the Emergency Judges Act of 1925. He also recommended that the state pay the traveling expenses of members of the Judicial Conference to all its regular meetings. [26] On January 12, 1927, Representative A. D. MacLean of Beaufort presented two bills to implement McLean's recommendations. One measure would divide the state into four sections and provide for four emergency judges in each to serve two years or until a constitutional amendment could be adopted. The second would amend the constitution so as to give the General Assembly control over all courts save the Supreme Court. In spite of the administration's endorsement, neither bill gained support and both were left to die in committees. [27]

In spite of these failures, the debate over additional districts and judges was renewed two days later. On January 14, Senators Smith, Horton, Woltz, and Hines introduced a bill increasing the number of judicial districts from twenty to twenty-seven and providing seven new judges and solicitors, a measure very much like the one introduced by Everett in 1925. On February 9, the senators approved the bill and sent it to the House. In the House an amendment reduced the number of districts and judges from twenty-seven to twenty-four and deleted a $750 expense allowance for solicitors. The Senate accepted the reduction in districts but remained adamant on the expense allowance for solicitors. The bill died in this stalemate. [28]

As in 1925, the legislators accepted a temporary remedy and postponed any permanent changes in the courts and judicial procedures. There had been considerable dissatisfaction with the Emergency Judges Act and the General Assembly was reluctant to try the same plan again. There had been criticism from those who felt the law enabled the governor to select certain lawyers to hold court and thereby gain prestige over others, as well as those who wanted a permanent reorganization of the judicial districts. The legislature asked Governor McLean for a full account of what the emergency judges had cost for the two years, and assemblymen harangued many hours before they agreed on a bill. Finally, they approved a measure authorizing the governor to appoint six special judges, three for the western circuit and three for the east. These were to be full-time judges to be assigned to both regular and special terms. An amendment to the original bill allowed the governor to limit his appointments to four if he thought that number sufficient. [29]

Reforms in the state election laws, especially the adoption of the Australian or secret ballot, were subjects of continuing debate during the four years of the McLean administration. Such reforms had been endorsed by Josiah W. Bailey in the Democratic primary in June 1924, and the women's clubs and liberal newspaper editors kept the issue before the public year after year. The *Raleigh News and Observer*, the *Greensboro Daily News*, Clarence Poe of *The Progressive Farmer*, and Livingston Johnson of the *Biblical Recorder* gave full support to the movement. In the 1925 session, Senator Johnson of Robeson County and Representative B. T. Falls of Cleveland County sponsored a bill providing for the secret ballot, but it was defeated. [30] In 1927, Senator J. Melville Broughton of Wake County joined Representative Falls in the fight, but their efforts were no more successful than they had been in 1925. [31] The opposition declared the system would make it harder for the average person to vote and that providing the ballots and private voting booths would cost the state nearly $500,000 every two years. The real reasons for their objections, of course, lay in their fear of the black vote in the eastern counties and in their desire to protect the interests of the party machine. Governor McLean refused to support either bill.

The legislators not only rejected the secret ballot but a group of them even tried to repeal the state primary law and restore the old system of nominating all candidates in party conventions. In 1925, Representative W. W. Neal of McDowell County introduced a bill to repeal the state primary law, and Representatives Walter Murphy and T. C. Bowie joined forces to secure its adoption. Governor McLean intervened, however, and threw all his influence against the measure. He recommended that they amend the law to eliminate its faults but declared it must never be repealed. His intervention helped save the primary. [32]

Only one constructive change was made in the election laws during McLean's administration. In 1925, the General Assembly passed an amendment to the constitution which made it possible for all elective officers to be installed on January 1, and in 1927, the legislature adjusted the election laws to coincide with the amendment. These changes made it possible for the governor to assume leadership from the beginning of his first session of the General Assembly instead of having to wait until late in January. [33] Other bills to regulate absentee voting, to authorize election officials to rope off the polling places, and to change the primary from June to August and from Saturday to Tuesday were defeated. A highly political measure taking away the governor's power to fill vacancies in the United States Senate was approved. [34] The politicians were anticipating the death or retirement of Senators Simmons and Overman and they wanted to be able to control the selection of new men. They did not know what to expect of O. Max Gardner, who was slated to be the next governor.

Although North Carolina was a leader in the New South and had experienced a remarkable growth in industry, very little had been done in behalf of industrial workers. In his report for 1923-24, the Commissioner of Printing and Labor, M. L. Shipman, noted this fact and asked that the legislature enact a workman's compensation law, that it provide for public inspection and enforcement of proper standards of safety in mines and in the maintenance of boilers, and that it reduce the working hours for children and for workers in hazardous occupations. Moreover, he recommended that the legislature study the advisability of providing a voluntary system of mediation for the settlement of industrial disputes. [35] In his message to the General Assembly on January 21, 1925, Governor McLean also asked the legislators to enact a workman's compensation law "that will meet the peculiar needs of our state, and, at the same time, be fair and just to all concerned."

In response to these requests, two bills were presented to the General Assembly. One bill sponsored by Senator Mark Squires of Caldwell County and Senator Johnson of Robeson County would have created the Industrial Commission of North Carolina and given it original jurisdiction over all claims for compensation for injuries sustained on the job. A tax of 2-1/2 percent on insurance premiums under the act was to provide the necessary funds. [36] A similar bill was introduced by Representative J. E. L. Wade in 1925 and others were presented in 1927; but all of them were turned down. Governor McLean, for some reason, withheld his support when the measures came up for discussion.

Efforts were made in 1925 and again in 1927 to secure improvements in the state's child labor law. In 1925, Senator Harris of Wake County introduced a bill prohibiting the employment of children under sixteen years of age in factories for more than eight hours a day or six days a week, or to work at night in mines or quarries. In the committee hearing, Senator W. C. Heath of Union County charged that child labor laws were "backed by Soviet Russia in order to communize American youth and ultimately the American government." Only one vote was cast for a favorable report. [37] In 1927, Senator L. C. Grant of New Hanover presented a bill forbidding the employment of children between the ages of fourteen and sixteen for more than eight hours, if they had not completed the fourth grade. The bill was passed; but the last clause nullified its significance, since most children would have finished the fourth grade before they reached the age of fourteen. [38]

In 1925, an attempt was made to consolidate the Child Welfare Commission with the Department of Charities and Public Welfare. Many people believed that the Child Welfare Commission was a tool of the textile industries and wanted to place the supervision of child labor laws under Mrs. Kate Burr Johnson, who had a reputation as an able administrator and as one who believed very strongly in promoting the social well-being of all classes. However, when Representative Graham of Orange County presented a bill providing for the consolidation, industrialists of the state sent letters of protest to Governor McLean's office. [39] In the face of this protest, the legislature refused to act and the Child Welfare Commission remained an independent agency. The same kind of protest prevented a survey of the working conditions of women and children in industry during the summer of 1926.

During the mid-twenties, North Carolina experienced some of the national hysteria resulting from the revival of the Ku Klux Klan and from arguments over science and religion. In 1925, the General Assembly received a measure which forbade the organization or operation of any secret society requiring members to conceal their identities by hoods or masks and made the punishment for violation of the law the same as that for grand larceny. The bill passed the House but was killed in the Senate. In 1927, the whole state was shocked by the report that the Imperial Wizard had attempted to influence members of the legislature to pass a number of bills, one such bill making membership in the Catholic Church a felony, another prohibiting marriage between Catholics and Protestants, and others of equally obnoxious nature. Whether the report was correct or not, it had its effect and a bill outlawing the Ku Klux Klan passed in the Senate without opposition. By the time it reached the House, however, the opposition won a postponement and in the end it was tabled. [40] Pressure from local organizations and a lobby organized and directed by high officials of the Ku Klux Klan caused the House to hesitate and then to surrender.

The teaching of Darwin's theory of evolution precipitated another tense debate, but the conclusion did not reflect so shamefully on the wisdom of North Carolina legislators as did their decision on the Ku Klux Klan bill. On January 8, 1925, Representative D. Scott Poole of Hoke County introduced a resolution which read:

> Resolved by the House of Representatives, the Senate concurring, that it is the sense of the General Assembly of the State of North Carolina that it is injurious to the welfare of the people of North Carolina for any officer or teacher in the state, paid wholly or in part by taxation, to teach or permit to be taught as a fact either Darwinism or other evolutionary hypotheses that links man in blood relationship with any lower form of life. [41]

This resolution grew out of a fear that the Bible and its teachings, as they were understood, was being threatened by science and Modernism. Statements made in *The Journal of Social Forces*, edited by a number of professors at the University of North Carolina, and one specific lecture by Dr. Albert S. Keister of the North Carolina College for Women, precipitated the debate in 1925. The January issue of *The Journal of Social Forces* had carried such statements as: "they created their gods as they created their mythical history"; "an alleged sacred book which is held to embody commands directly delivered by God"; "their ideas have been but the product of the folkways and mores of the primitive Hebrews, in the case of the Old Testament, and of the personal views of religious reformers of all grades from Jesus to Paul" and; "two thousand years of religion, philosophy, and metaphysics have left us no reliable and definite body of rules for conduct." [42] In an extension class for teachers in Charlotte, Dr. Keister was reported to have called the Book of Genesis an Israelitic myth. [43]

Large crowds attended the public hearings on the resolution. At the first hearing on February 10, President Harry W. Chase of the University of North Carolina spoke against the resolution on the grounds that it was a threat to human liberty. Dr. H. R. Pentupp of Concord, Representative Poole, and Miss Julia Alexander, a representative from Mecklenburg County, defended the measure. The vote of Chairman H. G. Conner, Jr. prevented a favorable report, but a minority report kept the bill alive. A second hearing on the evening of February 17 had to be adjourned because such a crowd filled the hall that the aisles could not be cleared. Finally, on February 19, after a debate characterized by facetious bickering as well as serious thought, the House rejected the minority report by a vote of forty-six to sixty-four. [44]

As both a compromise measure and a reassurance to the friends of the Poole resolution, Representatives Everett and Greer introduced "An Act to Renew Religious Liberty in North Carolina," which reaffirmed a belief in complete religious liberty, but provided for the removal of any officer, civil or political, who by word or act brought discredit upon any person's religion or sacred book or books. Representative Connor presented a similar resolution without the penalty for violation. Both of these died in the committee. [45]

The state as a whole had been greatly stirred by the legislative debates on Darwinism. Community gatherings in a number of towns continued the discussion, and men lined up on either side to fight for the principles which they thought were being threatened, the scriptures on the one hand and the freedom of thought and speech on the other. Whatever its appearance to later generations, the debate was a matter of serious thought and concern to many people in 1925. An editorial in the *Raleigh News and Observer*, on February 20, perhaps expressed the feeling of a majority of North Carolinians. The writer declared the legislators who voted the Poole resolution down did not mean to endorse "half-baked professors

whose intolerant expressions are largely responsible for the introduction of the measure to prescribe what is or is not to be taught in
the public schools and colleges of North Carolina." They voted
against it because they wanted to preserve liberty of thought. [46]

An attempt to renew the debate in 1927 failed. In April 1926, a
group of clergymen in Charlotte organized the Committee of One
Hundred to combat all influences that "tend to destroy faith in the
Bible." In May, the Anti-Evolution League of America opened a campaign in preparation for the fight in 1927, and the North Carolina
Bible League employed Representative T. C. Bowie to draft a bill to
present to the legislature. When the assembly convened in January
1927, Representative Poole introduced Bowie's bill. However, when
the Committee on Education returned an unfavorable report, no
effort was made to secure a minority report and the measure died
without a fight. [47]

The McLean administration inherited some unfinished business;
one item dated back to the 1750s, others to the War of 1812, and still
others to the period of the Civil War and Reconstruction. The oldest
problem concerned the boundary line between North and South
Carolina, and at the time, a specific area along the line in New
Brunswick County. In November 1927, two groups of clam diggers
were arrested by South Carolina officers in the Little River section
and charged with trespassing. The people at Southport, who had
fished and dug clams in the area for 100 years (thinking they were in
North Carolina), asked the state to define the border. South Carolina
had questioned the boundary line in New Brunswick County a number of times before, and twice since 1900, the North Carolina
General Assembly had passed bills authorizing the appointment of a
commission to survey the line and secure a permanent settlement,
but no action had been taken. The clam diggers episode revived the
issue and Governor McLean took steps to solve the dispute. He
opened negotiations with Governor Richards of South Carolina and
recommended that the two states appoint a commission to survey
the line again and define the legal boundary. Governor Richards
passed the recommendation on to his General Assembly and they
passed a bill authorizing the survey. In turn, Richards appointed a
surveyor, Colonel J. Monroe Johnson, to serve on the commission;
McLean appointed George F. Syme. [48]

After almost three months of reviewing old records and studying
an old map drawn up in 1775, the surveyors located the remains of
what was purported to be the Boundary House and a 355-year old
longleaf pine tree with markings made in 1729. [49] From these accepted points they were able to retrace the original line. Syme made a
preliminary report to McLean on November 1 and, on December 7,
the last granite marker was erected fixing the boundary line as it
had been drawn in 1735. Each state had agreed to pay its share of

the expenses. When all accounts were settled, the survey had cost each of them a total of $6,161.45 plus the salary and expenses of its surveyor. [50]

Other problems involved old debts and bonds issued before the Civil War. In August 1927, the comptroller general of the United States Government issued a ruling that no state failing to pay its obligations to the federal government would receive its share of federal aid funds. This ruling would deprive North Carolina of $1,713,356 which the state expected to use building roads and for welfare relief. [51] The state's debt to the federal government included railroad bonds with a face value of $41,000 issued in 1856 and others with a face value of $58,000 issued after the Civil War, as well as bonds issued between 1832 and 1855 to pay for wars with American Indians. [52] Governor McLean contested the comptroller's ruling on the grounds that the United States Government owed North Carolina a sum larger than all of her federal debts. During the War of 1812 and again during the Spanish American War in 1898, North Carolina had advanced money for raising and equipping troops but had never been repaid. Moreover, the federal government still owed the state for 24,000 pounds of cotton seized illegally in 1865. [53]

McLean and State Treasurer B. R. Lacy went to Washington in January 1928 for a conference with Comptroller General McCarl and presented a plan for settling all debts. An agreement was worked out and, in June, Lacy received a check for $118,035.69, an adjusted balance of the state's claims against the federal government. [54] North Carolina officials went to Washington to witness the cancellation and destruction of the old bonds. In the meantime, Senator Overman had introduced a resolution in the U. S. Senate relieving North Carolina of all claims for redemption of old bonds.

A few prewar bonds were still in the hands of states and private individuals and these were to create other problems for the McLean administration. Following the Civil War North Carolina was bankrupt with no money to pay off old debts and little for the current needs of the state. When bonds issued before the war began to mature, the state worked out a compromise with most of the bondholders in 1879. By this agreement, the state would redeem bonds in groups at forty, twenty-five, and fifteen cents on the dollar. The bondholders who refused to accept the terms of the compromise demanded payment in full.

In 1901, South Dakota brought suit against North Carolina demanding full redemption of ten railroad bonds ($10,000) and the Supreme Court, by a five to four vote, upheld the suit. [55] A new compromise had to be worked out and North Carolina agreed to pay $892 on each thousand-dollar bond. Again in 1926, South Dakota presented, on behalf of Miss Cora Sheehan, bonds valued at $17,000—bonds she had found in her father's old papers. On May 20,

McLean ordered payment for these bonds according to the 1901 formula and so closed the South Dakota case. [56] As far as state records indicated, there were only six more prewar bonds in existence and these were generally thought to have been lost or destroyed.

Bonds issued to pay expenses during the Civil War and those sold during Reconstruction had never been included in any of these settlements. The Fourteenth Amendment added to the United States Constitution in 1868 forbade southern states to repay any monies spent on the war, but a number of European countries, Great Britain in particular, still held some of these bonds and wanted them redeemed. In 1926, the Association of British Chambers of Commerce launched a drive to collect on these defaulted bonds, and, in 1927, a Scottish law firm appealed to the United States Senate for the redemption of bonds valued at $75,000,000. [57] There was some support for redemption of these bonds, but the federal government held that it was not responsible for debts incurred by individual states. These requests for redemption, therefore, got no further than the State Department.

One other group of bonds was left to cause trouble, bonds issued during Reconstruction and authorized by a legislature composed chiefly of recently freed blacks and carpetbaggers from northern states. In the summer of 1868, the legislators, under the guidance and "buying power" of lobbyist Milton S. Littlefield, a carpetbagger from Maine, had approved the sale of bonds for $6,333,000 to finish the Western North Carolina Railroad. [58] A few months later, in January 1869, George Swepson, president of the western division of the railroad, and his collaborator, Littlefield, both disappeared and with them went $4,000,000 worth of bonds. Governor William W. Holden appointed Augustus S. Merrimon, district attorney of western North Carolina, to find them, but after two years of fruitless search in towns and cities across eastern America and in major cities in England and France, he gave up the task. Nothing more was heard about the stolen bonds until the 1920s. Early in his term, Governor Morrison received a request from a number of Cuban businessmen asking that the state redeem some bonds they were holding—some of the Reconstruction bonds. Since individuals cannot sue a state, Morrison rejected the request.

Early in 1928, Governor McLean was informed that the State of Connecticut had filed a petition with the Supreme Court seeking permission to sue North Carolina for recovery on bonds they were holding. McLean went to Washington to seek advice and to find out what bonds were in question. When he discovered that these bonds were some of the bonds stolen in 1869, he asked Attorney General D. G. Brummitt to prepare a brief to submit to the Supreme Court. In his presentation, Brummitt explained that North Carolina had not agreed to be sued; that the bonds had been procured by fraud and corruption; that the state had declared them invalid and had publicized the fact throughout the United States; that in 1870, and again in 1874, the General Assembly had passed legislation forbidding their redemption; and that in a general election held in 1870, an amendment forbidding the legislature to redeem them had been added to the state constitution. Moreover, Connecticut was no longer the owner of the bonds because they had been given to a hospital. When Connecticut officials learned the facts about the case, they agreed to withdraw their motion before the Supreme Court. [59] In their investigations, state officials learned that some of the bonds had been offered to other states but in no other case had they been accepted.

Chapter XIII

—·•◆•·—

CONCLUSION AND EVALUATION

—·•◆•·—

In spite of Governor McLean's conservative policy toward social legislation and political reforms, his administration left an unusual record of achievement: inauguration of the Executive Budget System and other fiscal reforms in the state government; reorganization of the administrative departments and the establishment of a new unit, the Department of Conservation and Development; initiation of major reforms in county fiscal affairs; provision for increased aid to the public schools and improved facilities for teacher training; continuation of the Good Roads Program; preparation of a code of traffic regulations; and intensification of the movement to diversify both industry and agriculture. McLean's policy of efficiency in government and expanded public services was a continuation of the program begun immediately after the World War by Governor Thomas W. Bickett and continued by Governor Morrison, a program which won for North Carolina a place of leadership among the southern states. Dr. George B. Tindall in an article, "The Metamorphosis of Progressivism: Southern Politics in the Twenties," says:

> North Carolina was at the forefront of the movement, and it was more in the twenties than in the so-called progressive era that the state established its reputation as "the Wisconsin of the South," the leading progressive state of the region. It was during this period that it developed under President Harry Woodburn Chase the leading state university in the South, embarked upon the most ambitious highway program in the South, and developed extensive programs in education, public health, and welfare. In the war and postwar years the state had a succession of governors, Thomas W. Bickett, Cameron Morrison, and Angus W. McLean, who carried forward a consistent tradition of moderate progressivism reaching from Charles B. Aycock at the turn of the century. In the active expansion of public services, North Carolina set the pace for other southern states and ranked high in the nation at large. [1]

Statements from governors of other states support this conclusion. Governor Ralph O. Brewster of Maine wrote in December 1928:

"Maine has followed your development program with tremendous interest as you have blazed the trail for so many of the states." [2] A letter from Governor Huey P. Long of Louisiana stated: "The fine management accorded the State of North Carolina under your administration has attracted the favorable comment of the whole United States, and it, no doubt, is quite encouraging for you to know that several states are undertaking to pattern after some of the policies which are in vogue in your state at this time." [3] Another letter from Governor Henry Horton of Tennessee said: "North Carolina's forward-looking program during the last few years has been a revelation to the South and to the rest of the nation and Tennessee congratulates the Old North State for the way in which its public affairs have been administered." [4]

Perhaps as important as any of the specific accomplishments of the McLean administration were the changes made in the office of chief executive. The governor of North Carolina had remained one of the weakest state executives in the nation, but under McLean, the office gained powers no previous governor had ever enjoyed. In 1925 and again in 1927, the General Assembly yielded authority which the legislature had retained through the years, authority which gave the chief executive far-reaching power over almost all government operations. As the director of the budget, the governor was vested with authority to supervise and control the spending of all appropriations allotted to the several departments and agencies. Furthermore, a specific act of legislation in 1927 gave him the authority to investigate, through the office of the attorney general, the management of or conditions within any department, agency, bureau, division, or institution of the state. [5] Another act empowered him to appoint the boards of all state institutions. [6] Other legislation gave him control over state printing and made him the chairman of the Board of Directors for Central Prison, of the Board of Conservation and Development, and of the State Sinking Fund Commission. These powers, it is true, were relative and not absolute; moreover, the General Assembly still controlled the purse and could withdraw powers it had given. Nevertheless, the governor no longer had to depend on the prestige of his office as his greatest source of authority.

The explanation for this significant growth in executive power lies in two main factors: widespread concern over the great increase in government spending and confidence in the administration's policy of economy and efficiency as an effective remedy, and McLean's ability as a political leader. The large deficit in the state treasury and the bonded debt had caused an uneasiness mounting to a state of alarm in 1924. McLean's promise to spend only what North Carolina could pay and to bring efficiency into the conduct of state business won his election, and his dedication to that end after he assumed office created confidence in him as a leader. Business people, farmers, editors, as well as legislators, liked his approach to the job and were willing to trust him with the powers necessary to carry out his program.

Governor McLean's natural ability as an executive and as a leader also played an important role in shifting the balance of power. McLean had never had any legislative experience, but he displayed a remarkable capacity to impress his way of thinking on the General Assembly and to do so without causing friction. His messages were never examples of great oratory, but they stated the facts simply and clearly. In recommending legislation, he made it a policy to confine his requests to those measures for which he had made thorough preparation and to avoid becoming involved in propositions with which he was not immediately concerned. Furthermore, he had an unusual ability to sense how far he could lead the legislators and when to retreat. He gave up his fight for a constitutional convention, because a fight to the death on that issue would have lost him support for his other measures. He kept in personal contact with all the members of the legislature, before and during the sessions, and he carefully refrained from working through small groups. He did not use an administration leader to sponsor his bills; instead, he sent them all directly to the regular committee chairmen and then worked with the several groups as they prepared their reports. Such straightforward methods were simple but very effective; in fact, few governors have been so successful with their legislatures. In 1925, he lost only two of the measures he requested and in 1927 only three.

As for the state's business, McLean left office with all in good order. Through the application of strict rules of efficiency and cautious spending, he was able to maintain a balanced budget for the two biennial periods and to leave a surplus in the treasury. Moreover, his policies had won respect for North Carolina's credit in all the money markets of the nation. The written testimony of his successor in office, O. Max Gardner, discloses just what his efforts to bring good business methods into the government meant to North Carolina. In March 1946, Gardner wrote to Dickson McLean:

> I have never failed to say in private and in public that except for the wisdom, foresight and judgment of Wilton McLean in creating and establishing the Executive Budget Act, North Carolina would have gone bankrupt during the depression. I tried to exercise the power his wisdom created, and with everything I could do, we frequently verged on collapse. In my judgment, when the historian comes to write the story of North Carolina and to honestly assign responsibility for the preservation of the character and credit of the state, he will be compelled to recognize Governor Wilton McLean as the architect of our salvation. I know probably better than anyone else living that the Executive Budget Act was his work, without

which nothing I could have done would have availed to avert default during my administration; and if we had defaulted, you and I would never have lived long enough to have known the day when North Carolina bonds would have sold at or above par. As it is today, the credit of North Carolina is unequaled and unexcelled . . . [7]

McLean's ability and leadership were also demonstrated in activities outside the state. As a young lawyer, he became an acknowledged leader in the Democratic party, on local, state, and national levels. He served with distinction on the Board of Directors for the War Finance Corporation and as assistant secretary of the treasury during the Wilson administration. His one unfulfilled political ambition was that of becoming a United States senator, but he gave that up out of respect for his friend, Senator Simmons. In 1930, many of his friends and political associates urged him to run against Simmons, but he refused to do so. [8] In 1932, he was considered for a position in the United States Treasury Department, but he declined. His business interests had suffered rather acutely from the depression and he felt that he could not leave them at the moment. [9]

When he left office as governor in January 1929, he returned to his law firm and business interests in Lumberton; after some time, he also opened a new law office in Washington, D. C. His health, however, had become a problem and he no longer had the energetic drive which had characterized his earlier years. At times he found it necessary to take recuperative periods of rest away from the office. On April 19, 1935, while en route from Washington to Atlantic City, he suffered a thrombosis from which he never recovered. He was taken to the Emergency Hospital in Washington and, after several weeks, his condition seemed to improve; but on the morning of June 21, as he sat on the porch with Mrs. McLean, he suddenly sighed, bowed his head over the morning newspaper, and died. [10] Following a brief service at the Central Presbyterian Church in Washington, he was carried back to Lumberton to be buried among the other Scotsmen whom he had known and loved.

NOTES

Chapter I

1. Angus Wilton McLean et al., *Lumber River Scots and their Descendants* (Richmond: William Byrd Press, 1942), 1ff.
2. Ibid., 23.
3. Ibid., 134ff.
4. Robert C. Lawrence, *The State of Robeson* (New York: J. J. Little and Ives Company, 1939), 127.
5. *Raleigh News and Observer*, 15 January 1925.
6. *The Robesonian*, Lumberton, N.C., 10 May 1904.
7. Ibid.
8. Ibid.
9. *The Robesonian*, Lumberton, N.C., 16 October 1913.
10. Ibid., 16 November 1913.
11. Ibid., 3 July; 14 July 1913.
12. Ibid., 14 April 1897.
13. Ibid., 13 March 1911.
14. H. Hoyle Sink, Superior Court Judge, author interview, Greensboro, N.C., 16 November 1961.
15. *Proceedings of the Nineteenth Annual Session of the North Carolina Bar Association, 1917* (Wilmington: Wilmington Printing Company, 1917), 195.
16. Her grandfather left her half ownership of an estate with an estimated value of between $150,000 and $200,000.
17. Margaret McLean Shepherd, author interview, Lumberton, N.C., 24 November 1961.
18. *The Robesonian*, Lumberton, N.C., 19 April 1904.
19. *Raleigh News and Observer*, 15 June 1924.
20. *The Robesonian*, Lumberton, N.C., 26 July 1909; an unidentified newspaper clipping in a scrapbook (1910-1912), in Angus Wilton McLean Papers, Southern Historical Collection, University of North Carolina, Chapel Hill, N.C.
21. *Raleigh News and Observer*, 27 November 1924.
22. *The Robesonian*, Lumberton, N.C., 12 May 1897.
23. *Second Annual Report of North Carolina Corporation Commission for the Year Ending December 31, 1900* (Raleigh: Edwards and Broughton and E. M. Uzzell, Printers, 1901), 386.
24. *The Robesonian*, Lumberton, N.C., 1 January 1904.
25. Ibid., 20 May 1909.
26. Ibid., 12 January 1911.
27. *Annual Report of the Comptroller of the Currency, December 7, 1914*, 2 vols. (Washington: Government Printing Office, 1915), II, 16.
28. *Raleigh News and Observer*, 26 May 1922.
29. *The Robesonian*, Lumberton, N.C., 10 May 1904.
30. Ibid., 23 March 1906.
31. Ibid., 17 February 1910.
32. *Thirty-Fifth Report of the Department of Labor and Printing of the State of North Carolina, 1915-1926* (Raleigh: Mitchell Printing Company, 1926), 36ff.
33. Ibid., 52-53.
34. *The Robesonian*, Lumberton, N.C., 1 March 1909.
35. *The Robesonian*, Lumberton, N.C., 20 February 1906.
36. *Greensboro Daily News*, 3 June 1924.
37. *The Robesonian*, Lumberton, N.C., 31 May 1909.
38. Ibid., 13 January 1910.
39. Ibid., 10 February 1910.
40. Ibid., 16 January 1911.
41. *Raleigh News and Observer*, 11 June 1922. McLean severed his relations with the road in January 1924.

42. *The Robesonian*, Lumberton, N.C., 21 October 1909.
43. Ibid., 10 May 1904.
44. Ibid., 31 January 1910.
45. Ibid., 7 March 1910.
46. Ibid., 30 January 1908.
47. Ibid., 2 November 1911.
48. Ibid., 6 May 1915.
49. *Raleigh News and Observer*, 1 January 1912.
50. Ibid., 21 October 1915.
51. Ibid., 9 May 1910.
52. *Raleigh News and Observer*, 15 January 1925.
53. H. Hoyle Sink, author interview, Greensboro, N.C., 18 November 1961.
54. Margaret McLean Shepherd, author interview, Lumberton, N.C., 24 November 1961.
55. A. W. McLean to Hector McLean, 5 January 1935, in possession of Hector McLean, Lumberton, N.C.
56. Mrs. Furman K. Biggs to Evelyn Underwood, 15 November 1961, in the possession of the author.
57. Mark Sullivan to Martin Gillen, 12 August 1923, in letter book, A. W. McLean Papers, the Southern Historical Collection, University of North Carolina, Chapel Hill, N.C.

Chapter II

1. *The Robesonian*, Lumberton, N.C., 17 December 1913; *Raleigh News and Observer*, 9 June 1924.
2. *The Robesonian*, Lumberton, N.C., 27 May 1904.
3. *Proceedings of the Nineteenth Annual Session of the North Carolina Bar Association*, 1917 (Wilmington: Wilmington Printing Company, 1917), 195.
4. *The Robesonian*, Lumberton, N.C., 10 June 1912.
5. Ibid., 1 July 1912.
6. Ibid., 2 September 1912.
7. Ibid., 12 June 1916.
8. *Raleigh News and Observer*, 17 March 1917.
9. *The Robesonian*, Lumberton, N.C., 8 March 1917.
10. Ibid., 7 May 1917.
11. Ibid., 2 July 1917.
12. Ibid., 22, 29 October 1917.
13. Ibid., 14 January 1918.
14. Ibid., 7 January 1918.
15. Clipping entitled "The Southern Banker" (n.d.) in a scrapbook, A. W. McLean papers, Southern Historical Collection, University of North Carolina, Chapel Hill, N.C.
16. *The Robesonian*, Lumberton, N.C., 2, 13 May 1918.
17. Ibid., 6 May 1918.
18. Woodbury Willoughby, *Capital Issues Committee and War Finance Corporation*, The Johns Hopkins University Studies in Historical and Political Science, series LII, no. 3 (Baltimore: The Johns Hopkins Press, 1934), 67. (Hereinafter referred to as Willoughby, *Capital Issues Committee and War Finance Corporation*.)
19. Ibid., 47-48.
20. Angus Wilton McLean, "Activities of the War Finance Corporation," *Winston-Salem Twin City Sentinel*, 20 August 1919; *Raleigh News and Observer*, 10 June 1919.
21. *The Robesonian*, Lumberton, N.C., 7 April 1919; *Winston-Salem Twin -City Sentinel*, 20 August 1919; *Charlotte Observer*, 22 August 1919 .
22. Willoughby, *Capital Issues Committee and War Finance Corporation*,104.
23. Minutes of the War Finance Corporation, 2 June 1920, vol. VI (National Archives, Washington, D.C.), 23.
24. *The Robesonian*, Lumberton, N.C., 12 June 1919.
25. Minutes of the War Finance Corporation, 21 July; 4 August 1921, vol. IX (National Archives, Washington, D.C.).
26. Minutes of the War Finance Corporation, 15 May 1922, vol. XXXIV (National Archives, Washington, D.C.), 1-2.
27. *The Robesonian*, Lumberton, N.C., 22 May 1902; J. O. Carr Papers, Southern Historical Collection, University of North Carolina, Chapel Hill, N.C.
28. Minutes of the War Finance Corporation, 7 December 1920, vol. VII (National Archives, Washington, D.C.), 135.

29. *The Robesonian*, Lumberton, N.C., 10 June 1920.
30. Woodrow Wilson to A. W. McLean, 21 February 1921, the A. W. McLean Papers, Southern Historical Collection, University of North Carolina, Chapel Hill, N.C.
31. D. L. Houston to A. W. McLean, 3 March 1921, the A. W. McLean Papers, Southern Historical Collection, University of North Carolina, Chapel Hill, N.C.
32. A. W. McLean to J. O. Carr, 10 February 1920, in the J. O. Carr Papers, Southern Historical Collection, University of North Carolina, Chapel Hill, N.C.
33. A. W. McLean to J. O. Carr, 4 March 1920, in the J. O. Carr Papers, Southern Historical Collection, University of North Carolina, Chapel Hill, N.C.

Chapter III

1. *Raleigh News and Observer*, 1 January 1924.
2. Claude Kitchen to A. W. McLean, 7 December 1921, in letter book on microfilm, A. W. McLean Papers, the Southern Historical Collection, University of North Carolina, Chapel Hill, N.C.
3. Charles H. England to A. W. McLean, 12 October 1923; Charles H. England to Frank Hampton, 22 October 1923; and other correspondence on the matter in Furnifold M. Simmons papers, Duke University, Durham, N.C.
4. A. W. McLean to F. M. Simmons, 12 September 1923, Furnifold M. Simmons Papers, Duke University, Durham, N.C.
5. *Raleigh News and Observer*, 17 February 1924; see also *Charlotte Observer*, 16 February 1924.
6. Josiah W. Bailey to F. M. Simmons, 20 March 1924, Josiah W. Bailey Papers, Duke University, Durham, N.C.
7. *Raleigh News and Observer*, 13, 17 January 1924. His platform is in the January 17 issue.
8. Ibid., 18 March 1924.
9. *Charlotte Observer*, 9 March 1924.
10. A. W. McLean to J. O. Carr, 21 March 1924, J. O. Carr Papers, Southern Historical Collection, University of North Carolina, Chapel Hill, N.C.
11. *Raleigh News and Observer*, 6 April 1924.
12. *Greensboro Daily News*, 19 April 1924.
13. The scandal involved drunkenness and immorality. The accounts appeared in the *Raleigh News and Observer*, 30 January 1923.
14. *Raleigh News and Observer*, 18 April 1924; *Greensboro Daily News*, 19 April 1924.
15. *Greensboro Daily News*, 19 April 1924.
16. *Raleigh News and Observer*, 19 April 1924.
17. Ibid.
18. *Greensboro Daily News*, 18 April 1924.
19. *Roxboro Courier*, 12 December 1923, copy in Josiah W. Bailey Papers, Duke University, Durham, N.C.; see also *Raleigh News and Observer*, 29 December 1923.
20. A mailing list for the *Courier* article is in the Josiah W. Bailey Papers, Duke University, Durham. N.C.
21. A. W. McLean to J. O. Carr, 28 March 1924, J. O. Carr Papers, the Southern Historical Collection, University of North Carolina, Chapel Hill, N.C. McLean was sending materials for an article in the *Wilmington Star*.
22. R. A. Doughton to A. L. Brooks, 18 January 1924, in A. L. Brooks, "Correspondence Relating to Work of A. W. McLean," a bound folder of photocopies of the letters Brooks received, University of North Carolina; see also letter book on microfilm, in the A. W. McLean Papers, Southern Historical Collection, University of North Carolina, Chapel Hill, N.C. A. L. Brooks, *A. L. Brooks Replies to Anonymous Attack on Angus Wilton McLean* (n.p.: 1924) supplies other letters. There is a letter from Eugene Meyer, Jr., Director of the War Finance Corporation, dated 6 July 1922 and written in answer to McLean's request that Meyer recall the circumstances under which the Corporation's activities were suspended in 1920. Meyer's letter supports McLean's statement that he opposed suspension of loan in 1920.
23. *Raleigh News and Observer*, 11, 18, 30 March; 17 April 1924. These statements are taken from his speeches as reported in the Raleigh paper. Bailey also published one of these speeches in pamphlet form, under the title, *The Way of Progress in North Carolina* (Raleigh: Mitchell Printing Company, 1924).
24. *Raleigh News and Observer*, 17 April 1924.
25. James O. Carr to A. W. McLean, 23 February 1924, James O. Carr Papers, the Southern Historical Collection, University of North Carolina, Chapel Hill, N.C.

26. *Raleigh News and Observer*, 30 May 1924; see also G. K. Grantham, When Did Mr. Bailey Become the Friend of the Farmer? (n.p., 1924).

27. Bailey's answer to "mule and dog, hogs and ham" circulars, in the Josiah W. Bailey Papers, Duke University, Durham, N.C.; see also *Raleigh News and Observer*, 12, 16, 27, 30 May 1924.

28. Extract from an address at the University of North Carolina, 29 April 1924, J. O. Carr Papers, the Southern Historical Collection, University of North Carolina, Chapel Hill, N.C.

29. *Raleigh News and Observer*, 23 May 1924.

30. Extracts from address at the University of North Carolina, 29 April 1924, J. O. Carr Papers, the Southern Historical Collection, University of North Carolina, Chapel Hill, N.C.; *Raleigh News and Observer*, 14 May; 5 June1924; *Charlotte Observer*, 15 April; 31 May 1924.

31. *Raleigh News and Observer*, 22, 26, 28 March 1924.

32. Clipping from the *Wilmington Dispatch*, September 1919, in scrapbook (1918-1919) in A. W. McLean Papers, the Southern Historical Collection, University of North Carolina, Chapel Hill, N.C.

33. *Raleigh News and Observer*, 24, 25, 30 April; 16 May; 2 June 1924; *Charlotte Observer*, 13 March 1924.

34. *Greensboro Daily News*, 3 June 1924.

35. Josiah W. Bailey to Stacy Brewer, 9 February 1924, Josiah W. Bailey Papers, Duke University, Durham, N.C.

36. Josiah W. Bailey, *The Issues of the Campaign* (n.p., 1924); Josiah W. Bailey, *How the Political Machine Works* (n.p., 1924). These were pamphlets used as campaign literature.

37. Cameron P. West, ed., *A Democrat and Proud of It* (n.p., 1959), 13-14.

38. A. W. McLean to J. O. Carr, 3 February 1923, J. O. Carr Papers, The Southern Historical Collection, University of North Carolina, Chapel Hill, N.C. In this letter, McLean expresses distress over the Watts affair and tells Carr he had written Watts telling him his only hope was to give up his bad habits and lead a Christian life.

39. *Raleigh News and Observer*, 12 May 1924.

40. Ibid., 10 May; 4 June 1924.

41. Ibid., 4 June 1924.

42. Ibid., 5 June 1924.

43. Ibid., 25 May 1924.

44. [O. M. Mull], *Bailey the Crank-Shaft of Machine* (n.p., 1924), a political handbill in the Josiah W. Bailey Papers, Duke University, Durham. N.C.

45. Brock Barkley to Josiah W. Bailey, 15 February 1924, a public letter in the Josiah W. Bailey Papers, Duke University, Durham. N.C.; see also *Charlotte Observer*, 17 January 1924.

46. *Raleigh News and Observer*, 17 February, April 20, 30, 1924; Extracts from the address given at the University of North Carolina, 29 April 1924, James O. Carr Papers, the Southern Historical Collection, University of North Carolina, Chapel Hill, N.C.

47. *Raleigh News and Observer*, 20 May 1924.

48. Josiah W. Bailey to John V. Whitesides, president of the State Council of Carpenters, 15 January 1924; Josiah W. Bailey to Tom P. Jimison, chaplain of North Carolina State Federation of Labor, 15 February 1924; also a pamphlet, *Josiah W. Bailey: A Friend of the Laboring Man*, in the Josiah W. Bailey Papers, Duke University, Durham, N.C.

49. *Raleigh News and Observer*, 14 May 1924; [A. W. McLean], *Attitude of A. W. McLean, Candidate for Governor, in Regard to Labor* (n.p., 1924), pamphlet used as campaign literature.

50. John G. Dawson, author interview, Kinston, N.C., 21 November 1961.

51. *Greensboro Daily News*, 28 May 1924.

52. *Raleigh News and Observer*, 19 June 1924; see also Robert B. House, ed., *North Carolina Manual*, 1925 (Raleigh: Edwards and Broughton Printing Company, 1925), 364.

53. *Greensboro Daily News*, 9 June 1924.

54. *Asheville Citizen*, 9 June 1924.

55. Ibid., 30 May 1924.

56. A. W. McLean to Furnifold. M. Simmons, 15 September 1924, in the Furnifold M. Simmons Papers, Duke University, Durham, N.C.

57. *Raleigh News and Observer*, 12, 19 September 1924.

58. Ibid., 16, 17 September 1924.

59. Ibid., 8, 12 October 1924.

60. Ibid., 8 October 1924.

61. Ibid., 20 March 1924.
62. Ibid., 10 September 1924; 10 October 1924.
63. Ibid., 12 September 1924.
64. Ibid., 24 September 1924.
65. Ibid., 15, 16, 22, 23, 30 October; 4 November 1924.
66. His daughter Margaret told the author that no one in their family ever made long distance telephone calls except in the case of death or serious illness, and that her father never in his life took them on an opossum hunt.
67. *Raleigh News and Observer*, 4, 26 November 1924; see also Robert B. House, ed., *North Carolina Manual*, 1925, 366.

Chapter IV

1. David Leroy Corbitt, ed., *Public Papers and Letters of Angus Wilton McLean, Governor of North Carolina*, 1925-1929 (Raleigh: Edwards and Broughton Company, 1931), 3-15. (Hereinafter cited as Corbitt, ed., *Public Papers and Letters*.)
2. *Raleigh News and Observer*, 15 January 1925. The same reaction was reported in the *Charlotte Observer*, the *Asheville Citizen*, and in other dailies of the same date.
3. Hugh Talmadge Lefler and Albert Ray Newsome, *North Carolina, The History of a Southern State* (Chapel Hill: University of North Carolina Press, 1965), 569.
4. *Raleigh News and Observer*, 2 February 1923.
5. *The North Carolina State Budget for the Biennium*, 1925-1927 (Raleigh: Bynum Printing Company, 1925), 3.
6. *Public Laws of North Carolina*, 1921 Session, Chapter 229.
7. *Public Laws of North Carolina*, 1921 Session, Chapter 34.
8. *Raleigh News and Observer*, 5 February 1925.
9. Charles A. Webb to Cameron Morrison, 28 September 1925, in Governor's Papers, A. W. McLean, 1925-1929, State Department of Archives and History, Raleigh, N.C. (Hereinafter cited as Governors Papers.)
10. Santford Martin to Cameron Morrison, 7 October 1925, in Governor's Papers.
11. *Raleigh News and Observer*, 22 January 1925.
12. Corbitt, ed., *Public Papers and Letters*, 21.
13. A. W. McLean to Frank O. Lowden, 12 December 1924; A. W. McLean to Luther Gulich, Director of Municipal Research in New York, 18 December 1924; Luther Gulich to A. W. McLean, 20 December 1924; George R. Cooksey, Director of War Finance Corporation, to A. W. McLean, 6 February 1925, in Governor's Papers.
14. *Public Laws of North Carolina*, 1925 Session, Chapter 89.
15. *Public Laws of North Carolina*, 1925 Session, Chapter 112.
16. *Public Laws of North Carolina*, 1925 Session, Chapter 275, secs. 6, 7, 8. Neither the Executive Budget Act nor the Appropriations Act applied to the State Highway Department and the Department of Agriculture was exempted by ruling of the director.
17. *Public Laws of North Carolina*, 1925 Session, Chapter 128.
18. *Public Laws of North Carolina*, 1925 Session, Chapter 62.
19. *Raleigh News and Observer*, 21 June 1925; also H. Hoyle Sink, author interview, Greensboro, N.C., 18 November 1961.
20. Corbitt, ed., *Public Papers and Letters*, 769-70; see also *Raleigh News and Observer*, 21 May 1925.
21. Two laws passed in 1921 placed certain limitations on these rights. Chapter 37, sec. 37a, gave the governor the power to cut appropriations exceeding $50,000 per year if it became apparent that state revenues would be insufficient to pay the full amount of all appropriations; and Chapter 232 forbade directors or administrative officials to expend for maintenance any funds granted for permanent improvement and vice versa.
22. *Raleigh News and Observer*, 24 March 1925.
23. Ibid., 18 March 1925.
24. Corbitt, ed., *Public Papers and Letters*, 786; also *Public Laws of North Carolina*, 1925 Session, Chapter 101.
25. Corbitt, ed., *Public Papers and Letters*, 768.
26. *Raleigh News and Observer*, 21 May 1925.
27. Henry Burke, memorandum to governor, 6 November 1925, in Governor's Papers.
28. *Raleigh News and Observer*, 8 May 1925.
29. Ibid., 15 August 1925.
30. *Public Laws of North Carolina*, 1923 Session, Chapter 162, sec. 8.

31. *Memorandum on Overdrafts of the first Quarterly Allotments*, 1926-1927, 13 October 1926, in Governor's Papers.
32. *Memorandum to Governor on State Hospital*, 17 February 1927, in Governor's Papers.
33. Henry Burke to A. W. McLean, 10 March 1927 and other correspondence relative to the same matter, in Governor's Papers.
34. C. F. Harvey to A. W. McLean, 5 March 1927, in Governor's Papers.
35. Nathan O'Berry to A. W. McLean, 2 January 1926, in Governor's Papers.
36. E. C. Branson to A. W. McLean, 24 January 1927, in Governor's Papers.
37. *Raleigh News and Observer*, 8 July 1926; see also Corbitt, ed., *Public Papers and Letters*, 545ff.
38. A. W. McLean to P. W. Williams, Chairman of the Senate Appropriations Committee, and Z. V. Turlington, Chairman of the House Appropriation Committee, 25 January 1927, in Governor's Papers.
39. *Public Laws of North Carolina*, 1927 Session, Chapter 80.
40. Everett B. Sweezy, president of the First National Bank of New York, to A. W. McLean, 18 January 1927, in Governor's Papers.
41. *Raleigh News and Observer*, 13 June 1925; address given to the representatives of investment houses on 5 June 1925, in Governor's Papers.
42. *Greensboro Daily News*, 17 December 1925.
43. Ibid., 3 December 1926.
44. Ibid., 26 April 1927.
45. *Raleigh News and Observer*, 11 April 1928; see also *Greensboro Daily News*, 21 December 1928. Tom Bost, Raleigh correspondent for that paper, gave McLean full credit for the favorable terms, as did Chester B. Masslick, the state's bond attorney in New York.
46. Corbitt, ed., *Public Papers and Letters*, 614ff.
47. Ibid., 808.
48. Ibid., 615.
49. Ibid., 792, see also *Raleigh News and Observer*, 19 January 1928.
50. *State of North Carolina, The Budget for the Biennium 1929-1931* (New Bern: Owen G. Dunn Printer, 1928), 50.

Chapter V

1. Frank Nash, assistant attorney general, *Memorandum on Repairs to Governor's Mansion*, 20 May 1926, in Governor's Papers, A. W. McLean, 1925-1929, State Department of Archives and History, Raleigh, N.C. (Hereinafter cited as Governor's Papers.)
2. Angus Wilton McLean to Mr. H. Pier Giovanni [17 March 1925], in Governor's Papers.
3. *Raleigh News and Observer*, 22 November 1925.
4. Ibid.
5. H. E. Miller to W. S. Rankin, 13 February 1925. A memorandum in Governor's Papers.
6. Frank Nash, a memorandum, 20 May 1926, in Governor's Papers.
7. H. E. Miller to W. S. Rankin, 13 February 1925; N. E. Carmady to Stacy W. Wade, 16 March 1925, in Governor's Papers.
8. *Public Laws of North Carolina*, 1925 Session, Chapter 192; *Raleigh News and Observer*, 26 April 1925.
9. Frank Nash, *Memorandum on Repairs to Governor's Mansion*, 20 May 1926, and other memoranda in Governor's Papers; *Raleigh News and Observer*, 26 April 1925.
10. Margaret McLean Shepherd to Evelyn Underwood, 4 June 1985; also a tape from Margaret Shepherd, in possession of the author.
11. *Raleigh News and Observer*, 11 August 1925.
12. A. W. McLean to Hollaway Cabinet Shop, 8 September 1925; A. W. McLean to Henry Burke, 1 October 1925, in Governor's Papers.
13. Council of State, Minutes, 9 January; 26 August 1925, in Governor's Papers.
14. A. W. McLean to W. D. Terry, 10 June 1925, in Governor's Papers.
15. Margaret McLean Shepherd, author interview, Lumberton, N.C., 24 November 1961; also tape in possession of the author.
16. *Raleigh News and Observer*, 7 March 1928.
17. Margaret McLean Shepherd, author interview, Lumberton, N.C., 24 November 1961.
18. *Raleigh News and Observer*, 7 March 1928.
19. Hector McLean, author interview, Lumberton, N.C., 16 October 1970.
20. H. Hoyle Sink, author interview, Greensboro, N.C., 18 November 1966.
21. Hector McLean, author interview, Lumberton, N.C., 16 October 1970.
22. [B. R. Lang] to George W. Meredith, 14 December 1927, in Governor's Papers.

23. Hector McLean, author interview, Lumberton, N.C., 16 October 1970.
24. Margaret McLean Shepherd to Evelyn Underwood, 22 May 1985, a letter in possession of the author.

Chapter VI

1.   Baxter A. Durham, *Plan of Reorganization of State Departments, Boards, and Commissions* (Raleigh: Mitchell Printing Company, 1923).
2.   David Leroy Corbitt, ed., *Public Papers and Letters of Angus Wilton McLean, Governor of North Carolina*, 1925-1929 (Raleigh: Edwards and Broughton Company, 1931), 21ff. (Hereinafter cited as Corbitt, ed., *Public Papers and Letters*.)
3.   *Raleigh News and Observer*, 4, 5 March 1925.
4.   Furnifold M. Simmons to A. W. McLean, 26 February 1925, in Governor's Papers, A. W. McLean, 1925-1929, State Department of Archives and History (Hereinafter cited as Governor's Papers.)
5.   North Carolina, Senate Journal (1925), 479.
6.   Ibid., 360.
7.   *Public Laws of North Carolina*, 1925 Session, Chapter 125.
8.   *First Report of the Salary and Wage Commission*, 1925 (n.p., 1928), 3.
9.   *Raleigh News and Observer*, 31 March 1925.
10. *First Report of the Salary and Wage Commission*, 1925, 18.
11. Ibid., 54ff.
12. *Raleigh News and Observer*, 23 October 1925.
13. Ibid., 19 December 1925.
14. Ibid., 21 February 1926.
15. A supplemental report of the Salary and Wage Commission to Governor McLean, December 1926, in Governor's Papers.
16. *Raleigh News and Observer*, 27 February 1927; see also North Carolina, House Journal (1927), 282, 482.
17. H. Hoyle Sink to Evelyn Underwood, 16 February 1962, in possession of the author.
18. *Raleigh News and Observer*, 29 January 1925.
19. *Public Laws of North Carolina*, 1925 Session, Chapter 239.
20. *Public Laws of North Carolina*, 1925 Session, Chapter 158. Another enactment, Chapter 258, enlarged the first.
21. The most notorious case of fraud was one in which the Fisheries Products Company mulcted hundreds of North Carolinians of hundreds of thousands of dollars. The Bailey Company, a tobacco manufacturing company of Winston-Salem, had also been charged with defrauding the public.
22. *Public Laws of North Carolina*, 1925 Session, Chapter 190. A 1927 revision of the law reduced the filing fees and removed certain requirements that had served to prejudice the sale of approved securities.
23. *Raleigh News and Observer*, 28 April 1925.
24. Ibid., 17 June 1925.
25. University of North Carolina, News Letter, XII, no. 41 (25 August 1926).
26. *Raleigh News and Observer*, 14 February 1925; see also North Carolina, *House Journal* (1925), 220.
27. W. H. Wood [president of American Trust Company in Charlotte] to A. W. McLean, 13 November 1926, and A. W. McLean to W. H. Wood, 17 November 1926, in Governor's Papers.
28. *Public Laws of North Carolina*, 1925 Session, Chapter 119.
29. *Public Laws of North Carolina*, 1925 Session, Chapter 112.
30. *Public Laws of North Carolina*, 1927 Session, Chapter 113.
31. Edmund Platt to A. W. McLean, 10 March 1925, in Governor's Papers.
32. A. W. McLean to H. Hoyle Sink, 1 February 1926, in Governor's Papers.
33. *Public Laws of North Carolina*, 1925 Session, Chapter 50.
34. *Public Laws of North Carolina*, 1925 Session, Chapter 207.
35. Corbitt, ed., *Public Papers and Letters*, 31ff.
36. *Public Laws of North Carolina*, 1925 Session, Chapter 122.
37. *Public Laws of North Carolina*, 1927 Session, Chapters 51, 57, 250.
38. *Raleigh News and Observer*, 26 March 1927.
39. Ibid., 4 July 1928; see also report of Wade H. Phillips to the Board of Conservation and Development, 1 January–30 June 1928, in Governor's Papers.
40. *Raleigh News and Observer*, 6 February 1925.

41. Frank Page to A. W. McLean, 19 February 1926, in Governor's Papers; memoranda for files, 15 February; 9 March 1926, Department of Commerce, Bureau of Navigation, documents from Record Group 173, Part IV on microfilm, Southern Historical Collection, University of North Carolina, Chapel Hill, N.C.

42. J. O. Smith [engineer from The Radio Corporation of America] to A. W. McLean, 23 October 1926; J. G. Harbard [president of The Radio Corporation of America] to A. W. McLean, 7 October 1926; and other correspondence relative to the matter, in Governor's Papers.

43. *The North Carolina State Budget for the Biennium, 1927-1929* (Raleigh: Bynum Printing Company, 1928), 18, 246.

44. *Greensboro Daily News*, 10 January 1927.

45. *Raleigh News and Observer*, 26 February 1927.

Chapter VII

1. *Twenty-Second Biennial Report of the North Carolina State Board of Health*, July 1, 1925-June 30, 1928 (n.p., 1928), 27.

2. David Leroy Corbitt, ed., *Public Papers and Letters of Angus Wilton McLean, Governor of North Carolina, 1925-1929* (Raleigh: Edwards and Broughton Printing Company, 1931), 19ff. (Hereinafter cited as Corbitt, ed., *Public Papers and Letters*.)

3. *Public Laws of North Carolina*, 1925 Session, Chapter 18.

4. *Public Laws of North Carolina*, 1925 Session, Chapter 286.

5. *Public Laws of North Carolina*, 1925 Session, Chapter 114.

6. *Twenty-Second Biennial Report of the North Carolina Board of Health*, July 1, 1926-June 30, 1928, 27ff.

7. *Indenture of James B. Duke Establishing the Duke Endowment with Provisions of the Will and Trust of Mr. Duke Supplementing the Same* (n.p., 1932), 16, 43, 51.

8. *Public Laws of North Carolina*, 1925 Session, Chapter 306.

9. *Raleigh News and Observer*, 11 December 1925.

10. *Public Laws of North Carolina*, 1925 Session, Chapter 120.

11. Memorandum from Dennis G. Brummitt to A. W. McLean, 4 April 1925, in Governor's papers, A. W. McLean, 1925-1929, State Department of Archives and History, Raleigh, N.C. (Hereinafter cited as Governor's Papers.)

12. *Report of the Committee on Caswell Training School in Its Relation to the Problem of the Feebleminded of the State of North Carolina* (Raleigh: Capital Printing Company, 1926), 34ff.

13. *Raleigh News and Observer*, 27 January 1928.

14. *Public Laws of North Carolina*, 1925 Session, Chapter 29.

15. Corbitt, ed., *Public Papers and Letters*, 861.

16. *Report of the Office of the Commissioner of Pardons*, 1925-1929, in Governor's Papers.

17. *Charlotte Observer*, 26 March 1924.

18. *Raleigh News and Observer*, 20 February 1925.

19. North Carolina, *House Journal* (1925), 363.

20. North Carolina, *Senate Journal* (1925), 65.

21. *Public Laws of North Carolina*, 1925 Session, Chapter 1963. An Act in 1927 provided for classification of all prisoners in county convict camps and city jails and that accurate records be kept for all persons committed to these places; *Public Laws of North Carolina*, 1927 Session, Chapter 178.

22. Minutes of Meeting of Board of Directors, 7 April 1925, in Governor's Papers.

23. *Biennial Report of the State's Prison, 1923-1924* (Raleigh: Edwards and Broughton Printing Company, 1925), 15ff.

24. Corbitt, ed., *Public Papers and Letters*, 49.

25. Ibid., 52ff.

26. North Carolina, *Senate Journal* (1925), 279.

27. A copy of the letter mailed to the chairman of the boards of the county commissioners in June 1925, in Governor's Papers.

28. George Ross Pou to A. W. McLean, 13 June 1925, in Governor's Papers.

29. *Report on Examination of Plant Sites for State Prison*, 7 May 1925, in Governor's Papers.

30. *Raleigh News and Observer*, 29 February 1928.

31. Ibid., 27, 28 December 1928.

32. No appropriation was made for Central Prison other than its own income in 1927. A contingent fund was provided but none of it was used.

33. *Biennial Report of the State's Prison*, 1927-1928 (Raleigh: The State's Prison Printery, 1928), 5, 12; see also an account of Governor McLean's tour of Caledonia Prison Farm, in *Raleigh News and Observer*, 25 October 1927.
34. *Raleigh News and Observer*, 5 December 1927.
35. Ibid., 12 December 1927.
36. *Biennial Report of the State's Prison*, 1927-1928, 10.
37. *Raleigh News and Observer*, 4 January; 3, 20 February 1925.
38. *Public Laws of North Carolina*, 1927 Session, Chapter 219.
39. *Raleigh News and Observer*, 3 September 1927; see also "The Members of the Board of Directors to Governor McLean," 22 July 1927, in Governor's Papers.
40. *Raleigh News and Observer*, 5 March 1927; *Public Laws of North Carolina*, 1927 Session, Chapter 79.
41. *Raleigh News and Observer*, 20 June 1925.
42. Ibid., 2 January 1925.
43. Ibid., 3 February 1925.
44. Ibid., 26 February 1925.
45. Ibid., 27 March 1925.
46. Ibid., 31 August 1928.
47. Ibid., 7 July 1927.
48. *Biennial Report of the North Carolina State Board of Charities and Public Welfare*, July 1, 1924-June 30, 1926 (n.p., 1926), 13ff.
49. *Raleigh News and Observer*, 4 April 1925.
50. Ibid., 4 May 1925.
51. Ibid., 15 November 1925. On the same day, a mob in Mississippi seized a young black charged with assault and burned him, and the governor of that state said he could do nothing about it.
52. Ibid., 10 February 1926; see also Corbitt, ed., *Public Papers and Letters*, 529.

Chapter VIII

1. David Leroy Corbitt, ed., *Public Papers and Letters of Angus Wilton McLean, Governor of North Carolina, 1925-1929* (Raleigh: Edwards and Broughton Printing Company, 1931), 5. (Hereinafter cited as Corbitt, ed., *Public Papers and Letters.*)
2. *Biennial Report of the Superintendent of Public Instruction of North Carolina, 1924-1925 and 1925-1926*, Part I (Raleigh: n. p., n. d.), 13, 15, 16, 43, 174.
3. Samuel Huntington Hobbs, Jr., *North Carolina Economic and Social* (Chapel Hill: University of North Carolina Press, 1930), 266. (Hereinafter cited as Hobbs, *North Carolina Economic and Social.*)
4. *State School Facts*, vol. III, no. 4 (January 1932).
5. University of North Carolina *News Letter*, vol. VII, no. 4 (1 December 1920).
6. Ibid., vol. XI, no. 49 (21 October 1925); Hobbs, *North Carolina Economic and Social*, 183.
7. University of North Carolina *News Letter*, vol. X, no. 20 (2 April 1924)
8. Hobbs, *North Carolina Economic and Social*, 183.
9. *State School Facts*, vol. I, no. 14 (1 April 1925).
10. *Charlotte Observer*, 14, 15 March 1924.
11. Ibid., 2 May 1924.
12. *Biennial Report of the Superintendent of Public Instruction of North Carolina, 1922-1923 and 1923-1924* (n. p., n. d.), 23, 30, 31.
13. *Raleigh News and Observer*, 28 February; 5 March 1925.
14. Ibid., 23 January 1925.
15. *Public Laws of North Carolina*, 1925 Session, Chapter 275.
16. *Public Laws of North Carolina*, 1925 Session, Chapter 201.
17. *Public Laws of North Carolina*, 1925 Session, Chapter 297.
18. *Public Laws of North Carolina*, 1925 Session, Chapter 265.
19. North Carolina, Senate Journal (1925), 391.
20. *Public Laws of North Carolina*, 1925 Session, Chapter 203.
21. *Raleigh News and Observer*, 3 March 1926. Later Warren, Webb, and Robinson resigned and Edgar W. Pharr, Stanley Winborne, and Nathan O'Berry replaced them.
22. *Raleigh News and Observer*, 23 March 1926.
23. Ibid., 25 August 1926.
24. Ibid., 1 October 1926.
25. *The Progressive Farmer*, 12 June 1926.
26. *Raleigh News and Observer*, 3 January 1926.

27. *Charlotte Observer*, 2 January 1926.
28. *Raleigh News and Observer*, 13 August 1926.
29. *Charlotte Observer*, 28 January 1927.
30. A. W. McLean to J. O. Carr, 11 August 1926, J. O. Carr Papers, The Southern Historical Collection, University of North Carolina, Chapel Hill, N.C.
31. North Carolina, *Senate Journal* (1927), 100ff.
32. *Report of the State Educational Commission on the Public School System of North Carolina*, 15 January 1927 (Raleigh: Edwards and Broughton Printing Company, 1927), 5 and passim.
33. Ibid., 30ff.
34. North Carolina, *Senate Journal* (1927) 689.
35. *Raleigh News and Observer*, 19 February 1927.
36. Ibid., 22 February 1927.
37. Ibid., 27 February; 1 March 1927.
38. Ibid., 18 February 1927.
39. A. H. Bahnson to A. W. McLean, 17 February 1927, in Governor's Papers, Angus Wilton McLean, 1925-1929, State Department of Archives and History, Raleigh, N.C. (Hereinafter cited as Governor's Papers).
40. J. O. Carr to A. W. McLean, 18 February 1927, in the Governor's Papers.
41. William W. Dawson to A. W. McLean, 8 February 1927, in the Governor's Papers.
42. *Greensboro Daily News*, 1 March 1927.
43. *Raleigh News and Observer*, 20 February 1927.
44. *Public Laws of North Carolina*, 1927 Session, Chapter 256; *Raleigh News and Observer*, 9 March 1927.
45. *Public Laws of North Carolina*, 1927 Session, Chapter 199.
46. *Raleigh News and Observer*, 10 March 1925.
47. Ibid., 23 June 1927.
48. Ibid., 9 July 1927.
49. Ibid., 23 July 1927.
50. Ibid., 4 June 1928.
51. *Biennial Report of the Superintendent of Public Instruction of North Carolina, 1918-1919 and 1919-1920* (Raleigh: Edwards and Broughton Printing Company, 1921), 14.
52. *Asheville Citizen*, 3 March 1927.
53. Elizabeth C. Morris to A. W. McLean, 27 February 1926, in the Governor's Papers.
54. *Raleigh News and Observer*, 12 June 1927.
55. *Charlotte Observer*, 26 February 1925.
56. A. W. McLean to Furnifold M. Simmons, 22 December 1924, in Governor's Papers.
57. *The North Carolina State Budget for the Biennium 1925-1927* (Raleigh: Bynum Printing Company, 1925), 11, 15; see also *Raleigh News and Observer*, 1 January 1925.
58. *Public Laws of North Carolina*, 1925 Session, Chapter 275.
59. *Raleigh News and Observer*, 8 January 1927.
60. *Public Laws of North Carolina*, 1927 Session, Chapters 79, 147; see also *State of North Carolina Budget*, 1929-1930, and 1930-1931 (New Bern: Owen G. Dunn, 1928), 85, 90.
61. *Raleigh News and Observer*, 12 October 1926.
62. Ibid., 21 November 1926.
63. A. W. McLean to E. C. Branson, 28 January 1927, in Governor's Papers.
64. *The North Carolina State Budget for the Biennium, 1927-1929* (Raleigh: Bynum Printing Company, 1926), 67. The Morrison Administration had appropriated $10,929,000 for permanent improvements.
65. *The Report of the State Educational Commission on the Public School System of North Carolina*, 211.
66. Ibid., 134ff.
67. *Public Laws of North Carolina*, 1927 Session, Chapter 147.
68. In April 1927, the trustees of the university shattered a precedent of 133 years when they voted to add a woman to the faculty to instruct elementary teachers and supervisors.
69. United States Department of the Interior, Bureau of Education, *Survey of Negro Colleges and Universities*, Section of Bulletin, 1928, no. 7, Chapter XIV, "North Carolina" (Washington: United States Printing Office, 1928), 36, 92, 101.
70. *State School Facts*, vol. VIII, no. 8, (May 1931).
71. *Raleigh News and Observer*, 17 June 1928.
72. *State School Facts*, vol. VII, no. 8 (May 1931).
73. Ibid., vol. IX, no. 1 (October 1936); vol. XIV, no. 2 (November 1941).
74. Ibid., vol. VII, no. 11 (August 1931).

75. Ibid., vol. VII, no. 8 (May 1931); vol. VIII, no. 9 (June 1932).
76. Hobbs, *North Carolina Economic and Social*, 254.

Chapter IX

1. Paul W. Wager, *County Government and Administration in North Carolina* (Chapel Hill: The University of North Carolina Press, 1928), 99. (Hereinafter cited as Wager, County Government.)
2. Ibid., 126.
3. *North Carolina Club Year Book 1917-1918*, 7
4. Willard B. Gatewood, Jr., *Eugene Clyde Brooks: Educator and Public Servant* (Durham: Duke University Press, Durham, N.C., 1960), 179ff. (Hereinafter cited as Gatewood, Eugene Clyde Brooks.)
5. Ibid.; *Raleigh News and Observer*, 18 January 1925.
6. North Carolina, *Senate Journal* (1925), 445.
7. *Raleigh News and Observer*, 25 February 1925; E. C. Branson to A. W. McLean, 27 February 1925, Eugene Cunningham Branson Papers, Southern Historical Collection, University of North Carolina, Chapel Hill, N.C.
8. *Raleigh News and Observer*, 13 August 1925; see also, *Resolutions passed by the State Association of County Commissioners of North Carolina*, 20 August 1925, at Blowing Rock, in Governor's Papers, A. W. McLean, 1925-1929, State Department of Archives and History, Raleigh, N.C. (Hereinafter cited as Governor's Papers.)
9. David Leroy Corbitt, ed., *Public Papers and Letters of Angus Wilton McLean, Governor of North Carolina, 1925-1929* (Raleigh: Edwards and Broughton Company, 1931), 114. (Hereinafter cited as Corbitt, ed., *Public Papers and Letters*.)
10. *Raleigh News and Observer*, 12 August 1926.
11. A. W. McLean to Chester B. Masslich, 18 May 1926; A. W. McLean to Chester B. Masslick, 3 November 1926; Charles England to A. C. McIntosh, 24 December 1926; A. C. McIntosh to A. W. McLean, 25 December 1926; A. W. McLean to W. F. Willoughby, 11 January 1927; Charles B. Masslich to A. W. McLean, 20 December 1926; E. C. Brooks to A. W. McLean, 24 January 1927, in Governor's Papers.
12. Corbitt, ed., *Public Papers and Letters*, 115ff.
13. Ibid., 112ff; see also *Charlotte Observer*, 16 February 1927.
14. North Carolina, *House Journal* (1927), 850. The amendment was tabled after its second reading.
15. *Public Laws of North Carolina*, 1927 Session, Chapter 91.
16. *Public Laws of North Carolina*, 1927 Session, Chapter 146. This act was officially known as the County Fiscal Control Act.
17. *Public Laws of North Carolina*, 1927 Session, Chapter 81.
18. *Public Laws of North Carolina*, 1927 Session, Chapter 213.
19. *Consolidated Statutes* (1919), 8024, 8038.
20. *Public Laws of North Carolina*, 1927 Session, Chapter 221.
21. *Public Laws of North Carolina*, 1927 Session, Chapter 214; *Raleigh News and Observer*, 27 February 1927.
22. *Raleigh News and Observer*, 15 June 1927.
23. Ibid., 13 March 1927. *Report of County Advisory Commission*, 1928 (n. p., 1928), 22.
24. *Raleigh News and Observer*, 17, 19 March 1927.
25. Ibid., 21 April 1927.
26. *Report of County Government Advisory Commission*, 1928, 23.
27. Ibid., 22; John Alexander McMahan, "History of Development of the Local Government Commission," *1960 County Yearbook*, North Carolina Association of County Commissioners, 96.
28. *Report of County Government Advisory Commission*, 1928, 23
29. George A. Eyer to Ben R. Lacy, 19 September 1927; A. W. McLean to Chester B. Masslich, 23 September 1927; Chester B. Masslich to A. W. McLean, 26 September 1927, in Governor's Papers.
30. Baxter Durham to A. W. McLean, 11 February 1928, in Governor's Papers.
31. *Raleigh News and Observer*, 8 June 1928; see also *The Independent*, Elizabeth City, N.C., 15 June 1928, *Greensboro Daily News*, 8 June 1928, and the *Charlotte Observer*, 9 June 1928. *The Independent* and the *Charlotte Observer* expressed approval of Grady's action; the other two papers condemned it.

32. *Raleigh News and Observer,* 11 June 1928; see also *Greensboro Daily News,* 11 June 1928.
33. Hartsfield v. Commissioners of Craven County, 194 N.C. 358 (1927); Frazier v. Commissioners of Guilford County, 194 N.C. 49 (1927).
34. Report of County Government Advisory Commission, 1928, 13ff.
35. Ibid., 18.
36. Wager, *County Government,* 164.

Chapter X

1. David Leroy Corbitt, ed., *Public Papers and Letters of Angus Wilton McLean, Governor of North Carolina, 1925-1929* (Raleigh: Edwards and Broughton Company, 1931), 246ff. (Hereinafter cited as Corbitt, ed., *Public Papers and Letters.*)
2. Ibid., 422.
3. Ibid., 68.
4. *Public Laws of North Carolina,* 1925 Session, Chapter 142.
5. *Public Laws of North Carolina,* 1927 Session, Chapter 182.
6. *Public Laws of North Carolina,* 1925 Session, Chapter 223.
7. *Public Laws of North Carolina,* 1927 Session, Chapter 101.
8. Corbitt, ed., *Public Papers and Letters,* 344ff.
9. "The Cotton Situation," a manuscript for a speech delivered to the Civitan Club of Greensboro, 15 October 1926, in Governor's Papers, A. W. McLean, 1925-1929, State Department of Archives and History, Raleigh, N.C. (Hereinafter cited as Governor's Papers.)
10. *Raleigh News and Observer,* 1 October 1926.
11. Ibid., 18 October 1926.
12. Ibid., 15 October 1926.
13. Ibid., 12, 14, 24 October 1926; A. W. McLean to A. C. Williams, 15 October 1926; Eugene Meyer, Jr. to A. W. McLean, 20 October 1926, in Governor's Papers.
14. *Raleigh News and Observer,* 5 November 1926; 24 May 1927; 23 March 1928; John W. Simpson to A. W. McLean, 3 December 1926; A. W. McLean to John W. Simpson, 5 December 1926, in Governor's Papers.
15. *Raleigh News and Observer,* 27, 29, 30 October; 4, 6 November 1926.
16. E. C. Brooks to A. W. McLean, 28 October 1926, in the Eugene Clyde Brooks Papers, Duke University, Durham, N.C.
17. *Raleigh News and Observer,* 9 November 1926.
18. Ibid., 20 November 1926.
19. Ibid., 11 December 1926; 5, 11, 22 January 1927.
20. Ibid., 23 March 1928.
21. Ibid., 3 April 1928; University of North Carolina *News Letter,* vol. XIV, no. 31, (13 June 1928).
22. Corbitt, ed., *Public Papers and Letters,* 33.
23. *Greensboro Daily News,* 27 June 1926; Corbitt, ed., *Public Papers and Letters,* 32.
24. Corbitt, ed., *Public Papers and Letters,* 234ff.
25. *Public Laws of North Carolina,* 1925 Session, Chapter 122.
26. *Public Laws of North Carolina,* 1925 Session, Chapter 168; 1927 Session, Chapters 51, 60.
27. *Public Laws of North Carolina,* 1925 Session, Chapter 61.
28. *Public Laws of North Carolina,* 1925 Session, Chapter 175; Brent S. Drane to A. W. McLean, 19 January 1925, in Governor's Papers. Small's letter was included in the correspondence from Drane.
29. *Raleigh News and Observer,* 5 January 1926.
30. Corbitt, ed., *Public Papers and Letters,* 540ff.
31. *Raleigh News and Observer,* 29 April 1925; Herbert Hoover to A. W. McLean, 24 April 1925, and Frank Wood to A. W. McLean, 8 May 1925, in Governor's Papers.
32. Corbitt, ed., *Public Papers and Letters,* 74; *Raleigh News and Observer,* 8 November 1925; A. W. McLean to Council of State, 11 April 1927, in Governor's Papers.
33. *Raleigh News and Observer,* 25 May; 6 October 1927; 31 March, 6 April 1928.
34. Governor A. W. McLean to Chairman of the Board of County Commissioners, 2 September 1925, in Governor's Papers.
35. A. W. McLean to Major Wade Phillips, 19 May 1927; A. W. McLean to Frank Page, 19 May 1927, in Governor's Papers.
36. *Raleigh News and Observer,* 3 September 1926.
37. Ibid., 2, 3 November 1926; Wade K. Phillips to Fred N. Tate, 10 November 1926, in Governor's Papers.

38. *Raleigh News and Observer*, 16 June 1928.
39. A. W. McLean to Indiana Condensed Milk Company, 26 October 1928, and similar letters to Pet Milk Company and Carnation Milk Company; D. B. Hilliard [president of the Rayon Company of America] to A. W. McLean, 25 October 1928; P. A. Rockefeller to A. W. McLean, 31 May 1928; P. A. Rockefeller to A. W. McLean, 31 May 1928; A. F. Lodeizer [American Enka Corporation] to A. W. McLean, 2 June 1928, in Governor's Papers.
40. Willard B. Gatewood, Jr., *Eugene Brooks, Educator and Public Servant* (Durham: Duke University Press, 1960), 204ff. (Hereinafter cited as Gatewood, Eugene Clyde Brooks.); *Raleigh News and Observer*, 5 December 1924.
41. Gatewood, *Eugene Clyde Brooks*, 206.
42. Ibid., 207ff; Minutes of the Campaign Committee, meeting in Asheville, 21 October 1925, in the Eugene Clyde Brooks Papers, Duke University, Durham, N.C.; *Asheville Citizen*, 11, 14, 17 December 1924; *Raleigh News and Observer*, 22 October 1925; 20 November 1925.
43. *Raleigh News and Observer*, 15 May 1926.
44. North Carolina, *Senate Journal* (1927), 140; *Asheville Citizen*, 4 February 1927.
45. A. W. McLean to Charles A. Webb, 4 February 1927; Charles A. Webb to A. W. McLean, 31 January 1927; Charles A. Webb to A. W. McLean, 8 February 1927, in Governor's Papers.
46. A. W. McLean to Hubert Work, 8 February 1927 in Governor's Papers.
47. *Raleigh News and Observer*, 16, 23 February 1927; *Public Laws of North Carolina*, 1927 Session, Chapter 48; Gatewood, Eugene Clyde Brooks, 212ff.
48. Gatewood, *Eugene Clyde Brooks*, 213ff.; *Raleigh News and Observer*, 7, 9 March 1928; Resolution passed by the Governor and Council of State, 8 March 1928, in Governor's Papers.
49. Minutes of the Council of State, 12 September 1928, in Governor's Papers.
50. Everett B. Sweezy to A. W. McLean, 3 December 1924; Eldredge and Company to A. W. McLean, 5 December 1924; Warren J. Hayscradt to A. W. McLean, 5 December 1924; Curtis and Sanger to A. W. McLean, 6 December 1924; Everett B. Sweezy to B. R. Lacy, 12 December 1924, in Governor's Papers.
51. *Raleigh News and Observer*, 31 January 1925; *Asheville Citizen*, 7 February 1925.
52. *Raleigh News and Observer*, 19 February 1925; *Public Laws of North Carolina*, 1925 Session, Chapter 35.
53. *Public Laws of North Carolina*, 1925 Session, Chapter 35.
54. *Public Laws of North Carolina*, 1925 Session, Chapter 45.
55. *Public Laws of North Carolina*, 1925 Session, Chapter 74; *Raleigh News and Observer*, 4, 27 February 1925.
56. *Public Laws of North Carolina*, 1927 Session, Chapter 95; *Raleigh News and Observer*, 13 March 1927.
57. *Public Laws of North Carolina*, 1927 Session, Chapter 41.
58. Frank Page to A. W. McLean, 16 November 1927, in Governor's Papers.
59. Corbitt, ed., *Public Papers and Letters*, 429ff.; *Raleigh News and Observer*, 31 March 1928; 31 July 1928.
60. *Raleigh News and Observer*, 22 January 1927.
61. Ibid., 17 March 1927.
62. Ibid., 24 February 1927; *Public Laws of North Carolina*, 1927 Session, Chapter 44.
63. *Public Laws of North Carolina*, 1925 Session, Chapter 266. The issue turned on the fact that North Carolina needed a direct railroad connection with the West and the charge that the railroad companies had intentionally prevented such a connection.
64. North Carolina Cotton Manufacturers Association, *Report of Committee on Taxation*, at fall meeting held at Pinehurst, N.C., 27 November 1926, in Governor's Papers.
65. In March, Governor McLean asked Dr. Albert S. Keister of the North Carolina College for Women to review the matter of corporation taxes. His investigation, along with the findings of the National Industrial Corporation Board of North Carolina, revealed that North Carolina Corporations paid a smaller percentage of their net income in taxes than corporations in any state in the Union except four.
66. *Public Laws of North Carolina*, 1927 Session, Chapter 157.
67. *Public Laws of North Carolina*, 1927 Session, Chapter 71.
68. *Public Laws of North Carolina*, 1927 Session, Chapter 216. It was rejected in the November election.
69. *State of North Carolina Report of the Tax Commission* (Raleigh: n. p., 1928), 42ff.

Chapter XI

1. A. W. McLean, "Highland Scots in North Carolina," 2 vols., a bound manuscript in State Department of Archives and History, Raleigh, N.C.
2. *Raleigh News and Observer*, 3 May 1928.
3. Ibid., 13 August 1925.
4. Ibid., 23 September 1925.
5. A. W. McLean to Olmstead Brothers, 23 January 1928, in Governor's Papers, A. W. McLean, 1925-1929, State Department of Archives and History, Raleigh, N.C. (Hereinafter cited as Governor's Papers.)
6   Meeting of the Board of Public Buildings and Grounds, 16 October 1928, in Governor's Papers.
7. *Raleigh News and Observer*, 16 December 1928.
8. Ibid., 21 February 1925; 3, 11 March 1925.
9. Ibid., 24 September 1928.
10. Ibid., 14 February 1925; 22 August 1926.
11. J. S. Holmes to Rev. Joseph Blount Cheshire, president, Roanoke Colony Memorial Association, 29 October 1926, in Governor's Papers.
12. *Raleigh News and Observer*, 7 March 1925.
13. Ibid., 11 July 1925.
14. A. W. McLean to Furnifold M. Simmons, 30 December 1927; 22 February 1928, Furnifold M. Simmons Papers, Duke University, Durham, N.C.
15. David Leroy Corbitt, ed., *Public Papers and Letters of Governor Angus Wilton McLean, 1925-1929* (Raleigh: Edwards and Broughton Company, 1931), 366-71. (Hereinafter cited as Corbitt, ed., *Public Papers and Letters*.)
16. *Raleigh News and Observer*, 19 January 1927; 9 March; 23 July 1928.
17. Ibid., 21 May 1925.
18. Ibid., 11 February 1925.
19. Ibid., 21 May 1925; *Charlotte Observer*, 21 May 1925.
20. *Raleigh News and Observer*, 18 December 1926; 3 March 1927.
21. Ibid., 4 February 1928. This controversy was later solved and the Wright plane was returned to the Smithsonian Institute in Washington, D.C.
22. *Raleigh News and Observer*, 18 December 1928.
23. Lindberg had recently returned as a hero from his solo flight across the Atlantic.
24. *Raleigh News and Observer*, 18 December 1928.
25. Corbitt, ed., *Public Papers and Letters*, 504-7.
26. *Raleigh News and Observer*, 18 December 1928. The wind and sand had moved the hill almost a half mile from the actual site of the flight.
27. *Raleigh News and Observer*, 18 December 1928.
28. Ibid., 15, 19 August 1926.
29. Ibid., 11 April 1926.
30. Ibid., 18 September 1927.
31. Ibid., 3 August 1928.
32. Ibid., 17 December 1926; A. W. McLean to Franklin W. Ward, 13 January 1928, a telegram, in Governor's Papers.
33. *Raleigh News and Observer*, 11, 18 February 1927.
34. Ibid., 18 April 1926.
35. Ibid., 15 April 1926.
36. Ibid., 16 February 1927.
37. Ibid., 14, 18 June 1926.
38. Ibid., 11 October 1926.

Chapter XII

1. University of North Carolina *News Letter*, vol. XII, no. 38 (4 August 1926); *Raleigh News and Observer*, 22 January 1928.
2. *Public Laws of North Carolina*, 1927 Session, Chapter 148.
3. *Public Laws of North Carolina*, 1927 Session, Chapter 122.
4. *Public Laws of North Carolina*, 1927 Session, Chapter 43.
5. *Public Laws of North Carolina*, 1927 Session, Chapter 120.
6. *Public Laws of North Carolina*, 1927 Session, Chapter 64.
7. *Public Laws of North Carolina*, 1927 Session, Chapter 230.
8. North Carolina, *Senate Journal* (1927), 165.

9. *Public Laws of North Carolina*, 1925 Session, Chapter 50; *Raleigh News and Observer*, 8, 28, 30 January; 5, 18, 19 February; 5 March 1925.

10. *Public Laws of North Carolina*, 1925 Session, Chapter 231.

11. *Raleigh News and Observer*, 23 February 1927; *Public Laws of North Carolina*, 1927 Session, Chapter 136.

12. *Raleigh News and Observer*, 10 February 1925; 4 March 1925.

13. Ibid., 10, 20 November 1926.

14. Ibid., 7, 28 January; 21 February 1927.

15. David Leroy Corbitt, ed., *Public Papers and Letters of Angus Wilton McLean, Governor of North Carolina, 1925-1929* (Raleigh Edwards and Broughton, 1931), 25. (Hereinafter cited as Corbitt, ed., *Public Papers and Letters.*)

16. Copies of these letters are found in Governor's Papers, A. W. McLean, 1925–1929, State Department of Archives and History, Raleigh, N.C. (Hereinafter cited as Governor's Papers.)

17. A. W. McLean to A. B. Andrews, 26 November 1924; A. W. McLean to Henry M. London, 9 December 1924, in Governor's Papers.

18. *Raleigh News and Observer*, 19 February 1925.

19. A. B. Andrews to A. W. McLean, 12 December 1924; A. W. McLean to A. D. Watts, 17 December 1924, in Governor's Papers.

20. North Carolina, *House Journal* (1925), 190; *Raleigh News and Observer*, 27 February 1925.

21. North Carolina, *Senate Journal* (1925), 328; *Raleigh News and Observer*, 27 February 1925.

22. *Raleigh News and Observer*, 3, 10 March 1925; *Public Laws of North Carolina*, 1925 Session, Chapter 216.

23. *Public Laws of North Carolina*, 1925 Session, Chapter 244; *Raleigh News and Observer*, 15, 24 February 1925.

24. *Raleigh News and Observer*, 20 January 1927.

25. Ibid., 15 February 1927.

26. Corbitt, ed., *Public Papers and Letters*, 70.

27. *Raleigh News and Observer*, 12 January 1927.

28. Ibid., 14 January; 25, 26 February; 6 March 1927.

29. Ibid., 11 January; 6, 9 March 1927; *Public Laws of North Carolina*, 1927 Session, Chapter 206.

30. *Raleigh News and Observer*, 11, 26, 27 February 1925.

31. Ibid., 21 January; 24, 26 February; 13 March 1927.

32. Ibid., 3 March 1925.

33. *Public Laws of North Carolina*, 1925 Session, Chapter 88; 1927 Session, Chapter 260.

34. *Raleigh News and Observer*, 18, 19 February 1927; *Public Laws of North Carolina*, 1927 Session, Chapter 50.

35. *Thirty-Fourth Report of the Department of Labor and Printing of the State of North Carolina, 1923-1924* (Raleigh: Mitchell Printing Company), III-V.

36. *Raleigh News and Observer*, 27, 28 January 1925.

37. Ibid., 14, 25 February 1925.

38. *Public Laws of North Carolina*, 1927 Session, Chapter 251; *Raleigh News and Observer*, 24 February; 4, 9 March 1927.

39. North Carolina, *House Journal* (1925), 705; *Raleigh News and Observer*, 11 March 1925; E. C. Dwelle to A. W. McLean, 6 March 1925; C. D. Welch and others of Cramerton Mills to A. W. McLean, 6 March 1925; M. L. Long to A. W. McLean, 7 March 1925, and other correspondence on the matter, in Governor's Papers.

40. *Raleigh News and Observer*, 22, 23, 26 February 1927; 5 March 1927.

41. Ibid., 18 February 1925; North Carolina, *House Journal* (1925), 18.

42. *The Journal of Social Forces*, III (January 1925), 208, 214, 218. These statements were taken from two articles: "The Development of the Concept of Progress," by L. L. Bernard and "Sociology and Ethics: A Genetic View of the Theory of Conduct," by Harry Elmer Barnes.

43. *Charlotte Observer*, 19 February 1925.

44. *Home Journal* (1925), 271; *Raleigh News and Observer*, 11, 20 February 1925.

45. *Raleigh News and Observer*, 18, 27 February 1925.

46. Ibid., 20 February 1925.

47. Ibid., 26 January; 16, 24 February 1927.

48. Ibid., 8 February; 27 April 1928.

49. Ibid., 3 June 1928; George F. Syme to A. W. McLean, 28 May 1928, in Governor's Papers. Other correspondence relating to the survey is also included in the Governor's Papers.

50. *Council of State Minutes,* 1925-1929, in Governor's Papers. A certified copy of the survey-
     ors' report and a map of the boundary line are included.
51. *Raleigh News and Observer,* 30 August 1927.
52. Ibid.
53. Ibid., 31 August 1927; Frank Nash to A. W. McLean, 17 September 1927, in Governor's
     Papers.
54. Lee S. Overman to A. W. McLean, 22 June 1928; A. W. McLean to J. R. McCarl, 3 July 1928,
     in Governor's Papers.
55. *Raleigh News and Observer,* 20 May 1926.
56. Ibid.
57. Ibid., 3 April 1926; 20 February 1927.
58. Hugh Talmadge Lefler and Albert Ray Newsome, *North Carolina: a Southern State* (Chapel
     Hill: University of North Carolina Press, 1973), 493-4.
59. *Raleigh News and Observer,* 11 April; 10, 28, 29 May 1928.

Chapter XIII

1.   George B. Tindall, "The Metamorphosis of Progressivism: Southern Politics in the
     Twenties," 8ff, an unpublished manuscript in the possession of the author.
2.   Ralph O. Brewster to A. W. McLean, 11 December 1928, in letter book in the McLean
     Collection, Southern Historical Collection, University of North Carolina, Chapel Hill,
     N.C.
3.   *Greensboro Daily News,* 2 December 1928.
4.   Ibid.
5.   *Public Laws of North Carolina,* 1927 Session, Chapter 234.
6.   *Public Laws of North Carolina,* 1927 Session, Chapter 306.
7.   O. Max Gardner to Dickson McLean, 20 March 1946, in letter book on microfilm, in A. W.
     McLean's Papers, the Southern Historical Collection, University of North Carolina,
     Chapel Hill, N.C.
8.   H. Hoyle Sink, author interview, Greensboro, N.C., 18 November 1961.
9.   Hector McLean, author interview, Lumberton, N.C., 24 April 1961.
10. *The Robesonian,* Lumberton, N.C., 22 June 1935.

BIBLIOGRAPHY

Primary Sources

I. Manuscripts

Bailey, Joseph William. Papers, 1835-1948. Duke University, Durham, N.C.

Branson, Eugene Cunningham. Papers, 1899-1933. Southern Historical Collection, University of North Carolina, Chapel Hill, N.C.

Brooks, Eugene Clyde. Papers, 1775-1944. Duke University, Durham, N.C.

Carr, James Osborn. Papers, 1743-1938. Southern Historical Collection, University of North Carolina, Chapel Hill, N.C.

Clarkson, Heriot. Papers, 1862-1945. Southern Historical Collection, University of North Carolina, Chapel Hill, N.C.

Governor's Papers, Council of State Minutes, 1925-1929. State Department of Archives and History, Raleigh, N.C.

Hall, James King. Papers, 1751-1947. Southern Historical Collection, University of North Carolina, Chapel Hill, N.C.

McLean, A. W. Governor's Papers, 1925-1929. State Department of Archives and History, Raleigh, N.C.

———. Papers, 1910-1933. Southern Historical Collection, University of North Carolina, Chapel Hill, N.C.

Simmons, Furnifold McLendel. Papers, 1890-1931. Duke University, Durham, N.C.

Small, John Humphrey. Papers, 1720-1946. Duke University, Durham, N.C.

War Finance Corporation: Minutes. Vols. VII, IX, and XXXIV. National Archives, Washington, D.C.

II. Interviews

Biggs, Mrs. Furman K. Interview by author. Lumberton, N.C., 24 November 1961.

Dawson, John Gilmore. Interview by author. Kinston, N.C., 21 November 1961.

MacLean, Hector. Interview by author. Lumberton, N.C., 24 April; 28 October 1961.

McLean, Alexander Torrey. Interview by author. Lumberton, N.C., 24 November 1961.

Shepherd, Margaret McLean. Interview by author. Lumberton, N.C., 24 November 1961.

Sink, H. Hoyle. Interview by author. Greensboro, N.C., 18 November 1961.

III. Printed

A. Public Documents

Department of Agriculture. *Biennial Report of the North Carolina Department of Agriculture, 1924-1930.*

State Auditor of North Carolina. *Annual Report of the State Auditor of North Carolina,* 1924-1929.

The North Carolina State Budget for the Biennium, 1925-1929. Raleigh: Bynum Printing Company, 1925.

The North Carolina State Budget for the Biennium, 1927-1929. Raleigh: Bynum Printing Company, 1928.

Commission on Caswell Training School. *Report of the Commission on Caswell Training School in its Relation to the Problem of the Feebleminded of the State of North Carolina, 1926.* Raleigh: Capital Printing Company, 1926.

State Board of Charities and Public Welfare. *Biennial Report of the North Carolina State Board of Charities and Public Welfare, 1924-1930.*

Corbitt, David Leroy, ed., *Public Papers and Letters of Angus Wilton McLean, Governor of North Carolina, 1925-1929.* Raleigh: Edwards and Broughton Printing Company, 1931.

Corporate Commission. *State of North Carolina Report of the Corporation Commission for the Biennial Period, 1925-1928.*

Department of Conservation and Development. *Biennial Report of the Department of Conservation and Development of the State of North Carolina, 1925-1929.*

County Government Advisory Commission. *Report of County Government Advisory Commission,* 1928. n.p., 1928.

State Education Commission. *Report of the State Educational Commission on the Public School System of North Carolina, 1927.* Raleigh: Edwards and Broughton Printing Company, 1927.

——. *Consolidated Report of the Educational Commission on the Public School System of North Carolina, 1927.* Raleigh: Edwards and Broughton Printing Company, 1928.

North Carolina State Board of Health. *Biennial Report of the North Carolina State Board of Health, 1924-1928.*

North Carolina State Highway Commission. *Biennial Report of the State Highway Commission of North Carolina, 1925-1929.*

North Carolina House of Representatives. *House Journal,* 1925-1927.

State of North Carolina Department of Justice. *Fiscal Code for County Affairs of North Carolina.* Raleigh: 1927.

Department of Labor and Printing. *Report of the Department of Labor and Printing of the State of North Carolina, 1923-1928.*

McLean, A. W. *Financial Condition of the State of North Carolina, Balance Sheet, and Operating Statements for the Fiscal Year ended June 30, 1928.* n.p., 1928.

Superintendent of Public Instruction. *Biennial Report of the Superintendent of Public Instruction of North Carolina, 1924-1929.*

Salary and Wage Commission. *First Report of the Salary and Wage Commission to Honorable Angus W. McLean, Governor of North Carolina, October 1, 1925.* n.p., 1925.

——. *Report of the Salary and Wage Commission to Honorable Angus W. McLean, Governor of North Carolina, 1928.* n.p., 1928.

Secretary of State. *Biennial Report of the Secretary of State of the State of North Carolina for the Fiscal Years 1924-1928.*

North Carolina *Session Laws,* 1925-1927.

North Carolina Senate. *Senate Journal,* 1925-1927.

State Ship and Water Transportation Commission. *Report of the State Ship and Water Transportation Commission.* Raleigh: Edwards and Broughton Printing Company, 1924.

State Prison. *Biennial Report of the State's Prison, 1923-1928.*

Consolidated Statutes of North Carolina, 1919, 2 vols. Raleigh: Commercial Printing Company, 1926.

Supplement to the Consolidated Statutes of North Carolina, 1924, 1 vol. Raleigh: Edwards and Broughton Printing Company, 1924.

Tax Commission. *Report of the Tax Commission to Governor Angus Wilton McLean* [1928], Raleigh: 1928.

Transportation Advisory Commission. *Report No. 1, 6 July 1927, to Governor A. W. McLean.* A photocopy.

——. *Report No. 2, 7 January 1928, to Governor A. W. McLean.* A photocopy.

Treasurer of North Carolina. *Biennial Report of the Treasurer of North Carolina for Fiscal Years 1925-1929.*

B. Miscellaneous and Semi-Official Reports

Branson, Eugene Cunningham et al. *County Government and County Affairs in North Carolina in the North Carolina Yearbook, 1917-1918.* Chapel Hill: University of North Carolina,1918.

Association of Business Officers in Schools for Negros. *Proceedings of the Fourth Meeting of the Association of Business Officers in Schools for Negroes, 7-9 May 1942.* n.p., n.d.

State of North Carolina Department of Conservation and Development. *Analysis of North Carolina Taxes and Debts.* Raleigh: [1928].

——. *North Carolina Resources and Industries.* Raleigh: 1929.

State Board of Education. *Regulations Governing Certificates for Teachers in North Carolina, 1929.* Raleigh: 1929.

State Historical Commission. *North Carolina Manual,* 1925, comp. and ed. by Robert B. House. Raleigh: Edwards and Broughton Printing Company, 1925.

———. *North Carolina Manual*, 1927, comp. and ed. by Ray Albert Newsome. Raleigh: Edwards and Broughton Printing Company, 1927.

United States Department of the Interior, Bureau of Education. *Survey of Negro Colleges and Universities*, Section of Bulletin 1928, no. 7, Chapter XIV, "North Carolina." Washington: United States Government Printing Office, 1928.

University of North Carolina, Extension Division. *North Carolina Commerce and Industry* I-III (1923-1926).

University of North Carolina. *News Letter* X-XVIII (1923-1932).

State Superintendent of Public Instruction. *State School Facts* I-VIII (1924-1932).

Wager, Paul Woodford et al., *Studies in Taxation in the North Carolina Club Yearbook, 1927-1928.* Chapel Hill: University of North Carolina Press, 1928.

C. Newspapers

Asheville Citizen, 1924-1929.

Asheville Times, 1924-1929.

Charlotte Observer, 1924-1929.

Greensboro Daily News, 1924-1929

The Independent, Elizabeth City, N.C., 1924-1929.

The Robesonian, Lumberton, N.C., 1897-1914.

Raleigh News and Observer, 1924-1929.

The Union Republican, Salisbury, N.C., 1924-1929.

D. Pamphlets

Josiah W. Bailey Battling for Certain Great Causes. [*The People's Advocate*] Fayetteville, N.C.: [1924].

[Bailey, Joseph W.] *Announcement of Candidacy of J. W. Bailey for Governor in the Democratic Primary, June 7, 1924*. Raleigh: Bynum Printing Company, 1924.

———. *Four Services of Progress*. Raleigh: Mitchell Printing Company, [1924].

[———.] *Josiah W. Bailey: A Friend of the Laboring Man*. n.p., n.d.

———. *The Issues of the Campaign*. n.p., n.d.

———. *The Way to Progress in North Carolina*. Raleigh, 1924.

Brooks, Aubrey L. *Replies to Anonymous Attack on Angus Wilton McLean*. n.p., 1924.

Grantham, G. K. *When Did Mr. Bailey Become the Friend of the Farmer?* Dunn, N.C.: [1924].

Gully, Needham Y. *Josiah W. Bailey, a Brief Sketch of His Career and Activities*. n.p., [1924].

McNeill, Franklin. *Angus Wilton McLean*. Raleigh: 1924.

McLean, A. W. *Statement of Angus Wilton McLean, Candidate for Governor of North Carolina, March 17, 1924*. n.p., n.d.

[McLean, A. W.] *Attitude of A. W. McLean, Candidate for Governor, in Regard to Labor*. n.p. [1924].

Secondary Sources

I. Monographs and General Works

Betters, Paul V., ed. *State Centralization in North Carolina*. Washington: The Brookings Institute, 1932.

Brown, Cecil Kenneth. *The State Highway System of North Carolina*. Chapel Hill: University of North Carolina Press, 1931.

Donovan, Clement Harold. "The Readjustment of State and Local Fiscal Relations in North Carolina, 1929-1938," Ph.D. diss., University of North Carolina, 1940.

Gatewood, Willard B., Jr. *Eugene Clyde Brooks: Educator and Public Servant*. Durham: Duke University Press, 1960.

Hobbs, Samuel Huntington. Jr. *North Carolina Economic and Social*. Chapel Hill: University of North Carolina Press, 1930.

Henderson, Archibald et al. *North Carolina: The Old North State and the New*. 5 vols. Chicago: The Lewis Publishing Company, 1941.

Joubert, William Harry. *Southern Freight Rates in Transition*. Gainesville: University of Florida Press, 1949.

Klontz, Harold Emerson, "An Economic Study of the Southern Furniture Manufacturing Industry," Ph.D. diss., University of North Carolina, 1948.

Lawrence, Robert C. *The State of Robeson.* New York: J. J. Little and Ives Company, 1939.

Lefler, Hugh Talmage and Albert Ray Newsome. *North Carolina: The History of a Southern State.* Chapel Hill: University of North Carolina Press, 1954.

Long, Hollis Moody. *Public Secondary Education for Negroes in North Carolina.* New York: Teachers College, Columbia University, 1932.

McLean, A. W. et al. *Lumber River Scots and Their Descendants.* Richmond: William Byrd Press, 1942.

Morrison, Fred Wilson. *Equalization of the Financial Burden of Education Among Counties in North Carolina: A Study of the Equalizing Fund.* New York: Teachers College, Columbia University, 1925.

Rankin, Robert S. *The Government and Administration of North Carolina.* (W. Brooke Graves, ed., American Commonwealth Series.) New York: Thomas Y. Crowell, 1955.

Soule, George Henry. *Prosperity Decade from War to Depression: 1917-1929.* (vol. VIII, Henry David et al., eds., The Economic History of the United States.) New York: Rinehart, [1947]

Strayer, George Drayton. *Centralizing Tendencies in the Administration of Public Education.* Concord: Rumford Press, 1943.

Tilley, Nannie Mae. *The Bright-Tobacco Industry, 1860-1929.* Chapel Hill: University of North Carolina Press, 1948.

Wager, Paul Woodford. *County Government and Administration in North Carolina.* Chapel Hill: University of North Carolina Press, 1928.

West, Cameron P. *A Democrat and Proud of It.* n.p. 1959.

Willoughby, Woodbury. *Capital Issues Committee and War Finance Corporation* (Series LII, no. 3, *Johns Hopkins University Studies in Historical and Political Science.*) Baltimore: The John Hopkins Press, 1934.

Wilson, Louis R. *The University of North Carolina, 1900-1930.* Chapel Hill: University of North Carolina Press, 1957.

Woodward, C. Vann. *Origins of the New South, 1877-1913.* (vol. IX, Wendell Holmes Stephenson and E. Merton Coulter, eds., A History of the South.) Baton Rouge: Louisiana State University Press, 1956.

II. Articles

Bardin, B. N. "A Son of Carolina and a National Figure." *University of North Carolina Magazine* LII, no. 9 (June 1922): 20-21.

Brown, Cecil Kenneth. "Industrial Development of North Carolina." *The Annals of the American Academy of Political and Social Science* CLIII (1931): 133-40.

Matherly, W. J. "North Carolina Becomes a Great Furniture State." *North Carolina Commerce and Industry* I, no. 5 (January 1926): 41-44.

Mathewson, Park. "Forest Resources and Industry." *Tarheel Banker* VIII, no. 10 (April 1930): 34-37.

McMahan, John Alexander. "History and Development of the Local Government Commission." *North Carolina Association of County Commissioners Yearbook* (1960): 95-99.

Ryan, J. T. "The Furniture Industry in North Carolina." *The Wachovia* XIX, no. 7 (July 1926): 1-5.

Tindall, George B. "The Metamorphosis of Progressivism: Southern Politics in the Twenties." An unpublished manuscript in the possession of the author.

Varser, Lucurgus Raynor. "Angus Wilton McLean." *Proceedings of the North Carolina Bar Association* XXXVII (1935): 195-7.